THE RESURRECTION MEN

A Thomas Potts historical mystery

It is 1826, and in the town of Redditch in Worcestershire, Thomas Potts, reluctant Parish Constable, battles to keep the peace. With the notorious 'Needle Pointers' up in arms at the news of a cut in their rate of pay, and a mysterious criminal gang, known as the 'Rippling Boys', robbing, murdering and body-snatching with impunity, gentle, timid Tom has his work cut out...

THE RESURRECTION MEN

A Thomas Potts Mystery

Sara Fraser

Severn House Large Print
London & New York

This first large print edition published 2010
in Great Britain and the USA by
SEVERN HOUSE PUBLISHERS LTD of
9-15 High Street, Sutton, Surrey, SM1 1DF.
First world regular print edition published 2008 by
Severn House Publishers Ltd., London and New York.

British Library Cataloguing in Publication Data

The resurrection men.
   1. Potts, Thomas (Fictitious character)--Fiction.
   2. Police--England--Worcestershire--Fiction. 3. Great
   Britain--History--George IV, 1820-1830--Fiction.
   4. Detective and mystery stories. 5. Large type books.
   I. Title
   823.9'14-dc22

   ISBN-13: 978-0-7278-7886-1

Severn House Publishers support The Forest Stewardship Council
[FSC], the leading international forest certification organisation. All
our titles that are printed on Greenpeace-approved FSC-certified paper
carry the FSC logo.

Mixed Sources

Product group from well-managed
forests and other controlled sources
www.fsc.org Cert no. SA-COC-1565
© 1996 Forest Stewardship Council

FSC

Printed and bound in Great Britain by the
MPG Books Group, Bodmin, Cornwall.

One

Hopwood Hamlet, Worcestershire
Thursday, 3 August 1826

It was two o'clock in the morning and foggy darkness shrouded the isolated canal-side cottage when the stranger came to hammer on its door and rouse its sleeping occupants.

'All right all right, I'm coming, I'm coming, blast you!' the old man shouted querulously as he shuffled along the stone-flagged corridor towards the door, which was shaking under the impact of the thunderous knocking. The noise ceased, and the old man came to a halt, shielding the wavering flame of his candle from the draught hissing through the cracked door panel.

'Who am you? And what do you want coming here at this hour to wake honest folks in their beds?'

'If you'm Sid Marsden, then I've brought you a parcel o' meat from the Needle Man,' a hoarse voice informed.

'I'm Sid Marsden all right, but how does I know that the Needle Man sent you?' the old man demanded suspiciously.

'He told me to tell you to ask me the questions you agreed on last time.'

'All right. Where does the cockchafer start from?'

'It starts from Warwick Jail.'

'And where does it end?'

'It ends on the gallows tree.'

'And what does you get for making the journey between 'um?'

'After you've swung from the gallows tree, you shares your first supper wi' Old Nick and Jack Sheppard.'

'Wait a minute.' Marsden grunted, and shuffled back along the corridor, to reappear a few moments later with a lighted lantern in his left hand and a bell-mouthed blunderbuss cradled within his right arm.

He placed the lantern on the stone flags some 4 yards from the door, then with a speed belying his advanced years darted to slam open the door bolts and retreat to stand beyond the light of the lantern, aiming the blunderbuss menacingly at the burly man who entered with a sack-wrapped limp bundle slung across his shoulder.

'Jesus Christ!' The newcomer grunted indignantly. 'There's no need to point that bloody thing at me. I've proved meself, aren't I? I've give you the proper answers.'

'Just lay it down there, on your side of the lamp,' Marsden ordered.

The newcomer carefully laid the limp bundle down in the pool of pale lamplight and deftly stripped the sacking to disclose the crumpled naked body of a young man.

'Move back now, go outside!' the old man commanded, and, once alone, knelt and carefully examined the corpse, noting the swollen abdomen, face and neck and the livid green and purple staining of much of the skin. He checked inside the mouth, tutting angrily when he found that all the teeth had been removed, then laboriously rose upright and shouted, 'I'll give you two on account.'

The burly man re-entered, protesting forcefully. 'The Needle Man says the price is eight sovs. He says it's worth at least sixteen to any sawbones because it's so fresh and sweet.'

'Fresh and sweet, d'you say? Fresh and sweet?' Marsden jeered derisively. 'It's been in the ground a week or more and dead a week afore that, or I'm a fuckin' Dutchman! And two on account is all I'm offering because you've pinched all its teeth as well. If you don't like it, then you can fuck off and take that piece o' rotted meat with you! I've seen more than enough o' you for this night!'

For a brief instant the other man's eyes narrowed murderously, but he spread his arms wide in acceptance.

'Oh all right then, you thievin' old bastard. But it's only been dead a week, and that's the gospel truth, that is. When shall I come back for the rest?'

'This same time a sennight from now.' Marsden tossed gold sovereigns, which rang upon the flagstones and rolled glinting in the lamplight to collide with the burly man's heavy iron-shod boots. He bent and lifted them in his thick fingers, biting down on one and then the other with strong yellowed teeth, then turned on his

7

heel and went from the house.

Head cocked, listening carefully, Marsden cautiously moved forwards, finger crooked on the blunderbuss trigger. Then he quickly slammed the door closed and shot home the heavy iron bolts. Only then did he exhale a long drawn out sigh of relief and allow his tense body to relax.

'Who was that?' The wizened-featured old crone came from the dark-shadowed end of the long corridor, rubbing sleep from her eyes.

'A bloke bringing a parcel o' meat from the Needle Man.'

'You didn't oughter have no more dealings with that bloody Needle Man!' The old crone berated angrily. 'He's pure evil, so he is. I once saw the devil standing at his shoulder, so I did. I see'd the pair of 'um just as plain as daylight, standing there looking just like twin brothers. As like as two pins they was!'

Her bare feet padded on the flags as she came to stand and stare down at the corpse, and declare challengingly, 'I hope this poor chap died peaceful in the bosom of his family, and had a proper decent Christian burial.'

'Now don't you fret your head about that, my duck,' Marsden told her soothingly. 'We'll be saying a prayer for his immortal soul, won't we, like we always does.'

The crone's lips pursed thoughtfully. 'I'm wondering where this chap's come from. I mean, the Needle Man lives somewhere near Redditch, don't he? How can we be sure that this chap aren't been lifted from the Redditch graveyard?

8

If he has, then five miles is too close for comfort, aren't it?'

Her husband shook his head and stated positively, 'Don't talk so sarft, woman! The Needle Man knows what he's doing! He knows you don't shit on your own doorstep!'

'I aren't bothered about him shitting on his own doorstep, you bloody old fool, you! It's having him shit on our doorstep that worries me!'

He smiled at her fondly. 'Now don't you fret yourself, my duck. I'll go down now to the wharf and fetch the barge alongside. I'll take this 'un up to our Charlie straight off, and be back wi' our share afore suppertime.'

A hundred yards along the towpath from the old couple's house, the burly man was being indignantly confronted by a youth.

'A sov, Master Watts! You promised me a sov at the least, and you said it might even be more if we got a good price.'

'Well I didn't get a good price, did I? So a shilling is all I can afford to give you. And if you keeps on whingeing about it, I won't give you fuck all.'

'It aren't fair, not after all the work I've done,' the youth whined. 'And you said we'd get a good price, so I can't see why you didn't get it.'

'Am you calling me a liar, Kinchin?' Watts hissed, and raised his clenched fist menacingly.

William Kinchin cowered fearfully. 'No! No I aren't.'

'Oh yes, you am.' Watts swung his fist, catching the youth on the side of his head and knocking him to the ground. Then he sent his heavy boot thudding into the squirming body.

'No, Master! No!' Kinchin squealed. 'I'm sorry! I'm sorry!'

'You'll be more than sorry if you crosses me again,' Watts spat out. 'And if I hears that you breathes so much as a whisper about what's happened this night, then I'll cut your balls off and make you eat 'um afore I kills you.'

He dealt a final savage kick, then turned and walked away.

Two

Redditch Township, Parish of Tardebigge, Worcestershire. Monday, 7 August 1826

Redditch Town stretched across hillsides which sloped east, west and north down into the broad meandering valley of the River Arrow. To the south, the hillsides narrowed into a long high ridgeway, passing through the satellite villages of Headless Cross, Crabbs Cross and Astwood Bank. The town centred around a triangular open space, 'the Green', and at the Green's eastern point stood the lock-up, a two-storey, crenellated building which was the parish prison and also the living quarters of the head constable of Tardebigge parish.

Within the lock-up in the early dawn, Tom

Potts lay on his narrow cot staring up at the cracked plaster of the whitewashed ceiling of his bedroom, pondering, as he so frequently did, the imponderable mysteries of human existence.

'Thomass? Thomass? I need you, Thomassss?'

The strident shouting from the adjoining bedroom penetrated the thin lath and plaster wall to din into his ears. He sighed resignedly, and called. 'I'm coming directly, Mother. Calm yourself.'

'Calm meself? Calm meself?' The strident shouts raised in pitch and became a howling scream of rage. 'How can I calm meself when I've been cursed with such a wicked, ungrateful, unfeeling blaggard like you for a son? Tell me that! Tell me!'

Tom pushed back the bedclothes and swung his feet on to the floor, groaning as his stiff cramped muscles painfully stretched. He stood up and mentally promised himself, yet again, that as soon as he had money enough he would buy a bed wide and long enough to accommodate his exceptionally long body and legs in comfort. He saw his elongated reflection in the badly stained wall mirror, and grimaced regretfully as he regarded the lean features topped with a long-tasselled nightcap, and the skinny, weakly body enveloped in a flannel nightshirt that reached only to bony thighs.

'Let's face it, my lad, you've never been any oil painting, have you? And the older you get, the plainer looking you become.'

'Thomasssss? Thomasssss?' The screeching dinned into his ears.

11

'I'll be with you in a moment, Mother.' He hastily dressed in his long drawers, knee breeches, long woollen stockings, shirt, waistcoat and ankle boots.

'How can it be possible that I birthed such an ugly, useless streak of a thing as you? Me, the belle of all Worcestershire, and your father such a fine handsome figure of a man?' The Widow Potts scowled disagreeably and noisily sucked her toothless gums as she regarded her only living child. Propped up in her double bed by heaped pillows, she presented a grotesque appearance. Short, hugely fat, her face a purple-hued balloon framed by the capacious floppy mob cap, her small pig-like eyes almost buried in puffs of flesh.

She shook her head, and her hanging jowls swung from side to side. 'I can only think that the Lord sent you to me as a punishment for my youthful, innocent vanity. That's the only explanation I can find to explain my birthing of you. You were sent as my cross to bear.'

Tom's lips twitched in an ironic smile. 'Well Mother, at least you can draw comfort from the fact that you have borne that cross with exemplary fortitude and grace for these past thirty-three years. I'll bring your breakfast shortly, after I've fetched the milk.'

'And what about my commode? It's stinking the place out. You should have emptied it last night, but you were out at all hours again, weren't you, you gad-abouting no-good!'

'I'm the parish constable, Mother. I have to attend when I'm sent for, no matter what hour it might be.'

Before she could reply, Tom had extracted the foul-smelling bucket from the commode and made his escape down the steep narrow stairs to the ground floor. The gloomy central passageway ran the length from the front to the rear of the building, and was flanked by rows of cell doors. At the front end was the large, arched, iron-studded entrance door; to his immediate left was a smaller door which led into the rear yard. The only daylight came from the arrow slits which flanked both doors.

Tom unlocked the rear door, went out into the high spike-crowned walled yard and emptied the bucket into the doorless privy in the far corner, then crossed to the opposite corner and cranked the handle of the pump which was situated there. The water gouted in haphazard spurts and Tom half-filled the bucket and carried it back to the privy to swirl and empty the soiled liquid.

He returned the bucket to his mother's commode, making no answer to her diatribe of complaint and insult, and pausing only to put on his coat and top hat and take up a jug, went from the lock-up. Outside, he drew long breaths of the cool, fresh early morning air and walked quickly towards the cowshed and dairy of Owen Morgan.

The bells of the town's needle mills were tolling their summons to the crowds of grimy, unwashed men, women and children hurrying towards yet another fourteen, fifteen, sixteen or even eighteen hours of gruelling, badly paid, unhealthy toil. Yet, despite that grim prospect, men

13

coalesced in groups, chattering and laughing as if they were heading towards a merrymaking; women and girls walked arm in arm, humming and singing popular songs; and young men and boys catcalled and scuffled light-heartedly.

Tom passed them, envying their camaraderie and marvelling at the resilience they displayed in face of the hardships of their lives. He wished wistfully that his own life had contained more of such companionable comradeship, instead of the comparatively solitary and friendless existence it had been. 'Good morning, Master Potts.' The swarthy, stocky Welshman greeted him at the entrance to the dairy shed.

'Good morning to you, Master Morgan.' Tom could not hold back a sleepy yawn as he returned the greeting.

'Up late last night, were you, Master Potts? Chasing villains, were you?'

Tom nodded and grinned wryly. 'Chasing, yes, but catching them, no. Someone was trying to break into Hemming's warehouse down Fish Hill, and the watchman raised the alarm. But whoever it was, was long gone by the time I got there.'

'It'll be them bloody Rippling Boys, I'll take my oath on it,' Morgan nodded sagely. 'I'm certain sure that it's them buggers who're responsible for all the thievery and robbery in these parts.'

'You could be right,' Tom agreed ruefully. 'But who are the Rippling Boys, and where are they from, Master Morgan? I've not been able to find any proof that such a gang actually exists.'

14

'Well, Master Potts, I reckon that if any man on God's earth can lay the buggers by their heels, it'll be you. Just look how you copped that bloody maniac who was slaughtering them women. People don't call you, Tommy Artful for nothing, does they?'

'Don't forget that people call me a great many other names as well,' Tom chuckled wryly. 'And none of them half as flattering as Tommy Artful.'

'Well, I know that a lot of people makes mock of you, but remember that it's God's will that you're such a queer-shaped, lanky, gangly cratur, and it aren't your fault you lack strength, and aren't much good at fist fighting,' the Welshman offered in comforting tones. 'But your mate, John Hollis, can always do the fighting for you, can't he? That's when he's not being afflicted with one of his lunatic turns, o' course.'

Made uncomfortable by how this conversation was progressing, Tom requested quickly, 'Might I have a pennorth of milk please, Master Morgan. I need to get back to the lock-up.'

'O' course you do.' Morgan grinned genially. 'How are you going to catch them bloody Rippling Boys else? You won't catch them if you spends all your time keeping me talking to you here, will you?'

He disappeared inside the building with the jug, and brought it back filled almost to overflowing with milk still warm from the cow's udder.

'There you go, Master Potts. Plenty o' cream in this, I'll tell you. It'll put lead in your pencil,

15

if you get my meaning.' Morgan winked salaciously as he gave Tom the jug. 'And you'll be needing plenty o' that if and when you gets wed to young Amy Danks. She's such a ripe little peach, she is.'

Tom felt his face reddening with embarrassment, and to hide it, turned and walked quickly away.

Back at the lock-up, he broke bread into a small bowl, poured milk over it and took it upstairs to his mother. Her expression radiating disgust, she stirred the mess with her spoon, and complained bitterly. 'Stale bread and watered milk! It's no wonder that I'm in such poor health, is it. You're slowly starving me to death. You should hang your head in shame for treating your own mother so badly.'

'It's good fresh cream milk, and it's what I'll be breakfasting on myself,' he rejoined defensively. 'And it's better food than what a great many other poor souls in this town will be eating this morning. A lot of them will be going to their work with no food at all in their bellies.'

'That's as maybe,' she retorted scornfully. 'But they weren't born the son of a gentleman, were they? They've not had your education, have they? They're pauper born, and pauper bred, and they'll lay in a pauper grave.'

She suddenly screwed her eyes tightly shut, hurled the bowl of milk and water to splash out across the floorboards, and raising her arms high, emitted a long wailing screech. 'And that's what's waiting for me, isn't it! A pauper grave! And it's all your fault, you useless, idle wretch!'

16

Tom sighed resignedly, and knowing from bitter experience that nothing he could say or do would placate her when she was in this mood, went back down to the ground floor.

In the alcove next to the rear door, which served as both storeroom and pantry, he stood staring glumly at the contents of the virtually empty shelves. The jug of milk, the remnants of a stale quartern loaf, a small piece of even staler hard cheese, one solitary onion, and on the upper shelving, a meagre collection of pots, pans, plates, bowls and mugs. His mother's outcry had left him with no appetite for breakfast, and now a wave of depression swept over him.

'It's true, isn't it? I really am an utter failure. Not a penny piece in my pockets, and no prospect whatsoever of improving my fortunes.' The image of a girl's smiling, pertly pretty face came into his mind, and his depression intensified. 'And Amy? What of Amy?

'Half the young bucks in the parish are setting their caps for her. She's certain sure to accept one or other of them this year. And who can blame her if she does? Because I'll never have anything other than poverty and hardships to offer.'

He felt a pressure on his calf and looked down to see the black cat rubbing its flank against him, purring loudly, tail held high. His eyes softened.

'Well, at least you seem to be content, Bathsheba. I'm sure you're ready for your breakfast, aren't you?'

He took a bowl from the shelf, filled it with broken pieces of bread and milk, and set it down on the floor. The cat sniffed at it, then arched its back and stalked away as if with haughty repugnance.

Tom couldn't help laughing aloud with rueful amusement. 'Dear God! Has it come to this? Even the damn cat spurns the food I'm offering!'

He self-mockingly called after the animal. 'I'm sorry it's such poor fare, Bathsheba. I'll leave your breakfast here anyway; you might feel hungry later on. And if anyone comes to find me, then please tell them I'm doing my patrol, so they must try again later.'

Tom walked southwards from the Green crossroads along the flat Evesham Street, which at this hour was almost deserted, and came to the steep upward slope of the Front Hill. Halfway up the hill, there was a young man outside the door of a small house.

Tom stared hard at him and smiled in surprised recognition. Andrew Adamson, surgeon and man-midwife, fixed the shingle bearing his ornately scrolled name and professions upon the doorpost and stepped back to consider its effect.

'Yes, that will do very well. Indeed it will.' He had unwittingly spoken aloud, and was surprised when another voice repeated after him.

'Yes indeed it will, Dr Adamson.'

The young man swung round and his eyes widened in shock. 'Good Lord! It's Tom Potts! What brings you here?'

'I live in Redditch, Andrew.' Tom grinned.

'Good Lord!' Adamson shook his head in amazement. 'Let me shake your hand, Tom. The last time we met, I recall you were three years into your medical studies. I didn't know you practised here.'

'Unfortunately I don't,' Tom told him regretfully. 'After my father died, there wasn't money enough for me to complete my studies. So I'm currently earning my bread in the post of constable of this parish.'

'You? A parish constable?' Adamson was incredulous. 'What a sad waste of your talents, Tom. You were the cleverest scholar in the school by far. Everyone believed you'd rise to fame and fortune, in whatever field you chose.'

'Well, I must now seek fame and fortune as a lowly parish constable.' Tom smiled ruefully. 'And I'm not a very efficient one, I confess. I don't strike terror into the hearts of the local bad lots. Quite the contrary in fact; it's they who sometimes strike terror into my heart. I'm still a weakly, cowardly sort of fellow, I regret to say.'

Still gripping Tom's hand, the fair-headed, slightly built younger man shook his head in firm rebuttal. 'Oh no, my friend, that is a statement that I must contradict. I remember only too well that when I was a very small and frightened new boy at school, it was only you who did your best to protect me against the bullies.'

'If I remember rightly, those same bullies then thrashed me also. So my protection was of little use to you,' Tom chuckled.

'Maybe not, but at least I had someone to compare my bruises with.' Adamson laughed and invited, 'Now will you step into the house and take some wine with me?'

Tom regretfully declined. 'I'm sorry but I can't at this moment.' He lifted his truncheon. 'I'm on official business, but I'm sure we'll have ample opportunities to have a drink and chat now that you're living here. I still have a great interest in medical matters, and spend a lot of time studying other subjects which interest me.'

'To hear you say that really pleases me, Tom.'

'What made you choose here to set up in practice?' Tom queried.

'An old acquaintance said that he that he could rent me suitable premises and also recommend me to a great many people to enable me to build up a practice.' Adamson grinned happily. 'And I'm pleased to say that he's been as good as his word. I moved in here about a week ago and already have some patients.'

'Who is your landlord?' Tom was curious.

'Jonathan Crowther, Esq. A very pleasant, gentlemanly sort of fellow. Do you know him?'

'By sight only.'

'He has a very beautiful stepdaughter, name of Mary.' Adamson winked suggestively. 'At one time she and I were very close, and I was half-crazed with love for her. The folly of youth, eh Tom! But for now I must love and leave you. I've a pressing need to earn money and start to pay off my creditors before they commit me to the debtors jail.'

The two men parted warmly and Tom continued up the hill, filled with pleasure at having met once more with his old schoolmate.

Three

In the village of Headless Cross, Jonathan Crowther stood in the small snug bar of the White Hart Tavern sipping his breakfast drink of hot rum toddy, listening intently to the information being whispered into his ear by the youth stretching up on tiptoe beside him.

They were an unlikely pairing. The middle-aged Crowther, tall, sinewy-bodied, dressed like a gentleman-dandy in a green swallowtail coat with red collar and cuffs and rows of bright brass buttons. A long silk waistcoat, ruffled shirt and silk cravat. Kerseymere breeches and polished top boots. A fashionable low-crowned top hat upon his barbered grey hair.

The rat-faced, weedy, undersized William Kinchin. Pallid, grimy skin showing through the rents in his tattered greasy clothing. A squared brown-paper cap set at a rakish angle on long lank hair, and clogs on dirty bare feet.

Kinchin came to the end of his recital and stepped back a pace, staring up at the older man with an expression constantly metamorphosing between hope and trepidation. Crowther's chisel-jawed features displayed no reaction, and he carried on sipping his drink without answering, or even glancing at the youth.

21

Time passed; tens of seconds lengthened into minutes. The youth's trepidation began to overpower his hope, and he started to fidget uncomfortably. Several times he drew a deep breath and opened his mouth to speak, but each time thought better of it, and closed his lips without uttering a sound.

Eventually Crowther's glass was empty, and he rang the handbell on the bar counter. The landlord, Nail Styler, a noted prizefighter with the battered features and flattened nose of his calling, came from the recesses of the house, placed a fresh glass of hot rum toddy on the counter before Crowther and left again, without a word being exchanged.

Crowther tasted the fresh drink, nodded appreciatively, then turned to his companion and smiled grimly. 'There's no doubt about it, William. I can declare without fear or favour that Nail Styler serves the best rum toddy in the whole of the Midlands.'

Kinchin's sensation of relief was so intense he felt his entire body sag, and he gasped weakly. 'If you says so, Master Crowther, then it must be so.'

'Oh it is so, William, for I never gild the lily. When I say something is black, then black it is.'

'I knows you do, Master Crowther. In fact everybody in these parts knows that when you says something, then it's the gospel truth,' the youth hastened to assure him fervidly.

With the grim smile still playing around his lips, Crowther hissed sibilantly. 'So you can be sure, William, that if what you now tell me isn't the gospel truth, then I'll be having your guts for garters before this day is out.'

'It's the truth, Master Crowther! On my life, it's the truth!' Fear caused the youth to gabble frantically. 'Johnny Watts told me that you'd said I was to go with him to the old graveyard and help him lift the stiff, which I did. And then we took it to that house on the canal at Hopwood, like I've told you. Only Watts made me wait for him some ways from the house and he took the stiff the rest of the way by hisself, and when he come back he 'udden't pay me for me work.'

'Why are you whining to me about it?' Crowther challenged. 'The bargain was struck between you and him, not between you and me.'

'Because it's well known that you'm a man of honour, Master Crowther, and the more I've thought about it, the more I've thought that you 'udden't have let him cheat me like he did, and punch and kick me like I was a dog, and swear that he'd kill me if I ever breathed a word to anybody about it.'

'But you're not a man of honour, are you, William? So why should I believe your story?' Crowther scowled threateningly, and his light-coloured hazel eyes glinted with menace. 'If you lifted the stiff last Wednesday night, why have you waited so long to tell me of it?'

'Because I was too feared to, Master Crowther. And that's the truth! I'd never lie to you, Master Crowther. I'd do anything to be one o' your men,' the youth pleaded fervently.

'You'd even peach on your own flesh and

23

blood, would you?' There was a calculating gleam in Crowther's dark eyes.

'I'd peach on anybody if you told me to, Master Crowther. But I'd swing afore I'd inform on you. May God strike me dead this instant, if I aren't telling the truth on that! So 'ull you take me into your service? 'Ull you, please?'

Crowther appeared to be deep in thought for some moments, before nodding. 'Perhaps. Where exactly are you living these days?'

'Under the hedges, or anywhere else I can creep into of a night time. Me Uncle Joe kicked me out a couple o' months past. He said I was thievin' from him.'

'And were you?'

'O' course I was.' Kinchin grinned, displaying rows of broken teeth blackened with decay. 'The bastard took me in after me mam and dad died, and he's had me slaving at the needles ever since, and never paid me not a single penny piece. The miserable tight bastard said that because he was giving me bed and board that was payment enough; and that was more than I was worth.'

Crowther nodded again. 'I'll tell you what I'll do, William. I'll give you a trial run for a few weeks, and see if you might prove to be of some worth to me.'

Beaming with delight, the youth began to gush profuse thanks, but Crowther silenced him with an angry frown.

'The first thing you'll do, is to keep quiet unless I give you permission otherwise. Understand?'

24

Kinchin nodded and clenched his lips tightly shut.

'Good!' Crowther smiled. 'I see that you're a fast learner. Now go to Bocker Duggins's doss house down in the Silver Street, and tell him from me that he's to give you free bed and board, until I say otherwise. Here's a couple of bob for tobacco, but don't go spending it on the pongalo. You're no use to me if you're a lush. So you stay indoors until you hear from me again. Understand?''

Kinchin nodded his head, and mimed with his hands to show that no alcoholic drink would pass his lips. Crowther jerked his head in dismissal and lifted the glass of rum toddy to his mouth.

Kinchin stayed silent until he was outside and some 20 yards away from the inn, then clapping his hands and jumping up and down, he hurled loud squawks of glee into the air.

Crowther rang the handbell and the stocky landlord came once more from the recesses of the building.

'I've a little job for you, Nail.'

Styler nodded. 'All right.'

'I want you to take note of whatever Johnny Watts spends here, and who he spends it with. And keep an ear out for any talk that he's flashing the rhino in the other pubs. But be discreet about it!'

'All right,' Styler grunted. 'Does you want another drink?'

Crowther lifted his glass and drained it, then shook his head regretfully. 'I've not got time for another one now, Nail. I've got a bit of business to attend to.'

'That bit o' business'll mean a loss for somebody, I'll bet.' Styler grinned.

Crowther's ivory false teeth gleamed wolfishly. 'That's as may be, but never forget, Nail, that one man's loss is always another man's gain, and the more widespread the losses, the more opportunities there are for a man like me to have gains. I'll see you later.'

Outside, Crowther mounted his smart trap and turned the glossy-groomed pony's head northwards towards the neighbouring village of Crabbs Cross, a mile and a half distant. The narrow road known as the Rough was made gloomy by the overhanging branches of the thick woodland bordering its sides, but it was even-cambered and well-maintained and the pony went at a brisk pace, the iron-rimmed wheels of the trap loudly crunching the freshly laid gravel.

A mile into the woodland, Crowther brought the pony to a halt outside a tumbledown cottage which stood a little way back from the road behind a pair of ancient yew trees. He sat for some moments staring with angry contempt at the broken rag-stuffed windows and ragged rotting thatch roof of the dilapidated building. Then his frown abruptly metamorphosed into a genial smile, as the cottage door opened and a petite young woman stepped out from it and came towards him.

'Good morning, Mary,' he greeted her. 'Are you come to welcome your loving stepfather?'

She came right up to the trap before answering challengingly, 'I've come to find out what my poor dead mother's husband wants with me?'

Her expression was sullen; her long black hair hung loose and uncombed around her shoulders. But the shabby threadbare gown accentuated the lush curves of her body, and her dark lucent eyes highlighted the beauty of her features.

Crowther kept smiling genially. 'What I want with you is just to help you in any way that I can, my dear.'

She tossed her head scornfully. 'Humph! I'll believe that when you actually do something to help me.'

Sudden anger flashed in Crowther's eyes, but the genial smile still curved his lips, and his voice was warm and friendly.

'That's the very reason I'm here now, my dear. I've come to offer your husband some work. So will I wait here for him, or shall I come into the cottage?'

'It's no use you doing either, because he's not here,' she snapped.

'Master John Watts is not here?' Crowther feigned surprise. 'But he's normally still in his bed at this hour of the morning, isn't he? It's widely known among his acquaintances that early rising taxes his delicate constitution.'

'You can spare me the sarcasm,' she hissed.

'Then where can I find him, my dear?' Crowther enquired pleasantly.

'God might know, but I don't,' she spat out angrily. 'So you've had a wasted journey.'

'Oh no, my dear. No journey is wasted that

brings me into your company,' Crowther assured gallantly, but his words were directed at her back as she ran into the cottage and slammed the door shut behind her.

Crowther turned the pony's head and went back the way he had come, but all pretence of smiling geniality had now disappeared and he was scowling with fury.

'You'll be swilling down the pongalo in some stinking alehouse won't you, Watts, while I have to undo the damage you've done to me. Well enjoy it while you still can, you stupid bastard!'

Four

On the southern side of the Redditch Green in the Fox and Goose Inn, landlord Tommy Fowkes's fat red face was glistening with sweat and indignation. 'You'm late again, Amy Danks! I'm not sure that I can keep on letting you get away wi' this sort o' service!'

'I'm sorry, Master Fowkes. Truly, I am.' The pertly pretty young woman lifted her hands to the strings of her bonnet. 'Shall I not take me bonnet off then? Have you given me the sack?'

'I ought to! If I warn't so soft-hearted, I'd give it you on the spot!' he blustered.

Her white teeth shone in a beaming smile. 'Now don't be so hard on me, Master Fowkes. I do work very hard for you, don't I?'

'Oh yes, when you deigns to come in here and do your work.'

She instantly detected the softening tone in his voice, and came towards him and lifted her hands to touch his bulbous cheeks. 'Oh Master Fowkes, it's no fault of mine that I'm late coming back. Me mam is sickly with the birthing almost on her, and me Dad was out all night chasing poachers. I couldn't leave her until he got back, now could I?'

The innkeeper tried to refuel his anger, but faced with her beguiling smile was forced to surrender. 'All right Amy. But don't you do it again, or by God I'll sack you on the bloody spot! Is that understood?'

She dropped a curtsey. 'Of course it is, Master Fowkes. And it'll not happen again. I promise!'

His bulbous, bloodshot eyes roamed up and down her shapely body, and his breathing quickened. 'Well now, since I'm being so kind to you, Amy, don't I get a reward for it?'

She appeared puzzled by his question, but in the depths of her blue eyes there lurked a gleam of amusement. 'I don't know what you mean, Master Fowkes. How could a poor serving girl like me be in any position to offer a gentleman like yourself a reward?'

'Well, you could give me a kiss.' He reached out for her, but with practised ease she evaded his groping hands.

'Oh Master Fowkes! How could you take advantage of an innocent young girl who is so partial to you? And your wife upstairs directly over our heads. Supposing she found out that you wanted to kiss me? And what about me Dad! You know that he'd kill any man who tried to take advantage of my weakness, don't you? Just look what he did to me last boyfriend. There's nothing can stop me Dad when he wants vengeance, Master Fowkes.'

Tommy Fowkes swallowed hard, and muttered resignedly. 'Just get the bar well stocked up will you, Amy, and check how much vittles we've got. We've a busy night ahead of us. The needle masters are having an important meeting, and I reckon nearly all of them will turn up for it, so business will be brisk.'

'What are they meeting for?' she asked.

'I'm not at liberty to disclose what the gentlemen have confided to me. Especially not to a little chit of a mere serving girl.'

'That's phooey, that is!' She giggled, and her blue eyes glinted mischievously.

'They haven't confided anything to you, if the truth be known. That's why you can't tell me, because you know nothing yourself. You're just a blowhard.'

'You cheeky little cat! Don't you dare speak to me like that.'

But she only giggled again, and retorted, 'Well, I shall know soon enough what they're about, shan't I? Because I'll be serving them their drinks, and I'll hear everything, won't I?'

For a brief moment he glowered at her, but then chuckled throatily, and accepted. 'So you will, but don't let on to anybody what I'm telling you, will you?'

'Of course I shan't, Master Fowkes. You know

how close with secrets I can be, don't you?'

'Oh yes, I know,' he nodded wryly. 'Well the secret is that the masters am going to decide on how much they're going to be cutting the pointing rates.'

'Cutting the pointing rates!' She echoed his words disbelievingly. 'When?'

Pleased with the impact his news had had, Tommy Fowkes grinned, and nodded. 'That's what I said, my girl. The rates are to be cut just as soon as the masters reaches agreement on the amounts. Mind you, they'll have trouble agreeing, like they always does. It could take weeks for it to happen.'

'It'll cause bloody ructions! They cut the rest o' the needleworkers' rates only weeks since, didn't they, and now they'm set on cutting the pointers rates!' Amy was still wide-eyed with surprise. 'The pointer lads aren't likely to just lie down under rate cuts like the others did. They'll kick up a storm when they hears about this, you just wait and see if they don't.'

For the first time a note of concern entered Tommy Fowkes's voice. 'I'm sure they will. I just hope that they leaves my windows in one piece. Because the last time they went on a randy, I had the whole of my front glass smashed to bloody smithereens.'

'Then you'd better hope that we do extra good business tonight, so that when they smashes it again you'll have enough money to replace it,' she giggled.

Five

The north-western point of the Green was the start of the long steep decline of the Fish Hill which fell away northwards, and at the very top of the hill stood the imposing Red House, the residence of Joseph Blackwell, Esq.

Joseph Blackwell was clerk to the magistrates, select vestry clerk, senior overseer to the poor, and the part-time coroner for the entire Needle District.

Small in stature, with deeply lined pale features and pedantic mannerisms, he was physically insignificant, which caused many new acquaintances to underestimate his true potency. Joseph Blackwell, however, was locally a very powerful and influential figure, who often likened himself to the spider lurking in the centre of his own widespread web.

Trained in the law, exceptionally shrewd and hardbitten, he was the custodian of many secrets concerning the ruling aristocracy and master manufacturers of the Needle District. Now in the mid-morning, sitting behind his desk in the large, book-lined study, hands clasped on his narrow chest, chin resting on steepled forefingers, he listened intently to Tom Potts report on the previous night's happenings.

'...and truth to tell, Sir, at this moment I've not the slightest idea who it was who tried to break into the warehouse. Although I've heard opinions expressed that it must be the gang called the Rippling Boys,' Tom finished with a doubtful frown.

'Am I correct in assuming that you do not believe that such a gang actually exists, Master Potts?' Blackwell queried.

'I've yet to discover any proof that they do, Sir.'

A wintry smile briefly touched Blackwell's thin lips. 'There is a wealthy gentleman named Jonathan Crowther residing in Crabbs Cross about whom there have long been whispered rumours concerning his knowledge of the Rippling Boys' evil doings. Register his name in your mind, Master Potts.

'Now however, I've something else to discuss with you. I've received a complaint from the Widow Craig concerning the grave of her son who was recently interred in the paupers section of the Old Monks Graveyard down in the Abbey Meadows. She is infirm and cannot easily visit the grave herself, so her neighbour goes in her stead to lay a posy and keep the mound tidily shaped. It seems that when the neighbour last went there, vandals had scattered the previously laid posy and damaged the grave mound. The Widow Craig begs my assistance in finding the vandals responsible.'

'I've much sympathy with the poor old woman, Sir,' Tom replied. 'But the old graveyard is used as a playground by street urchins,

33

and trampers sometimes doss down there for the night. I fear it might prove to be impossible to discover the vandal who scattered Widow Craig's posy.'

Even as he spoke, Tom knew that Blackwell was not concerned with the scattering of posies, and he waited expectantly for his Machiavellian-minded employer to elucidate further.

'I'm sure you're right, Master Potts, and scattered posies do not concern me in the slightest,' Blackwell admitted. 'But what does concern me is the possibility that the Widow Craig's son may have been taken by resurrection men.'

'Why do you suspect that, Sir?' Tom queried.

Once more Blackwell's thin lips curved in a bleak smile. 'The spider who wishes to eat well and live long must always investigate even the merest tremor on his web. I sense a tremor on my web, Master Potts.'

'So what do you want me to do, Sir?' Tom experienced an uncomfortable sense of foreboding.

'You must open the grave. However, no trace of your doing so must be left, and whatever you discover must remain strictly confidential between our two selves. I don't wish to cause the Widow Craig any distress, or to create alarm in the parish. Act without any delay, because I'll expect your report tomorrow.

'On a happier note, I'm pleased to inform you that my Lord Aston has graciously consented to accept my numeration of the fees owed to you for last month, and has authorized me to pay you the said sum immediately. Namely, two pounds, five shillings and five pence ha'penny.'

Relief flooded through Tom. 'Many thanks, Sir. I truly do appreciate the efforts you make on my behalf.'

The other man waved the thanks aside. 'You owe me nothing, Master Potts. You are only receiving what is due to you.'

He opened a drawer and took out a cash box from which he counted out the coins.

'Sign here, if you please, Master Potts ... Thank you ... I think that is all our official business for now. I bid you good day.'

With the comforting weight of the coins in his breeches pocket, Tom left the house and stood on the brow of the Fish Hill, staring northwards over the rooftops of the buildings beneath him to where the wooded fields of the Arrow Valley stretched to the distant gently rising horizon.

'I'll not get much sleep tonight,' Tom thought ruefully. 'Pray God that it rains to keep people indoors. I don't want to be discovered digging up Widow Craig's son, and be taken for a body snatcher and lynched!'

He could fully understand why Blackwell was insisting on secrecy. The vast majority of people shared the superstitious belief that a dismembered body would be unable to rise again whole and perfect on the final day of judgement. In consequence, resurrection men were feared and loathed for their desecrations of the dead.

The irony of the situation was that in law a human corpse was not classed as property, and therefore anyone who stole a corpse had committed no crime. A charge of theft could only be brought against a body snatcher who also took the corpse's shroud or personal jewellery or cosmetic adornment such as a wig or false teeth, since these were personal items and as such were classed in law as property.

Tom was not a sentimentalist about corpses. During his years of helping his surgeon father and his own medical studies, he had come to know how essential it was to practise anatomical dissection and considered it to be perfectly acceptable, with the proviso that eventually the corpse should be accorded a respectful burial. But the greatest difficulty for the various schools of anatomy was in obtaining a sufficient supply of dead bodies for study and dissection. This severe shortage meant that many professors and surgeons who taught anatomy didn't ask searching questions as to the origins, and paid well for the corpses, making body snatching a lucrative source of income for those who dared to do it.

Tom understood and strongly empathized with those who abhorred the thought of having their dead loved ones cut to pieces. People like the aged Widow Craig who had adored her son in life, was grieving bitterly for his loss, and wished only for him to lie in peace in his final resting place, no matter that it was only a shared pauper grave in a derelict graveyard.

Tom scanned the distant skies, hoping to see rain clouds approaching, but there were only clear blue horizons. He was walking slowly back towards the lock-up when he heard his name being shouted. He stopped and turned to see a young woman running towards him, and called anxiously, 'Amy? Are you all right? Has something bad happened?'

She reached him and came to a standstill, and was forced to catch her breath before telling him. 'Not yet, but something bad could happen before very long. From what Tommy Fowkes was saying, the masters are going to cut the pointers' rates, and sooner rather than later.'

Tom frowned in concern. The pointers were the men who dry ground points on to needles, day after day breathing into their lungs a fine dust of stone and steel, which in scant years mortally lacerated the soft tissues of air-sac flesh, until a man literally drowned in his own blood.

They demanded very high wages, which the needle masters had no other choice than to pay, because it was only the most reckless and life-careless men who would dare to do such deadly work.

Unfortunately for the more respectable and sober elements of the Needle District's population, the pointers' drink-fuelled excesses propelled them into frequent outbursts of wanton violence, and they brawled with the savagery of wild beasts.

Since being reluctantly forced into taking the post of constable, Tom had had several dealings with one or other of the local pointers, and although some of these encounters had been amicable enough, others had been painful to his body, and damaging to his morale.

He forced a smile, and assuming a confidence he was far from feeling, told the young woman,

'I'm sure that there won't be any serious repercussions, Amy. And if there are, then I shall just have to deal firmly with them, won't I? That's what I'm paid for.'

'But you don't get paid for being constable,' Amy protested. 'You only gets some bits o' fees and suchlike, don't you?' Then her manner became petulant. 'If you were getting regular wages, then you'd be able to get wed and have a wife and kids.'

He felt driven to defend himself. 'I didn't ask to become a constable, Amy. I was forced into it, as you well know. If I had money and prospects enough, then I'd like nothing better than to get wed.'

Again her manner changed instantly. She smiled coquettishly. 'And who would you want for your wife, Tom?'

An intense yearning filled him. 'Why you, of course,' he admitted huskily.

Yet another lightening-like change of mood altered her expression, and she snapped at him irritably. 'Then you'd best be quick about asking me to marry you, Tom Potts, because I'll not wait much longer for you. Not with so many others queuing up to wed me.' With a swirling of petticoats she hurried from him, and he stared miserably after her, bitterly castigating himself.

'You're a bloody fool, man. Ask her this very day, why don't you?' But then from the depths of his mind another voice questioned scornfully, 'And will you drag the poor girl down with you into poverty? Be selfish enough to ask her to share miserable quarters in a jailhouse, with your mother there to make both of your lives a misery with her evil tongue and vile tempers? Will you have children that you can't afford to even clothe and feed well, never mind pay for their educations, or provide for their futures?'

He shook his head, and sadly answered this interlocutor. 'No, I won't. I care too much for Amy to drag her down into such a life.'

He continued on his way, walking very slowly, depression weighing heavily upon him.

Six

Lozells parish, Birmingham

It was nearing midnight and Jonathan Crowther had been waiting in the back room of the tavern for several hours. The door opened and a man clad in dark clerical style clothing entered.

Crowther rang the handbell on the table before him, telling the waiter when he came. 'Bring us in a bottle of brandy, a jug of water and a couple of pipes of Turkish.'

The newcomer seated himself at the table, and no words passed between them until the drinks and pipes of tobacco had been served, and they were alone once more.

Crowther poured the brandy and measured water into it, then lifted his glass. 'Here's to your very good health, Charlie.'

There was a scowl on the saturnine features of Charlie Marsden and he did not lift his own glass in acknowledgement.

Crowther gusted an impatient sigh. 'Come now, speak out! Why have you kept me waiting here? I sent word to you hours since.'

'It's that parcel of meat you sent to me!' Marsden hissed. 'Eight sovs is too bloody dear by far, Jonno. And I thought we'd got an agreement that you'd always leave me the teeth. That last bugger hadn't got so much as a bloody stump left in his head. And don't try telling me he'd already lost 'um, because they'd been fresh pulled. It aren't fair trade, Jonno!'

Crowther lifted his palms outward in a placatory gesture.

'Now calm down, Charlie, and just tell me, how much rhino have you paid out for the parcel?'

'Me Dad give your man two sovs on account. But I'm not prepared to pay eight sovs for inferior goods, Jonno. And I thinks badly of you for trying to pull such a stroke on me.'

Again Crowther lifted his hands in the placatory gesture. 'All right, Charlie, you've every right to be angry. But surely you've known me long enough to know full well that this couldn't have been any of my doing. But I know for sure who's responsible for it, and they're going to be taught a lesson they won't forget in a hurry.' He paused momentarily to give full emphasis to his next words. 'And as compensation for your trouble, you won't have to pay a penny piece more for that parcel. I'll take the loss myself.

Now I can't be any fairer than that, can I?'

For a few seconds, the other man sat mulling over what he had been told. Then he nodded his head and conceded, 'It looks like I've been a bit too hasty. So let's say no more about it, and put this all behind us. And you don't have to stand any loss, Jonno. I'm prepared to pay eight sovs for the parcel, and what's more I'll give you the six sovs that I still owes on it right this minute.' He pulled gold coins from his pocket and counted six of them into Crowther's hand.

Crowther chuckled with satisfaction, and applauded. 'This is how it should be between old friends. Here's to your very good health, Charlie, and to plenty more profitable dealings between us.'

'I'll gladly drink to that,' Marsden rejoined.

Both men tossed back their drinks, and Crowther replenished the glasses. 'Tell your dad not to worry about that bastard coming for the rest of the money. I'll see to it that he don't get within a mile of your dad's house.'

Marsden chuckled grimly. 'I'll tell him, but he won't be worried anyway. The evil old bugger keeps a blunderbuss ready loaded, and he's quick to use it.'

Crowther laughed appreciatively, then invited, 'Let's get to business. How do you feel about handling some more top-quality needles? I'll be having a shipment before too long, and I'll let you have them cheap.'

The other man nodded. 'That sounds all right to me, Jonno. I can always find a market for Redditch Fancies. Only trouble is, I have to get

41

rid of them in bits and drabs. It's not such a quick return as I can get for a nice parcel of meat.'

'Don't you worry, Charlie, you'll be having more parcels of that commodity, and there'll be no more cock-ups like this last one.'

Marsden winked salaciously. 'Well now, seeing as it's a bit late for you to be going back home, how about a visit to Sally Dykes's place. She took delivery of a fresh little country wench just a couple of days since, what'll give you the sweetest night of your life.'

'You can personally vouch for that, I take it.' Crowther returned the wink.

'O' course I can,' his companion laughed.

Seven

In the hedge-enclosed old graveyard which bordered the Abbey Meadows, Tom Potts moved cautiously, circling the ancient yew trees, trying not to trip and stumble across the grave mounds and the few remaining tumbled gravestones as he searched for any trampers who might be dossing there for the night.

Once satisfied that he was alone, he lifted his lantern shutter and went to find the grave of Widow Craig's son. The feeble beam fell on the crudely fashioned wooden cross with the name carved on the cross piece. Tom moved the beam along the length of the mound and noted the slight declivity beneath the cross at its western end.

'That's where I must dig. I just hope the coffin isn't too deep.'

Tom knew how the resurrection men – the body snatchers – went about their gruesome business. They dug down to the head of the coffin, smashed a hole through the lid, hooked the corpse around its neck and hauled it bodily through the hole. They then stripped the corpse of any burial shroud or clothing, which they threw back into the hole and refilled the grave. Re-fashioning the mound and replacing any stone or cross, they went away with their spoils, leaving the grave apparently untouched.

There came a sudden gust of wind, eerily shivering the branches of the yew trees and carrying with it a spattering of raindrops.

'I'll be bloody well soaked before I'm finished here,' Tom thought unhappily, but consoled himself with the knowledge that the inclement weather would deter any insomniacs from taking midnight strolls in the vicinity.

He unrolled and laid out a large square of canvas, and moved the cross. He took off his top hat and coat and laid them carefully to the side, then began to dig into the mound with his spade and pitch the dirt on to the canvas. The wind repeatedly gusted, bringing more spatters of raindrops, then the gusts ceased and the raindrops became a steady downpour.

Within scant minutes Tom was soaked to the skin, and the sweat engendered by his hard

43

labour mingled with the rainwater chilling his body. He breathed a heartfelt sigh of relief when at a depth of about 3 feet his spade struck wood. A few spadefuls more and he could crouch and feel with his fingers the jagged edges of the hole in the coffin lid. He lay face downwards and tentatively inserted his hand into the coffin, to find only the bundled shroud.

'The bastards!' Tom cursed the body-snatchers. 'It'll break poor Widow Craig's heart if she comes to know of this.'

By the time he had refilled the grave, re-fashioned the mound and replaced the cross, he was liberally plastered in mud. He went to the nearby Pigeon Brook and immersed himself in its chill waters, gasping for breath as he washed the mud from his clothing and body. Shivering violently, he exited the brook, put on his coat and top hat, picked up his spade and the roll of canvas and jogged away.

Back at the lock-up, he kindled a fire in the grate of his room and stripped, rubbing his goose-pimpled flesh hard with a strip of rough towelling, sighing with relief as he felt warmth returning.

In bed, although bodily weary, sleep eluded him. He lay staring up into the darkness, his mind filled with mental images and racing thoughts. He pictured Joseph Blackwell's lined features, and could not help but acknowledge admiringly.

'You're truly the king of spiders enthroned upon your web, Master Blackwell. You seem to gather information from all manner of sources. I just hope you can point me in the right direction of these body snatchers. Because truth to tell, I've not the slightest idea of where to begin looking for them.'

The first palings of dawn had entered his room before he drifted into uneasy sleep, which was very shortly disturbed by the screeching voice from the adjoining room.

'Thomassss? Thomassss? Where are you, you lazy hound? Are you going to leave me near dying from thirst and hunger? God damn and blast you, you unnatural, cruel, useless blaggard! A mother's curse on you!'

Tom blearily dragged himself from his narrow cot.

'I'm coming, Mother. Calm yourself, do.'

Eight

Tuesday, 8 August, mid-morning

Joseph Blackwell sat with steepled forefingers in front of his chin, eyes closed, listening intently to Tom's report on what he had discovered in the old graveyard.

When Tom fell silent, the older man sighed heavily and opened his eyes to stare keenly at Tom. 'Poor Widow Craig. No good can be served by telling her what has happened, so it's best if it remains our secret, Master Potts. Are

45

you agreeable to that?'

'Most willingly, Sir,' Tom confirmed. 'Unfortunately, at this time I've not the slightest notion who the robbers might be. But I'm sure that they've local knowledge and connections.'

'It would appear so,' Blackwell concurred. 'Have you any thoughts on how to proceed with the investigation?'

'All I can think of at this moment, Sir, is to wait for the next death in the parish and then keep a covert surveillance on the grave, in the hope of catching the scum in the act.'

'Very well.' Blackwell nodded. 'Do you have anything else to report?'

'There's a stray cow near to the Unicorn Inn, Sir, which I'm going to catch and take down to the pound.'

'Good day to you, Master Potts.' Blackwell opened the leather bound ledger on the desk before him and started reading it.

'Good day, Sir.'

As Tom headed for the central crossroads, he saw a scarlet-coated soldier entering the Fox and Goose, and smiled.

'I wonder if he's got a billeting order. That'll please Tommy Fowkes, I don't think! Having to give free bed and board to a redcoat.'

It was noon when Jonathan Crowther brought his pony and trap to a halt outside the Fox and Goose, where a long row of horses and other pony traps were already tied to the wall-mounted hitching rings.

'Will I take charge of it for you, Sir?' a poorly

46

clad old man hurried to offer.

Crowther dismounted and handed the man a coin, then entered the inn. He did not go into the inn's best room, the large bar-parlour favoured as the meeting place of the needle masters and rich farmers, but instead entered the shabbier tap room which was patronized by the respectable artisan classes of the town.

Behind the counter, Tommy Fowkes was helping his staff of men and girls to fill trays with freshly filled glasses and tankards, which they hurried to take into the bar-parlour.

Fowkes's fat red face was glistening with sweat, and he was breathing hard with effort, but his eyes were gleaming with satisfaction. He saw the incomer and greeted him.

'You're more than welcome here, Master Crowther. I'll see to you in two ticks.'

'There's no hurry, Master Fowkes.' Crowther smiled. 'I've plenty of time to spare. It looks like you're doing good business.'

The innkeeper winked broadly. 'It's an ill wind that blows nobody any good. What's bad news for the pointers has been good business for me.'

'The masters have cut the pointing rates then, I take it?' Crowther queried casually.

'They have indeed,' Fowkes chuckled. 'They had another meeting here this very morning, and it turned out to be a gold mine for me, because all that argufying makes 'um real thirsty. They went at it hammer and tongs so they did. But you can take it from me that there'll be plenty o' weeping and wailing in this town when the news spreads, because the cuts am deep.'

47

'How will that affect your own trade?'

Fowkes shrugged his meaty shoulders. 'Not a bit, Master Crowther. I don't get any pointers drinking in my place. I get a better class of custom than them animals.'

'Indeed you do,' Crowther agreed equably. 'I'll tell you what, Master Fowkes. I could do with something to eat. I've an errand to do which will take me a couple of minutes, so perhaps you could have a beefsteak broiled for me. I'll not be long.'

He walked quickly eastwards from the inn towards the lock-up, where the road forked into Alcester and Red Lion Streets, and took the latter route. Some distance further he reached the Red Lion Inn, to the side of which was the arched entrance to the most notorious slum in the town, the Silver Street. Reluctant to soil his highly polished boots with the thick layered filth of the long fetid alley, he beckoned a ragged urchin.

'Go to Bocker Duggins's house and bring William Kinchin here to me. When you come back with him I'll give you a penny.'

The child ran through the archway whooping with delight and returned quickly with Kinchin. Crowther tossed the urchin the coin and then whispered rapid instructions to Kinchin, who saluted like a soldier and hurried away.

Well satisfied, Crowther strolled at a leisurely pace back to the Fox and Goose.

Nine

Wednesday, 9 August 1826

It was fifteen minutes past five o'clock in the morning and the sun was barely rising over the eastern horizon when Tom Potts was roused from sleep by the loud discordant jangling of the lock-up bells. Dragging himself from the cramped cot, wincing from the painful stretching of stiff joints and muscles, he hurried down to open the front door and poke his night-capped head around its edge.

Unaware of the opened door, the diminutive man on horseback, dressed in the green uniform coat and jockey-cap badged with the ciphered bugle horn of His Majesty's Mail, continued tugging the iron-rod bell pull.

'Can you stop doing that please!' Tom begged. 'You'll wake my mother else!'

The man let go the rod and stared unbelievingly at Tom's face.

'Bugger me! Be you standing on a ladder, or summat?'

'No, of course not!' Tom snapped irritably. 'I'm merely quite tall.'

'Quite tall!' the man exclaimed. 'Fuck me, I've seen shorter steeples!'

'What do you want?' Tom demanded.

'You! That's if you're Potts the constable?'

'I am.'

'Then you're wanted straightaway at that cottage with the yew trees in front that's on the road between the Crosses. It's a gent who calls himself Dr Adamson what's sent for you.'

Tom felt bemused. 'But why does he want me?'

'I'm fucked if I know,' the man shrugged carelessly. 'I was just passing on me way when he come out and shouted me.' With that he cantered away.

Tom hastened to wash and dress, then took up his constable's staff – the 3-foot long crown-topped, blue, red and gold-painted truncheon which denoted that he was on official duty – and after checking that his mother was sleeping soundly, left the lock-up.

'My God, Tom, but you've taken your time!' Andrew Adamson's youthful features displayed a hint of resentment.

'Considering I was roused from sleep, and it's over a mile and a half to walk, I think that I've made good time,' Tom retorted with his own twinge of resentment. Tom was forced to bow his head in the low-ceilinged bedroom of the tumbledown cottage.

Adamson pointed at the naked body of the heavily bandaged man who was lying on his back upon the low bed, snorting stertorously through his slack-jawed mouth.

'It's Jonathan Crowther's son-in-law, Johnny

Watts. At about two o'clock this morning George Jolly the Carrier and his man were travelling along the Rough and they found Watts lying on the road. Jolly knew him so they brought him here, and eventually I was sent for.

'He's taken several heavy blows on the top and both sides of his head and has a fractured right forearm, a smashed nose and left-side cheek-bone. He could well have cracked ribs and internal injuries also.'

'Has he been able to speak about the attack?' Tom questioned.

'No, I've not been able to rouse him.' Adamson shook his head, and a hint of cynicism entered his tone. 'Crowther thought it might be robbers who did this.'

'Do you doubt that?' Tom had noticed the change in tone.

Adamson swept his hand to indicate the dirty room. 'Crowther's paying my fees for treating the bugger, so I'm not going to argue with his opinion. But does this pigsty look like the habitation of a man worth robbing? He's stinking of drink so I reckon it was a drunken brawl.'

'Where's his wife now?' Tom asked.

'She's at Crowther's house. It's the three-storied one opposite the Fleece at Crabbs Cross. And when you see her, please tell her from me that her husband is to be kept as still and quiet as possible, and that I'll return this afternoon. Now I'm going to have my breakfast.'

He lifted his medical chest and went downstairs and out of the front door to his tethered horse. As he mounted and heeled the beast into motion he shouted in parting. 'The head injuries are severe, so it could be a few days before he'll be recovered enough to be questioned, Tom. I'll let you know as soon as he does. Goodbye now.'

Tom went to the corner of the room and carefully examined the small heap of bloodstained clothing which had been stripped from the injured man, paying particular attention to the pockets in the coat, waistcoat and breeches. He frowned thoughtfully when he could find no signs of cuts or tears in them.

'Footpads wouldn't take the time to carefully turn every pocket inside out, they'd rip or cut them open. So perhaps Andrew's right and it was only a drunken brawl?'

'Was it you who had him waylaid, Crowther?' Mary Watts demanded for perhaps the hundredth time, and for perhaps the hundredth time Jonathan Crowther sighed and denied it.

'Of course it wasn't me. How can you think that when I've always been such a fond parent to you?'

'Fond parent?' Her pretty face was flushed with angry resentment. 'Fond parents don't try to get into their stepdaughter's, bed do they! I know you've done this! You've always hated John, haven't you!'

'God save me,' Crowther groaned wearily. 'I was in the snug bar of the White Hart all last night. Just go and ask Nail Styler or any other of the lads who were there. They'll confirm what I say.'

'Oh yes,' she scoffed angrily. 'They'll confirm

it all right. Because you've got them all in your pocket, haven't you? They'll swear black is white if you tell them to. They'll rob and cripple and...'

The door knocker rapped loudly, and Crowther wagged his forefinger and placed it across his lips, frowning warningly at the young woman, who instantly fell silent.

The knocking came again.

'Now act the dutiful daughter,' Crowther hissed and gestured to her to go and open the door.

As she moved to obey, he slipped his hand into the inner pocket of his coat and gripped and cocked the small pistol hidden there.

'Good morning, Ma'am,' Tom greeted politely. He had heard her raised angry voice but had not been able to distinguish what she had been shouting. 'My name is Potts, and I'm the constable of Tardebigge parish. Am I addressing Mrs Watts?'

'You are indeed, Constable,' Jonathan Crowther's voice sounded from within. 'Show the gentleman in immediately, Mary, there's a good girl.'

Tom's eyes quickly scanned the room as he stepped through the door. It was well furnished, its chairs upholstered, coloured prints on the walls, brocade curtains at the window. A costly, gleaming black leaded oven grate with burnished brass fittings. Staffordshire ornaments on the mantelshelf and in one corner a fine, sonorously ticking grandfather clock. He noted that the several candlesticks held expensive wax candles,

53

not the cheap tallow candles or the even cheaper fat-impregnated rush lights.

Jonathan Crowther rose from his fireside chair, hand outstretched in greeting. 'I assume you've come to ask us about the terrible outrage committed upon my son-in-law, Master Potts. Do please sit down.' He waved Tom to a chair facing his own. 'Can I offer you some refreshment? Ale or wine perhaps?'

'No, I thank you. The doctor asked me to tell you that Master Watts must be kept as quiet and still as possible, and that he himself will return this afternoon. I'm afraid that I must ask you both some further questions.' Tom was finding it difficult to reconcile the whispered rumours of evil doings with the personable reality of this hospitable man.

'Of course, Sir. Mary, come and sit beside me.' Crowther patted the arm of his wide chair. 'I know that it's very painful for you, my dear, but if we are to have any hope of catching the miscreant who injured our poor John, then the constable must be told everything that you can recall.'

She perched on the arm of the chair, and with her stepfather's arm comfortingly supporting her, told Tom in tearful, halting tones how she not seen her husband since the previous day, and had been asleep in her bed when the carriers had brought her husband to the cottage.

Always susceptible to beauty in distress, his heart softened by the sight of the tears falling from her dark, doe-like eyes, Tom had to force himself to reluctantly request, 'Did the carriers

54

tell you exactly where they found your husband, Ma'am?'

'No. But they said he had his arms stretched out sideways, just like Our Dear Saviour on the cross.' She wailed, and covering her face with her hands, burst into loud sobbing.

'I'm truly sorry that my question has caused you such distress, Ma'am.' Tom felt mortified. 'I do apologize most sincerely for adding to your troubles like this.'

Crowther waved his hand in gracious dismissal. 'You've nothing to apologize for, Master Potts. You're only doing your lawful duty. Jolly showed me the spot and I shall take you there myself.'

'Step-papa, I must go back to my John,' Mary Watts beseeched chokingly. 'I must be with him.'

Crowther smiled fondly and planted a kiss on her tear-streaked cheek. 'I wouldn't dream of letting you be by yourself, my dear. I shall show the constable where John was found and then we'll go directly to your cottage.'

The trio made the journey with stepfather and daughter riding in the trap and Tom walking alongside. When Crowther had solicitously helped Mary Watts into the trap, Tom had noted her patched, threadbare gown and shawl and the clumsy clogs on her dainty feet. Now he was wondering why such an apparently doting and prosperous step-parent should allow his step-child to be so poorly clad and shod.

Some 30 yards past Watts cottage towards the Headless Cross end of the Rough, where the track was closely hemmed in by thick shrubbery and trees, Crowther reined the pony to a halt and pointed his whip.

'There, Master Potts, that's the spot.'

'Please can you tell me what direction his head was towards?' Tom requested.

'I believe Jolly said he was face downwards towards Headless Cross,' Crowther informed him. 'Now I must take my stepdaughter to her husband. I trust that you'll keep me informed as to any progress your investigation makes.'

'Certainly I will.' Tom assured him. Witnessing Mary Watts's distress had made him determined to help her.

'Many thanks.' The other man nodded, turned the pony's head and drove back towards Crabbs Cross, his stepdaughter sobbing heart brokenly beside him.

Tom moved to the site pointed out by Crowther in the centre of the roadway, and carefully scrutinized the pooled, still-damp bloodstains on the hard-gravelled surface, dipping his finger into them and tasting the metallic saltiness for confirmation.

Crouching low and peering hard at the ground, he moved away from the stains, slowly quartering the trackway, his excitement burgeoning as he discovered more spattered blood droppings, which metamorphosed into a distinct trail leading slantwise across the roadway and in the direction of Crabbs Cross. The blood spoor came to an end very close to a large, densely leaved bush next to the clearing were the cottage stood. He turned his attention to the bush,

56

minutely examining its outer layers, and found spattered spots on the upper leaves. Again he used his tongue to confirm that they were blood.

For almost an hour he traversed crabwise around the blood spoor and its vicinity, before coming to certain conclusions. 'Watts was first attacked next to that bush. His forearm was broken in the first attack, because that's likely to be a defensive wound. He took blows on the face and nose, sending the blood flying to spatter across the bush. He ran towards Headless Cross and was brought down by the other blows to his head. He lay face downwards and was hit about the head some more, the blood spraying and then pooling. The weapon might be a cudgel or perhaps an iron bar.'

Tom Potts began to walk back to Redditch. He passed several people along the way, some of whom greeted him, but he returned those greetings absently, engrossed in his own musings.

'Motive for the attack? Robbery? Drunken quarrel? Attempted murder? But why choose to make the attack so close to Watts's home, where there was every likelihood his wife would have heard the commotion? And why didn't Watts run towards his home?'

Inside the cottage, Jonathan Crowther was urging Mary. 'Let me send Annie Kelper here to nurse him. You can come back and keep house for me. Come now, what do you say?' he coaxed. 'I'll buy you your own pony and trap, and you'll eat and drink whatever you fancy, and be dressed as a lady.'

'And have to share your bed!' she retorted

sharply. 'Not to mention I'd never be given a moment's freedom to be myself, and to do what I want to do, when I want to do it.'

'And what did you do when you wanted to do it? Why you ran off and married that animal who's kept you in rags and near starving ever since.'

'Only because you wouldn't help us!'

'Why should I have helped you when you only married him to spite me, and only made a fool of yourself by doing it.'

The truth struck home to her, and she reddened and blustered, 'It's your fault that we've fallen on hard times. He had good prospects when we got wed.'

Crowther drew a long deep breath, and fought to control his rising temper. 'Look, there's nothing to be gained by you and me being at each other's throats like this. I admit I was hard on you and him when you got married, and I'm sorry for it. But what's happened to him now is none of my doing. I swear on my mother's grave that I've had no hand in it!'

'Well, if it wasn't you, then who was it?'

Sensing that he was winning her over, Crowther smiled grimly. 'At the moment I've not got the slightest idea. But I'm going to find out!'

He paused to see what effect his promise had, and after a few moments she nodded.

'All right, Crowther. I'll believe you this time. But don't you dare be lying to me again.'

'I'm not! Now let me send Annie Kelper here to look after him, and you move back in with me. Listen, I promise I won't try anything on

58

with you. I only want to help you.'

Mary shook her head. 'No, I'm going to stay here and look after John myself. But if you really want to help me, then give me some money so I can buy some necessaries.'

He immediately handed her some coins, then told her. 'I'll start enquiring straightaway into who might have served your man out. I'll call later.'

Outside he mounted his trap and drove directly to the White Hart Inn.

'How's your son-in-law. Is he dead?' Nail Styler greeted him immediately he entered the snug bar.

'No, worse luck.' Crowther rejoined. 'I'll have a rum toddy, Nail.' Frowning thoughtfully, he went to sit down.

As Tom passed through the toll gate at the top of the Mount Pleasant, he was startled from his reverie by the frantic shouting of the man who came hurrying to block his path.

'Thomas Potts! Thomas Potts! I've been looking for you all over the place!'

Tom forced a smile. 'Well, you've found me now, Charles. What service can I do for you?'

Charles Bromley, the middle-aged, pot-bellied, sole proprietor of Bromley's Stationery Emporium for All Articles of Stationery, Rare and Antique Books and New Literature and third in rank of the trio of Tardebigge parish constables, took off his crumpled top hat and mopped his pink bald pate with a grubby handkerchief.

'A moment, Thomas, I beg of you. Allow me

59

to catch my breath,' he beseeched mellifluously, his eyes alarmingly magnified by his bulbous-lensed spectacles, and his ill-fitting bone false teeth slipping up and down as he spoke.

He carefully stretched and plastered long strands of greasy grey hair across his pate, replaced his hat, and brushed the dust from his threadbare clothing with his pudgy hands, before going on, 'You need to warn the pointers not to cause trouble, Thomas. I'm quite sure they're intent on mischief. There are a gang of them who've gone on strike because their rates have been cut.'

Tom's throat instantly tightened, his heart thudded nervously, and he snapped involuntarily, 'If you're sure that they intend mischief, then why didn't you confront them? Were you too afraid to?' The next instant, impelled by the shamed realization that he had levelled the accusation because of his own fear, Tom apologized, 'I'm sorry. I didn't mean that.'

His embarrassment deepened when Charles Bromley quietly told him, 'You don't have to apologize for speaking the truth, Thomas. I freely admit that my mother didn't birth a hero.'

This man truly puts me to shame, Tom thought glumly. *Unlike me, he at least possesses moral courage enough to admit that he's a physical coward.*

Aloud, he asked gently. 'How many were in that gang that you met with, Charles, and where do you think they might be heading?'

'Bonny Southall was leading a dozen or more, and they were coming up from Bredon.'

'Has there been any violence?' Tom was dreading what the answer might be, and was relieved when Bromley shook his head.

'Not yet.'

'Does Joseph Blackwell know what's happening?'

'I don't know.'

'Oh my God! Then we'll have to act on our own initiative.'

'Oh no!' Bromley's head shook so hard in rebuttal that his top hat fell off. 'Oh no! I'm not acting on anybody's initiative! I'm not going within a mile of those buggers!'

'But it's our lawful duty to warn them against causing a riot,' Tom protested.

'Bugger our lawful duty!' Bromley was adamant. 'If those buggers cripple us the only reward we'll get from the parish is a ticket to the bloody poorhouse!'

He crammed his hat tightly down on his head, then urged, 'Come with me, Thomas. We can say that we were chasing a vagrant across the parish boundary to make sure he was gone. And now I'm gone as well!'

He hurried away at a puffing, shambling trot.

Tom stared after the fleeing man, and smiled wryly. *Fear lends wings to the feet. And the way I'm feeling I could easily fly past him.*

He drew in several deep breaths to calm his jangled nerves, summoned all his resolve, turned on his heel and began to walk rapidly towards Redditch. Halfway down the long gently sloping Mount Pleasant his mouth dried with fear when he saw the crowd approaching him.

61

'Oh my God! There must be forty or more of them!'

They looked to be all young men, the vast majority of them wearing red shirts, leather waistcoats and breeches, ribbed woollen stockings, and iron-bound clogs, with bright-coloured neckerchiefs around their throats and square brown paper caps on their shaggy heads; the virtual uniform which proclaimed to the world that these were the notoriously savage-natured pointer lads of Redditch Town.

Some of them spotted Tom and howled threats and abuse.

'Oh my God! What can I do against so many?' Every atom of Tom's being was clamorous with the desire to escape from this threatening violence. But he stubbornly refused to surrender to that clamouring, and moved forwards to confront them.

The crowd came on until only yards distant Bonny Southall, the tall, strongly built, handsome young man leading them, threw up his arms and brought them to a halt.

'What do you want with us, Constable Potts?' he challenged.

'I want to know what you intend doing, Master Southall.' To Tom's surprise his voice sounded firm and steady.

'We're on strike, and we're calling for all the other pointers to join us.' Southall exuded confidence. 'And now that the Combination Acts have been abolished, we can't be arrested any more for combining together to demand our lawful rights to our wages and employments, unless we uses violence to further them demands.' He turned and asked his followers. 'Am we going to use violence, lads?'

'Noooo!' they roared in unison.

Southall grinned at Tom, displaying fine white teeth. 'Does that satisfy you, Constable Potts? Can we pass you now?'

Knowing that what the man had said was accurate, Tom nodded.

'You may pass, Master Southall, but I would urge you to continue to act peacefully. Good day.'

He stepped aside, and Bonny Southall led his jubilant followers onwards.

Feeling weak with relief, Tom continued his own journey.

Ten

Sunday, 13 August 1826

It was mid morning, the sun was high and hot in a clear blue sky and the population of the Needle District were celebrating the Sabbath day. The God-fearing, respectable inhabitants were attending the morning service in church or chapel. Those God-ignoring disreputable in-habitants not still sleeping off the effects of the previous night's drunken debaucheries, were in the alehouses seeking alcoholic salve for their aching heads and brawl-gained bruises. Yet others were wandering through the woods and fields enjoying relief from their drudgeries in mills and factories and workshops, while those fortunate domestic servants who had kindly employers were hurrying homewards to briefly see their loved ones.

Tom Potts was doing none of these things, however. Instead he was pursuing one of his esoteric interests.

Firstly, he pressed his finger and thumb pads against the sheet of paper lying on the table before him. Then took a small bowl of finely powdered charcoal and using a small soft brush, delicately dusted a little of the powder across the place where he had pressed his finger and thumb pads.

Slowly the dark shapes emerged and he laid aside the bowl and brush and gently blew the excess powder from the paper. Lifting his magnifying glass, he examined the results. A warm glow of satisfaction brought a smile to his face, as he compared the papillary patterns of his finger and thumb pads with the charcoal imprints. His thoughts raced wildly.

'They're almost perfectly recognizable. My technique is improving. What it could mean is, supposing I find fingerprints left by a burglar or suchlike, then I could arrest a suspect, take his prints to the site of the crime and compare them. If they are the same pattern, then it will prove his guilt!'

When a little later Amy Danks came to call, he welcomed her eagerly.'Amy, come over here and look at what I've discovered.'

He was sitting on a three-legged stool staring through a magnifying glass at the sheet of paper placed on the small sunlit table beneath the leaded window. She came to stand at his shoulder and looked down at the paper.

'It's naught but a sheet of paper, Tom.' She was distinctly under-impressed.

'No it's not, Amy!' His lean face was flushed and smiling with excitement. 'Look.' His long finger pointed. 'Look here, and here, and here! Can't you see what these are?'

'Black smudges, like coal marks.' She shook her head impatiently. 'Honest to God, Tom! Can't you find naught better to do than to stare at smudged bits of paper all day? No wonder your mam is so mad at you always! You tries my patience as well sometimes!'

He chuckled, and explained. 'These aren't mere smudges, my dear girl, they're finger-prints.'

'So what if they are? When I get the coals in for me mam, I leave dirty finger marks on things I touches until I washes me hands clean again. Now are you coming out for a walk with me instead of wasting your time with this tom-foolery?'

'Sweetheart, you don't understand what these fingerprints really are.' His enthusiasm was not diminished by her attitude. 'I've been studying people's fingerprints and they all differ from each other. Each set of prints has distinct patterning: some are like arches and some like whorls, while yet others are loops and there are

65

even some that appear to be a mixture of all three patterns. I've been experimenting to find the best method of showing up these prints. On light surfaces I use powdered charcoal, but for dark surfaces powdered chalk. Don't you see what this means?'

'No, I bloody well don't see, and what's more I've no interest in such nonsense.'

'But let me try and demonstrate to you what it means...' he began, but she cut him short.

'I'm fed up with this nonsense, Tom. I came here to take you out for a walk, but instead I find that you want to waste my time looking through that bloody silly spyglass at a load of coal smudges. Well I'm off! I'm fed up of you paying more attention to all sorts of dull books and things than you do to me. There's plenty more men in this town who want to pay me all their attention! So don't ever speak to me again!'

With that parting shaft, she was gone in a flurry of skirt and petticoat and tossing blonde curls.

'You see, now even that empty-headed flibbertigibbit is tired of you, and I don't blame her one little bit!' Widow Potts' corncrake voice sounded loud and clear from the adjoining room.

Tom could only sigh in weary resignation and turn back to his studies, but even that pleasure was abruptly curtailed when the bells jangled and the small boy to whom he opened the door told him, 'You'm come to Yorks Yard. There's been a robbery at Batesshed.'

When Tom arrived at the small warehouse

situated at the end of a narrow alley of tenements which led off the hill directly behind the
Duke of York tavern, a cluster of slatternly
women with snot-nosed infants hanging on to
their skirts greeted him mockingly.

'Come a bit too late, aren't you, Master Constable?'

'Didn't want to risk running into them robbers,
did you?'

The door of the single-storied warehouse was
wide open, and as Tom neared it a man charged
out of the building to confront him.

'Above 200,000 finished needles I've lost!
Above 200,000! If I warn't a God-fearing Christian man, I'd bloody well use bad language! I
bloody well would! And that's God's truth, that
is...!'

The elderly Needle Factor Jasper Bates was
literally foaming at the mouth as he ranted his
fury, and although Tom was much the taller man,
the spittle spattering against his face drove him
to take a backward step to avoid the bombard-
ment.

'...200,000 or more finished needles! All on
'um packed and ready for selling! And the fair
opens next week! My customers 'ull be coming
for their bloody needles, and I aren't got any for
'um! If I warn't a Chapel elder I'd use foul
language, so I bloody well 'ud! May the Good
Lord strike the thievin' bastards dead! Above
200,000 I've lost! No wonder me heart's playing
me up!'

Bates clutched his chest with both hands and
gasped hoarsely.

Tom seized the opportunity to voice his first words. 'I'm sorry for your loss, Master Bates.'

'Sorry for me loss?' Bates screeched in a high falsetto. 'You'm sorry for me loss, am you? How the fuckin' 'ell does you think I'm feeling? I'm fuckin' well ruined, and me fuckin' heart's broke to bits!' He flung out his arm. 'And so's me fuckin' roof! Look at the fuckin' great hole the bastards knocked in it!'

'That's how whoever robbed you gained entrance then?' Tom surmised.

'How the bloody 'ell do I know?' Bates challenged furiously. 'They could have dug a bloody great tunnel and come up through the floor, for all I knows.'

'Or you might have been pissed out o' your yed again and left the bloody door open for 'um to just walk in,' a woman jeered and was applauded by her companions.

'You just shut your bloody mouth, Maggie Cull, afore I does it for you,' Bates threatened.

'Come on then, you old cunt! Just you try it!' Maggie Cull stepped forwards, brandishing her fists. Flat nosed, brawl-scarred, beefy-shouldered and fists like hams, she was a notorious female pugilist who fought with both men and women for prize money.

'Go on, Maggie! Trim his lamps for him!' The women laughingly urged her on.

Dreading the onset of violence, Tom swallowed hard and stepped between the pair.

'Stop this! In the King's name, I'll arrest the first one who strikes a blow.' He tried desperately to sound authoritative, but to his dismay

68

the words came out in a breathy whinny.

'Ooooh, hark at her!' Maggie Cull jeered mockingly. 'Her's going to arrest the first one who strikes a blow.' She squared up aggressively to Tom. 'Come on then spindle-prick, try and arrest me in the fuckin' King's name, why don't you. I been waiting for the chance to put you on your arse, you stuck-up, fancy-talking bugger. Come on then!'

Enthralled by the drama, no one had noticed the man who was coming rapidly towards them, until he burst through the cluster of spectators.

'Where's me breakfast, you slut?' He squared up to Maggie Cull, dodged the blow she aimed at him and punched her on her jaw.

She staggered sideways and thudded upon the cobbles.

Ernie Cull faced the shocked onlookers and invited, 'Anybody else want some?'

No one spoke, and after a brief moment he grabbed his wife by the hair and pulling her upright, dragged her away.

Tom breathed a heartfelt sigh of relief, and told Bates, 'I need you to clarify a few things for me, if you please, Master Bates. To enable me to proceed with my investigation.'

Bates gruffly assented, and Tom asked a series of questions, listening very carefully to the answers he received.

'Thank you, Master Bates, I think that's all for the present. I'll not need to detain you further if you've other business to attend to.'

'Other business.' Bates seemed near to shedding tears. 'The only other business I can look forwards to attending to, is how best to arrange my affairs to deal with my bankruptcy. Close the door when you've finished here, will you, even though there's nothing left worth pinching.' He walked disconsolately away.

Tom went into the warehouse and found it virtually empty but for a few old rags and broken pieces of wooden roof laths. He looked up at the gaping hole in the tiles, and since Bates had vehemently insisted that the door had been chained and padlocked, was confident that the thieves had entered through the gabled roof. He theorized on what had happened.

'It's likely there were three of them because of the height of the roof. They boosted one man up on to the roof. He removed the tiles and passed them down, trying to be as quiet as possible. When the hole was big enough, he dropped inside. A second man went up on the roof and the man inside threw the packets of needles up to him, which he then passed to the third man outside the building.

'Once they had all the needles, the man on the roof leaned through the hole and pulled the man inside back out. He would have been the smallest and lightest of them, and the man who pulled him out must have been the strongest.'

Tom grinned wryly. 'And now that I've solved how it was done, all I need to do is to identify the culprits.'

He went outside and stood staring thoughtfully at the red-clay roof tiles which had been neatly stacked against the wall.

'If only you could speak to me.'

He bent and lifted a tile which was partially covered in greenish black damp-mould, and excitement burgeoned when he saw the indented imprints of fingers upon the mould. Carefully sifting through the remaining tiles, he found others with hand and finger imprints in the mould.

'These must be left by the thieves' hands. I might discover distinctive marks on these indents, such as a cut scar or something similar.'

He fashioned a crude tray from the broken roof laths and carefully arranged selected tiles upon it. As he carried his load along the row of tenements, a woman poked her head from one of the windows and shouted, 'Hey, come and look at this, girls. The bloody constable's robbing old Bates' tiles now. You can't trust any bugger these days, can you?'

Face burning with embarrassment, Tom bent his head against the storm of catcalls and laughter which erupted from the tenements, and quickened his pace. With Tom's departure, the prospect of further excitement receded and the cluster of spectators dispersed.

Concealed among them, William Kinchin had been watching and listening with avid interest. Now he headed towards Crabbs Cross, to make his report to Jonathan Crowther.

Eleven

Mary Watts opened the door to Kinchin's frantic knocking.

'I must speak to Master Crowther right away, Missus.' He tried to move past her, but with a strength belying her petite body, she violently pushed him backwards.

'You can stay outside! You stink too bad to step foot into a decent house.'

'Who is it, my dear?' Crowther's voice sounded from inside.

'It's me, Master Crowther, and I'se got important news for you,' Kinchin shouted, and then bared his teeth defiantly at the young woman. 'And it's news that's for your ears only, Master Crowther.'

'Let him in, Mary,' Crowther instructed,

She stood aside with a bad grace, and spitefully kicked Kinchin's shin as he went past her.

'Ouch! There's no call for you to do that, you bloody bitch!' Kinchin protested, then shouted out in alarm as Crowther's hand gripped hard on his throat and he was slammed back against the wall.

'Don't you dare speak to my daughter in that manner, you filthy gutter rat!' Crowther's eyes blazed with fury. 'I'll break your bloody neck for you!'

Choking, Kinchin desperately struggled to draw breath, but was too mortally afraid of this man to try and fight free.

'Leave him go, Crowther,' Mary Watts intervened. 'It was my fault. I shouldn't have kicked him like I did.'

After a few seconds, Crowther released his grip, and Kinchin stumbled outside to bend over, dragging in wheezing gasps of air.

Mary Watts sat on a stool before the fire, while Crowther reseated himself at the table and called, 'Come inside, William.'

Kinchin entered and stood rubbing his throat with his fingers, warily regarding his employer, who was wolfing down a large platter of fried bacon and mushrooms, smacking his lips and smiling with satisfaction. When he had finished eating and the platter was empty, Crowther beamed genially at the nervous youth.

'Do you know, William, I can state without any fear of contradiction, that my dear Mary brings me the finest and freshest mushrooms in the whole of Christendom. She also cooks them to perfection with butter and grated cheese. They're a feast fit to lay before His Majesty himself.'

'Yes, Master. I'm sure they be,' Kinchin croaked submissively.

'So, tell me your news, if you please, William.'

The youth glanced uneasily at Mary Watts, who was gazing into the flames of the fire.

'Well Master, well, it's, it's, well...' Kinchin

stammered nervously.

'Spit it out, damn you!' Crowther frowned. 'I've no secrets to hide from my dear daughter here. You may speak freely, Boy.'

'It's Bates's warehouse in Yorks Yard, Master. It's bin broke into in the night and thousands and thousands o' sharps bin robbed. At least that's what Bates is saying is how many.'

Crowther's eyes glared, and his lips tightened into a thin harsh line. For a brief while he stayed silent, then he gritted out, 'Bring me my writing gear, Mary.'

She hurried to fetch him the articles he needed. He filled a sheet of notepaper with neat copperplate handwriting, folded and sealed it, and beckoned Kinchin to him.

'You'll take this to Worcester. You're to go to the Horn and Trumpet coach inn there, and ask for Benjamin and Thomas Fairfax. Do you know them by sight?'

'I do, Master.'

'Good. When you find either one of them, you give this letter to him. But you don't show it or speak of it to any other living soul, or I'll have your guts for garters. Do you understand?'

'I do, Master.'

'Get going then.'

'But how do I get to Worcester?' Kinchin asked plaintively. 'I've never been further than Bromsgrove in me life.'

Crowther bared his teeth in a savage grin. 'You go to Bromsgrove and ask the way to Droitwich. And when you get to Droitwich you ask the way to Worcester. It's only 20 miles or so. When I

74

was your age I used run that far for fun.'

'I'll run all the way as well,' Kinchin promised fervently.

'Good lad.' Crowther chuckled, and handed the youth a coin. 'Here's a shilling to buy some grub with after you've given the letter to my nephews. Don't go spending it on the pongalo!'

'I won't, Master. I swear I won't.' Kinchin exited at speed.

Twelve

'Thomassss! Thomassss! Where's my supper? Do you mean to starve me to death, you wicked, unnatural hound? And it's getting dark. I need my candle lighted, and my fire needs tending to. The devil definitely stole my own dear baby from his cradle, and put you in his place when I gave birth! There's no doubt of that! No doubt at all!' Widow Potts's screeching resounded through the lock-up.

'Dear God, give me strength,' Tom sighed resignedly, and laying aside the magnifying glass through which he had been studying the tiles, went from his own room to his mother's adjoining it.

'Oh there you are!' She glowered from her bed, and for a brief moment Tom was reminded of the pictures of ogres he had seen in his child-hood books of fairy stories. He shook his head to dispel the images, and told her quietly, 'I'm cooking a mutton broth for you, Mother. Please be patient, it'll be ready within about a half hour.'

He stoked up the fire and used a taper to light the wall-sconced candle.

'Phwaw! Phwaw! Phwaw!' She ballooned her fat cheeks and blew out a series of loud explosive raspberries, then screeched derisively. 'Half an hour, he says! Do you hear him, Dear Lord? Half an hour! How can he know how time is passing, when he's got his nose stuck in some stupid book, or he's fiddling with all sorts of bits of rubbish every day and night, instead of finding a decent employment and earning enough money so that he can repay me for all of the sacrifices I've made for him?'

She paused to draw breath, and then abandoned her one-sided conversation with the deity, and recommenced her direct verbal assault on her son.

'You're a disgrace! You're a worthless scoundrel! Your poor dear father would rise from his grave if he could only know how cruelly you treat me, the woman who has slaved for you all her life. This woman who has sacrificed everything for you. This woman who has known only suffering and misery since the death of my beloved husband...'

'I'll bring you your food as soon as it's ready,' he told her, and returned to his own room, asking himself for the thousandth time why he should be stupid enough to put up with this woman's constant verbal, and at times physical, abuse.

Tom had greatly loved and revered his father, but even as a child had found nothing to love or revere in this unpleasant woman, who from his earliest memories had always been a vicious-tongued, evil-tempered and violent shrew. Then, as always, came the reason why he did put up with her, as in memory he could hear his own youthful voice promising his dying father that he would care for his mother until death should take one of them.

Now with the ease of long practice, he mentally detached himself from the continuing screeching next door, and concentrated on what he had discovered on the damp-mould of the tiles. Among the smears of hand and finger prints there were two clear sets of finger indents, in which a finger appeared to be truncated. He lifted his magnifying glass and spent some time closely studying the two sets in the wavering light of the candle. Then took his brush and bowl of charcoal powder and dusted them. But strain his eyes though he might, he could not distinguish any definite pattern on these indents and eventually abandoned his scrutiny.

'Ah well, at least I know now that mould isn't a good surface for fingerprints. But definitely whoever's imprint this is, the top joint of the ring finger on their right hand is missing. But with all the machinery that's operated in this district, missing fingers are common.'

He pondered for a few moments, then painstakingly measured the indents and noted down the figures. 'A smallish hand judging from these measurements, but that doesn't take me much further.'

He mentally reviewed the list of possible suspects, convinced that they would be local people who would have known that Bates had the stock of ready-for-sale needles in his warehouse. After a couple of minutes, he grimaced. With the pointers on strike, and numbers of them probably getting short of money, the potential list was long.

He sighed, laid down the magnifying glass, and went to serve his mother her dinner. After he had eaten his own bowl of mutton broth Tom felt a sudden urge to escape from his austere room and go to see Amy Danks.

'I have to go out, Mother. I'll not be long.'

'That's right! You go out and leave me all alone, why don't you? I hope that the Good Lord takes me to his bosum while you're out gallivanting. It'll be a merciful relief from my loneliness and suffering. Go out, and be damned to you!'

'Would you like me to bring Bathsheba to keep you company?' he asked.

'Bathsheba? Keep me company? Do you think that I'm a witch and that evil black imp of Satan is my familiar? It's your bloody cat, so let it keep you company! If I have my way I'll wring it's bloody neck the first chance I get!'

Tom couldn't help but chuckle wryly. 'I'll warn her to keep well away from you then, Mother.'

He went downstairs and out the front door, with his mother's parting diatribe still assaulting his ears.

* * *

The bar-parlour of the Fox and Goose held only a few customers, and Tom was disappointed to find that Tommy Fowkes was alone behind the bar counter.

'Is Amy not working tonight, Master Fowkes?' he asked.

'Oh yes, Constable, she's here all right, but I wouldn't say that she's working at present.' The innkeeper's tone was offhand, and a hint of malicious enjoyment glinted in his bloodshot eyes. 'You might say that she's engaged elsewhere.'

Tom knew that Fowkes disliked him personally, and he could accept this fact with equanimity, so stayed civil.

'Can you tell me when she's likely to be coming back in here, please?'

'You may ask her that yourself, Constable. She's in my private parlour keeping my soldier nephew company. Feel free to go there.' Now the malice was in his sneering grin and voice. 'But you'd best knock the door afore you goes in, because you don't want to catch her doing anything that she didn't oughter be doing, does you? You know how these young girls can kick over the traces when they catches the scarlet fever at sight of a redcoat.'

Tom felt a flush of anger at the other man's leering attitude, but bit back the urge to rise to the bait and demand what he was insinuating, so merely nodded.

'Thank you, Master Fowkes, I'll make sure to knock before I enter.'

He went down the corridor to the rear of the inn, and as he reached the private parlour door heard the tones of a man's voice and Amy's tuneful laughter.

Tom came to an abrupt standstill. A sickening sense of dismay flooded through him as he was racked with the memory of Tommy Fowkes's sneering words and grin.

Dear God! Has she caught the scarlet fever, I wonder?

The man's voice sounded again, the words muffled by the thick wooden door panels, and again Amy's laughter rang out.

Tom lifted his fist to rap on the door, and then let it drop to his side before his knuckles touched the panels. His heart was pounding and his throat felt unbearably tight. For a brief instant the urge to turn away and leave was almost overwhelming.

Stop acting like a damned fool, he castigated himself furiously. *It's all perfectly innocent, I'm sure.*

He raised his fist once more and this time he managed to knock, but he was so distraught that his knuckles crashed jarringly against the panels, causing the door to shake on its hinges.

'Lord God Almighty! Be you using a bloody sledgehammer?' Mrs Fowkes shouted irately as she swung the door open and thrust her red, sweaty, multi-chinned face up at Tom's. 'Is the bloody house on fire, Master Potts, that you must needs make such a din and frit to death respectable people at their supper?'

Absolutely mortified, he could only stammer,

'I do most sincerely apologize, Mrs Fowkes. I never meant to alarm you.'

'He doesn't know his own strength, do you, Tom?' Amy giggled from her seat at the table strewn with the remnants of a meal and bottles and glasses. She told her companion, 'This is my old friend Thomas Potts, Sergeant Sullivan. He's the constable of this parish.'

'I'm sure that any friend of yours, Miss Amy, is a most worthy gentleman.' The soldier rose from his chair and bowed. 'I'm honoured to make your acquaintance, Master Potts.'

Tom stiffly returned the bow. 'And I yours, Sergeant Sullivan.'

'Sergeant Sullivan has just returned from India, Tom. He's had such wonderful adventures there. You must persuade him to tell you of them.' Amy was flushed with excitement, her eyes shining , her pretty features animated. 'He's hunted wild elephants and tigers and fought the black savages in a score of battles, haven't you, Sergeant Sullivan?'

Tom's heart sank as he saw her reach out and clasp the other man's hand.

Sullivan's fine teeth flashed down at Amy, and Tom could not help but enviously acknowledge that the sergeant, resplendent in scarlet coatee, white trousers, shining gold chevrons and glittering braid and buttons, cut an exceptionally dashing figure. Added to which his suntanned face was handsome, his dark hair thick and glossy, his shoulders broad, his waist slim and taut.

'I'm sure that Master Potts has had equally

exciting adventures of his own in foreign parts to relate to us, Miss Amy. Is that not a fact, Sir?'

Sullivan turned his gleaming smile on to Tom, who suddenly felt uncomfortably stiff and awkward and could only stammer a disclaimer.

'I'm afraid, Sergeant, that I'm not able to lay claim to experiencing any exciting adventures, either here or abroad.'

Amy tugged on Sullivan's hand and demanded, 'Do sit down and tell me some more stories.'

'What was it you wanted with us, Constable Potts?' Mrs Fowkes frowned. 'Only we'd like to get on with our little party.'

Tom was made diffident with embarrassment, 'I just wanted a word with Amy, Ma'am.'

'Well?' The woman lifted her thick eyebrows interrogatively, and all eyes turned expectantly to Tom.

Tom could feel himself blushing as he met Amy's smiling gaze. 'I only came to ask if you wanted to go to the fair with me, Amy.'

She tossed her head and exclaimed impatiently, 'Oh Tom! You know very well that I have to work on fair days. It's one of our busiest times.' She waved her hand in a gesture of dismissal and turned her eager attention to the dashing soldier once more. 'Now do carry on with the story you were telling me, Sergeant Sullivan. The one where you challenged the Rajah to fight you in single combat.'

A wave of despondency swept over Tom, and he muttered, 'Perhaps it's better that I should go now.'

They all totally ignored him, and croaking a strangled, 'I bid you all a good night, then,' he made his exit.

Outside on the street, he dragged in gasps of the damp night air to ease the tight constriction in his chest. *I'm going to lose her, aren't I?* he told himself miserably. 'That soldier is sweeping her off her feet. And it's all my own fault for being such a dull, timid wretch. It's my own fault, and I deserve to lose her.'

Unable to face going back to the lock-up to be subjected to more of his mother's corncrake diatribes, he wandered off aimlessly into the darkness.

Thirteen

Thursday, 17 August 1826

It was almost noon of the day of the August Livestock Fair in Redditch. At the bottom of the Unicorn Hill, the Pound Meadow was a discordant bedlam of lowing cattle, bleating sheep, honking pigs, barking dogs and the loud voices of men and women disputing the ages and conditions of the beasts, haggling prices, sealing bargains with a spit on palms and clap of hands between buyer and seller.

At the entrance to the broad flat meadow stood a line of men and servant maids seeking to be hired by the wealthier farmers and their wives. Each man wore an emblem to denote his occupation or skill: whip cords for the ploughmen and carters, cow hair for the dairy men, shepherds crooks and sheep wool, and common labourers rakes and spades. The women wore the white aprons of cooks and domestic maids, the blue aprons of dairy maids, nursery girls carrying baby rattles, and the lowliest menials with their brooms and scrubbing brushes. All standing in stoic silence, waiting hopefully for the approach of a prospective employer, knowing from bitter experience that should they make the first approach it would be construed as being disrespectful and acting above their lowly station in life.

Among the thronging crowd there were some men who had not come here to buy or to sell, or to seek to be hired. They moved inconspicuously, drawing no attention to themselves. Wandering apparently aimlessly, stopping occasionally to listen to the bartering, watching until the deal was done and taking careful note of the seller stowing money in purse or pocket.

Tom Potts and Joseph Blackwell were also in the Pound Meadow. They made an incongruous coupling: the tip of Blackwell's top hat reaching only to Tom's shoulder, with the added inches of Tom's top hat exaggerating their discrepancy in height even more. They also seemed to be wandering aimlessly, but at intervals Blackwell would tug on Tom's coat sleeve, and tell him quietly, 'Over to your left, Master Potts. The middle-aged fellow wearing the brown jacket, white waistcoat and brown beaver hat, do you see him?'

'Yes, Sir.'

'Mark him well. He's called Gloucester Jack. He's a Ticket-of-Leave man, and returned from transportation a year past. He used to be a pickpocket until his fingers lost suppleness, then he turned to foot padding. He'll have others with him today, and they'll be selecting potential targets for robbing.

'That elderly woman wearing the costly-looking widow's weeds who is talking to the young girl. She's a procuress for the Birmingham brothel keepers, and calls herself Lady Amelie Smyth-Fothergill. She was born Sally Dykes and to my knowledge has never been married. If you should see her leaving here in company with any young girl, then challenge her and demand to know what she's about, and question the girl closely about her own antecedents and parentage.

'Those gypsies over there are members of the Lee family. They should have been hung for horse thieving years since. But like all their cursed tribe they're as cunning as rats.

'Look there at that young ragamuffin. Name, William Elkin. Father hung, mother transported for life, two sisters working as prostitutes in Birmingham, and a brother serving hard labour in Warwick Jail. He's been born for the gallows, and hopefully it won't be too many more years before he's swinging from them.'

Tom concentrated hard, storing names, faces, clothing and physical stature into his visual memory, marvelling at the older man's almost encyclopedic memory for wrongdoers.

'Stand here for a moment, Master Potts. There are twin brothers clad like dandies to our rear right. Observe them closely when they pass us. They're Thomas and Benjamin Fairfax, the maternal nephews of Jonathan Crowther. I'm convinced that like him, they're involved in all manner of criminalities; but again like him, it's been impossible to lay them by the heels.'

Tom covertly studied the pair as they walked past, emitting a wave of scented pomade. In build they were above average height and athletic-bodied. He was struck by their familial likeness, both having the chisel jaw and high sharp cheekbones of their uncle. They were dressed alike in fashionable dark blue swallow-tailed coats, heavily padded at the chests and shoulders, with white waistcoats and trousers, silken shirts and cravats and costly white beaver top hats.

When they had passed, Tom remarked, 'I must say, Sir, that their cousin is very dowdy dressed in comparison to them, yet much prettier to look at.'

The older man chuckled drily. 'She's not their blood cousin, Master Potts. However, I would say that if she returns to the house of Jonathan Crowther, and her behaviour towards him is amenable once more, then she'll undoubtedly be garbed fashionably.'

'Yes, he did act as if he was very fond of her,' Tom mused aloud.

Joseph Blackwell nodded slowly. 'Oh yes. But

86

I think he might be fond of her in a way that is not fatherly. I understand he was extremely angry when she ran off to wed John Watts. But then, he is not the first stepfather to covet the ownership of a stepdaughter's body.'

'Do you think then that Crowther might be responsible for the attack on Watts?' Tom queried.

'He might well be, Master Potts.' Blackwell frowned severely. 'However, John Watts is a ne'er-do-well, thief and poacher. When criminal scum fall out and do damage to each other then that is all to the good for the law-abiding elements in our community. So don't expend a deal of effort in trying to track down whoever it was who laid Watts low. I would much prefer you to concentrate on bringing to book the still active criminal elements in the parish.'

He looked around him, and snapped tetchily. 'I see that Grier is coming at last to cry the reward for information concerning the rogues who robbed Bates's warehouse. Now I want you to remain on constant patrol during the fair's hours of opening, and I've sent word to Hollis that he is to come down and assist you in keeping order. So I suggest that you fetch your staff and immediately commence your duties. Good day to you, Master Potts.' Blackwell touched the brim of his top hat and walked away.

Resplendent in green tailcoat, scarlet waistcoat and ostrich-plumed tricorn hat, the elderly Jimmy Grier, town crier, shuffled stoop-shouldered through the crowd. He came up to Tom and complained querulously, 'These fuckin'

87

rheumaticks 'ull be the death o' me. I'm getting too old to do all this walking and hollering.'

Tom smiled sympathetically. 'Well Jimmy, as soon as you've cried the reward, then you'll be finished work, won't you?'

'Will I buggery!' the old man contradicted indignantly. 'Lord bloody high and mighty Aston is going to preach in the chapel this Sunday next, and he's sent word that I'm to cry it all through the fair 'til the finish tonight.'

In an abrupt change of mood he bared his toothless gums and cackled gleefully. 'Mind you, the more I cries it, the fewer folk 'ull go there, because it's well known that his bloody sermons am bloody rubbish.'

'That's very true, Jimmy,' Tom chuckled in agreement.

'Right then, I'll make a start.' Grier swung his brass bell, ringing out the summons to pay attention, then bawled hoarsely.

'Oyez, oyez, oyez, a reward of ten guineas is offered to any person giving information which leads to the capture and conviction of those who committed the robbery of finished needles from Master Jasper Bates's warehouse in Yorks Yard during the night of Saturday the twelfth of August... The Reverend the Lord Aston will be preaching in the Chapel on the Green this coming Sunday evening service, the twentieth of August ... God Save the King!'

He shuffled on, leaving Tom standing alone.

Mindful of what Blackwell had told him, Tom strolled through the crowd looking for the woman who called herself Lady Amelie Smyth-

Fothergill, and was relieved to see her walking towards the meadow entrance by herself. Keeping his distance, he followed and watched as she climbed into a pony and trap driven by a swarthy-featured man wearing a footman's livery, who then whipped the pony into motion and drove away northwards down the road leading out from the town's confines.

'Tom, I've been looking all over for you.'

Amy Danks came up to him and when he saw the smile on her rosy face, a warm glow of pleasurable relief struck through him, and he blurted. 'Oh Amy, I'm so pleased to see you.'

'And I'm pleased to see you, Tom Potts. Have you forgotten that you promised to take me round the fair? It's in full swing around the Green, and the fiddlers and drummers are already playing for the dancing.'

'But I thought you were working today, Amy,' he said in dismay.

'Not all day, I'm not. I told you ages ago that Tommy Fowkes said I could have a couple of hours off. So we can do the fair and have a dance as well, can't we?' She reached out to take his hand. 'Come on, Tom, it's naught but smelly beasts and boring business down here. There's all sorts of show booths and stalls up town.'

'Don't you remember? When I came to the pub to ask you, you told me that you'd be working all day. And now I can't take you round the fair. Joseph Blackwell has just this minute past told me to commence my duties immediately. I'm sorry, sweetheart. Really I am.'

Her blue eyes hardened and she pouted with

petulant anger. 'But you promised me ages ago that you'd take me to the fair! I've had to pester Tommy Fowkes for these last days to give me the time off, and now you've let me down again.'

'I'm sorry, truly I am,' he told her miserably. 'I'm just as disappointed that I can't go to the fair with you as you are, sweetheart.'

'Oh no!' She shook her head forcefully, causing her long blonde ringlets to dance wildly upon her cheeks. 'I'm not disappointed! Because I've got lots of other beaus who're begging me to go to the fair with them. And they're all of them much younger and handsomer than you. And they've got more money to spend as well. I'm finished with you for good this time, Tom Potts! I shall go to the fair with Sergeant Sullivan. So don't ever speak to me again! Don't even look in my direction!'

She turned on her heel and lifting her long skirts, ran from the meadow.

Tom could only gaze sadly after her.

Fourteen

It was four o'clock in the afternoon and the factories, mills and workshops throughout the Needle District had been left deserted. Redditch Green was a noisy seething mass of men and women, youths and girls, excited shrieking children and crying babes in arms. Garishly decorated stalls and booths lined the central triangle of roadways, and the gaily painted caravans and carts of the show people cluttered the adjoining streets, guarded by the old and infirm while their younger, stronger brethren plied their trade.

Depressed by his encounter with Amy Danks, Tom moved slowly through the crowd, his crown-topped, yard-long truncheon of office borne like a musket on his shoulder. He was keeping a sharp lookout for suspicious characters, and periodically stopping to check the varied goods and knick-knacks being offered for sale by the many pedlars and hucksters, paying particular attention to any packets of needles on their trays, but finding none with the telltale wrappers of Jasper Bates.

All types and conditions of humanity were here. Fine clothed dandies reeking of Macassar oils, their scented womenfolk in costly bonnets and gowns of silk and satin. Soberly clad respectable artisans and trades people with their wives and children, faces clean and shining, linen freshly washed and ironed. Prosperous farmers in broadcloth and riding boots and their embroidered-smocked, clod-booted labourers. Young working girls and women chattering and laughing in their best finery and bonnets, eagerly eyeing potential sweethearts among the young men and youths also dressed for the occasion in their flash waistcoats, striped kicksy-up trousers and rakishly cocked caps and hats.

Ragged beggars swarmed, displaying their sores and mutilations, the stench of their unwashed flesh emanating from them like a foul miasma, causing the myriad vendors of sweetmeats, ginger snaps, meat pies and fruit pies to turn viciously on them and drive them away from their stalls.

'Fuck off, you smelly bastards! You're turning my foodstuffs rotten with your stinks!'

'I can tell your fortunes. I can see the future. Step into my tent and in my magic crystal I will see when you're to be rich and famous! When you'll find true love. When fortune will smile on you,' a gold bangled, spangled-shawled gypsy woman promised, and for a brief instant Tom was tempted by her offer.

'Might she really be able to foretell what the future holds for Amy and me?'

'Roll up! Roll up! Roll up! See the twin sisters who are giantesses! The tallest women in the whole world! Twice as tall as the famous giant of the beanstalk,' the showman claimed, and seeing Tom passing, accosted him. 'Come now Sir, wouldn't you like to see women who are human steeples like yourself, but twice as high?'

His listeners laughed raucously at his sally, and Tom thought it best to just ignore him and pass on.

'Ride my swing boats. Fly like a bird through the air. Swoop as fast as the speed of lightning. Ride my swing boats!'

'Cummon, lads, let's see who can go the highest.' A gang of youths swarmed into the rope hung boats.

'Broadsheets! Buy my broadsheets! Just a paltry penny for the news of all the town!'

'Gallop my cock horses. One ha'penny for a gallop on my roundabout. One ha'penny only for a gallop on my fine spirited cock-horses.'

'Ohhh Dad, let me go on n'orses! Let me go on n'orses!' a small boy pleaded.

'Will you give over moithering me. I'm not made o' money!' his father scolded.

'Don't be so bloody mean! You'll have money enough to get drunk on afore this night's done, I've no doubt,' the wife attacked.

'It's being married to you that sends me on the bloody drink in the fust place!' the husband riposted.

'A penny piece, my lords, ladies and gentlemen, just a single penny piece to see the albino family. Every one of them whiter than snow, their eyes glowing red like the fiery furnace that burnt poor Shadrach! Only a penny piece and for another measly penny you can touch them as well!'

'Can we go in and see 'um, Willy' A young woman coaxed her sweetheart, who was cuddling her tenderly. 'I've never seen albinos afore.'

'O' course you shall see 'um, my honey.'

'Can I touch 'um as well?'

'O' course you shall touch 'um, my honey.'

'You're all bound for damnation! Leave this place of sinful pleasures now, before the Lord God sends his thunderbolts to destroy you like he did the evil cities of Sodom and Gomorrah!' An itinerant hellfire preacher howled his warnings from the box he stood on, until drunken pointers kicked the box from under him and drove him from the Green with kicks and blows amid a storm of jeering applause.

'Ginger snap! Ginger snap! Come buy my luvverly sweet ginger snap!'

'Roll up! Roll up! Roll up! Exhibited for the first time in this country, the amazing pig-faced lady found only one month ago in far-off Russia,' a showman dressed as a Cossack claimed. 'She comes from a tiny remote village in Siberia, which is the only place in the world that such women are to be found. And I've spent a fortune to bring her here.'

'You're a fuckin' liar,' one of his listeners shouted, 'because my missus and her sisters has all got faces like pigs, and they all been born and bred in Crabbs Cross.'

'Mam, Mam, I wants a toffee apple, Mam.'

'Here you are then, my duck. You shall have this one. Ohhh bless him. Just look at his little face. I could eat him,' a proud mother lovingly exclaimed.

'And afore too many years has passed, you'll be wishing that you had. He's naught but a spoiled brat!' her own toil-worn mother told her sourly.

'Three shies a penny. Knock off a box and win a fine prize. Three shies a penny. Knock off a box and win a fine prize!' a gypsy showman promised, his white teeth flashing in his dark-skinned face.

And gullible men paid their money for the three sticks, which no matter how many times they hit the targets would never knock the cunningly secured cigar boxes off their poles. Other gullible men gathered around the 'find the lady' and 'pea and tumbler' tables and put their bets down in fruitless attempts to beat the expert sleight of hand.

Tom stopped for a while outside one booth to listen to the spiel. 'Step inside, ladies and gentlemen, and see the one and only, the miracle of the ages, the world famous Miss Charity Murrell, who has appeared before all the crowned heads and nobility of Europe and the Emperors of China and Japan and India.

'She was born with no hands or arms, but can use her feet with such phenomenal, such miraculous, such unbelievable, such stupendous ambidextrousness that the King himself, our own good King George, offered to make her his personal valet.

'Her next performance is about to begin, so pay your tuppence and come inside before the crush is so great that I have to close the doors against all comers. The remarkable Miss

Charity Murrell is about to demonstrate her amazing talents. Please form an orderly queue. No pushers-in or shovers-in, or any other sort of jumpers-in will be admitted.'

Intrigued by what he had heard, Tom promised himself that should opportunity arise in the future he would witness the feats of this remarkable woman himself.

'In fact, why shouldn't I take a little time off now, and go in and see her?' he decided on impulse.

He was moving to join the queue when a middle-aged, respectably dressed man ran up to him and grabbing his arm, demanded breathlessly, 'Am you the constable?'

'Yes, I am,' Tom nodded. 'You can see my staff, can't you?'

'Well you've got to do something! Somebody's stole my missus, and I wants her back!'

'What?' Tom was momentarily nonplussed.

'Am you bloody deaf or what?' The man shook Tom's arm agitatedly. 'I've just told you, aren't I? Somebody's stole my missus, and I wants her back!'

Tom was still puzzled. 'Do you mean that your wife has been abducted by someone?'

'I don't know what you means by abducted.' The man's face was red and dripping with sweat, and his agitation was increasing by the moment. 'Her's been stole! How many times does I have to tell you, you great lanky stupid bugger you? Her's been stole! Somebody has stole her!'

'But how do you know that she's been stolen?' Tom tried desperately to get some clarification.

'Could she not have gone with someone of her own free will?'

'How could her go of her own free will, when her was laying dead in her bloody coffin?' the man shouted.

By now a sizeable crowd had collected around Tom and his new companion, including all those who had been in the queue, and the irate show-man bawled, 'Will you two just fuck off from here and stop pinching my customers!'

'Come with me, Sir, please.' Tom took the man's arm and led him in the direction of the lock-up, knowing from past experience that the only way to lose the crowd of avid listeners was to escape behind a locked door.

'What about my missus? What am you going to do about her?'

'Say nothing more until we're alone, if you please, Sir.'

Inside the lock-up, with the iron-studded door firmly closed and the noise of the crowd muted, Tom said, 'Now try to keep calm, and give me all the details, if you please, Sir. What is your name? Where do you live? Where has your wife's body been stolen from?' He kept the ques-tions coming in a steady stream, and the answers came volubly back.

'I lives in the cottage at the back of the Metho-dist Chapel at Headless Cross ... Me name's Harry Gould ... Me missus died fust thing yester-day morning ... Young Billy Oakley come up wi' the box and we put her in it in me shed out back ... Her'd been bedridden for months so it was a blessing that her went at last ... All her did was

97

moan and groan, and I never had a bit of "How's your father" off her for years ... Well, with her out the way I thought that I'd go to the pub and have a bit o' fun ... I had a good piss-up, so I went straight to bed when I got back home, and took a lie-in this morning ... Then Trevor Hardwick has just come and knocked me up ... He's the seckeratary o' the Oddfellows Burial Club, and has to check that the dead 'un is really dead afore he can pay out the funeral money ... Well, bugger me if we didn't go to the shed and when we looked in there she was! Bloody well gone!

'I been paying the subs on me missus for bloody ages, and if I can't get her back, I shan't get a penny! Not even so much as a bloody farthing! All me money wasted, just because some thieving bastards of resurrection men has stole me missus! It don't bear thinking on, so it don't!' he finished in an aggrieved rush of words.

While Tom listened his initial sympathy for the other man's bereavement inexorably ebbed away because of the callous attitude Gould was displaying.

'I wants you to catch whoever's done this, and see 'um hang for it!' Gould blustered fiercely. 'I swear to God, I'll hang 'um meself if I gets me hands on 'um!'

'This is not a hanging offence, Master Gould,' Tom said quietly. 'To steal a corpse is not even classed as a crime under the law at present. However, I shall do all that I can to track down the perpetrators. We'd better go directly to your home, and I'll examine the scene.'

98

* * *

Tom was forced to remove his top hat and bend his head beneath the low rafters when he stepped inside the small narrow shed. The crudely-fashioned, unvarnished coffin with its rope handles was little more than a rectangular box, its only lining the discarded patched and torn sheet which had served as the dead woman's shroud. The coffin lid was propped against the side wall, one of its panels still bearing the scribbled chalked information, *Dried Yarmouth Bloaters*.

Tom stepped back outside and examined the door fastening. 'Did you have a padlock on this, Master Gould?'

'O' course I never. There warn't nothing worth pinching in here, was there? So I just left it on the latch like any sensible Christian 'ud do.' Gould looked as if he could hardly believe that he had been asked such a stupid question.

'Well, there was something in here that someone quite obviously thought to be worth stealing.' Tom could not bite back the rejoinder, and immediately felt a surge of guilt. 'I'm sorry, Master Gould, that was a cruel thing to say, and I hope that you'll forgive me for it.'

'I suppose I'll have to, won't I? After all, you'm the only chance I got of getting her back,' Gould conceded grudgingly.

Tom pondered for a short while before asking. 'Tell me, what weight was your wife? Was she a small- or a large-built woman?'

'Her was about twice my size. Her was so fat that me and Oakley had to squeeze her into the coffin. We near on ruptured ourselves having to drag her out from the house.'

Again Tom thought hard for some moments, then requested. 'Can I take the coffin lid away with me, please?'

'Why? What good 'ull that do?' Gould questioned suspiciously.

'It may help me in my investigations, Master Gould.'

Gould considered the request for a while before reluctantly acquiescing. 'Ahr well, all right then. But remember it's cost me good money, and even if I don't get her back, I shall be needing it. So don't do it any damage.'

'Thank you. In the meantime could you padlock this door and keep people from entering, because I shall need to return and make a further examination.'

The other man emitted a gusty sigh of exasperation. 'All right, but I can't see what good that'll do. It's shutting the stable door arter the horse has bolted, aren't it?'

'Nevertheless, Master Gould, I'd much appreciate your doing so. Will you allow me to make use of this old rope? I want to make a sling to carry this lid back to Redditch.'

'Bloody hell! How much more does you want me to do for you?' Gould demanded irritably. 'I suppose that next thing you'll be wanting is for me to give you a bloody pick-a-back into Redditch?'

Tom controlled his own irritation at this man's attitude, and said quietly, 'I'll return the rope to you together with the coffin lid, Master Gould.'

'Make sure that you does, or I'll be having

words with the select vestry about you. Some on 'um am good friends o' mine.' With that parting threat he stamped away.

By the time Tom had stowed the coffin lid safely in his room at the lock-up and finished his report to Joseph Blackwell at the latter's house, it was past eight o'clock and the sun had set.

'It appears that we are experiencing something of a crime wave in our parish, Master Potts, with all this body snatching and warehouse breaking.' Blackwell smiled bleakly. 'How do you propose to proceed with your investigation into this latest outrage?'

'With your permission, Sir, I'd like to take John Hollis with me and begin immediately to make door-to-door enquiries at Headless Cross to find out if anyone heard or witnessed anything suspicious during last night.'

'Surely it will be a waste of time to go knocking on doors tonight, Master Potts? Everyone will be at the fair, or in the taverns,' Blackwell objected.

'The vast majority will be, Sir,' Tom readily accepted. 'But some will be at home. And as you know, many of the aged or infirm who are confined to their homes take a great interest in what their neighbours are doing. They'll be alert to what's happening in the road outside their doors.'

'That's well reasoned, Master Potts.' Blackwell nodded. 'I would prefer, however, that yourself and Hollis remain on duty at the fair tonight. The respectable citizens need protecting from the roughs and scoundrels roistering here. You may both begin to make the door-to-door enquiries tomorrow. The news of the theft will undoubtedly have spread far and wide by then, and it may well help to spark people's memories.'

Tom didn't argue his point further. He knew Blackwell's polite request was a command.

On the southern outskirts of the rapidly expanding industrial city of Birmingham stood the Edgbaston Academy of Anatomy, a large, imposing red-brick house set in secluded grounds. Just after sunset the Academy's resident porter opened its rear door and demanded irritably, 'Can't you stop that soddin' beast making such a bloody racket? It's enough to wake the dead!'

The man standing beside the braying donkey savagely beat the animal's head with his cudgel until the loud braying subsided into whinnies of pain, then laughed and told the porter, 'I don't reckon any racket 'ull wake this 'un up.' He prodded the large sack-wrapped bundle which hung across the donkey's back. 'See what I mean, Cully? It's dead to the bloody world, aren't it? Now, the letter I brought you was all right I'm sure, so how much longer are you going to keep me waiting here? Where's me money?'

The porter nodded. 'I've got it. My master was satisfied with the letter, and we'll accept the goods.'

He gave gold coins to the other man, who counted and carefully examined them in the light of the door lantern, biting each one in turn as he did so.

The porter scowled indignantly. 'Do you really think that my master would pay you in snide money?'

The man shrugged. 'Better to be safe than sorry, aren't it, Cully? He wouldn't be the first gentleman I've come across who passed lead off as gold. Anyway, let you and me part on good terms, Cully. I'll give you a hand to carry this 'un inside. Her's bloody heavy, I'll tell you.'

Fifteen

Late afternoon, Friday 18 August

In Headless Cross, Tom Potts and John Hollis had been separately knocking on doors and asking questions since early morning, and now met outside the White Hart Inn to share their findings. Hollis, in his mid-thirties, was eccentrically strange in his physical appearance and mannerisms. He was tall, with a skeletal body, his chin and nose so long and hooked that they almost met. He always wore a military style, floppy-topped peaked cap upon his longish hennaed hair, a countryman's rough-sewn smock, knee breeches and highly polished top boots with golden knee tassels.

He also suffered from periodic attacks of

lunacy, during which he laboured under the delusion that he was a poet of genius, the cloned inheritor of William Shakespeare's talents. He would spend hours, days, even weeks, creating and publicly declaiming his abysmal verses, until the insanity receded and his mind recovered equilibrium once more.

Hollis lived near the hamlet of Webheath with his twin brother James, a stonemason who loved and cared for his sibling during John's lunatic fits. Equally fortunate for John was the fact that Joseph Blackwell had used his influence to keep him in the post of a parish constable for the dozen last years, thus enabling him to earn a living, however meagre that might be.

Blackwell had not done this purely from motives of charitable kindness, however. He reasoned that because of the difficulty of finding suitable men to undertake this highly unpopular and unwanted task, it was to his own advantage to have a man like John Hollis to almost permanently fill the post. Hollis was highly intelligent and erudite, possessing exceptional physical strength and acrobatic capabilities, and also brave and incorruptible, attributes which outweighed any difficulties his mental affliction might occasionally cause.

Since Tom's appointment as head constable, he had forged a firm and close friendship with Hollis.

'Nothing of any use to us, I'm afraid, John,' he now reported. 'Most took one look at my staff and shook their heads. They just don't like constables, do they?'

104

'The same here,' Hollis agreed ruefully. 'About the only civil speech I had was with John Tanner. He's an old blind man who lives in the cottages just down the road from Gould's. He said he'd heard a donkey braying outside his window some time after two o'clock Thursday morning, and what sounded like a drunken row between men and women.'

'Well, that certainly gives us a lead to follow,' Tom chuckled in wry amusement. 'All we have to do is to pick out which one of perhaps a hundred drunken rows between men and women, and find which donkey it was that brayed. I'm sure it must have a very distinctive...' His voice abruptly stilled as another thought struck him, and when he spoke again he was very serious.

'Do you know, John, I'm wondering if it might be possible that it could be a lead of sorts. Mrs Gould was a fat heavy woman according to her husband. It would take at least two men to lift her from the coffin and out of the shed. Now Gould himself is no weakling, and young Billy Oakley is a coalman, so he's well used to carrying weights. But Gould said it was all that the two of them could do to carry her a short distance only. So it's perfectly feasible that whoever stole the body slung it over a donkey's back to get it away. Where's this blind man's cottage, did you say?'

'Down there, towards the Webheath road.' Hollis pointed.

'Come on, let's go and have another talk with him. It might prove useful to us after all.'

John Tanner's cottage was at the end of a

tumbledown terraced row and it was the blind man himself who answered the door to John Hollis's knock.

Before Hollis could speak, Tanner cocked his white-haired head to one side, sniffed loudly, and queried pettishly, 'What's you come pestering me again for, John Hollis. And who's this other bloke you've brung wi' you?'

'I'm Thomas Potts, the head borough constable, Master Tanner,' Tom introduced himself, and asked curiously, 'How could you tell that it was John here, who'd come again to your door?'

The old man grinned, and with his gnarled forefinger tapped his ear and nose. 'Me eyes aren't no use any more, Master Potts, but me ears and nose am in fine fettle still. I could hear two men's footsteps on the cobbles, and when I had a sniff I could recognize his stink, and another man's stink as well. Man stink is different to woman stink, and a babby stink is different to a grown-up, and an old bugger stink is different to a young bugger. And each and every soul on God's earth carries their own special stink with 'um. And if you don't know such simple things as that, then you aren't as clever as you might think.'

'No, perhaps I'm not,' Tom admitted wryly. 'Because I certainly don't possess your skills in this matter.'

'No you don't, nor never will do.' Satisfied that he had established a degree of superiority, Tanner's manner became pleasant. 'Right then, you'd best come inside and sit yourselves down, and ask me what it is you've come to ask me.'

The room was sparsely furnished, but neat and clean, and seeing the chiming clock on the wall, Tom was satisfied that the old man was fully cognizant with the passage of time.

He questioned Tanner at length, and listened intently to the answers he received. There had been two men and a woman arguing heatedly as they passed the cottage going towards the Webheath road, and all of them had sounded to be the worse for drink. While they argued the donkey had brayed repeatedly. Judging from their accents the trio were locals. From the brief snatches of their slurred speech that he had heard, the old man gathered that they were arguing over how far they should travel that night.

'I heard the one bloke say that he warn't going to walk 13 miles or more wi'out getting some sleep first, and the woman called him a useless lazy bastard, and said that if he didn't do as he was told, then she'd find somebody else the next time there was a job to do.'

When the pair thanked the old man and left, Tom was fully satisfied with the accuracy of what he had been told.

'It could have been them who snatched Mrs Gould, John,' Tom mused aloud. 'Thirteen miles or more to walk? As the crow flies where would that distance take them from here? Which places where they might be able to sell a corpse?'

John Hollis considered for some moments, before suggesting. 'It would take them near to Warwick, or over halfway to Worcester, and through or into Stratford, Henley, Pershore, Evesham, Droitwich or Birmingham. To possible selling locations at all points of the compass, in fact.'

Tom shook his head and grinned wryly. 'They'd be quite spoilt for choice, wouldn't they? And for us it's become like looking for a needle in a haystack.'

'We'd best get ourselves a strong magnet then, Tom,' Hollis laughed.

While Tom was questioning Tanner, a conference was taking place in Jonathan Crowther's parlour, and as usual it was the patriarch of the family who was dominating the proceedings, while his two fashionably clad nephews and a third man, Eddie Harris, sat dutifully listening.

'Somebody is trying to take over my territory. They're deliberately interfering in my business and causing me a great deal of trouble and expense,' Jonathan Crowther announced grimly. 'Now I want them found out and dealt with before they ruin my good name.'

'What makes you think that you're being deliberately targeted then, Jonno?' Eddie Harris, wearing the rig-out of a needle pointer, was a thick set shaggy-haired man in his mid-twenties, with brawl-scarred features and extremely bloodshot eyes.

'It's bloody obvious, isn't it, Eddie?' Crowther snapped angrily. 'To begin with, John Watts must have been put up to lifting that parcel of meat from the old graveyard. He'd never have had the gumption to do it off his own bat.

'Then there's the job at Jasper Bates's warehouse. More than 200,000 fancies taken, and

I've not so much as heard a whisper about who did it. And to add insult to injury, it was a job I'd earmarked for ourselves.

'Now, to top it off, there's this body snatch at Headless Cross. They took Harry Gould's wife from out of his own shed. She was going to be put in her family's grave plot at Feckenham, and that would have been easy pickings for us. The bastards didn't even have the common decency to wait until after she'd had a Christian burial. Which is something that I've always insisted upon before lifting anyone.'

He shook his head in disgust. 'Standards of behaviour are slipping fast nowadays. It wouldn't have happened when I was a boy. We were brought up to show respect for others. Not like the kids today, who're spoilt to death and allowed to run riot!'

He sat fuming in silence for some seconds, then sighed regretfully. 'She would have fetched a good price as well. A fine plump specimen is always much sought after among the anatomical gentlemen. They believe they're getting more value for their money than if they have a skinny one.'

Sixteen

Saturday, 19 August 1826

As soon as full day came to give him sufficient light to see clearly, Tom carefully positioned the coffin lid beneath his bedroom window and began to dust its surface with charcoal powder. As he had hoped, a myriad of smudgy hand and finger prints showed and he studied them closely through his magnifying glass. Some of the prints were exceptionally clear, and he experienced a feeling of gratified vindication when he managed to find several partial handprints which bore what appeared to be an identical scar running diagonally across the left hand palm.

Using a finely pointed quill pen, ink and paper he spent a considerable time trying to make as accurate copies as he was able of these magnified prints and also some of the clearer fingerprints.

Turning the lid over, he dusted the other side and again pored over the resulting disclosed prints. Suddenly, as he traversed the magnifying glass along the outer edges of the lid, his heartbeat quickened with excitement, and he deliberately straightened up and drew long deep breaths to steady himself, before bending to examine his latest find again.

'It's there! It's really there! I'm not imagining it!' He wanted to shout exultantly, wishing that he had someone with him who could share this moment of discovery. He couldn't stop from repeatedly re-examining the row of four clear imprints of the upper finger phalanges of a right hand, with the ring finger's top joint missing.

Next he carefully studied the opposite edges of the wooden boarding and again found a set of four upper finger phalanges, this time from the left hand.

'Whoever left these must have been the one who lifted the lid off and propped it against the wall.'

He took precise measurements and compared them to the measurements on the tile mould, and was satisfied that they matched.

'Now, all that I have to do is to find the man whose prints match these, and I've not only got my body snatcher, but also my needle thief. I must tell John what I've found, and we can begin the search for him straightaway.'

The bells began to jangle, and from the adjoining room his mother screeched irritably. 'Thomassss! Thomasssss! You great idle beast. Will you answer those bells, they're deafening me! If ever a poor benighted woman suffered the agonies of hell, then I'm that tragic soul! And it's all your fault, you cruel unnatural swine! It's all your fault!'

'All right Mother, all right. I'm going down directly.' Tom hastily shed his nightgown and tasselled night cap, and pulled on a shirt and breeches; then, still barefoot, he hurried down and opened the front door to find Amy Danks, youthfully fresh and pretty in her best silk bonnet and gown, blonde ringlets framing her rosy features, white even teeth gleaming between her slightly parted succulent pink lips.

'My God, but you're a mess.' Amy Danks frowned angrily. 'Your hair looks like a mouldy haystack, you're stubbled like a tramp, and your feet are the biggest and ugliest that I've ever set eyes on. Couldn't you at least have put your boots on and spared me the sight of them?'

Disconcerted by her aggression, Tom could only mutter apologies, which she dismissed with a contemptuous toss of her bonneted head.

'There's no need for you to say sorry to me, Thomas Potts, because I don't care to listen to anything you have to say. I'm only come here to tell you that I want nothing further to do with you.'

'Oh Amy!' he exclaimed with dismay. 'What have I done to deserve this treatment from you?'

'What have you done?' she demanded as if not believing what she had heard. 'What have you done? It's what you've not done that you should be asking about.'

He stared miserably at her, fumbling for words. 'But you know why I couldn't take you to the fair, Amy. I was ordered to remain on duty by Master Blackwell and the vestry. I had to obey that order and patrol the fair.'

'But you weren't at the fair, were you? I never saw you there, and I looked high and low for you,' she snapped. 'Had you gone to enjoy yourself elsewhere?'

'Of course I hadn't. There was a body-snatching at Headless Cross, I had to go there to investigate it. And next day I was continuing with the investigation. You may ask John Hollis, he was with me all that time.'

'Don't bother giving me excuses.' She waved her hand dismissively. 'And anyway, I don't care what you were doing, because I've found another sweetheart now. And it was him who bought me this fairing.'

For the first time, Tom became aware of the brightly coloured cockade of ribbons pinned on to the shoulder of her gown.

'Who was it who bought you that?' he asked.

'That's for me to know, and for you to find out. I've said what I came to say, and I don't want to ever speak to you again. So goodbye and good riddance to you, Thomas Potts.'

She turned and flounced away and he went after her.

'Wait, Amy! Please wait!'

Then his bare foot came down heavily upon a sharply pointed stone, and he cried out in shocked pain and began to hop awkwardly on one leg as he clutched at his injured foot.

She glanced backwards over her shoulder, then hurried on, giggling mischievously.

Tom lost his balance and came down heavily upon his knees, crying out again at the painful thudding impact on the iron-hard ground.

In the nearby houses windows opened, and a man shouted.

'What's up, gaffer? Be you having a bloody fit or summat?'

113

'No, he's doing St Vitus's dance. The sarft lanky bugger thinks that it's all the rage now,' a second voice bawled, and raucous howls of laughter greeted the sally.

Face flaming with embarrassment, Tom clambered to his feet and limped despondently back to the lock-up. With the memory of Amy's scathing criticisms of his physical appearance still coursing through his mind, he stripped off his clothes and went to the pump in the rear yard, sluicing his head and body beneath its gouts of icy cold waters. Then he filled a bucket and took it upstairs to his room. He lathered his face and neck with harsh gritted soap, stropped his cutthroat razor and shaved carefully in the cracked and mottled mirror. He dressed fully, brushed and combed his hair, buffed his ankle boots until their cracked leathers gleamed, and told himself, 'There now, at least Amy won't be able to charge me with being dirty and unkempt if we should ever meet again. She'll see that I still have my pride. She may break my heart, but she'll never break my spirit.'

The next instant he couldn't restrain a chuckle of rueful self-mockery. 'Dear God! Will you just listen to yourself, Thomas Potts. You sound like a self-pitying schoolboy. Just remember how many times Amy has behaved towards you like this. She's forever threatening to find and marry another sweetheart. And how can you blame her for doing so? If this time she has really found someone she prefers to you, then it's your own fault entirely, and she can't be blamed for it. And I truly hope that she'll be happy.'

Again he could not help but chuckle. 'Stop trying to behave with such noble self-renunciation, you hypocritical swine you, Potts. You know very well that you'd hate it if she ran off and married someone else.'

The bells jangled and Tom went downstairs and opened the front door to find Joseph Blackwell's manservant there.

'Master Potts, my master's told me to tell you that there is no need for you to report to him today. He says that you may employ your time more usefully continuing enquiries into the other matters he has discussed with you.'

'All right, Sim, thank you.'

Tom spent the next hour doing household chores and preparing a breakfast of onion porridge for himself and his mother. Despite his release from reporting to Blackwell he still faced a busy day: there were summonses to deliver and checks on hawkers and hucksters licenses to be made. But after he had eaten he decided to go firstly to Crabbs Cross and visit John Watts, in the hope that the man had recovered sufficiently to be able to tell him about the assault.

As Tom walked up the Front Hill, Andrew Adamson came out from his house carrying a bag, and hailed him.

'Good morning, Tom, and it's a fine one is it not?'

'It is indeed.' Tom halted. 'I'm on my way to see John Watts.'

'That's a happy coincidence. I'm going there myself. I have to dress his wounds.'

'I shall be glad of your company.' Tom smiled.

'How is Watts?'

'His wounds aren't healing well and he's suffering a deal of pain. As for his mental state, his wife tells me that he's suffering frequent fits of violent lunacy, when he rants and raves and convulses severely. Undoubtedly he is apoplectic. I've tried various treatments but none seem to have had much effect so far.'

Tom's continuing interest in medical matters impelled him to ask, 'What treatments are those, Andrew?'

'Firstly, of course, I bled him several times. He made little progress so next I purged him with tincture of aloes combined with calomel. Then I tried mustard plasters with added chillies applied to the soles of his feet and the insides of his thighs and calves. On my last two visits, I've administered doses of acetate of strychnine. Nothing has worked, I'm sorry to say.'

'Well, you've certainly proved that you're very up to date in your practice. But how will you proceed now?'

The other man smiled happily. 'I've another trick up my sleeve, Tom. You've heard of Dr Holland, of course.'

'Indeed I have. A remarkable young physician!'

'Well, I'm going to try one of his latest treatments.' Adamson opened his leather bag and lifted out a small glass bottle which contained wriggling worm-like leeches. 'I'm going to apply these little beauties to the verge of the anus. Dr Holland has achieved some marvellous results using them like that.'

116

Tom nodded, suitably impressed, then enquired, 'How does his wife manage Watts when he's
having one of these fits?'

'Mainly she fears that he might do himself
serious injury when he has these attacks, so I've
advised her to keep him well dosed with laudanum when she senses that another fit is
coming on. Which is pretty often because most
times I've been there to dress his wounds he's
virtually comatose from its effects.'

'I hope that he's not under its influence this
morning. I need to ask him some questions about
the attack on him.'

Adamson grimaced doubtfully. 'Well don't
raise your hopes, Tom. On my first visit I did ask
him about it, but he just reacted like a drunken
lunatic, shouting that he could see cows shitting
in the corner of the room. His wife blamed me
for upsetting him with my questions. She gave
me a real dressing down, I can tell you. I haven't
risked asking him again. There's a very fiery
temper hid behind that pretty face of hers.'

'Well, I'm going to have to risk enraging her.'
Tom smiled. 'Because I really do need to know
if he can tell me anything at all about what
happened that night.'

'Well don't stand too close to him, because
twice now he's vomited over me while I was
changing his dressings. His wife says that he's
always suffered with a bilious affliction.'

With a willow basket on her arm, Mary Watts
was standing by the yew trees in front of her
cottage talking with a tall, well-built young man,

who was holding the lead rope of a pair of donkeys laden with panniers of wood logs. She saw the two men coming nearer, and told her companion. 'You'd best unload the wood round the back now, Billy, and thanks again for helping me collect these mushrooms.'

Billy Oakley was reluctant to leave her. 'Are you sure there's nothing else I can do for you, Mary?'

'Look, there's the doctor coming to examine my husband, and he's got the constable with him so it's best that you should leave me now.' She smiled seductively. 'We don't want to give anybody cause for gossip, do we?'

His eyes were shining with infatuated desire. 'I don't care what anybody might say about us.'

'But I do!' She frowned. 'I'm a respectable married lady and a faithful wife, Billy. My good name means everything to me.'

'Oh I knows it does, Mary, and I'm awful sorry if I've upset you,' he hastily apologized. 'I'd sooner cut me right hand off than upset you.'

She allowed herself to be mollified, and smiled once more. 'I know that, Billy. Now get off with you.'

'Shall I see you later? There must be some job or other needs doing, that I can help you with?'

'Come tomorrow morning, Billy, and we can go and collect some more of these.' She patted the willow basket, then with the same hand touched his face in a brief caress.

He grabbed her hand and pressed his lips upon it in a passionate kiss.

'Leave me go.' She snatched her hand away.

118

'I loves you, Mary, with all me heart I loves you.'

'Get off with you now!'

Reluctantly, he walked away, crossing the road and into the woodland, constantly looking back over his shoulder at her.

Adamson had not noticed the interchange between the couple, but Tom had. He made no comment on what he'd seen, merely remarking, 'I hope Billy Oakley hasn't been sent for in his more melancholy role capacity, Andrew. He and his father are not only coalmen, but also trade as undertakers.'

'Oh well, if Watts has popped his clogs I can always earn a fee for certifying the cause of death in the parish register, can't I? So my journey won't be completely profitless.' Adamson grinned.

Tom wasn't disturbed by this display of callous gallows humour. He knew that the vast majority of doctors' patients died no matter what medical treatments were administered. To protect their own sanity, doctors had to quickly learn to accept the deaths of their patients as a mere routine occurrence.

'Good morning, gentlemen,' Mary Watts greeted them as they reached her.

Tom was struck by the change in her appearance since their last meeting. Her shabby threadbare clothing had been replaced with a new silken gown and fine woollen shawl, and instead of clogs, the toe-tips of leather bootees peeped out from under the hem of her gown. Beneath the beribboned, wide-brimmed straw

119

sun hat, glossy tresses of raven-hued hair cascaded downwards to frame her smiling face.

My God, but she's a beautiful woman, was Tom's initial thought, almost instantly superseded by memories of Joseph Blackwell's barbed allusion to her relationship with her stepfather. *I wonder if it's Crowther who's bought her these new clothes?*

'They look to be a fine mixture of mushrooms you have there, Mrs Watts,' Adamson remarked.

'They should be, it's taken me a deal of time and trouble to collect them this morning.' She smiled fondly. 'But it's worth it just to watch my Johnny enjoy them. He's always been very partial to a dish of mushrooms.'

'There are so many different sorts of fungi, I don't always know which ones make good eating or bad,' Adamson told her.

'I'm still learning, and sometimes make mistakes which leave me feeling rather sickly,' she laughed self-deprecatingly. Then she asked, 'Are you both come to see me? Or are you merely passing by, Constable Potts?'

'I'm hoping that your husband has recovered sufficiently to answer some questions about the attack on him, Ma'am,' Tom told her.

'Thanks to the doctor's treatment my John is slowly recovering.' She smiled gratefully at Adamson. 'But I don't think that he's strong enough yet to be badgered with a lot of questions.'

'I've no intention of badgering him, Ma'am,' said Tom. 'But I do feel that it's in both you and your husband's best interests that I find out

120

whether he can recall anything, no matter how vague it may be. Whoever attacked him mustn't be allowed to escape scot-free, Ma'am. They might still be a danger to him, and perhaps to you also.'

Anger sparked in her dark eyes. 'Don't deliberately try to frighten me, Constable Potts. My John is not strong enough in his mind yet to be worried with questions. So leave him in peace.'

Tom's instinct was urging him to persist and he indicated his staff. 'I'm on the King's business, Mrs Watts. I need to question your husband urgently. You said that he was carrying money, yet when he was found he had none with him. So, if he was robbed on the King's Highway, then that's a hanging matter, and for that reason, if no other, I need to question him.'

'And I say that you shan't badger him at this time, Constable, because he's not yet recovered enough in his mind to bear it.'

'Would you really force me to obtain a warrant to gain entrance to him?' Tom was feeling increasingly puzzled by her attitude.

'You shan't badger him,' Mary Watts snapped curtly, and turned to Adamson. 'Will you come now and see to my John please, doctor. He was in great pain this morning, and I had to give him laudanum.'

'Mrs Watts, please be reasonable,' Tom entreated. 'Your husband was attacked and I am legally bound to investigate this crime. I'm only trying to do my duty.'

'And I'm only trying to protect my husband

from any more distress.' She didn't look at Tom as she spoke, but kept her dark eyes fixed on Adamson's face. 'Please doctor, will you come inside?'

She turned and went into the cottage.

Adamson grimaced. 'I must go to my patient. Tom.'

'Of course. Look Andrew, I realize that you are bound by oath to respect the wishes of your patients for discretion, but I really would appreciate if you will tell me if you manage to glean any information from John Watts about the attack on him. I have to go about other business now, but perhaps I could call on you later tonight?'

The other man shook his head. 'Tonight won't serve, Tom. When I'm done here I have to go directly to my uncle in Birmingham, and I shall probably be there for some days. But if I should find out anything from Watts then I'll let you know.'

He followed Mary Watts into the cottage.

Tom slowly walked back towards Redditch. Frustration burned through him, coupled with puzzlement that Mary Watts was so determined not to allow him to question her husband.

'Why won't she? Has whoever attacked him threatened and frightened her into keeping silent?'

The questions reverberated over and over again. Then another question rose unbidden into his mind. 'Or could she be protecting his attackers, I wonder?'

'Shame on you for that suspicion!' he instantly

castigated himself. 'You witnessed her distress after the attack. The poor girl was heartbroken and half out of her mind with worry!'

Yet despite all his efforts to cast the suspicious thought from his mind, at odd moments during the following hours it persisted in returning in nagging reiteration.

Seventeen

Tuesday morning, 22 August 1826

It was the thirteenth day of the pointers strike. Increasing numbers of men, women and children were being forced to survive on whatever charity their relatives, friends and neighbours could spare from their own straitened means, and hunger and want were stalking the mean alleys and courts of the Needle District.

At a quarter to ten o'clock in the morning the Reverend John Clayton, curate to Lord Aston, came out of the parsonage house on the Fish Hill and walked reluctantly up the steep slope towards the central Green and the Chapel of St Stephen. A tall, powerfully built man whose muscular physique strained against his threadbare black clerical clothing, John Clayton commanded the grudging respect of the majority of the parish inhabitants because of his physical strength and boxing skills, rather than his religious calling. At 33 years of age he was still a bachelor, and his remarkably ugly features, material poverty and complete lack of any future prospects of advancement above his present lowly position in his profession were not attractions for the socially eligible unmarried ladies of the parish. John Clayton had long since sadly accepted that his chances of ever finding a suitable wife were very limited.

The reason for his present feeling of reluctance to go to the chapel was the fact that today was the regular weekly session of the committee of select vestrymen and overseers to the poor, who decided on the cases of the applicants for parish relief. As the incumbent curate of Redditch Chapel, Clayton was obliged to attend these sessions as the representative of his employer, The Reverend Lord Aston, Vicar of Tardebigge parish, and as such was charged to report to the committee upon the moral and religious character of the individual supplicants for parish relief.

Clayton was a kindly natured man, and had great sympathy with the sore plight of the impoverished and dispossessed masses that existed within his own nation. He had always hated the hypocrisy of those well-born social reformers and politicians who while campaigning against black slavery in the British colonies, chose to turn a blind eye and profit from the white slavery that millions of their own low-born countrymen/women/children were subject to within the industries and agriculture of the British Isles.

Now, walking slowly towards the Green, he

was resigning himself to yet another day of witnessing harsh judgements taken by the committee upon which he could wield little or no influence. As a humble curate, bereft of any powerful familial connections, his lowly status in life ensured that the rulers of this parish could carelessly disregard whatever he said.

As he neared the Green he saw Thomas Potts walking ahead of him and called, 'Wait for me, Tom.'

Tom was more than happy to take a brief respite from the laborious climb uphill and wait for the other man to catch up.

The two men enjoyed a mutual feeling of friendship and respect, and they shook hands before walking on side by side.

They came to a standstill some 20 yards distant from the chapel doors, outside which a large crowd of men and women – many with babes in arms and older children hanging on to their skirts – had already gathered.

'I hate these relief sessions,' Tom stated glumly, and fidgeted with the long truncheon he carried. 'I just hope that I don't have to arrest some poor soul today who's been driven by desperation to speak their mind to the committee.'

'I hope the same,' Clayton agreed feelingly, and gestured towards the crowd. 'There are more here than ever, and if the strike doesn't end soon there'll be nigh on the entire parish coming to seek relief. Another five mills in the district laid off their workers in the last few days, and none of the masters have given out any steel wire to the outdoor workers to take home to their workshops since over a week ago. Lord Aston fears that we might have trouble if the strike lasts for much longer, and he's already sought permission from the Earl to place the yeomanry on full alert to deal with any violent outbreaks.'

'What about the masters? Are they showing any hint of restoring the old rates?' Tom asked.

A grim smile momentarily touched the curate's lips. 'In public most of them are full of bluster, vowing that they'll never give in, and they'll starve the pointers back to work. But I gather that in private some of these same blusterers are bewailing their loss of profits, and expressing dismay that the pointers are showing no signs of surrender. Anyway, I see that the committee are arriving, so we'd best join them.'

In the vestry room beneath the cupola of the chapel, the quorum of three committee members were seated ranged behind a long trestle table. Joseph Blackwell, acting in the dual capacities of senior overseer to the poor and parish clerk, had a large leather bound ledger, inkwell and quill pens on the table before him. On his left side sat George Boulton, the assistant overseer to the poor, a gentleman of independent means. On his right hand the ageing, white-haired Richard Chillingworth, needle master and select vestryman. At the far end of the table, John Clayton sat upon a tall, three-legged stool, waiting to be called upon to testify.

Because he shared Lord Aston's expectation of violent outbreaks, Joseph Blackwell had ordered the entire police force of the parish to be on duty this morning. Tom Potts and John Hollis were standing guard outside the chapel's main door, while Charles Bromley took a post inside at the vestry room door.

'Shall we begin, Gentlemen?' Joseph Blackwell smiled bleakly. 'This will prove to be a long day's business I fear. The numbers of applicants has greatly increased.'

When his companions nodded their assent Blackwell rang a small handbell, and Charles Bromley shouted.

'Let the first one in, if you please, Master Potts.'

Outside, the crowd began to frantically push and jostle to get to the front, babies bawled and small children cried out in fear.

Tom shouted, 'Please form an orderly queue. If you fight each other then no one will gain admittance. Please form an orderly queue!'

John Hollis was less polite and took forceful action, using his long truncheon like a lance, jabbing its lead-weighted, crowned top into ribs and stomach, shouting threateningly.

'Do what you're told, or none of you will get any relief today. Get into line, damn you! Get into line!'

When one man angrily lifted his clenched fists, Hollis said, 'Yes, come on Harry Berwick! Take a swing at me, why don't you. And I'll break your bloody head afore chucking you into the lock-up.' Knowing that Hollis was willing and able to carry out that threat, Berwick wisely dropped his fists and got into line.

Tom walked along the queue, repeatedly telling the desperate people, 'Everyone will be seen by the committee, but you must be patient.' He looked unhappily into sullen faces gaunt with want and prematurely aged by hardship, and as the acrid stench of unwashed flesh and greasy, ragged clothing filled his nostrils, he felt his anger rising at the bitter injustice of this modern world, which lavished obscene amounts of wealth and privilege upon the fortunate few and condemned so many other millions to short, brutish lives of poverty and despair.

Inside the vestry room, the business of the day was being conducted briskly and brusquely. 'The Widow Chapman.' Joseph Blackwell, spectacles perched on his thin nose, peered down at the open ledger, tracing the entries on the page with the feather of his quill pen. 'Two shillings and five pence, one farthing. That being the total for three quartern loaves at the price of nine pence, three farthings per loaf. Sixpence for one week's room rent. Two pence for a mustard plaster to ease her cough. One penny ha'penny for three buckets of fresh water drawn from the Fox and Goose well. That totals the sum of three shillings and four pence three farthings. Are we agreed on that amount being paid, gentlemen?'

Without waiting for any reply, he counted the coins out from the cash box, which was on a low stool at the side of his chair, and placed them on the table. Pointing to a spot on the ledger page, he said, 'Will you make your mark here, please Widow Chapman, to signify you have received this amount?' The bent-shouldered old crone moved to obey, but was suddenly brought to a halt by Richard Chillingworth's irritable command.

'Stay still, woman!'

His companions stared at him with shocked surprise, and he scowled around at them. 'What I want to know is, why must we pay for water drawn from the Fox and Goose well? Why in hell's name cannot she draw any water she needs from the Big Pool? That costs nothing, as far as I remember.'

'Come now, Master Chillingworth,' John Clayton remonstrated indignantly. 'You must also remember, I'm sure, that the Big Pool is a rancid, disease-laden disgrace to this parish and a shame on the gentlemen of the select vestry who will not vote the necessary few shillings it would cost to clean out the filth and rubbish it contains. You surely cannot expect this poor old soul to take her water from there?'

'I can expect any damn thing that I choose to expect.' The other man was unabashed. 'And I'll not be taken to task by any psalm-chanting parasite who lives off the tithe and chapel rates that I and my fellow select vestrymen are forced to pay. If you're so concerned about the Big Pool, then I suggest you do a real day's work for a change, and clean the damned thing out yourself.'

'Gentlemen! Gentlemen!' Blackwell reproved sharply. 'Please remember where you are, and don't indulge in such unseemly bickering in front of your inferiors.'

Face flushed with anger, John Clayton bit back

129

the heated rejoinder he wanted to make, and instead told the old woman. 'Please, Widow Chapman, pick up your money and make your mark.' Then he spoke directly to Blackwell. 'If the committee is unhappy with the total to be paid this lady, Master Blackwell, then withhold the penny ha'penny for the water, and I will pay it out of my own pocket.'

'With the tithe money robbed from my pocket!' Chillingworth snorted. 'If it was up to me I'd accept his offer.'

Blackwell raised his eyebrows at George Boulton in silent enquiry and receiving a nod in reply, told the Needle Master, 'You have been outvoted on this point, Master Chillingworth. The money in dispute will be paid from the Poor Relief Fund.'

He beckoned the old crone forward and she made her mark in the ledger, scrabbled the coins up with her swollen arthritic fingers and hurriedly left the room, to be quickly replaced by a worried-looking woman with a squalling baby in her arms and three snot-nosed, frightened, half-clad children clinging to her skirts.

For Tom, the time was passing with an almost agonizing slowness. More than an hour had passed and the queue had hardly diminished, as new arrivals continually joined it. Applicant after applicant entered and emerged from the chapel door, some clutching their money with relief etched on their faces, others cursing furiously at having received little or nothing from the committee.

A small pony and trap drew up alongside Tom and a female voice greeted him, 'How are you, Master Potts?'

Hannah Anstiss, the widowed daughter of Richard Chillingworth, was around Tom's age. Tall for a woman, full-breasted and robust in build, she was not conventionally pretty but her rosy complexion, thick glossy dark brown hair worn in a loose chignon , white even teeth and soft, pleasant voice made her a very desirable woman.

Hannah Anstiss smiled warmly at Tom, and he experienced a frisson of pleasure as he looked into her brown eyes, an emotional reaction which paradoxically left him feeling somewhat uneasy.

'Indeed I'm very well, I thank you Ma'am. And how are you?'

'I'm well. Is my father inside?'

'Yes, he is. Do you wish me to tell him that you're here?'

'No.' She frowned slightly. 'I'd prefer to wait here until he's finished. What I've got to tell him will only sour his mood I'm afraid, and that might make it go hard for these poor people seeking relief.'

Even as she spoke a woman came out of the chapel sobbing and complaining angrily. 'The bastards won't give me nothing, they says it's me husband's fault that we've no money for food. That rotten bastard Chillingworth says that my man chooses not to work, so we can't get any thing from the parish. How am I going to feed my kids now? I'm going to do meself in, I am! I swears it! I'm going to end it all!'

'Oh God!' Hannah Anstiss sighed. 'That's Henry Atkins's wife. He's one of our pointers. We were forced to shut down and lay off everyone at the start of last week. My father is very angry with the pointers, and when he hears my news it'll do nothing to soothe his temper.'

'Is it anything that I could be of help with?' Tom offered.

'I doubt it, Master Potts. I've just received a message from one of our customers threatening to cut their connection with us because we're unable to deliver their current order on time, due to the strike.'

She glanced at the length of the queue, and decided, 'It could be hours before my father is done here. I think I'll wait to tell him until he comes back home. A good meal will perhaps help to reconcile him to the bad news.' She smiled at Tom. 'I'm pleased that we've met again, Master Potts. If ever you're in the vicinity of my house, then do call in and say hello.'

'I'd be honoured to, Ma'am,' Tom bowed, feeling quite inordinately gratified by her invitation.

'Good day, Master Potts. Don't neglect to call on me.'

'Indeed I won't, Ma'am.'

He watched her drive away with very mixed feelings. He was confused and troubled by the fact that although he believed he was in love with Amy Danks, he was feeling such a strong physical and mental attraction towards Hannah Anstiss.

Eighteen

Thursday morning, 24 August 1826

In his private lecture theatre in the leafy Birmingham suburb of Edgbaston, professor of anatomy Dr Semprimus Monkland visibly preened with self-satisfaction as he rested his hand on the forehead of the naked corpse lying on its back upon the table.

'You will note ladies and gentlemen, that the subject is a particularly fine plump member of the female gender, and exceptionally fresh. I am confident that there will not be a finer specimen to be found this day throughout the kingdom.' His listeners voiced appreciative agreement, and applauded with cheers and clapping of hands.

The room resembled a small amphitheatre, its centre piece the rectangular table serrated by hollowed narrow troughs which ran to holes at the four corners, each hole with wooden sawdust-filled boxes set on the floor beneath it. The table itself was closely surrounded with a steep rising horseshoe of wooden boarded tiers separated by iron railings.

The audience, closely packed together on the tiers, was a mixture of young medical students of Monkland's, and other non-medical men and women who had paid to view the spectacle as a macabre entertainment.

The room was well lit by large windows and the afternoon sunlight lanced through the panes of glass to warm the air, which was thick with the smoke of cheroots and pipes and the scents of ladies' perfumes, men's pomades, and the cloying fumes of the incense burners lit to overlay the rank stench of death impregnated in the very walls and furnishings.

'Today I intend to remove and display to you some of the major internal organs of the human body,' Monkland announced portentously. 'Now who shall serve as my assistant?'

He stared around the serried ascending rows of faces, smiling as the medical students erupted into loud clamorous pleadings to be selected. After a few moments, he raised his hands, gesturing for silence, and as the noisy outburst stilled, pointed his chubby hand at a young, fair-haired, slightly built man. 'Dr Adamson, will you render me your services?'

'It will be an honour, Sir.' Andrew Adamson flushed with pleasure.

Monkland turned slowly around as he addressed his audience. 'Dr Adamson was one of my finest students, and has recently established his own practice in the parish of Tardebigge, Worcestershire. He is, I am very proud to tell you, my nephew.'

The audience applauded politely, but there were resentful murmurs and muttered gibes among the medical students at what they saw to be another example of blatant nepotism.

Monkland beamed avuncularly, 'I shall now

call upon the doctor to open the abdominal cavity and display the intestinal tract.'

Glowing with pride, Andrew Adamson took the proffered scalpel, and with a confident flourish made a long cut down Mrs Gould's protuberant abdomen, then inserted his hand and pulled out a coil of the thick, glistening, worm-like intestines.

Shocked gasps and smothered screams sounded among the paying spectators, and one pomaded dandy rolled up his eyes and fainted, an act which was greeted with uproarious jeering applause from the medical students, and a sharp kick in the fallen gentleman's buttocks from the dainty shoe of his female companion, coupled with the hissed admonition, 'Gerrup, you bloody nancy boy, and stop showing me up!'

While Andrew Adamson was removing Mrs Gould's intestines, William Kinchin was sitting by the fire enjoying a late breakfast of fried tripe and onions in the smoke-filled, rancid-smelling communal kitchen of Bocker Duggins's lodging house. The proprietor, skin and clothing as grimed and grease-layered as the fabric of his establishment, came into the long, low-ceilinged room grinning with satisfaction.

'What's you so happy about, Bocker?' Kinchin gibed at the normally miserable-looking man. 'Has you just bin told that you'm the long lost brother o' Lord Plymouth, and bin invited up to Hewell Grange for your dinner?'

'Better than that, you little scab! I'se just bin

told that Chillingworth's storeroom bin broke into last night, and nigh on a quarter of a million stock's bin robbed. It'll be the ruin of the old bastard, you just wait and see if it won't.' Bocker Duggins's decayed teeth glistened black and green as he hooted with delighted laughter. 'That just serves the old bastard right for getting me brother transported like he did! A quarter of a million sharps robbed! Good for whoever did it, I says, and more power to their elbows.'

William Kinchin's chomping jaws stilled abruptly. He gulped down the mouthful of half-chewed food, causing the glottal of his scrawny neck to jerk violently.

'Am you sure, Bocker? Who is it who's told you that?'

'Ritchie Bint and Tommy Chance. They saw Chillingworth come tearing up to the lock-up on his horse, shouting and bawling the odds to that lanky bugger, Potts, not five minutes since. It's happened all right, and I'm fuckin' dead happy, I am! Fuckin' dead happy!'

William Kinchin looked far from happy. He abandoned his food and ran from the room to hurtle up the rickety staircases to the attic cubicles directly beneath the gables of the ramshackle building.

'Eddie? Eddie?' He wrenched aside the tattered curtain of the first cubicle's narrow doorway. 'Where the fuck am you?'

The bedding on the narrow wooden cot covered no sleeping man, instead it was Harris's fat slovenly woman, Maggie Murphy, staring up at him with bleary stupefaction.

'Where is he?' Kinchin grabbed her shoulders and shook hard. 'Wake up you fuckin' slut! Wake up 'ull you! Where is he? Where's Eddie?'

'I dunno. Now fuck off!' Her slurred voice was as rough-edged and deep as a man's.

'Where?' Kinchin's voice rose to a screech. 'Where's he gone?'

'I dunno. I've bin asleep, 'aven't I?'

'When did he leave? What time about?'

'I dunno. I've bin asleep, 'aven't I?'

'You useless cow!' Kinchin spat at her, then scurried downstairs and out into the Silver Square. He ran down the long fetid alley of Silver Street, asking men and women who were lounging at the doorways of the tumbledown terraced cottages if they had seen Eddie Harris that morning. None had, and Kinchin continued on his way out under the arched entrance and into Red Lion Street, which took its name from the tavern at the side of the archway.

Kinchin went into the tavern to be greeted by the landlord, Herbert Willis, with a snarling challenge.

'What does you want, you young hound?'

'I'm looking for Eddie Harris. Is he here?'

Willis assumed an expression of mock concern. 'Why didn't you tell me that you was blind, my boy?'

'I aren't blind.' Kinchin was momentarily baffled.

'Then why can't you see that he aren't here? Just bugger off, will you!' Willis scowled.

Kinchin went into the other inns and taverns that he knew Eddie Harris patronized, but at

137

each drew a blank. He then abandoned his search and hurried as quickly as he could to Jonathan Crowther's house at Crabbs Cross.

Nineteen

'Well, Potts? What are you going to do about this outrage?' Richard Chillingworth demanded irascibly.

'I'm going to investigate it to the best of my ability, Master Chillingworth.' As Tom replied he was standing staring hard at the method of the break-in, noting how it was almost identical to the robbery scene at Bates's warehouse.

The needle storeroom of the Forge Mill was a single-storied, windowless structure with no outer door jutting out from the main building, surrounded by a walled, gravelled yard with a single narrow-gated entrance. As in the Bates robbery, tiles had been removed from the roof and neatly stacked against the side wall. Because of the gravel underfoot there were no bootprints showing on the ground, so Tom couldn't make any judgement as to how many robbers might be involved, but he thought it probable that there were at least three of them. One to be let down inside, one to stay on the roof and pass the spoils down to the third on the ground. He knew that the needles in varying amounts and weights had been ready-wrapped and packaged in canvas.

Tom noted the scattering of lumps of animal

138

droppings inside the narrow entrance gate and crouched to examine them closely. 'Have you kept any beasts in this yard within the last couple of days, Master Chillingworth? These droppings appear to be quite fresh.'

'Goddamn your eyes, man!' the needle master exploded. 'Instead of wasting time here staring at lumps of shit, why aren't you scouring the parish to find the bastards who've robbed me?'

'Father, you've no call to take your temper out on Master Potts. I'm sure he has good reason to ask you that question.' Hannah Anstiss came through the entrance, and smiled at Tom. 'How are you, Master Potts?'

'I'm very well Ma'am, I thank you. And I hope I find you well, despite this loss?' Tom rose and bowed, and once more experienced both pleasure and guilt as he found himself thinking what an attractive woman she was, with her fine figure, rosy complexion, glossy brown hair and white teeth.

'I'm very well, and to answer your other question, to my knowledge there have been no beasts in this yard. Our workers come here to use the privies.' She indicated the row of half-door privies lining one wall. 'But since we've shut there's been none of them in here. Do you think the robbers brought a packhorse with them, perhaps?'

Tom nodded. 'A quarter of a million needles weigh heavily, so I think they might well have used a beast to carry the load.'

'Well now that you've established that fact to your satisfaction, Constable, will you kindly set

about finding these thieving buggers?' Chillingworth sneered sarcastically. 'I'm sure that as
soon as you begin to question every bloody
horse, ass and mule in the parish you'll discover
the culprits in no time.'

'I'll do my very best to find them, Master
Chillingworth.' Tom refused to allow himself to
take offence at this sarcasm, and requested
politely, 'Now can I have access into the storeroom, please?'

'You see to it, Daughter,' the old man snapped.
'I've more important things to be doing than
acting as a guide to this gangly fool.' He stamped away, muttering angrily to himself, and
Hannah Anstiss smiled ruefully at Tom.

'I hope you'll forgive my father's rudeness,
Master Potts. I'm afraid this robbery is a great
trial to him. It's cost us dearly.'

'I understand Ma'am. Say no more about it
please.' Tom returned her smile. 'Will your business be able to withstand this loss?'

'Only if we reopen the mill immediately. We
must if we are to survive. The stock we've lost
will have to be replaced as soon as possible, and
we've existing orders to meet,' she explained. 'If
that means giving in to the pointers' demands,
then so be it – no matter how much the other
Needle Masters object to us doing so.'

'Well, at least some good may come out of
this,' Tom could not help but remark. 'If your
pointers return to work, then the other Masters
will undoubtedly follow suit and reopen their
works, and that will be a blessing for the whole
of the Needle District.'

140

'You're right.' Hannah Anstiss frowned with concern. 'It's been very hard to see the women and children suffering want and hardships, Master Potts. I've been doing what I can to help our own workpeople, but could do little enough for them because I've only scant resources of my own to draw upon.'

'You are a truly good and kind woman, Ma'am!' Tom exclaimed on impulse, and a poignant yearning momentarily swept over him for a wife with her fine qualities to share his life.

In the storeroom there was a jumble of sacks, odd pieces of wood, a few wooden crates which were splintered apart, coils of wire and various parts and segments of mill machinery. The sunlight streaming through the hole in the roof enabled Tom to see into even the darker corners clearly. While Hannah Anstiss remained watching him from the doorway, Tom spent a considerable time searching through the room, using his large magnifying glass at intervals to study various marks on the grimed, oily brick floor and the solid pieces of the jumbled contents, but found nothing that he considered could help his quest.

At last he admitted defeat and told the woman, 'I've made no progress, I'm sorry to say.' He looked up at the hole above his head, and smiled wryly. 'Well, at least there's been no rain falling through this hole to soak me.'

Then he peered more closely as something gently moved on the end of one of the broken roof laths. 'Ma'am, could you come here please?' He beckoned Hannah Anstiss to him.

141

'Can I ask you to help me, Ma'am?'

'Of course I will.' She smiled 'What do you want me to do?'

'Allow me to lift you up, so that you can take that article dangling from the end of that roof lath there.' He pointed.

'Very well,' she agreed, but then a flash of doubt passed across her eyes.

'Do you think you will be able to lift me so high though, Master Potts? I'm not a small and dainty morsel.'

Tom grimaced ruefully. 'And I'm not a strong man, I admit. But I think I can manage to support your weight for one brief moment.'

She faced him and he bent low, wrapping his arms around her thighs, then grunting with effort as he raised her as high as he was able. Despite the strain, he was uncomfortably aware of the effect upon his senses of the pressure of her soft warm flesh through the thin fabric of her gown and petticoats.

'Lift me a fraction higher, Master Potts,' she urged. 'Just a fraction only, I nearly have it.' Without warning, she moved violently, shouting out, 'I've got it.'

The sudden displacement of her weight caused Tom to lose his balance and he stumbled backwards, lost balance completely and fell. Her weight crushed the breath from his body, and as she levered herself from him he felt waves of embarrassed shame at his own physical weakness.

Then he heard her peals of laughter, and felt relief course through him that she was not injured by the fall. 'I do beg your pardon, Ma'am!' he panted. 'I hope you're not distressed?'

'Not at all, Master Potts. I'm just happy that I haven't crushed the life out of you, because I'm become far too fond of you to want to crush you in that way. Come, take my hands.'

They clasped hands and she helped him to his feet, but did not release his hands, and they stood looking into each other's eyes, with only inches separating their bodies. Her fingers tightened on his and her laughter stilled. She lifted her face towards him, her eyes moistly gleaming in invitation.

'How can I show you just how fond of you I'm become?' she murmured.

Tom was suddenly consumed with a ravenous hunger to crush his mouth to hers, to hold her close and feel her soft warm body against him. Every instinct within him clamoured that she was as desirous for this as he was himself.

Then in his mind there sounded the voice of his beloved father saying as he had done so many times, 'Never be a blackguard by taking advantage of a woman's weaknesses merely to satisfy your own sexual appetite, Tom. The brothels and gutters are filled with the poor silly creatures brought to destruction by men who do take such blaggardly advantage of them.'

But she's a grown woman, Father! Driven by the fierce lust engendered by his long celibacy, Tom found himself mentally arguing with the dead man. *She's a widow who's experienced a man's loving. She wants me to, as much as I want to myself.*

143

She wants you to make love to her, Tom. Make love! Not merely to use her to satisfy your own desires. How will you feel when you've done that? Will you not feel guilty for using her so?

Of course I shall. The realization suddenly swept over him, and he was filled with disgust at his own lust. He stood for long moments perfectly motionless, his eyes filled with the image of his father's face as if his much-loved parent were standing there before him.

Then he felt the pressure on his fingers disappear, and became aware that Hannah Anstiss had released his hands and was staring at him with a resentful frown. 'Are you feeling all right, Master Potts?' she queried coldly. 'You've suddenly became very strangely distant in your manner.'

Utterly mortified, he could only fluster lamely. 'Yes! Yes I'm perfectly well, I thank you, Mrs Anstiss. I was engrossed in my thoughts. Please forgive me, I meant no offence.'

'I thought that you were a man of the world, Master Potts,' she snapped, her eyes glinting with anger. 'But it seems I was mistaken in my judgement.'

He could only shake his head and mumble, 'Perhaps that may be so, Ma'am.'

'Here, this is what was caught on that lath.' She pressed a scrap of cloth into his hand, then told him curtly, 'I must leave you now, and go to my father. You'll keep us informed as to any progress you might make in your investigation, I trust.'

'Oh most certainly I will,' Tom hastened to

144

assure her, but was only speaking to her back as she disappeared through the door.

Acute embarrassment flooded over him, and the thought of Amy caused him to feel even more ashamed of the emotions he had been experiencing.

'I believe myself to be in love with that girl, and yet I became like a dog in heat just because I was physically close to Hannah Anstiss. Well it'll not happen again,' he vowed. 'It'll not happen again.' He opened his tight-clenched fist and looked at the torn scrap of cloth that Hannah Anstiss had given him. It was red flannel, and had a button attached to it. A surge of excitement overlaid his guilt and shame.

'It's a bit of sleeve ending by the look of it, and it's the colour favoured by the pointer lads. Is it pointers who've robbed this place? God only knows they're daring and agile enough, and most of them must be in sore need of ready money after being on strike for so long.'

He stuffed the cloth into his pocket and went outside. He took his coat off and carefully wrapped it around the roof tiles, fashioning a clumsy bundle to carry them away with him.

'I'll examine these for prints. Maybe there'll be some with the top of the ring finger missing, and if that's the case then I'm going to check every pointer's hands in the whole of the bloody Needle District, even if it takes me 'til Christmas.'

He set off at a rapid pace, but within scant yards found that the heavy load he carried necessitated a slow, laborious plod, and frequent

145

halts to get his breath back and rest his aching muscles.

Halfway up the Fish Hill, he balanced the coat-wrapped tiles upon a convenient wall, and sank on to his haunches, dragging hoarse breaths into his straining lungs. He was wiping his sweating face with his handkerchief when he heard the raucous braying of a donkey. Tied head to tail, a caravan of eight donkeys with large panniers slung across their backs was coming up behind him, led by a young man wearing the capped leather shoulder cape and chain-mesh mittens of a coalman.

'What's up, Master Potts? Is that load making hard work for you to tote it up hill?' Billy Oakley asked as the donkeys reached Tom.

Tom grinned wryly. He had personally always found this open-featured young man to be jovial and good-natured, despite his reputation for being a habitual and at times aggressive drunkard, and so didn't mind admitting to him.

'It's beginning to seem so, Billy. In fact I'm wondering if I'll even manage to get it up this hill.'

One of the donkeys brayed loudly, showing its yellow teeth and shaking its coal-blackened head as if laughing uproariously at Tom's plight.

'Shut that rattle 'ull you.' Billy Oakley belaboured the noisy beast with his long stick until it subsided into indignant grunts. 'I swear to God, Master Potts, I'll slit this bugger's throat one day. He drives me near mad with the bloody rattle he makes. He's forever on bloody heat, so he is.'

Tom reluctantly pushed himself upright and lifted the bundle from the wall. 'I must get on, Billy, or I'll not get home before dark, the pace I'm making.'

'No need for you to rupture yourself toting that.' Billy Oakley grinned. 'This noisy bugger can carry it. '

He took the bundle from Tom and placed it across the tops of the donkey's coal-filled panniers, exclaiming as he did so. 'Bloody Hell, it weighs a bit, don't it! What's you got here? Tiles is it? Has you got a hole in your roof that needs stopping up?'

Tom told him about the robbery and Billy Oakley guffawed appreciatively. 'Couldn't happen to a better bloke, could it? That Chillingworth is one of the meanest, tightest buggers that God ever put breath into. Was it the Rippling Boys who done it, do you reckon?' Then his brow furrowed in puzzlement. 'But what's the use of taking these tiles home wi' you? Clay tiles aren't got tongues has they, so they can't tell you nothing.'

Tom couldn't resist teasing the young man a little. 'Oh yes they can, Billy. Clay tiles like these can be very garrulous sometimes.'

Billy Oakley laughed. 'I don't know what that word garrasummat means, Master Potts, because I aren't clever like you. I'se never had no book learning.'

'Don't put yourself down, Billy,' Tom hastened to tell him. 'Book learning isn't everything a man needs to be educated. There are a whole lot of ways in which you're far cleverer than me.'

147

They resumed the laborious climb up the steep slope and didn't speak again until they had reached the lock-up. Tom lifted the bundle from the panniers and thanked his companion.

'You'm welcome.' Billy Oakley grinned and led the donkey train away. Then he stopped some yards distant and turned his head to call back, 'Master Potts, how can them tiles tell you things?'

'Finger and palm prints, Billy,' Tom called back. 'They carry finger and palm prints, which I can read.'

'See, I said you was a clever man, didn't I?' Billy Oakley laughed. 'You can read everything can't you, and I can neither read nor write.'

He walked on, wondering in puzzlement. 'Fingerprints? Does he mean finger marks?' He grinned and glanced down at his mittened hand. 'He'd have a job reading a finger mark if there warn't a finger there.'

In the lock-up, Tom immediately started to examine the tiles. Delicately brushing finely powdered charcoal across the surfaces, gently puffing away the excess powder and minutely studying the resultant images through his powerful magnifying glass. Some two hours later, feeling deflated with disappointment he abandoned the search, having found only a few smudged partial palm and fingerprints, but none with a truncated ring finger of the right hand.

'Never mind,' he consoled himself. 'But I may as well record them, if only for the sake of practice.' He took up paper and charcoal crayons and began to carefully copy the prints.

148

Twenty

It was dusk when Eddie Harris came to Jonathan Crowther's house in company with William Kinchin. Crowther was in the lamplit kitchen with his nephews, Thomas and Benjamin Fairfax. He greeted Eddie Harris genially, inviting him to sit down at the table, and gesturing to the bottles of gin and large platters of bread and cheese upon it.

'Help yourself, Eddie. You must have had a hard day, doing lots of urgent business.'

Harris's brawl-scarred features frowned suspiciously as he seated himself. 'Why d'you say that, Jonno?' Crowther's demeanour changed in a flash, as he suddenly produced a small pistol, cocked it and levelled it at the other man's head.

'Because you'll be needing to get rid of those sharps in a hurry, won't you, you swindling bastard,' he snarled, baring his teeth like a feral beast.

As he spoke the Fairfax twins instantly moved in from both sides, pinioning Harris's arms, forcing him to remain seated.

Harris's face blanched. 'What's you doing this for, Jonno? What's I done to you?'

'Who did the job with you, you bastard?' Crowther hissed.

'What job?' Harris seemed genuinely baffled.

'I aren't had a job for weeks!'

'Who helped you to swindle me?' Crowther demanded.

'I don't know what you'm on about, Jonno. I swear on me mam's grave, I don't know what you means.' Harris was visibly shaking with fear.

'Truss him!' Crowther ordered.

The Fairfax twins dragged Harris from the chair and slammed him brutally face downwards on the stone-flagged floor. They swiftly and expertly bound his arms and legs, then turning him on to his back, used the ends of the rope to fashion a noose around his neck so that if he struggled to free himself it would tighten and choke him.

'Don't kill me, Jonno! Please don't kill me! I aren't done nothing against you! I swear on me mam's grave, I aren't done nothing!' Harris shrieked in terror.

'For Christ's sake, gag the cunt. He's making more rattle than a stuck sow,' Crowther spat out disgustedly.

Wadded rags were rammed into Harris's mouth and tied fast, muffling his high-pitched shrieks.

With his back to the wall, William Kinchin, wide-eyed and panting with mingled excitement and trepidation avidly watched what was happening to this tough brawler, whom he had always feared and disliked.

'Come here, my boy.' Crowther smiled and beckoned Kinchin to his side. 'Now you've no need to be afraid, William, because I'm sure that you didn't double-cross me by helping this lump of shit to rob Chillingworth's mill.'

'I never, Master!' Kinchin interrupted in fright. 'Honest, I never! I was doing what you told me to do. Waiting to go and help rob it when you told us to. I never knew that Eddie was going to double-cross you, Master. Else I'd have told you straightaway I found out. Honest I would. Honest!'

Muffled wailing sounded from the trussed man on the floor and his head frantically shook in denial.

'Take the gag out,' Crowther told Thomas Fairfax.

As the wadded rags came out, Harris shrieked. 'I never robbed the mill, Jonno. I never! I was waiting for you to give the word! I was waiting for you to give the word! I don't know who did it! I don't, I swear I don't!'

'Shove it in again,' Crowther barked, and the terrified shrieks again transmuted to muffled wailings.

'Now I'm going to give you the opportunity to demonstrate your loyalty to me, William.' Crowther smiled in a kindly fashion at the apprehensive youth. 'Would you like that?'

Kinchin nodded vehemently. 'I 'ud, Master! I'll do anything you tells me to!'

'Good boy.' Crowther's smile widened as he pushed the small pistol into Kinchin's hand. 'Now put a ball into this treacherous bastard's head.'

Kinchin looked at the pistol and then at Harris, and the glottal spasmed in his scrawny throat as he swallowed hard.

'Do it then!' Crowther urged.

Again Kinchin's glottal spasmed. The hand holding the pistol was trembling violently and with an audible groan Kinchin rammed the muzzle against Harris's forehead. Harris's eyes bulged with terror and he desperately rolled sideways, but cannoned into the wall. Kinchin stepped over to him again, his pistol still wavering wildly as he pointed it into Harris's face and pulled the trigger. The hammer cracked against the flint, sparks flew, flame and smoke jetted from the muzzle.

Harris slumped and urine flooded through his breeches to spread steaming over the stone-flagged floor, but he was still alive, his face unscathed.

Kinchin's face was a study in fearful dismay as he turned to face Crowther. 'I aimed it proper, Master! Honest I did! I aimed it true!'

Crowther's teeth bared in a ferocious snarl, and the youth cowered, lifting his arms to protect his head, pleading desperately, 'No Master! No! Don't kill me! Please don't kill me!'

Crowther's ferocious snarl abruptly metamorphosed into a grin of savage amusement, and he and the Fairfax twins erupted into uproarious laughter.

'The pistol wasn't loaded with ball, William. I was only testing you,' Crowther explained as his laughter stilled. 'And I'm very pleased with your loyalty. You'll go far with me, my boy. I'll make you a rich man before I'm done.'

Sobbing with relief, the youth slumped on to

152

his knees and wrapped his arms around Crowther's legs.

'God bless you, Master! God bless you!'

Crowther looked down at Harris and complained indignantly. 'Bloody hell! This dirty bugger's pissed himself all over my floor. William, get it cleaned up. Mary will be coming to cook my supper shortly, and I don't want her to see this mess.

'Thomas, Benjamin, take this bugger down the cellar, and chain him tight so he can't move around and make a rattle. I don't want him disturbing my mealtime.'

When the twins returned from the cellar, Thomas Fairfax asked, 'What makes you think it might be Eddie who did the job then, Uncle?'

Crowther was grimly thoughtful. 'Well, I've got strong suspicions about Bonny Southall. And Eddie has been a regular drinking mate of his lately. He might have let slip to Southall that Chillingworth's was ripe for the plucking, and they decided to beat us to it. If it is them who're cocking a snook at us, then I swear they'll be laying on slabs as specimens before they're too much older.'

'What about Harris, now?' Benjamin questioned. 'Do you want us to dispose of him?'

Crowther shook his head. 'Not until I know where those sharps are. They'll have to be sorted and counted and repackaged before they can be sold on. The sharps are still in this district, you may be sure of that, and I think Harris might lead us to where they're hidden. So tomorrow we'll let him go, tell him that we no longer suspect him, and that he's still a trusted member of our gang. I'll give him a couple of sovs to soothe his hurt feelings – gentle, sweet morsel that he is.'

'Who's to keep tabs on him?' Thomas wanted to know.

'My right-hand man here will be doing that. William keeps a close watch on whoever I tell him to.'

Down on his hands and knees scrubbing the soiled flagstones, William Kinchin looked up at Crowther with an expression of slavish devotion. 'I does, Master. I sticks as close as glue, I does.'

Crowther grinned and leaned to pat the youth's greasy head as if he were a pet dog. 'William is the finest watchdog I've ever had, lads. He sneaks about so quiet and careful and he sees all and hears all. Then he comes to tell me all, don't you, William?'

Kinchin preened with gratified pride. 'I does, Master. I comes straight to tell you everything.'

'Now be quick and get that floor done, William. My darling stepdaughter will be here very shortly.'

Kinchin went back to cleaning with redoubled speed, and above his head Crowther winked at his nephews and with a contemptuous grin told them, 'This young man is a treasure, lads. Worth his weight in gold. He'll go far!'

The Fairfax twins took their leave, and once away from the house, Thomas laughed. 'Oh yes, Kinchin will go far all right. Bloody transported for the rest of his natural to Van Diemen's Land

154

before our beloved Uncle's done with him.'

'Oh you never know, our kid, he might only get to travel as far as Worcester or Warwick gallows,' Benjamin gibed.

'Well, if his neck gets stretched then he'll be travelling on the journey nobody's ever managed to come back from. I'd call that going far, wouldn't you?' Both roaring with laughter, they strode towards Redditch, arms linked, mutually devoted brothers.

At Mary Watts's cottage, fingernails were tapping in rapid rhythm upon the outside of a window pane.

In the black-shadowed unlit room, Mary Watts rose from the tableside stool and opened the outer door, calling softly, 'Who is it?'

'It had better be me, because if it's any other bugger I'll break his face for him.' Bonny Southall came chuckling out of the darkness of the cloud-shrouded night.

'Shhh! Keep your voice down,' she hissed and stepped outside, closing the door behind her. He tried to take her in his arms, but she angrily fended him off. 'No! Keep your hands off me!'

'Fuckin' 'ell! I was only going to give you a kiss. What's got into you?'

'I'm in no mood for kissing. And why have you come here anyway? I told you to keep away until I sent word to you, didn't I?'

'I'm missing you something cruel, honey, and I just couldn't help meself. I had to see you. I really love you, you knows that.' His tone was beseeching. 'Come away with me. We can go

155

anywhere that you want to. We can go out to me brother in America and make a new life for ourselves there.'

'And how would we make enough to live well on out there?' she demanded.

'I earns good wages.'

'Oh yes, I'm forgetting aren't I? You're a working man who earns good wages.' Her tone was ambiguous. 'I'm already married to a working man who's earning good wages, and look at the state of this cottage, and of me.'

'I'd look after you properly.'

Her tone softened. 'I know you would, sweetheart. But I couldn't desert my husband, it wouldn't be right. Adultery like that would be a mortal sin.'

'Mortal sin?' Southall grinned incredulously. 'You've let me bed you God knows how many times, and that's adultery, aren't it? You aren't worried about that being a mortal sin.'

'That's a different thing altogether.' She hid a sly smile. 'That was just me taking a bit of comfort from you when I was feeling very unhappy.'

'Well why don't you take a bit of comfort from me now,' he whispered hoarsely and tried once more to pull her close.

'No!' Again she fended him off.

'Why not?' he pleaded. 'Listen, I reckon you cares for me as much as I cares for you. If you was free then I'd marry you tomorrow. I swear on me mam's grave that should your husband die, then you and me will get married just as soon as it's possible.'

She shook her head and told him regretfully.

'We wouldn't be able to, Bonny. My stepdad wouldn't let us.'

He frowned in puzzlement. 'Why would he stop us? You'd be a widow woman. What would Crowther gain by trying to stop us?'

'He'd have me back at his beck and call. That's what he'd gain from it.' She spat angrily. 'The evil old bastard likes to have everything all his own way. He rules his gang with an iron hand, and he tries to do the same to me.'

Southall didn't reply, but stood uncertainly, mulling over what she had said. From inside the cottage there sounded a long, drawn-out wailing cry.

'He's woke up again, I'll have to go to him. He needs more laudanum to dull the pain,' Mary Watts whispered.

'Well what about me?' Southall challenged. 'I needs you a sight more than any other bugger does, believe me. So leave Watts, and I'll face up to Crowther and tell him about us and have done with it, because I aren't scared of him nor any of his lads.'

With an abrupt change of mood, Mary Watts smiled seductively, pressed close to Southall, wrapped her arms around his neck and kissed him passionately. Then she put her lips to his ear and whispered urgently for some time, before breaking free and darting back into the cottage, slamming and bolting the door behind her.

Bonny Southall stood staring at the closed door, shocked at the information her impassioned whispering had imparted to him. It was many long minutes before he turned and walked away.

Twenty-One

Saturday morning, 26 August 1826

The bar-parlour of the Fox and Goose was packed with seated and standing needle masters. Chillingworth, Milward, Holyoake, Turner, Hemming, Field, Thomas, Hollington, and a score more ranging from the prosperous proprietors of large mills and factories to the struggling entrepreneurs of back-alley workshops. The atmosphere in the room was tense and the smoky air filled with a hubbub of heated argument.

Presiding over the meeting, ensconced in an armchair, was vicar of Tardebigge and justice of the peace, the Right Honourable and Reverend Walter Hutchinson, Lord Aston. His purpled fat face glistened with sweat and the chair creaked beneath the vast expanse of his chest and huge belly.

Joseph Blackwell was seated on a stool beside him. His pale features were emotionless, but there was contempt in his eyes as he surveyed the noisy gathering. He leaned across and whispered into Aston's ear, 'Might I suggest, my Lord, that you call them to order, or we might well be here for the whole of this day.'

Aston nodded and shouted, 'Gentlemen! Gentlemen, can we have some silence please, and take a vote.'

'There's no need for a vote as far as I'm concerned.' Richard Chillingworth glared pugnaciously about him. 'On Monday morning I'm reopening my mill no matter what anybody here can say or think about it, because if I don't get production going again, I'll be ruined.'

'Then you'm a lily-livered traitor to us all, Chillingworth.' Samuel Thomas spat furiously at him. 'If you gives in now to the bloody pointers and restores the old rates, there's no saying what the buggers 'ull be demanding from us next! I says that we should starve the buggers back to their work.'

Once more the hubbub of voices resounded, some echoing Thomas's words, others supporting Chillingworth, and the general argument resumed.

In the passage outside the door, Tom Potts stood as sentinel to prevent anyone other than needle masters entering the room. Periodically, Amy would emerge from the rear of the inn and walk past him to the front entrance and back again, making a great play of ignoring his presence, and calling to any passers by outside, 'If you see Sergeant Sullivan will you tell him that I'm waiting for him.'

Although Tom longed to speak to her, his own pride prevented him from doing so, and when she passed him he forced himself to stare blankly over her head.

Amy had just completed another of her promenades when there erupted a sudden outburst of mingled cheering and booing from the bar-parlour. A few seconds later, the door was flung open and Samuel Thomas stamped out, his face red with anger.

'No good'll come o' this bloody giving in to the bloody pointers!' he was shouting back over his shoulder. 'Them as is cheering now, 'ull be weeping and wailing afore too long. You mark my words, if they won't! Bloody lily-livered fools that they be!'

He was followed in a continuous stream by the other needle masters, some smiling, others scowling, and Tom stood to one side to let them pass. When the last one had gone, Joseph Blackwell called, 'Will you step inside, Master Potts? My Lord Aston wishes to speak with you.' Tom stepped into the room to find only Blackwell and Aston remaining.

'Close the door please, Master Potts,' Blackwell requested. 'My Lord Aston requires our conversation to remain private to we three.'

Aston's purpled moon of a face glowered up at Tom and he growled. 'Well, Constable, what excuse have you?'

'Excuse for what, my Lord?' Tom, hating himself for it, as always experienced a frisson of anxiety when facing a potentially hostile situation.

'Excuse for being such a lanky, gangly, useless fool!' Aston's bloodshot eyes glared with fury, but he kept his voice low, so as not to be overheard by anyone outside the room. 'In this last month there have been two serious warehouse robberies and two incidents of body snatching that we know of, and maybe others that are still hidden. And how far have you progressed in discovering who committed these outrages? How near are you to laying the rogues by their heels? I'll tell you shall I, you gormless idiot! Nowhere near at all! Any constable with the intelligence of a gnat would have at least some inkling of who these thieving scum are by now. But not you! Goddamn and blast you for the useless brainless gawk that you are!'

The sheer injustice of this virulent assault sparked Tom's resentment and roused his determination to answer to these unwarranted insults. He opened his mouth to speak, then over Aston's shoulder saw Joseph Blackwell slyly shaking his head and winking. Knowing as he did so well the older man's Machiavellian deviousness, Tom instantly realized that there was a hidden agenda behind what was happening here, and closed his lips.

'Oh yes, that's right! You may keep your mouth closed, but I know what you're up to. You think that if you fail to catch these rogues then I'll dismiss you from your post.' Aston's hanging folds of jowls shook violently as he nodded with self-righteous satisfaction. 'Well I'm on to you, you lanky, gangly clown, and I'll tell you now that much as you might hate it, you'll stay as constable for just as long as I want you to. And the moment you try to refuse to remain in that post, then I'll make it my business to see that you go to jail for it. In the meantime, you'd better lay these thieving rogues by their heels in double-quick time, or I'll hound you to hell and back! Is that understood?'

Over Aston's shoulder, Blackwell's thin lips smiled in satisfaction and he nodded.

Tom tried to keep his voice neutrally submissive. 'I understand perfectly, my Lord.'

Aston struggled up from the armchair, grunting with effort, and wheezed hoarsely. 'See me to my carriage, Master Blackwell.'

'At once, my Lord.' Blackwell followed his waddling master from the room, whispering to Tom in passing, 'Join me outside when he's gone.'

'What's the sly old devil got up his sleeve this time?' Tom wondered. Peering through the bulbous, diamond windowpane, he watched the distorted image of the carriage move off, and then moved to join Blackwell outside.

Amy was standing blocking the front doorway with her back to Tom, and he asked politely, 'Could you let me pass please?'

She turned and uttered, 'Oh Tom, I thought you'd gone.'

'No, but I have to go now, Amy.' He essayed a tentative smile. 'That's if you'll let me pass.'

'Humph!' she snorted indignantly, and tossed her blonde curly tresses. 'Why should I want to keep you here? I'm only waiting for Sergeant Sullivan, that's why I'm looking out of the door. Not to see where you'd gone.' She lifted her skirt and pushing by him, ran down the passageway.

Despite her scathing words, a sudden surge of hope came pulsing through Tom. He had caught a look in her eyes that suggested she was not so estranged from him as she claimed to be.

'Could she still care for me, as I care for her?' he wondered happily, and greatly cheered went on to join Joseph Blackwell, who was waiting by the side wall of the chapel yard.

'Now Master Potts, I trust that you're not too disturbed by Lord Aston's harsh words. I fear that his appetite greatly outweighs his digestive tract's ability to deal comfortably with the resulting input of food and drink. In consequence, his temper becomes rather choleric.' Blackwell smiled thinly.

'No Sir, I'm not disturbed.'

'Good! Then let's to business. Have you discovered any clues yet about the robbery at Chillingworth's?'

'Only a scrap of shirt sleeve which could be from a pointer's shirt. But apart from that, nothing else of material use.'

'No titbits of information?'

'No Sir, what with my other duties I've had little time to chat with people who given encouragement might let something drop.'

'Yes, I understand.' Blackwell frowned thoughtfully. 'Well, I've persuaded my Lord Aston to use his influence with the vestry to vote sufficient funds to meet the fees of two constables on full-time duties, if this might be a help to you.'

'Of course it will, Sir,' Tom asserted enthusiastically. 'With both John Hollis and myself sharing the day-to-day duties, then I can devote much more time to investigating both the robberies and the body snatching.'

'Then so be it. You may go directly to Hollis and inform him that until further notice he is acting in a full-time capacity. I'm sure that he and your good self will come to an amicable agreement as to the particular duties you fulfil.'

'Indeed we shall, Sir, and I'm very much obliged to you. I'm confident that I'll make good progress with the investigation once I have more time to spare for it.'

'Make sure that you do, Mister Potts. I would be most distressed to find myself disappointed in the high expectations I have of you.' He lifted his finger to draw attention to the chapel bell as it rang out, and counted in cadence with each chime, 'One, two, three, four, five, six ... A woman's six tailors knell, Master Potts. That'll be to mark the Widow Asprey's death yesterday afternoon. I was well acquainted with her family and called with my condolences last night.'

The tolling recommenced, and Blackwell again counted aloud until the final chime and the bell fell silent, 'Eighty, eighty-one, eighty-two, eighty-three. She reached a ripe old age, did she not, Master Potts? Let us hope that we both do the same, so long as we remain hale and hearty. Because I've no wish to spend my dotage senile, drooling, and bed-bound.' He smiled expectantly at Tom. 'This means another burial very shortly, Master Potts.'

'Yes, Sir.' Tom smiled back. 'And you may rest assured that I shall be keeping a close watch over the poor lady's grave.'

'I'm happy to hear that.'

They looked at each other in surprise when the bell began to toll again. Now it was Tom who kept cadence.

'One, two, three, four, five, six, seven, eight, nine.' This time it had been the nine tailors knell rung, to mark the death of a man. If it had been a child, then the bell would have tolled a knell of only three chimes, followed by the number of its years. Now the bell recommenced single tolling for twenty-eight repetitions, and Tom remarked, 'That's a young man. I wonder who it might be?'

'You'd best find out quickly, Master Potts,' Blackwell advised. 'It may be that yourself and John Hollis will have to be mounting separate grave-watches these coming nights.'

Tom hurried to the front of the chapel and met the notoriously cantankerous Joseph Davies, sexton, bell ringer, and caretaker of St Stephen's, as he left the chapel yard gate. 'Master Davies, can you tell me please who it was that you rang the nine tailors for?'

'What's the problem? Was me belling not up to me usual standard? Am you trying to tell me that me usual toning or timing was lacking?' Davies challenged aggressively.

'Of course not! Your ringing was superb, Master Davies, as always. I'm merely curious as to who has died.'

'A chap name of Watts, from up the Rough. That chap, Crowther, from Crabbs Cross, come to give me the name and pay me for the knell money about an hour since. Now I got things to do and can't waste any more o' me time standing here wi' you. So good day to you.'

'Good day, Master Davies, and thank you for your information,' Tom replied absently, and stood motionless, pondering over this new de-

165

velopment as the other man walked away.

'This could give Aston another rod to beat me with,' Tom realized glumly. 'Depending on the actual cause of Watts's death, this could now have become a case of murder or a manslaughter.'

'Hello, Tom.'

Tom swung round to find John Clayton's pleasantly ugly features smiling at him. 'I've just been speaking to Samuel Thomas, Tom, and he's quite indignant that the vote went against him.' Clayton chuckled amusedly. 'Virtually spitting feathers, in fact.'

'Spitting feathers?' Tom had been so engrossed in his own thoughts that at first Clayton's words didn't penetrate. Then clarity returned. 'Oh yes indeed. He was very irate when he left the Fox and Goose.'

'You'll have your work cut out for you tonight.' Clayton grinned. 'When the pointer lads hear that the masters have given way they'll go on the randy for sure. There'll be plenty of blood and thunder in the pubs, I've no doubt.'

'Neither have I,' Tom agreed ruefully. 'And to tell you the truth, John, I really hadn't given a thought to that aspect of the masters giving way until this moment.' Then he added with grim humour, 'Thank you very much for bringing it to my notice. I think I shall try to find a very pressing reason to leave the town before nightfall.'

'Always pleased to be of service to you, Tom,' Clayton laughed, and walked on.

Tom tried to console himself. 'At least I'll have John Hollis with me tonight when the pointer lads kick up a ruction. Not that I'll be a deal of use to him when the fighting starts.' He decided to go firstly to notify John Hollis about his new duties, and afterwards to call in on Mary Watts. He sighed resignedly. 'It'll not be pleasant to have to question a grieving widow, but it must be done.'

Twenty-Two

Saturday afternoon, 26 August 1826

'Now then, young man, I've measured that coffin you delivered so don't try charging me for more wood than you've used,' Jonathan Crowther warned.

'I wouldn't dare try to overcharge you, Master Crowther,' Billy Oakley grinned, and baited cheekily, 'But I still think that it would have looked much nicer with that purple velvet lining I wanted you to have.'

'It looks nice enough as it is. Those brass handles cost a fortune and the wood's finest oak, isn't it? Never mind having purple velvet lining!' Crowther scoffed contemptuously. 'I'm sure he'll rest well enough on the boarding.'

'Ahr, they all does that, don't they?' Oakley light-heartedly concurred. 'Leastways I thinks they does, because none of 'um ever comes back to complain to me about having a hard bed to lay on. But you might give some thought to having velvet lining for your own coffin when the time comes, Master Crowther. It looks so fine, so it does.'

'If you give me any more of your cheek, my buck, you'll find yourself having a hard bed to lay on. So just button your lip and do what I'm paying so generously for you to do, before I get angry,' Crowther warned. 'Here's the key. When you've done there bring it straight back to me.'

The young man left and some minutes later Mary Watts came down from the upper floor and asked Crowther, 'Who was that talking to you?'

'Billy Oakley. He's going to clean your husband up and lay him in the coffin. He'll bring the key back here when he's done.'

Her dark eyes flashed with sudden fury, 'You've given him the key to my cottage? What the hell were you thinking of? He'll be poking his nose into every nook and cranny of the place.' Before Crowther could reply she ran from the house.

When Tom reached the Watts cottage, he was surprised to hear tuneful singing coming from inside it. The front door was ajar and Tom stood there for a few moments listening.

Farewell my lovely Nancy,
Farewell I must away.
For I hear the drums a beating,
And no longer can I stay.
We've orders out from Worcester Town,
For many's the long long mile.

We go to fight the French and the heathens,
On the banks of the River Nile...

Tom stepped into the room and applauded.
'Well sung, Billy.'

The young man started visibly. 'By God,
Master Potts! You give me a bloody fright. I
feared that the devil had come to claim this
bugger.'

He pointed to the naked body lying face upwards on the table. 'I was just about to start
washing some of the stink off him, and give him
a shave.'

Tom sniffed the rank stenches of vomit, excreta and death and grimaced. 'I think the whole
place could do with a thorough scrubbing.' He
came to stand by the younger man and looked
down, shocked at the sight of the emaciated
corpse.

'By God, he looks like a famine victim!'

'Well, from what his missus has told me, he
warn't able to keep any grub or drink down since
he got that hammering. He kept sicking everything up all the time, and shitting himself as well.
Funny thing is though, she told me a couple of
days past that he reckoned he was feeling ever
so much better. And then he upped and died
yesterday morning. Good job I had a coffin in
stock that fits him. But it just goes to show don't
it, none of us can ever know when we'll be
taken.'

'Do you know if Dr Adamson has ascertained
the cause of death?' Tom asked.

'What's that word mean? Ascertained?' Billy

Oakley grinned. 'You aren't half fond o' using them big words, aren't you Master Potts?'

'Apoplexy! A serious attack of apoplexy. That's what took my poor dear husband from me. Dr Adamson said his poor suffering brain could stand no more fits,' Mary Watts informed them from the doorway.

Tom took off his top hat and bowed. 'Please accept my sincere condolences on your sad loss, Ma'am.'

He looked keenly at her, noting the dark circles of tiredness beneath her eyes, which were reddened and puffy-lidded as if from shedding tears.

She nodded and with tremulous lips asked. 'Why are you here, Master Potts?'

'I needed to find out the cause of your husband's death, Ma'am. If it had resulted from the injuries he suffered then it would be a case of either murder or manslaughter.'

She lifted her hand to shield her eyes and muttered brokenly, 'No, Master Potts, Dr Adamson was quite positive that it was nothing to do with his previous injuries.'

Tom's sympathies were aroused by her obvious distress, and he told her gently, 'Very well, Ma'am. I'll not trouble you any further. Good day to you, and to you, Billy.'

He felt a sense of relief going out into the fresh air and escaping the rancid stenches, and the spectacle of grief.

'At least I haven't got a murderer to contend with,' he told himself. Then a voice from deep within his mind reminded sombrely, 'Don't

170

rejoice too soon. You've still got two serious robberies and two body-snatchings to solve, haven't you? And the pointer lads will be on the randy tonight, without a doubt.'

Twenty-Three

Saturday Evening, 26 August 1826

'Oh you can't have it tonight,
'cos the moon is shining bright,
and the stars are twinkling in
the skies eyes eyes eyes.
And somebody's awatching us,
a watching you and I,
so let's go round the corner,
and 'ave a bit on the slyyyyyyy!'

The roaring chorus ended with stamping of feet and hammering of pewter mugs upon table tops as the massed singers applauded themselves vociferously.

The large, low-ceilinged tap room of the Red Lion was packed with pointers and their women-folk celebrating their hard-won victory over the needle masters. Drink had been flowing freely since early afternoon, because the landlord, Herbert Willis, was once more allowing tick and still-to-be-earned wages were being rapidly spent in advance as the tallies were marked up in

171

ever-lengthening lines of chalked tick-strokes on the large black tally slate behind the bar. Sitting slouched in a dark corner, mainly ignored and un-noticed by the drunkenly roistering crowd, William Kinchin appeared to be stuporous with drink. But his eyes periodically flicked to the tally slate as he kept careful note of the chalk tick marks beside the column of names.

Four names had no ticks against them: Bonny Southall, Crem Fisher, Eddie Harris and Maggie Murphy. The first two, although regular customers of the Red Lion, were not there tonight. Kinchin knew that Fisher lay on his sickbed, but Southall's absence was unexplained.

Eddie Harris, with his fat sluttish woman beside him, had been standing at the counter for several hours, both of them swilling down pot after pot of beer which Harris was paying cash for.

'I wonder how much Master Jonathan gave that bastard?' Kinchin was wondering disgruntledly. 'A fuckin' sight more than he give to me, by the looks on it, the way they'm guzzling the pongalo.'

'What's that little rat doing now?' Eddie Harris asked his woman, Maggie Murphy, for the tenth time since they had come into the inn.

'He's just sitting there, looking gormless. I reckon he's well pissed.'

'Well I reckon he's spying on me again,' Harris growled. 'I'm going to learn him a lesson tonight. I'm going to blind the sneaking little rat so he can't spy on me ever again. I'm going to ram his eyes out and shove 'um up his stinking arse!'

'Don't talk so bloody sarft!' Maggie Murphy rounded on him angrily. 'Crowther 'ull have your guts for garters if you knocks the shit out of Kinchin. You was lucky he didn't bury you in his bloody cellar the other day.'

'I don't give a flying fuck for Crowther, or his bloody nephews.' Harris's bloodshot eyes were glaring with hate. 'If they hadn't took me off me guard, I'd have done for the three of 'um, and crushed Kinchin's yed wi' me bare hands.' His voice grew louder as his temper rose. 'I'll crush the sneaking rat's yed wi' me bare hands! You just wait and see if I don't. And I'll do it this very night! And fuckin' Crowther and his nephews yeds as well.'

Aware that the ever-watchful Herbert Willis was listening from his usual vantage point, perched on a tall stool behind the counter, Maggie Murphy put her mouth to her man's ear and hissed, 'Hold your tongue, you stupid bugger. Willis might hear you, and he'll grass you to Crowther as sure as God made little apples.'

'Grass me, will he? Grass me?' Harris's drink-inflamed brain was now past reason. 'Then I'll crush his fuckin' yed for him, as well.' He leaned over the counter and shouted at Herbert Willis. 'Does you hear me, you fat-gutted bastard? I'll crush your fuckin' yed for you as well!'

Willis hastily vacated his stool, moved to the far end of the counter and signalled to his pot man who was collecting empty tankards from the tables. The pot man immediately went out of the room. William Kinchin also slipped out of the inn and ran to the Fox and Goose.

Tom Potts was sitting in his candlelit room engrossed in reading a book he had borrowed from John Clayton's meagre library. The jangling of the lock-up bells caused him to sigh in mingled resignation and trepidation. This summons could only mean there was trouble to be faced. Tom glanced at his wall clock. It was barely half past nine and John Hollis was not due to come on duty for another hour, so whatever trouble there was, he must face it alone.

'Thomassss! Thomasss!' His mother screeched angrily from the adjoining bedroom. 'Will you answer the door, you great idle hound! How am I ever going to get the rest I need with that racket going on for hours without end? Oh almighty and merciful God, why did you send me such a cruel, unnatural villain to be my son?'

'I'm going directly, Mother. Please don't upset yourself so much,' Tom called as he put on his hat and coat and picked up his staff.

'Ohhhh, I'm more than upset, you evil beast!' she howled indignantly. 'I'm near to death's door, thanks to you! I hope you're satisfied! I hope you're happy now you've finally managed to destroy your own mother? Poor, tragic, accursed soul that I am!' Her voice followed him down the stairs and along the passage between the cells.

The large door creaked open, and the pot man shouted excitedly, 'You'm to come quick to the Red Lion. There's trouble there.' With that the

174

man was gone.

Tom locked the door behind him and walked reluctantly towards the Red Lion Inn. With every step his heartbeat quickened and he could feel his stomach churning with ever-increasing dread.

When he reached the small crowd clustered outside the inn, the uproar of shouting men and shrieking women coming from within its walls dinned in his ears, and for a brief moment he was sorely tempted to walk on past its door.

'Here he is, Jack the bloody Steeple hisself!' An old man cackled with scornful laughter. 'What use he'll be, Christ only knows. He can't fight his way out of a paper bag!'

Tom drew a long shuddering breath, gripped his staff tightly and went in. He was forced to push hard to get through the packed throng in the tap room and reach the clear space by the counter, where Eddie Harris was bellowing threats and curses at Herbert Willis, with Maggie Murphy struggling to restrain him.

'Eddie, me love! Eddie, me darlint! Don't cause no trouble! Eddie, sweetheart! Let's just go! Eddie, me darlint! For the love o' God, let's just go!"

Just as Tom entered the clear space, Harris gripped his woman by her throat with one hand, and with his clenched fist brutally clubbed her to the ground, then kicked her in her stomach with his iron-shod clog.

'Now it's your turn, Willis,' Harris bawled and with surprising agility for his drunken state, vaulted over the counter and moved threateningly towards the frightened innkeeper, who was trapped in the narrow aisle between the wall and counter.

Tom's mouth was dry, his entire body trembling, and he felt as if his insides were liquefying, but when he glanced down at Maggie Murphy writhing in agony, blood gouting from her smashed nose, he knew that come what may, he would not permit himself to surrender to his own fear.

'Stand where you are, Harris.' The command came out in a strangled wheeze, and he swallowed hard and tried again and this time succeeded in emitting a stentorian shout. 'Harris! In the King's name, stand where you are!'

The noise of the crowd hushed.

Enveloped in the sudden silence, Tom took a pace forwards, pointing his long crowned staff like a soldier would point a bayoneted musket. 'I'm arresting you in the King's name, Harris, and you'd best surrender quietly.'

Harris slowly turned to face this fresh adversary. Snatching up a tall stool by its legs and brandishing it above his head, he challenged, 'Or what, you long streak o' piss? What'll you do if I don't choose to come quietly?'

Inwardly Tom was praying desperately, 'Dear God, if he comes for me, please give me the courage to stand my ground and fight him.' Then to his own wonderment, he found himself stepping another pace nearer to Harris and saying aloud in a firm voice, 'I'll still be taking you in, Harris. You and anyone else who chooses to defy the King's laws. So if you know what's good for you, put that stool down and come quietly with me.'

'Just try and take me then, you long streak o' piss!' Harris shouted.

'Do what the constable says, Eddie, and put the stool down!' A voice advised firmly, and all eyes swung to the man standing framed in the tap room doorway.

The crowd parted to make way for Jonathan Crowther to walk up to the counter, closely followed by the Fairfax brothers. He glanced down at Maggie Murphy and told his nephews. 'Put this lady in the trap, boys, and take her to Dr Adamson's house. Tell him I'll pay the cost of any treatment he can give her.'

While they lifted and carried the woman out, Crowther frowned at Harris and calmly leaned across the counter and plucked the stool from him without any resistance being offered.

For an instant Tom could only gaze bemusedly at Crowther, who smiled back at him, and explained, 'I see you're wondering why I've intervened here, Constable. Well, I've a financial interest in this concern and no wish to see my business partner, Master Willis, injured, or the premises damaged.'

'I see,' Tom nodded.

Herbert Willis spoke up. 'And I've no wish to bring any charge against Eddie Harris, Constable. No harm's been done here. It was just a bit of a misunderstanding, that's all.'

'And Maggie won't be charging him with anything either. That's guaranteed, that is. They scraps every weekend, so they does,' one of the

177

spectators put in.

'That's right, that is. And her struck the first blow tonight, so her did. I saw her. But for once Eddie managed to duck afore he decked the cow,' another man asserted. His claim was greeted with uproarious laughter and shouted confirmations.

'Leave Eddie here with us. We'll keep him in order,' another voice urged, and again was greeted with laughter and shouts of confirmation.

'I'm also agreeable that the man should be allowed to stay here.' Crowther added his contribution. 'He's a good customer and this business can ill afford to lose such an enthusiastic drinker.'

Tom was now faced with something of a quandary. He knew that the claims about Maggie Murphy and Harris regularly coming to blows were truthful, and the likelihood of her pressing a charge was virtually non-existent. Also, with neither Willis nor Crowther wanting to press charges, then bringing Harris before the magistrates would serve no purpose because without independent witnesses the case would be dismissed.

Yet he was still reluctant to allow Harris to escape any consequences for so brutally beating Maggie Murphy. He stood undecided as to what to do. As the pause lengthened, the mood of the crowd began to darken, and one man shouted threateningly, 'You'll not be taking Eddie anywhere tonight, Potts. He's a pointer lad, and one of our own. So just bugger off!'

Immediately the pointers in the room began to

chant their traditional battle cry. 'Go it, lads! Go it, lads! Go it, lads!'

Tom's heart quailed within him. Drunk or sober, the pointers were notoriously volatile, and he realized that if any one of them made a move against him, then like a pack of ravening wolves the others would tear into the attack and he would end up at best seriously injured, at worst left for dead. Yet even now, inwardly quaking as he was, his stubborn refusal to surrender to his own fear kept him standing there.

'Master Potts, please go this instant!' Jonathan Crowther hissed urgently through tight lips. 'You can achieve nothing good by remaining here. Please leave for the sake of myself and Master Willis's business. You can only bring trouble and loss down on everyone's heads by staying.'

Tom silently blessed Crowther for offering him this honourable escape route. Aloud, he answered, 'Very well, Master Crowther, to avoid causing you any trouble or loss, I'll leave.'

'Thank you, Master Potts! I'm most grateful to you.' Crowther turned and shouted commandingly, 'Make a path there, lads. Clear the way for the constable.'

Feet shuffled and Tom passed through a narrow gauntlet of threatening scowls and hostile mutterings. When he had pushed through the cluster at the front door and was walking away from the inn, Tom vented a heartfelt sigh of relief. That sense of relief was strengthened when he reached the lock-up to find John Hollis sitting on the top board of the double stocks at

179

the side of the front door.

'Hello Tom. No doubt we'll have a queue of clients waiting their turn to be locked in these before tonight is done with,' Hollis greeted him genially.

'I thought we'd already got one a few minutes since,' Tom told him, and went on to relate what had happened in the Red Lion.

Hollis listened in intent silence until the narration finished, then chuckled appreciatively. 'Well Tom, there are those in this parish who claim that Crowther is a devil incarnate, but in this case I have to say that we must give the devil his due. He's acted like a friend towards you.'

'Oh I'm very grateful to Crowther, believe me,' Tom acknowledged, but added with a wry grin. 'However, what I'm bearing in mind still is that, "Who sups with the devil must use a long spoon."'

It was long past midnight, the doors of the inns and taverns and alehouses were closed and bolted and the drunken roisterers had staggered to their resting places. The streets, alleys and courts were still and quiet, with just the occasional gleam of a candle showing through window glass or shutter, and only the soughing gusts of the chill northeast wind disturbing the silence.

Tom Potts and John Hollis were making their last patrol of the night, which to their mutual surprise had turned out to be relatively peaceful, and they had not been impelled to make any arrests. They completed the final circuit at the central crossroads and halted there at the chapel yard gate.

'You'll get a good night's sleep tonight, Tom.' Hollis smiled. 'No drunks kicking up a ruction in the cells to keep you awake.'

'Thank God!' Tom agreed fervently. 'I confess, I'm happy to see the end of this night. I was expecting a lot of trouble.'

'So was I.'

'Will you come back to the lock-up and have something to eat and drink before you go home, John?'

'I'll gladly share a glass and a pipe with you, but I don't want any food.'

They walked side by side along the chapel yard wall. A sound like a cry of pain was suddenly carried on the gusting wind and Tom halted, listening hard. It came again, this time more drawn out.

'Can that be King William?' John Hollis wondered aloud. 'Is somebody mistreating him?'

'They'll answer to me if that's the case,' Tom vowed grimly.

Both men stared over the wall, eyes straining to pierce a darkness lightened only by starlight.

King William was a deranged, harelipped simpleton who spent most of his nights sleeping among the gravestones of the chapel yard. The vast majority of the townspeople treated him with rough kindliness, looking upon him as their proprietary village idiot. But there were some who tormented and abused him for their own brutal pleasure.

'There! Over there!' Tom spotted dim moving shapes.

Both men clambered over the wall and ran towards the shapes, which as they neared them solidified into two men grunting, gasping, cursing , punching, wrestling and falling to roll across the ground.

'Break it up, you two!' Tom shouted.

John Hollis grabbed the uppermost man by his hair and bodily heaved him away.

'You're under arrest, my bucko! You'd best come quiet!'

'And you also!' Tom shouted at the second man. 'Don't try anything, or it'll be the worse for you.'

'All right! All right! No need to get riled!' The second man struggled to lever himself into a sitting position, and Tom suddenly recognized Bonny Southall. 'I'll come nice and easy, Master Potts.'

He was slurring his words badly, and when Tom pulled him up on to his feet he could only stay upright by clutching Tom's arm, he was so helplessly drunk. John Hollis's captive was Eddie Harris, equally reeling drunk. Neither man made any effort to resist as they were led staggering to the lock-up and put into adjoining cells, where they slumped to the floor and within scant minutes were both loudly snoring.

'Well, that's two customers for the stocks after all,' Hollis remarked. 'Who's on the bench on Monday?'

'Aston and Timmins.'

'Then that'll be four days in the stocks at least

for this pair.' Hollis grinned with satisfaction. 'And four days padlock fees for us and our slice of prisoners' subsistence money besides.'

Tom shook his head. 'No John, I really can't bring Southall before the bench. I wouldn't feel right about doing so.'

'Why not? He's a regular troublemaker, isn't he? And Harris is rotten through and through. A dose of the stocks won't be undeserved by either of them.'

'There's no doubt of that fact, John. But Bonny Southall kept the peace during the strike and saved us a deal of trouble. I can't forget that, can I?'

'But it was his fault the strike started,' Hollis argued.

Tom shook his head. 'No, truth to tell, I sympathize with the pointers for going on strike when they did. They earn very good wages, I know, but the price they pay is to have their own lives cut short. The masters earn good profits, and don't need to cut the workers' rates as they continually do, solely to satisfy their own greed.

'No, John, I'll not bring Southall before the bench, and Harris can't be brought up without him. But I'll see to it that you won't lose out on the padlock fees. You can issue all the summonses and warrants for the next week, and take any strays into the pound. That should more than cover your losses.'

'Fair enough,' Hollis nodded and grinned. 'Now let's have that glass and pipe, shall we?'

Twenty-Four

Sunday, 27 August 1826

It was early dawn when Tom rose and dressed. Although he had spent a restless night of strange, vaguely troubling dreams and constant drifting in and out of sleep, he was feeling a sense of happy anticipation. Today he intended to devote all his time to investigating the thefts of Bates's and Chillingworth's needles, and the two body-snatchings. He decided that his first task of the morning, however, was to release his two prisoners.

'Wake up now, Master Southall. You don't want to spend the day in here do you?' Tom unlocked the first cell and roused its occupant.

Bonny Southall opened his bleary eyes, yawned hugely, stretched his arms wide and groaned, 'Oh it warn't a dream then. I really did get run in last night, didn't I?'

His head, arms, fists and clothing were caked with dried blood and his handsome features marred by swollen cuts and bruises. He gingerly fingered the side of his jaw. 'Christ! That bugger Harris packs a wallop. What state is he in?'

'You'll be able to judge for yourself if and when you see him again. But I expect he'll be looking just like you. What was the reason you were fighting?'

A wary gleam entered Southall's eyes, but after a moment he grinned bluffly and shook his head. 'God only knows. When has us pointer lads ever needed any reason to knock the blue mould off each other? It's well known that we likes a good scrap now and again. That's reason enough, aren't it?'

'Now I don't want any more trouble from either of you, so I'm warning you to go straight home and behave yourself.'

Southall frowned in puzzlement. 'Go home? But the magistrates are sitting tomorrow, aren't they? You'll be putting me up afore 'um, won't you?'

Tom shook his head. 'No. You and Eddie Harris were only damaging each other, and it was so late there was no one else around to see it.' He grinned wryly. 'From the look of you, you've already been punished sufficiently, without me loading any more troubles on to you.'

'So I'm not being charged wi' anything then?' Southall sounded as if he could not believe what he was hearing.

'Get out of my lock-up this instant, will you?' Tom ordered. 'Before I change my mind.'

Southall grinned and rose to his feet. 'Fair play to you, Master Potts. You'm all right, you am. I'll not be forgetting this in a hurry.' He followed Tom to the main door, and when it had been un-locked and opened he proffered his hand. 'Will you shake hands wi' me, Master Potts?'

'I'm happy to do so, Master Southall.'

They clasped hands firmly, and Bonny South-all jauntily left, whistling a lively tune. Tom stayed at the door, watching until the other man was gone from view, before going to unlock the other cell.

Harris presented a similar battered and bloody appearance to his opponent, and demanded aggressively as Tom entered the cell. 'Why have you let that bastard Southall go?'

'For the same reason I'm letting you go,' Tom told him. 'You were only harming each other. Why were you fighting, anyway?'

'Because he's been trespassing on my property,' Wright grunted.

'Your property? I thought you lived in Bocker Duggins's lodging house in Silver Street, so how can you own property?'

Harris made no reply, and Tom was not interested enough to press him further. 'You can go now, Master Harris. But mind what I say. If I catch you creating a disturbance again, I'll bring you in front of the magistrates.'

Harris shambled sullenly away, and Tom stood in the open doorway enjoying the fresh chill morning air, and mentally registering the fact that neither man was missing the top joint of a finger.

Some 30 yards distance from the lock-up, William Kinchin crouched behind a clump of bushes on the edge of the Green, his ragged clothes clutched tight around his scrawny body, cold, hungry and weary after his night-long vigil. As soon as Tom disappeared back inside and the lock-up door closed behind him, Kinchin rose stiffly and cursing his aching body, began the long trek to his master's house.

Twenty-Five

Wednesday Morning, 30 August 1826

Tom rose from his bed, feeling tired in body and depressed in spirits.

'What a waste of time it's all been. I'm not one step nearer to solving anything!'

During the whole of Sunday, Monday, and Tuesday from early dawn until late at night he had ceaselessly tramped the environs of the parish, talking to various people, asking seemingly casual questions, carefully evaluating the answers. Returning to the scenes of the robberies and body snatchings, desperately hoping to discover anything at all which would aid his search.

'Nothing! I've got nothing!'

Now, down in the rear yard, he stripped naked and sluiced his head and body repeatedly with buckets of pump water, gasping and shivering under its icy cold impact. Adding to his depression was the fact that he had on every night also called at the Fox and Goose and tried to speak with Amy Danks. On every night she had tossed her head disdainfully and told him she had nothing more to say to him, because she had now found a true and honourable suitor who was desperately eager to marry her on any day she chose.

'Unlike you, Thomas Potts, who keep on saying you love me, but never ever sets a date for the wedding! So go away and leave me be!'

In a fruitless effort to deaden the painful memory of her scornful expression and scathing words, Tom increased the speed of his bucketed dousing until his body at least felt deadened with cold.

The lock-up bells jangled furiously, and fearing the noise would wake his mother, Tom pulled his nightshirt over his nakedness and hurried to open the entrance door.

'Fuckin' 'ell! You'm bloody well soaking! Has you been pissing yourself?' Maggie Murphy's swollen blackened eyes stared in astonishment.

'No, of course not!' Tom snapped curtly, embarrassed to have been caught in this condition. 'I was merely bathing.'

'Barfing? You wants to be careful, long un. Barfing washes away your body oils and damages your health.'

'That's a matter of opinion,' Tom retorted irritably. 'Now what can I do for you, Mrs Murphy?'

'It's Miss Murphy, if you please,' she corrected him indignantly. 'I'll have you know I'm a maiden lady.'

For a brief instant a cutting gibe rose to Tom's lips, but he bit it back, feeling some shame that he should be acting so unpleasantly towards this woman who had done him no harm. In a softer

188

tone, he apologized. 'I'm sorry for my error, Miss Murphy. What do you need with me?'

'Is my man locked up in here again? Only the bugger aren't been home since he went out on Sunday night.'

'Do you mean, Master Harris?'

'Who the fuckin' else would I be asking after, you great lanky gowk!'

Tom shook his head. 'No. I've not seen Master Harris since I released him from here on Sunday morning last.'

'Am you sure?'

'Yes, I'm very sure. Good day to you, Miss Murphy.'

Tom went to close the door, but she pushed against it with her meaty arm, and growled. 'Well, if you does see the bastard, tell him I'm going to be having his fuckin' guts for garters!' She waddled away mouthing more threats of what she was going to do to Eddie Harris.

Tom's sigh of relief that she had gone was abruptly stifled in his throat.

'Thomassss? Thomassss? Why have you woken me up to my agonies at this ungodly hour? Dear Lord, why do I have to suffer so? Poor, pathetic, put-upon creature that I am! And when are you going to empty my commode, you lazy, useless wretch? It's stinking my room out.'

Tom summoned all his patience, and called, 'I'm coming directly, Mother. Pray don't upset yourself so.'

After sharing a breakfast of boiled eggs, bread and milk with his mother, Tom took up his staff and went across the road to the small barber shop with its massive protruding red and white striped pole, from which hung a large ornate sign proclaiming to the world that Professor Aloysius Parr, accredited barber surgeon of the University of Malheim, had dressed the hair of the royalty, nobility, and gentry of all the German states.

Since setting up his business in Redditch, however, Professor Parr had been forced to cater to the more lowly classes of society. He was much patronized by the needle pointers because of his expertise in using leeches to treat black eyes, swollen jaws and the various other contusions they suffered during their frequent brawling.

Tom, despite knowing very well that Parr's claims to university accreditation and high born patronage were totally false, nevertheless liked the garrulous, wig-wearing, dandified Parr, who was invariably replete with the latest gossip of the town.

Now he seated himself in the high-backed chair and felt his earlier depression lifting as the diminutive barber, prattling continuously, lathered sweet smelling soap and expertly shaved him with a huge cut-throat razor.

'I had the Oakleys in earlier, Constable Potts, father and son. Full barbering they wanted, because they're doing two funerals today. One this morning, and one this afternoon. Full haircut and shave for both of them. The young one even had me curl his side whiskers and apply a nicely scented Macassar oil. Got his eye on a young wench, no doubt. That's the thing about

190

funerals, isn't it? There are always young fillies coming with their families to the service. Mind you, if I was a girl I wouldn't relish marrying an undertaker. Too much of a morbid trade for my fancy. You never know where their hands have been dipping into, do you? If you get my meaning.'

'Which funeral are they doing this morning?' Tom enquired idly.

'Johnny Watts. He's to be buried in the old graveyard on top of his dad and mam, and three of his sisters. Old Tommy Oakley reckoned that there'll be hardly 6 inches of cover over him, the grave's that full. Old Tommy was becalling Crowther, I'll tell you. He said the drag down and up the Fish Hill will make the horse all sweaty and dusty and so it'll have to be fresh groomed afore it can draw Widow Asprey this afternoon. He said Crowther could well have afforded to buy a plot in the chapel yard and have Watts buried there. Tommy put it down to him being mean with his money.'

For some reason that he could not fully understand himself, Tom suddenly felt his interest spark. 'I've never heard tell that Crowther is a mean man with his money, professor.'

'Well, nor have I, Constable. But then young Billy Oakley told me it was nothing to do with Crowther being mean. It was Watts's own missus who insisted he must be buried in the old graveyard. She said it was Watts's own dying wish to be laid to rest with his family.'

'Well, a man's dying wishes must always be respected whenever possible,' Tom concurred.

'And in all truth the old graveyard is a pleasant enough spot to await the last judgement in, is it not, professor?'

'It most certainly is, Constable Potts, and that's you all shaved and shiny. Would you like me to apply some Polar Bear pomade of Muscovy? I've especially imported it from the steppes of Russia.'

'No, thank you. I've no wish to be mistaken for a Cossack,' Tom demurred with a chuckle. He paid the shaving fee of two pence.

'Will you be going to either of the funerals?' Parr queried.

Tom was on the verge of saying no, when on sudden impulse he found himself nodding. 'I do believe I shall be attending John Watts's funeral, professor.'

Twenty-Six

Tom stood at the gate of the old cemetery watching the approach of the sombre funeral cortege. Tommy Oakley headed the short procession, pacing with a stately gait. Behind him, a black-plumed horse led by Billy Oakley drew the crepe-swathed bier on which the laurel-wreathed coffin lay. On each side of the bier walked a line of three elderly mutes, carrying black banners. Directly behind the bier, in sumptuous black satin and velvet mourning clothes, the heavily veiled Mary Watts walked alone. Then came two open carriages, the lead carriage bearing Jonathan Crowther, his two nephews and a saturnine-featured man dressed in dark, clerical-style clothing. The second carriage was occupied by John Clayton and Andrew Adamson. These in turn were followed by a crowd of curious spectators, attracted by the unusual ostentation of this ordinary working man's funeral.

The aged gravedigger, Hector Smout, came to stand with Tom. He narrowed his watery eyes to stare hard at the oncoming procession, then hawked and spat derisively. 'Look at her showing herself off! Women aren't supposed to go parading themselves at funerals like her's doing. Funeral going is men's work, and always has been. And what the fuck is Crowther thinking of to go spending all this money on planting a lazy useless bastard like Johnny Watts? He must need his yed looking at!'

'Well certainly no one can accuse him of stinting payment for this funeral,' Tom acknowledged, and studied the passengers of the two carriages.

'I'se had a hell of a job making room for the bugger,' Smout grumbled self-pityingly. 'I'se had to lift out the youngest sister's coffin, her what died last Michaelmas, and then crunch down the buggers that was under her wi' me sledgehammer so as to make room for this bugger coming in now, and then slot her back in again. But he'll still only have a foot o' covering over him. Mind you, if it had been down to me I'd have boiled the bugger up wi' the swill and

193

fed him to the pigs, because I'se never liked him.'

Smout hawked and spat on the ground, before adding lugubriously. 'But I'se done me best for him today, and that's all any man can do for a blessed soul what the good Lord has took up to paradise.'

Tom was forced to hide a smile of wry amusement at his companion's bizarre recital.

The cortège reached the graveyard gate and Tom moved discreetly back with Smout as the mourners dismounted from the carriages, while the mutes laid aside their black crepe banners and prepared to carry the coffin to the open grave.

John Clayton led the procession into the graveyard, declaiming sonorously, 'Man that is born of woman hath but a short time to live, and is full of misery. He cometh up, and is cut down, like a flower; he fleeth as it were a shadow, and never continueth in one stay. In the midst of life we are in death: of whom may we seek for succour, but of thee, O Lord, who for...'

Tom watched the mutes in their new role of pall-bearers, noting that the men appeared to be exerting considerable effort to bear their load.

'They don't look to be particularly infirm, and there's six of them,' he thought. 'It's odd that the coffin seems to be weighing heavily, when Watts looked so thin and wasted.'

Almost as if he had heard Tom's unspoken thoughts, Hector Smout exclaimed in a hoarse whisper, 'Just look at them crafty old bastards! They always pretends that the dead 'uns are hard

194

to carry, because then they thinks they'll get a couple o' extra pennies for their trouble.'

'Do they now?' Tom accepted, and dismissed the matter from his mind.

The service eventually came to an end, and the mourners moved back towards the gate, leaving Mary Watts alone at the open grave, head bowed, hands clasped before her breasts, shoulders visibly heaving as she wept.

'I'd best go and stand across from her until she gets the hint and buggers off a bit quick,' Smout muttered sourly. 'Or else I might be waiting ages for her to go and leave me to fill the bloody hole up again.'

Tom was not repelled by the old man's apparent callousness. He could appreciate that anyone living and working daily with the constant presence of death and its aftermath became hardened to it.

As Smout left, Andrew Adamson came to greet Tom.

'What brings you here, Tom?'

Bidden by sudden impulse, Tom lied. 'Oh, I was walking in the Abbey Meadow and I saw the cortège coming, so I stayed to pay my respects.' He casually added, 'His wife told me you've diagnosed apoplexy as the cause of death.'

'Yes, I'm positive of it,' Adamson confirmed.

'It's a pity he was never able to tell us anything about the night he was attacked.'

'Indeed it was. Unfortunately, every time I saw him he was in no condition to tell me anything. He was either comatose, or continually vomiting, with severe stomach pains and diarrhoea. To make matters worse, the convulsive fits violently wrenched his limbs and I fear caused the knitting of the broken bones to be severely disrupted.'

'Do you know exactly what caused those fits?'

'The convulsions indicated severe congestion of the brain, which might also have affected his cognitive intelligence. Mind you, from what I'm told, Watts was never overburdened with intellect.' Adamson smiled. 'So any damage to that organ he may have suffered wouldn't have been very noticeable, particularly to any recent acquaintances such as myself. However, after I tried Dr Holland's recommended treatment for a couple of days, Watts appeared to be rallying and his condition improving tremendously. Then he suddenly up and died on me. Still, that's fairly common in cases of severe apoplexy, is it not?'

'How did his wife manage to cope with such awful troubles, so young as she is?' Tom wondered aloud.

'Very well indeed, ' Adamson declared. 'She cared for him as if he were her newborn babe. I only wish that when the time comes for marriage I might get wed to someone like her: a beautiful young woman who's absolutely devoted to her husband. What more could a man ask for in a wife? Apart from a sizeable dowry, of course.' He grinned. 'And now I'm going for my after-funeral refreshments, Tom. My throat is as parched as a desert.'

When the cortège departed, Tom remained standing alone, deep in thought, slowly dredging from the depths of his memory fragments of re-collection which Adamson's words had brought to mind. The fragments gradually accumulated, slotting one with another like a jigsaw, to form a coherent mental picture.

He frowned and shook his head, trying to dismiss an unwelcome conclusion. 'No! That can't be right. It can't be!'

But deep within his mind, the question persisted. 'Why not, Tom? Why not? Why not? Why not?'

In the leafy suburb of Edgbaston, professor of anatomy Dr Semprimus Monkland's face was glowing with satisfaction. With a theatrical flourish, he whipped the covering sheet from the emaciated corpse on the dissecting table, and announced portentously to his rapt audience, 'This morning, ladies and gentlemen, I am able to bring before you one of the rarest specimens it has ever been my pleasure to offer up for your edification and education. This subject is a male destroyed in the prime of his life, by multiple bone traumas, flesh member lesions and organic dissolutions. As I dissect it, this specimen will reveal and illustrate the remarkable capacity of the human form to struggle to sustain life and make attempts to repair itself after receiving the most extreme and varied abuse that can be envisaged. I am entirely confident, ladies and gentlemen, that for a great many years to come, in no other Academy of Anatomy throughout the continent of Europe will a specimen of such rarity be presented to such a distinguished audience as that which I have the honour to now see before me.'

The audience applauded with stamping feet, clapping hands and loud cheering.

In a wayside beer ken on the road midway between Edgbaston and Redditch, a dozing drunken man was being shaken awake by the beer ken keeper.

'Whass up? Whassa marrer?' the drunk growled angrily.

'What's up?' The keeper shouted indignantly, and pointed towards the broken, rag-stuffed window. 'Just listen to the racket that beast o' yours is making out front, will you! That's what's up! It's enough to rouse the dead! Now get it away from here, and don't come back, because it's driving me bloody mad!'

'All right, all right, keep your hair on,' the drunk snarled aggressively. 'I was going anyway, because I've had enough of this stinking place and your stinking, sour face.'

He staggered out of the ken, untied the frantically braying donkey from the hitching post and led the beast on towards Redditch.

Twenty-Seven

Wednesday, late afternoon, 30 August

For several hours, Tom had been carefully studying his father's medical case journals, gleaning all that he could find from the stained and faded handwriting concerning vegetable poisoning. He laid the final ledger back into the chest where he kept his father's mementos and rubbed his aching eyes.

'I really must get some reading glasses,' he reminded himself for perhaps the thousandth time.

From the adjoining room came the sound of his mother's grotesquely girlish giggling, interspersed with the irritatingly mellifluous tones of Charles Bromley relating some long-winded anecdote. Although Tom had little liking for his fellow constable, he was nevertheless grateful that the man had become a frequent caller at the lock-up, and spent many hours keeping the Widow Potts company.

'At least it gives me some respite from her constant nagging and complaining.'

Now Tom briefly pondered his course of action, came to a decision, put on his top hat and picked up his staff. He knocked on the door of his mother's room and called, 'I have to go out for a while, Mother.' But he received no reply because she was too engrossed with Bromley, who was at that moment professing his undying devotion towards her.

The small, tumbledown White Lion tavern which did little trade, stood almost opposite the Red Lion Inn. Its limited clientele were mainly aged and impoverished, as was its landlady, the Widow Poole. Who, when Tom came into her tap room, smiled toothlessly and told him, 'I hopes you aren't come here to ask me to lend you any money, Master Potts, because me lodger still owes me for his last month's bed and board.'

Tom, forced by the low ceiling to remove his hat and bend his head, smiled back, 'No Ma'am, I'm not here to ask you for anything. It's your lodger, Master Smith, I've come to consult. So at least he'll have my fee to enable him to pay you some of his arrears. Is he here?'

'He's out the backyard sitting on the privy. You'd best go there and give him a shout – he'll be sitting there all day else trying to have a shit.' She cackled with laughter. 'The bugger's no more use at moving his bowels than he is at finding a proper job to go to.'

'But you wouldn't be without him, would you Ma'am? You're very good and old friends are you not?'

'True enough. And in all fairness, whenever he gets money he always pays me all he owes and more besides.'

After Tom had called his name several times,

Jack Smith emerged from the privy fully dressed and glowering. He was an unusually eccentric character in his personal appearance, manners and habits: middle-aged and swarthy, with penetrating dark hazel eyes, hairless head and eyebrows and a pendulous lower lip. He stood less than 5 feet tall, with an exceptionally powerful upper body; his neck so short that his head appeared to grow straight from his broad shoulders. He was dressed always in an old black tailcoat and tall black hat, the coat tails reaching to his heels and the hat brim drooping over his tiny misshapen ears.

He was one of the Needle District's white witch men, and widely believed to possess occult powers and to be able to converse with spirits. People came to him to have their horoscopes cast, their futures foretold, their stolen property located. He was also a highly knowledgeable and skilled herbalist who had achieved many successes in treating the sick and afflicted with his own herbal potions. His failing in life was his inordinate liking for strong drink. Whenever he had funds, he would meticulously settle his debts, and then spend what money was left in the taverns, bingeing until he was penniless and in debt once more. His many esoteric volumes on occult matters were invariably in pawn at one tavern or another in exchange for drink.

'What does you want with me, Master Potts? Can't a man be left to have a shit in peace without being pestered by the constabulary?' Smith asked.

Tom hastened to apologize, and explained, 'I need to consult you professionally, Master Smith, on a confidential matter of some urgency to myself.'

The prospect of earning money mollified Smith a little, and he replied civilly enough, 'Well, if it's a horoscope that you want, we'll need to go to the Unicorn. Me books are being held there for the time being.'

Having been regaled many times with accounts of Smith's occult successes, for a fleeting instant Tom found himself toying with the idea of asking the man to identify the needle robbers and body snatchers. Then caught himself up and with wry amusement dismissed that notion, 'No Master Smith, it's not a horoscope I need. I merely want to draw on your knowledge, for which of course I'll pay your fee.'

'All right. Ask away.'

'Fungi, Master Smith? Do you know where any poisonous fungi might be found to be growing in this or the neighbouring parishes?'

'Oh yes,' Smith said, and held out his hand. 'And that question has cost you a crown piece, Master Potts.'

'A crown piece!' Tom exclaimed. 'You're charging me five shillings for a single question?'

Smith grinned, displaying large, widely gapped, yellowed teeth. 'Oh no, Master Potts. I'm charging you a crown in exchange for a lifetime's hard-gained knowledge.'

Despite Tom's initial reaction, a moment's reflection brought his innate sense of fairness to the fore, and he nodded. 'There's a degree of justice in what you say, Master Smith. But in all truth I've not got five shillings in my pockets.'

'How much have you got?'

Tom searched through his coat and breeches and counted out his scant store of coins. 'Three shillings and nine pence three farthings.'

'Well, I'm not a hard-hearted chap, Master Potts, and wouldn't want to see you with nothing at all in your pocket,' Smith declared magnanimously. 'So I'll take only the three shillings now, and you can owe me the other two.' His yellowed teeth bared in a mocking grin. 'After all, if we can't trust the parish constable to pay his debts, then in whomsoever can we trust?'

Tom ruefully placed the three silver coins in Smith's cupped palm, and watched them disappear like lightening into the capacious folds of the black topcoat.

'You drive a hard bargain, Master Smith.'

'It's a hard life that my lowly order of society have to live, Master Potts. The fine lords and gentlemen who rule us have one hand round our throats and the other hand digging into our pockets for the taxes they spend upon their own luxuries, while we go hungry.'

'True enough,' Tom was forced to admit. 'So I'll bid you good day, Master Smith.'

He reached the gate of the small backyard, and Smith called, 'You're a decent man, Master Potts, for all you're a servant of those who grind down people like me. If you bring me three shillings instead of two, then I'll answer any and all questions you want to ask me. Is that a bargain?'

The sheer incongruity of the situation tickled Tom's sense of humour and laughingly he accepted. 'It's a bargain, Master Smith, but it may be some time before I can raise that amount.'

'Take whatever time you need,' Smith chuckled. 'I won't be going anywhere. The spirits have told me I'm going to be staying right here in Redditch for the rest of me days.'

As Tom walked back to the lock-up fingering the nine pence three farthings left in his pocket, the grimmer aspect of his present financial condition began to over cloud his earlier humorous reaction to Jack Smith's demands.

'I'm going to have to ask grocer Groby for credit again,' he realized glumly. 'And Morgan and baker Scambler as well, or Mother and I will be starving before this week's done. Not to mention poor Bathsheba.'

He pulled his father's old pocket watch from its fob pocket and glanced at the time. 'Quarter to seven o'clock – it'll be sunset in about an hour. I'd best go and tell Blackwell what John and I intend doing, and then prepare for the night.'

He and John Hollis had secretly arranged that for the next nine successive nights they would maintain separate covert grave-watches, Tom over the grave of John Watts in the Old Monks Graveyard, and Hollis over the Widow Asprey's grave in the small burial ground at Crabbs Cross. After that period, buried corpses were generally accepted to have deteriorated too much to be of any saleable value for the resurrection men.

Joseph Blackwell sat behind his study desk resting his chin on steepled forefingers, showing no reaction until Tom had finished his recital. Then he nodded approvingly.

'Excellent, Master Potts! Does Hollis have access to any firearms?'

'He and his brother own sporting guns, I believe, Sir.' Tom was slightly puzzled at this question.

'Make sure that he takes them with him.' As he was speaking, Blackwell rose and went to the wall cabinet, from which he lifted out a brace of holstered pistols and a small leather satchel. 'You're already familiar with these, Master Potts, so I've no need to instruct you in how to prime and load them.'

'With all respect, Sir, I don't believe either John Hollis or myself will need firearms. It's only grave robbers we're lying in wait for, not garrotters or killers,' Tom pointed out.

'It's criminal scum that you're lying in wait for, Master Potts.' Blackwell frowned severely. 'And if they are killed while resisting arrest, then the world is a much cleaner and safer place for their being removed from it. Do you understand me?'

Knowing the futility of further argument, Tom obediently nodded.

A fleeting smile curved Blackwell's thin lips, and in a gentler tone he told Tom. 'I know that there are many misguided people throughout the Needle District who jeer at Hollis and yourself, and think you both to be figures of fun. In my opinion however, you and John Hollis are the finest constables this parish has ever had. Unlike the legendary Spartan mother, I want you both to always come back safely, with or without your shields.'

This totally unexpected demonstration of warm regard from such a normally austere and formal-mannered man touched Tom deeply and brought a lump to his throat. He took the pistols and satchel from Blackwell and as the older man reseated himself behind the desk, replied, 'Thank you, Sir. I'm grateful for your regard, and I shall go to see Master Hollis immediately and relate to him what you've said.'

Blackwell's head was bent over the large open ledger on the desktop, and he didn't look up, but only waved a hand in dismissal and grunted, 'Good night, Master Potts.'

When Tom arrived at the woodland cottage bordering the road to Webheath hamlet, he found his friend working in the small vegetable patch. John Hollis listened intently to what Tom had to tell him, and scoffed dismissively, 'Blackwell says I must take guns with me? I don't need a gun to arrest sneaking cowardly body snatchers. My staff is more than enough to scuttle the likes of them. It's not Dick Turpin and his gang we're going after, Tom. It's only yellow-bellied scum who haven't got courage enough to rob the living, so they needs must thieve the dead. I'd think myself to be as cowardly as them if I needed a gun to arrest them. No! I'll not take any gun with me, no matter what Blackwell says.'

His friend's forceful refusal caused Tom to experience a sense of shame that he himself had so readily accepted Blackwell's instruction. His honesty forced him to openly confess, 'I don't possess your bravery, John, or your fighting qualities. I freely admit that I'm taking Blackwell's pistols because the prospect of having to face resurrection men in a deserted graveyard fills me with utter dread.'

Hollis was instantly remorseful, 'Oh Tom, I meant no slight to you. I know you're not a coward!'

Tom grimaced ruefully and shook his head. 'But I am a coward, my friend. The mere prospect of facing any sort of conflict or confrontation causes my heart to thud, my stomach to heave, and my hands to shake.'

The other man's lean features grinned fondly. 'I can top that list, Tom, because I own the largest and smelliest collection of brown-stained breeches in this parish. So the only real difference between you and I is that I'm a terrible braggart who constantly lies about his own bravery, while you're man enough to admit to your own frailties, yet still stand and face whatever danger confronts you.' He stepped forward and hugged Tom close for a moment.

For the second time that day a lump rose to Tom's throat, and he was forced to swallow hard. The intensity of the moment made him feel uncomfortably self-conscious, and he coughed and said hurriedly, 'It's dusk, my friend, we'd best be getting to our posts.'

'Yes. I'll see you in the morning.' John Hollis

nodded, and turned to go into his cottage, adding jokingly, 'I'll just go get my musket and bayonet.'

Tom laughed and walked away.

When he arrived back at the lock-up, he was surprised to find the resplendently uniformed Sergeant Sullivan standing outside the front door. His unbidden initial reaction was the mental picture of the handsome sergeant and Amy Danks laughing together, and a surge of jealous resentment flooded through him, to be quickly superseded by uneasy apprehension as to what the soldier might be waiting here to tell him.

Sullivan saluted and requested politely, 'Good evening, Constable Potts. Might I have a word with you?'

Tom drew a long deep breath, fighting to control his disturbed emotions, and in a strained voice acquiesced with equal politeness, 'Certainly you may, Sergeant Sullivan. Perhaps you'd care to step inside and wait for a moment. I have to collect my staff and some other items.'

'No, thank you. What I've got to say will only take a moment or two.' Sullivan's tone became almost apologetic. 'I've no wish to quarrel with you, but I fear my news will undoubtedly cause you some annoyance. However, I hope we can both behave as gentlemen.'

Tom's apprehension deepened. He nodded and muttered, 'I'm sure we shall both behave so, Sergeant.'

'Amy has told me that for some considerable time you and she were very close friends, and

that there was some talk of eventual marriage.'
Sullivan's handsome features were very grave,
but bore no hint of hostility. 'She also tells me
you've always acted towards her with the utmost
propriety and behaved honourably.' A smile
briefly hovered upon his lips. 'As I've done so
myself.'

Tom was abruptly driven by the overpowering
need to cut short the other man's preamble, and
he couldn't stop himself from interrupting
curtly.

'I've no wish to be unmannerly, Sergeant
Sullivan, but I would greatly appreciate your
coming to the point, and telling me what you
have to without further delay.'

Sullivan frowned slightly, and with equal curt-
ness snapped, 'Very well, Constable Potts. In
short, this afternoon I asked Amy to become my
wife, and she honoured me with her acceptance.
Consequently I'm asking you, as the gentleman
that I'm assured you are, to in future stay away
from her, and no longer seek to pursue any
relationship with her.'

The impact of Sullivan's words struck Tom
like a physical blow, momentarily stunning him,
driving all thoughts from his mind. The soldier
regarded him keenly, tensed for any violent
reaction from his rival. Tom stood motionless
and speechless, desperately fighting to regain
control of his chaotic emotions.

Sullivan was by nature a kindly hearted man,
and he could plainly see the devastating effects
of his words. 'I'm truly sorry that you and I have
been forced into this situation,' he told Tom with

genuine sympathy. 'If we had met in any other context I'm sure that we would have become good friends. I'll say goodbye to you, Constable Potts.'

'Goodbye, Sergeant Sullivan,' Tom muttered automatically, his mind filled with vivid pictures of Amy's smiling face, his entire being aching with the pain of her loss. There were people walking past the lock-up, children playing near-by, and unable at this moment to face the prospect of having speech with anyone else and all thought of collecting his staff and pistols driven from his mind, Tom hurried away, taking the road which led eastwards to Bredon. He went through and beyond Bredon and when he was at a sufficient distance for the darkness to shield him from view of the houses he turned north-wards, desperately seeking solitude.

As he stumbled through fields and wasteland, crossed ditches, climbed over styles and hedge-rows, descending downwards into the Arrow Valley, it seemed that he had become two separate mental entities, one wallowing in maudlin self-pity, the other harshly condemnatory.

'What shall I do now that I've lost her?'

'Pull yourself together, and act like a man!'

'Now I've nothing in my life to look forward to.'

'Stop crying like a child over spilt milk!'

'How can I go on living an empty life?'

'By doing what you've always done, continuing to breathe.'

Gradually the initial impact of his encounter with Sergeant Sullivan lessened, and although

the pain of losing Amy still throbbed agoniz-
ingly through his being, he forced himself to
face the unwelcome reality that he was responsible for what had happened.

'It's my own fault that I've lost her. If only I'd
fixed a date for our wedding, she'd still be mine.
It's all my fault! Stupid cowardly idiot that I am!
I deserved this, and can only blame myself for
it!'

Then the self-pitying entity questioned plaintively, 'But what am I to do now that she's gone
from my life?'

'Your duty! You must do your duty! Do your
duty!' the other harsh hectoring voice thundered
ever more dominantly.

The entities slowly merged as Tom doggedly
struggled to reassert self-control until he was
able to resolve grimly, 'Duty! I shall do my
duty!'

He turned westwards and headed towards the
Abbey Meadows and the old Monks Graveyard.

Twenty-Eight

At Jonathan Crowther's house, by the early
evening the consumption of lavish post-funeral
refreshments had engendered a festive atmosphere and the room was noisy with talk and
laughter. The host sat at the top of a table laden

with bottles and the remnants of a feast, a benevolent smile on his lips, a lighted cheroot between his fingers, a glass of brandy in his hand. Around the table his four remaining guests lounged at their ease, smoking and drinking, exchanging anecdotes and jokes. Crowther's shrewd gaze moved continuously from one to another: Charlie Marsden, Benjamin and Thomas Fairfax, and the fourth man, Turpin Wright, whose youthful, fresh-complexioned face bore a long livid, jagged scar from hairline to jaw line, passing transversely across his left eye, nose, and right cheek.

'You didn't attend the funeral of Watts, Master Wright?' Charlie Marsden enquired. 'Can I take it you weren't a friend of his?'

'Whether I was friend or enemy of Johnny Watts is none o' your business.' Wright's steel-blue eyes held an aggressive glint.

Jonathan Crowther was quick to smoothly intervene. 'Turpin couldn't come to the funeral Charlie, because he was journeying back from Worcester. Otherwise he would most definitely have been with us, wouldn't you, Turpin?'

'If you says so, Jonno,' Wright replied in a surly voice.

Crowther's expression hardened perceptibly, 'Oh, I do say so, Turpin, and you'd do well to remember which side your bread is buttered on, and leave those jail bird manners where they belong.' He turned to Marsden and smilingly explained, 'Turpin has been a guest of His Majesty in the Worcester Bridewell for the last year or so and was only released this morning,

212

Charlie. Sadly, during his incarceration he seems to have forgotten how to behave in polite society. I'm sure you'll make due allowance for that unfortunate fact.'

'But of course I will, Jonno,' Marsden assured, and lifted his glass to Wright. 'I drink to your good health and continued liberty, Master Wright.'

Crowther frowned warningly at the young man, and after a fleeting pause Turpin Wright lifted his own glass and forced a strained smile. 'Many thanks, Master Marsden, and here's to you likewise.'

'That's it,' Crowther chuckled. 'Let's not forget we're all good friends and trusted companions here, and that being the case I may as well tell you all that Charlie and I don't believe that the sharps have been sold on yet, do we, Charlie?'

'No, I'm certain they haven't been. I've had some fly lads keeping their eyes and ears open, and they've seen nor heard nothing. Whoever took the sharps has got them stowed away still, I'll bet my life on that.'

'And we've got a good idea who it is, haven't we boys?' Crowther beamed at his nephews. 'And when we next lay hands on him, he'll cough to it. That I can guarantee.'

'Who is it then, Jonno?' Turpin Wright asked.

'It's somebody that you've had trouble with over a certain woman, Turpin.' Crowther winked slyly at the other men.

'Harris?' Turpin Wright snarled. 'Fuckin' Eddie Harris?'

'Got it in one, Turpin,' Crowther chuckled. 'And he's still shagging Maggie Murphy for free.'

Turpin Wright's face twisted with murderous fury, and the scar's lividity intensified. 'I'm going to have both them bastards, Jonno!' He spat viciously. 'I'm going to make 'um pay for how they cheated on me!'

'And so you shall, my boy, all in good time. But let's talk of other things now. Have you enjoyed your visit, Charlie?'

'I always enjoy my visits here, Jonno. But I have to confess I'm a trifle disappointed that Mrs Watts didn't choose to spend more time in our company,' Marsden said regretfully.

'Well, you must take into consideration how the poor girl is grieving for her husband, Charlie. It was best for her that she took a good dose of laudanum and went early to bed. She's in sore need of some respite and she was sleeping like an innocent babe when I looked in upon her. She'll not stir until well after sunrise tomorrow.'

'Well, I shall hope to say a farewell to her tomorrow at least,' Marsden accepted, and went on jocularly 'Now have you heard the one about the three paddies and the Liverpool judy? Well, these paddies come off the pig boat at the docks and go for a walk towards the infirmary, and at the same time this judy comes out of the infirmary and heads down towards the docks ... What happens next is...'

His recital was interrupted by a loud knocking at the outside rear door, and he scowled in frustration when Crowther gestured for silence,

214

then rose and went from the room.

After a few moments, Crowther returned in company with the ragged figure of William Kinchin. Crowther was smiling savagely as he announced. 'William's brought good news. Harris is back! He's gone into the White Hart, throwing money around and as drunk as a lord. Knowing him, it's guaranteed that he'll stay there until stop tap, so here's what we shall do...'

Hidden on the other side of the door which led upstairs, Mary Watts had her ear pressed to a crack in the warped panelling, listening intently to all that was being said.

Twenty-Nine

It was nearing midnight in the tap room of the White Hart, and the air was filled with a cacophonous noise.

*Now there's some likes a girl
who is pretty in the face,
and some likes a girl
who is slender in the waist...*

Eddie Harris drunkenly bawled the song at the top of his hoarse voice, stamping his foot to keep the time, waving the pewter flagon above his head.

But I likes a girl
who will wriggle
and will twist,
whenever I slaps me hand
on her cuckoo's nest...

The other drinkers in the room urged him on with shouts of encouragement and clapping of hands, while swilling down the drinks he had paid for.

Nail Styler stood watchfully behind the counter, but made no attempt to quieten the gathering. Instead he periodically shouted. 'Anybody want a top up? Eddie's in the chair!'

Drinks were eagerly gulped down and empty flagons and tankards slammed down upon the counter.

'I'll have a cider.'

'Gi' me another ale.'

'Drop o' gin for me, Nail, and none o' that watered down muck neither.'

One man beckoned Nail to him and asked curiously, 'Where's he got all his bloody rhino from? The bugger aren't done a tap of honest toil for weeks.'

'I don't know, and I don't care,' Styler grunted, 'just so long as he keeps putting it across my bar. Pity is it's getting so late that I'll to have to call stop tap soon.'

Then he shouted to the singer, 'Eddie? You've got another reckoning to pay.'

Harris blinked owlishly, and pulled a golden sovereign from his breeches. He pitched it on to the counter, 'Does that cover it, Nail, me old mucker?'

'Oh yes.' Styler grinned. 'And you'll have a bit o' change to come from it as well.'

'Ne'er mind the bloody change. Just you keep the drink coming, me old mucker.' Harris slurred. 'There's plenty more where that 'un come from. And now I got to go for a piss.'

'Well make sure you pisses in the privy, and not up my bloody back wall. I'se only just had it fresh lime-washed,' Styler admonished.

Harris staggered from the room and along the ill-lit corridor to the rear door of the tavern. Outside, he lifted his sweaty face to the rain, relishing its cool droplets on his overheated skin. He lurched down the long muddy yard, unlaced and let fall his breeches fly flap and opened the door of the low-roofed, stench-reeking privy. But before he could step inside, a voice whispered urgently.

'Eddie? Eddie?'

He swung round and squinted into the darkness, swaying from side to side, finding it difficult to focus on the dark figure which had materialized before him.

'What does you want wi' me now?' he demanded aggressively. 'And be quick about telling me, 'cos I'm busting for a piss, so I am.'

In two lightening strikes the razor sharp blade sliced deep into his naked lower belly and viciously ripped upwards, then smashed deep into his chest.

Harris's eyes bulged, his mouth gaped wide emitting a high pitched squeal, and he staggered and toppled forwards, his face slamming down

217

upon the cobbles with an audible crack of breaking bone.

The killer bent over the stricken man, hands expertly rifling through his pockets. Drunken laughter sounded, and the stumbling footsteps of men coming along the corridor and out into the yard. The killer climbed catlike over the wall and slipped away into the murk of night.

'Look at Eddie. A few pints and he's sleeping like a babby,' the first drunk bellowed with glee. 'Let's have a look in his pockets, and see if he's got any money left. I needs the bugger to pay for me next jar or two.'

But when he stooped low he saw blood slowly snaking from beneath Harris's twitching body, mingling with the rain to form an ever-widening pool, and gasped. 'There's summat happened! Fetch Nail out here quick!'

Thirty

Thursday, 31 August 1826

Soaked to the skin and shivering with cold, Tom fervently blessed the advent of the dawn which brought his wearisome night long vigil to its end. The hours had passed in a slow and seemingly endless progression, his thoughts dominated by the bleak sadness of losing Amy Danks forever.

Groaning, fingers kneading aching back and knees, he slowly straightened from his cramped hiding place in the thick hedgerow. The rain eased and petered out, birds fluted their calls, and lighter-shaded rifts began to split the dark canopy of the clouds.

His mood remained depressed as he tried without success to lift his spirits. 'My life has to go on, doesn't it? I just have to try and accept what's happened with as much fortitude and good grace as I can muster. Amy will undoubtedly be much better off materially with Sullivan than with me, and I truly wish for her to be happy.'

Not wanting anyone to know that he had been keeping watch here, he stood undecided as to which route to take when leaving the graveyard.

'Perhaps I should take the indirect way and go through the fields to Bredon again?'

An involuntary fit of violent shivering struck through his wet cold body. 'Damn it! I need a warming drink and a hot fire before I catch my death o' cold. I'll go straight back up the Fish Hill. There'll not be anybody about to see me leave here anyway, it's too early still.'

He walked along the twisting lane which led from the graveyard and past the Forge Mill, his gait made awkward by the painful twinges in his cold-stiffened muscles and joints. As he was passing the Chillingworth's house adjoining the mill complex, an upper window opened and Hannah Anstiss leaned out from it and called, 'Why Master Potts, what are you doing here at this early hour? You look to be absolutely satur-

219

ated. Why are you lurking around our premises?' Her handsome features were smiling, but there was a sarcastic edge in her tone. 'Is it too much to hope for, that at long last you're come to tell us that you've succeeded in tracking down the thieves who robbed us?'

Chagrin at being seen swept through him, but he halted, politely doffed his top hat and bowed. 'Regretfully not, Ma'am. But I do assure you that my investigations into the robbery are still ongoing.'

'But I thought you had completed whatever investigations you needed to make on our premises? So why have you come here again without our invitation?' She was deliberately goading him.

Tom, becoming increasingly ill at ease, was desperate to escape. 'If you'll be kind enough to excuse me, Ma'am, I really do have to be going now. I've a very pressing matter to attend to up in the town. I bid you good day, Ma'am.'

He walked on as quickly as he could.

Hannah Anstiss remained leaning out of the window watching until his tall figure had gone from her view. She half-angrily berated herself, 'Why must you still harbour fond feelings towards that passionless, bloodless, cold-hearted long streak? Why?' Then she smiled. 'Because you know very well that he would make a faithful and obedient husband.'

'Where have you been all night? Sharing some whore's bed, I'll be bound, you sin-soaked, dirty stop-out.' Widow Potts began shrieking accusations the moment Tom stepped inside the lock-up.

He sighed as he began to mount the stairs and called, 'I've been out on duty all night, Mother.'

The fat old woman had hobbled from her room to stand on the landing, leaning on her two walking sticks. As Tom reached the landing, she howled like the legendary banshee in a high-pitched keening torrent of words, 'You're a liar! Liar! Liar! Liar! Liar!' Her face purpled, veins throbbing in her temples, reddened eyes glaring madly.

Tom became alarmed that she might suffer some sort of seizure, and went to take her arms and try to calm her. 'I'm telling you the truth, Mother. I've been out on my duties all night. I swear it!'

'Oh no, you haven't been out on duty, you wicked beast!' She rebuffed his offered hands, waving one of her sticks threateningly at him. 'Don't you dare touch me with those sin-soiled hands! God only knows what filthy and corrupt flesh they've been delving into all night! Don't you dare lay one single sinful, unclean, whore-mauling finger upon my pure and sinless flesh!'

'How can you know that I've not been out doing my duty?' Tom, wet, weary, hungry, cold and thirsty, was trying to be patient, but finding it increasingly difficult.

'I know because all night long people have been coming here, ringing the bells, waking me up shouting at the tops of their voices, frightening me near to death, and each and every one of them was looking for you!'

221

'What did they want with me?' Tom asked.

'They wanted you because there's been a murder! A dreadful murder!' she announced, and cackled triumphantly when she saw the shock on her son's face. 'There now, that's shot you up where the monkey sticks his nuts, aren't it! That's caught you well and truly out, aren't it! That'll teach you to try and tell your own poor suffering, sainted mother a pack of lies, won't it! Hey, where are you going? Come back here, you un-natural fiend, I aren't finished talking yet! Come back here!'

Even as she shrieked the last words, Tom was through the front door and running across the Green towards the house of Joseph Blackwell.

Despite the early hour, Joseph Blackwell was fully dressed and working at his desk when Tom was shown in to the study.

A hint of a smile hovered on Blackwell's thin lips when he saw Tom's damp dishevelment.

'You look to have spent an inclement night, Master Potts.'

'Yes, Sir,' Tom joked wryly. 'With only the ducks on the mill pool to share it with.'

'Well, at least you've enabled John Watts to lie peacefully in his grave. I take it you have heard what occurred at the White Hart last night?'

'No Sir, my mother only told me that there has been a murder committed.'

'Edward Harris was found lying in the rear privy yard of the White Hart. It appears he was murdered. I'm afraid I must require you to give precedence to this case above your ongoing

222

investigations. My Lord Aston has been notified of my decision, and raises no objection. My Lord Aston's stated opinion is that he doesn't give a tinker's fart which case takes precedence because there is not a cat in hell's chance of you ever solving any of them.' Blackwell paused momentarily, and his faded hazel eyes twinkled with amusement at Tom's indignant expression.

'However, let me assure you, Master Potts, that I myself have complete confidence in your investigative abilities. Now tell me, have you any thoughts to share with me concerning this latest case? Any suspicions as to the culprit or culprits?'

Tom could only shake his head and admit, 'At this moment, Sir, my thoughts are a jumble. I've nothing whatsoever to offer.'

Blackwell nodded understandingly. 'That's only to be expected. What I would suggest is that you go and change your clothing, get some breakfast, have a few hours' rest, and then begin your investigation.'

The suggestion was overpoweringly tempting, but Tom knew he could not allow himself to surrender to that temptation.

'With respect, Sir, I think it best if I collect my bag of investigation tools and then go directly to the White Hart. Strike while the hammer still retains some heat, so to speak. You and I both know that with every hour that passes, memories can become increasingly distorted. It's essential that I talk to as many of those who were there as soon as possible.'

Blackwell smiled with satisfaction. 'Well said,

Master Potts. Yet again you justify my faith in you.' He pulled open a desk drawer and took out a small leather draw-purse, which he proffered to Tom. 'There is a total of ten guineas here. Pay Styler five shillings as a fee for the use of his tap room for the inquest, and the storing of the corpse on his premises until that takes place. Should the need arise, you may very discreetly use a little judicious bribery to loosen potential witnesses' tongues. But spend as sparingly as possible, because I have to make full account to my Lord Aston of any sums so disbursed. I bid you good day, Master Potts.'

Factory and mill bells were ringing out the summons to work when Tom reached the White Hart, but the inn was doing a roaring trade. Nail Styler was grinning contentedly as he served drinks, while his bold-featured, plump-bodied wife stood at the inn's rear door marshalling the queue of men and women in the corridor to whom she was charging two pence each to allow them into the small privy yard to gawp for brief seconds at the dead man, before chivvying them with stentorian commands.

'That's it! You've had your look, now get back in here and make room for somebody else!'

When Tom entered the noisy thronged tap room Nail Styler saw the crowned staff, frowned and challenged, 'I hope you aren't come to close us down?'

Tom shook his head. 'Not immediately at any rate, Master Styler. Now where is the dead man?'

'Out back,' Styler grunted sourly.

In the crowded corridor Tom pushed through to the rear door, shouting, 'Make way! Make way in the King's name!'

Maud Styler blocked him at the door. 'You can get back to the end of the queue and take your turn like everybody else is doing.'

'I'm here in the King's name, Ma'am.' Tom held his crowned staff in front of her eyes. 'And you shouldn't be doing this. So tell these people to go away, and let me pass.'

'I'll tell 'um nought of the sort,' she declared indignantly. 'Who the bloody hell does you think you am? How dares you to come into my pub like mister high and mighty, and try ordering me about? I'll take no bloody orders from you, my buck!'

Tom was taken aback by this unexpected resistance. 'But I'm here in the King's name, Ma'am,' he protested lamely.

'I don't give a bugger whose name you're here in. This is my pub, and I'm the boss here. I don't take orders from you nor the bloody king!' She was becoming increasingly aggressive.

Dismay struck through Tom as he heard the growls of support for her coming from behind him, and he realized that should he try to force his way past her there was every likelihood that violence would erupt. Deciding that discretion was the better part of valour, he tried to mollify her.

'If I've offended you, then I do apologize most sincerely, Ma'am, but I'm here by the express command of the magistrates. They have instructed me to investigate this unfortunate incident.'

'It aren't an unfortunate incident for the Stylers, Mister. They'm making a good profit from it,' a man shouted waggishly. 'But I don't doubt that Eddie Harris would agree with what you say.'

There was a burst of general laughter, and the atmosphere tangibly lightened. Heartened by this, Tom sought for a compromise with Maud Styler.

'If you'll permit me to pass and examine the body, Ma'am, you can still allow these good people through. I shan't impede their viewing, I promise you. Surely this is better for all of us, rather than have the magistrates issue a summons against you for obstructing a constable in the course of his lawful duty.'

Maud Styler mulled over his proposal for several seconds, then nodded. 'All right, Mister Constable, you can pass through.' She held out her hand. 'That'll be tuppence.'

Tom had to rummage through all his pockets before he could total a penny, a half-penny and two farthings.

'Bloody hell, it's like getting blood out of a stone,' Maud Styler complained loudly, and instructed the queue. 'Make sure you've got your money ready or we'll be here all bloody day else.'

She let another couple into the yard while Tom slowly paced around the corpse, which lay face downwards, almost completely surrounded by pooled, blood-reddened rainwater.

'Has anybody moved or touched the body,

226

Ma'am?' he called to Maud Styler.

'Only me husband. He felt for a pulse in the neck, but the bugger was dead so we just left him laying there. Come on you two, you can't stand there gawping all day, there's other folks wants their turn.'

The couple returned inside, to be instantly replaced by another onlooker.

Tom bent low over the body, and could smell the voided excreta in its breeches.

'You didn't manage to get into the privy then, Harris,' he thought, and grasping the dead man's shoulder, slowly turned the stiffening body. As he did so, a mass of bloodied intestines slithered out from the ripped lower belly. The onlooker turned away gagging and retching, being shouted at by Maud Styler.

'Don't you dare be sick in my yard, you kettle-stomached bugger!'

Tom's eyes locked on to the bloodied handle of the knife jammed into Harris's chest.

Behind him a fresh onlooker exclaimed excitedly, 'That'll be what killed him, won't it?'

Tom nodded thoughtfully. 'It certainly might be.' He took his magnifying glass and minutely examined the wooden handle but could find no discernible sign of fingerprints, only what appeared to be small deep scratches. He had to exert considerable force to pull the hook-curved blade free of the bones that entrapped it. He examined it curiously, asking, 'This looks to be an unusual type of knife, what would it be used for?'

'That's a spar hook, that is,' the onlooker

stated confidently. 'It's what thatchers uses to cut their brotches from the hazel bushes.'

'Are you sure that it's a thatching tool?'

'O' course I am. Me uncle was a thatcher and I used to help him when I was a nipper. I knows a bloody spar hook when I sees one.'

'Come on you,' Maud Styler shouted at the man. 'You've more than had your tuppence worth.'

'Let him stay a little longer, please Ma'am,' Tom requested on impulse. 'I'll pay for his extra time.'

'Well he's already had a tanner's worth, Mister Constable, so it'll cost you a shilling at the least. And I hopes that it don't take you so long to find it as you did to find the tuppence.'

'All right,' Tom conceded. He wiped the blood from the handle and found that the scratches were two small incised letters.

'A and S? Could they be initials?' he pondered aloud and asked the other man, 'Do you know of any thatchers hereabouts with the initials A and S?'

'I don't know about these days, but when I was a nipper there was two brothers called Sandford from Feckenham way who was thatchering. But they was grown men when I was just a nipper, so it's more than likely that they've been dead and buried long since.'

Tom felt a pang of disappointment, but thought resignedly, *Ah well, it was perhaps too much to hope for that I could trace the killer so easily.*

'I'll have to get to work, or I'll be having me sack give me,' his companion said regretfully

228

and walked away, but before he disappeared through the door turned his head and called back. 'There was another old bloke as well who was a thatcher, his name was Soother or Suther or summat like that. I reckon he come from Redditch.'

The memory of Bonny Southall and Eddie Harris's fight rose vividly into Tom's mind, generating a rush of excitement. 'Soother? Suther? Could that old thatcher's name really have been Southall? And could Bonny Southall be related to him and come by the knife in that way? Did Southall use this knife on Harris?'

'God strike me dead! What a mess he's in!' The loud horrified exclamation jolted Tom back into awareness of the unwelcome presence of successive eager onlookers.

'Now calm down and go about matters in an orderly progression,' he told himself sternly, and searched the dead man's pockets. He found only a short clay pipe, a twist of tobacco and a solitary coin, a copper farthing stuck in the deepest corner of a breech pocket.

'Could robbery have been the motive? Did the killer take money from him, or could Nail Styler have done so when he checked for life? But perhaps Harris hadn't got a penny piece in his pockets to begin with.'

Tom rose and stood back against the privy wall, staring at Harris's chalk grey face and bulging eyes, carefully considering his next move. He knelt again and taking the dead hands in turn, studied the fingers and palms.

A deep scar ran across the base of Harris's left

palm. Tom gasped in shock. He closed his eyes, desperately trying to visualize the scarred palm prints he had discovered on the coffin lid of Harry Gould's wife, and drew a long deep breath. It looked to be a possible match.

Now his heart was pounding with excitement. If the prints did prove to match then it meant that Harris was one of those who had stolen Mrs Gould's corpse.

'I need my drawings!' He went to the door and told Maud Styler. 'I'll be back in a little while, Ma'am.'

She held her hand under his nose. 'Never mind about you coming back. You pay what you owes me now. That's a shilling for Terry Elliot's extra viewing time.'

Driven by a mounting sense of urgency he tried to go past her. 'I'll settle what I owe when I return, Ma'am. I'll not be long!'

She obdurately blocked his path, 'You'll settle your reckoning now, or you'll not pass.'

'God give me strength!' he hissed impatiently, and knowing that the only money he had with him was Blackwell's purse of coins, took desperate measures.

'Here, take this,' he pressed the purse into her hand. 'There are ten guineas here. If I don't come back, then keep it. Will this allow you to trust me?'

Scowling suspiciously, she loosened the drawstrings and peered into the purse. Her eyes glistened greedily.

'I'll return shortly.' Tom pushed past her, and this time she made no attempt to stop him.

When he arrived back at the inn sweating and breathless from running, the queue of would be viewers was much diminished and the inn was starting to empty as men and women reluctantly dragged themselves away from the scene of such drama and went to their daily work.

Tom took the sheets of coarse paper from his bag and carefully compared his drawings against the dead man's scarred palm. To his gleeful satisfaction, he found the comparison with the coffin lid prints amazingly accurate. A source of added excitement was that he thought he could also find some varied similarities with certain of the partial palm prints he had taken from the tiles of Chillingworth's storehouse.

Fighting hard to hide his burgeoning impatience, he stood quietly waiting until the final viewer had had their two pence worth and only he and Maud Styler remained in the rear yard.

She gave him back the purse of guineas, telling him, 'I'll take the shilling you owes me now, Mister Constable, but I won't charge you for this second viewing you've just had.'

'I shall give you that shilling with pleasure, Ma'am,' he smiled genially, and gave her the coin. Then he extracted five more shillings from the purse and placed them on to her open palm. 'And this is your fee for storing Harris on your premises until the coroner holds his inquest in your tap room, Ma'am. Of course Harris must be kept under shelter and locked securely away from any further display as a peepshow, and I shall need a receipt for this sum.'

'You'll have to get that from Styler because none of this fee will be mine.' She grimaced resentfully. 'He keeps all the money we earns in his own pockets. I don't get to spend none of it on meself.'

'That seems very unfair, Mrs Styler.' Tom smiled sympathetically, then winked meaningfully. 'But I wouldn't be needing any receipt for the money I'd pay you if you and I came to a private understanding about a little matter that you might be able to help me with. I'd pay you well and no one else need know that money had changed hands. Not even your husband. It would remain strictly confidential between you and I.'

He saw the gleam of avarice in her eyes, and to win her confidence completely he extracted a gold sovereign from the purse and placed it upon the shillings in her open palm.

'That's for you alone to spend how you please, Mrs Styler, and should you give me satisfactory answers to a few questions I want to ask, you'll have another sovereign as well. Let me assure you once again that only you and I will ever know what passes between us. I give you my sworn oath on that.'

After only a momentary hesitation, she nodded. 'I think you're an honest man, Master Potts. So I reckon that both you and me are going to part satisfied, because my answering will be as straight as a die. Ask away.'

Tom fired a string of questions, and when he finished the interrogation he was satisfied that she had told him the truth.

'Thank you, Ma'am, I'm much beholden to

232

you.' He gave her the second gold coin. 'Could you please call your husband to help me put Harris wherever it is you want him stored?'

'I'll have to clear a space in one of our stables for him if he's got to be locked away. But I aren't got time to do that right now, Master Potts. Howsomever, I'll just get me chores done as quick as I can, and then me and Nail 'ull lock him up so tight that not even a mouse won't get near him.'

Tom instantly realized she was hoping for more people to come and pay for entry to this macabre peepshow, and opened his mouth to protest, but then a sudden wave of physical exhaustion washed over him and he decided against it. *It doesn't really matter for the time being where Harris lays, does it, and if I don't very soon get some food and sleep then I'll be keeling over.* He bowed to Maud Styler, and bade her a polite goodbye. 'Very well, Ma'am. Many thanks for all your help. I shall let you know as soon as possible when the inquest is to be held. I'll say good day to you.'

Jingling the coins in her hand, Maud Styler beamed with satisfaction at him, bobbed a curtsy and invited fulsomely, 'You must call again, Master Potts, but as a most welcome customer next time. Me and Nail 'ull be honoured to serve you, and you'll always find good drink and vittles and jolly company here.'

Thirty-One

'Don't stop, don't stop, don't stop...' Mary Watts moaned and writhed, digging her fingers into the taut buttocks of the man on top of her, arching her hips to meet his pounding belly.

Bonny Southall's harsh panting became a series of gasping grunts as he drove into her body harder and harder, faster and faster until with a shuddering groan he climaxed and collapsed down upon her, sweating heavily, dragging wheezing breaths into his straining lungs.

'Get off me!' Mary Watts snapped angrily, and pushed and wriggled out from under him.

'What's up?' He turned on his side to stare at her in puzzlement.

'You're not up, that's what's up!' She scowled resentfully. 'You only ever thinks of your own pleasure, don't you! I hadn't come, had I? But you was only thinking of pleasuring yourself, like you always does.'

'Now that aren't fair!' he protested. 'You knows very well that I always tries to make sure that you'm satisfied. It's your fault that I come so quick because you haven't let me have a bit for ages, have you? It's no wonder I got so excited, is it?'

He smiled and reached for her, telling her

coaxingly. 'Come here and let me cuddle you. I'll get a hard-on again in double quick time, and then I'll give you what you wants for as long as you wants.'

'Get off!' She struck his seeking hands away and rising from the bed, began to dress, pulling her gown over her head and shaking it down to cover her shapely body.

He rose himself and came to her, trying to draw her into his arms. 'Oh don't be like this, sweetheart. I've been missing you so bad. I just couldn't stop meself coming so quick, because I love you so much. Please, honey, take pity on me. I'm really sorry. Really I am.'

She appeared to soften, and allowed him to pull her close, but when his lips sought hers she jerked her head back and pushed his arms away. 'No, Bonny! There's no time for any more of that now. I've got to get back to Crowther's place.'

'Why?'

'Because!'

'Because of what?'

'Because! And that's all you need to know, Bonny.'

She lifted her long cotton stockings and rolled them into a ball, which she pushed into her willow basket. She slipped on her shoes and put on her bonnet, then snapped curtly. 'Come on, look sharp and get dressed. I need to lock up here.'

'I can lock up for you,' he offered.

'No you can't.' She frowned and shook her head. 'You're not having the key to my cottage,

235

Bonny. That's never been part of our agreement, has it?'

He also frowned, but with mingled puzzlement and exasperation. 'But now we're going to get married I should have the key, shouldn't I? Because as soon as we're wed it'll be my property.'

Her mood abruptly changed, and she smiled coquettishly. 'That's when we're wed. But for now all I want you to do is to get dressed and get out from here. Crowther will go mad if he finds out what we've been up to.'

'I don't give a bugger for Crowther, nor a dozen more doddering old bastards like him,' Southall scoffed contemptuously. 'In fact, I've a mind to go up there with you now and tell him straight and open that we're going to wed just as soon as I can get the banns called.'

He started to pull his clothes on.

'In fact, that's exactly what I'm going to do!'

'No, Bonny, you can't!' Alarm flashed in Mary Watts's eyes. 'I have to wait for my mourning time to end before we can wed.'

'Bugger the mourning time. We're getting wed, and that's that.'

Her mind raced, and she blurted out, 'Not yet, we can't, because Crowther's mad jealous over me! He's pestering me to be his mistress, and he's threatened to kill himself and me both if I should take any other man into my bed!'

Southall's handsome features hardened into a mask of fury, and he gritted out between clenched teeth, 'I'll teach that bastard not to threaten you! He's going to get what's coming to him this very hour!' He started to dress, snarling, 'It's him alone who'll be killed, and it's me who'll do the killing.'

'Listen to me!' She spoke sharply, and grabbed his hands to prevent him pulling his shirt over his head. 'Listen to me!'

He reluctantly became still.

She moved closer and wrapped her arms around his neck, looking up into his eyes, murmuring tenderly, 'I want to be your lawful wife more than anything else in this world, honey. But I can't be wed to you if you're hung for killing Crowther, can I?'

'No, but neither can you get wed to me if that bastard kills you first!' Southall riposted fiercely.

'He'll not get the chance to harm either of us if we box clever, sweetheart.' She kissed his mouth to stifle any reply, and he crushed her close and passionately returned her kiss, until she forced his head back and told him urgently. 'Now listen very carefully, because you must do exactly as I say...'

Thirty-Two

Night had come when Tom awoke from a sleep made uneasy by confused surreal dreams of desecrated graves, faceless men pitching handfuls of glittering needles into the air, and fleeting images of Amy Danks walking away from him towards a red-coated soldier.

For a while he lay staring up at the cracked, stained plaster of the ceiling, struggling to come to terms with the fact that Amy Danks was to marry another man, and angrily berating himself for having lost her.

Slowly he regained some degree of control over his rampaging emotions, and was able to concentrate his thoughts on what he had discovered from Maud Styler. She had told him that Crowther was rumoured to be closely involved with the mysterious Rippling Boys, maybe even their leader. When Tom had pressed her for more details about the gang she had given him other names: the Fairfax twins, Johnny Watts, Turpin Wright, Eddie Harris and Bonny Southall.

Eddie Harris and Bonny Southall had at one time been extremely close to Jonathan Crowther, but lately there had appeared to be a rift between the three men. But at the same time Maud Styler had stressed that these were only rumours and

238

she had no definite proof, except the knowledge that they had spent a great deal of time in each others' company, and on various occasions had drunk and gambled away large sums of money which they had obtained from some unexplained source.

'It was always a sight more than they could earn at the pointing, or any other honest work!' she insisted. 'And they used to throw it away as if they had the keys to the Bank of England in their pockets.'

Tom was prepared to give credence to what she had told him. He knew that every man she had named bore a reputation for being capable of using extreme violence and acting with reckless daring. He was now certain that Eddie Harris had been involved in both the Gould body-snatching and the Chillingworth needle robbery.

'Who might his accomplices have been? Old Tanner spoke of hearing two men and a woman arguing on the night that Mrs Gould was taken. Harris's woman, Maggie Murphy, is a tough nut, and I'd judge her to be capable of helping him to commit whatever roguery he'd a mind to. She's got to be the woman.

'Although Bonny Southall claimed that he and Harris were fighting for just the love of it, they could have been quarrelling about the split of the spoils. Southall is a strong candidate for the second man.'

Tom suddenly sat bolt upright as other questions drilled into his mind.

'Why hasn't Maggie Murphy come looking

for me to demand what I'm doing about his murder? She must know that he's been killed? Everybody throughout the parish will know about it by now.'

He threw the coverings aside, hastily dressed, took up his staff and then noticed for the first time the scrap of notepaper on his bedside stool. The scrawl of writing was only a few words long, 'To my heartless, unloving wretch of a son, from your martyred mama. I have gone to Birmingham with Charles Bromley Esq., to be introduced to his most tender-hearted sister and her loving family. I shall return at my pleasure. PS: Empty my commode. It's stinking my room out.'

Tom lifted his eyes to the ceiling. 'Thank you, Lord. Thank you for this blessed mercy.'

The entry of a staff-bearing constable into the smoky, evil-smelling, rush-lit gloom of Bocker Duggins's communal kitchen created an uneasy stirring among its denizens, and much furtive fumbling to conceal various articles beneath ragged greasy clothing. But its proprietor, enthroned on a high-backed chair in front of the cooking fire like a beggar monarch surrounded by his courtiers, greeted Tom with an ingratiating glistening of decayed black teeth.

'How d'you do, Master Potts? To what does we owe the pleasure of your company? I hopes that none o' my guests has been up to no good.'

'Good evening, Master Duggins.' Tom was equally courteous. 'Your guests have no need for alarm, I'm merely wanting to speak to Miss Murphy. Is she in the house?'

240

'I do believe her might be.' Duggins leered salaciously. 'But her said earlier that her was going to be busy entertaining a friend, if you get my meaning.' He used his fingers and thumbs to simulate sexual congress. 'So her won't take kindly to being interrupted at the minute.'

'Entertaining a man? But her own man has just been murdered.' Tom could not credit what he was hearing. 'This is a shameful way for her to behave!'

'Eddie Harris getting his guts sliced? Maggie said good riddance to bad rubbish! And I says the same!' Duggins hawked a gob of phlegm and spat it into the fire to give emphasis to his contempt for Harris. 'And you thinks it shameful for her to bed another bloke, does you? Well Maggie's still got her living to earn, Master Potts. Folks like us aren't got the luxury of taking time off from work to mourn for the dead. We has trouble enough keeping breath in the living.'

Tom was forced to accept that there was justification for the other man's bitter statement, but persisted quietly, 'I still have to speak to her, Master Duggins. What room is she in?'

'Oh I don't reckon I can rightly be letting you go up to her room, Master Potts.' There was a suggestion of a sneer on Duggins's leering face. 'Arter all, I have to respect my guests right to a bit o' privacy, if you get my meaning.'

A rustle of muted appreciative amusement from the listeners greeted his words.

Tom smiled pleasantly and leaning closer to the other man, whispered, 'But I don't have to

241

respect any keeper of an illegal bawdy house, do I, Master Duggins? A few words from me into the magistrates' ears and even the most privacy-respecting lodging establishment can be closed down, if you get my meaning.'

The leer instantly disappeared from Duggins's face, and he whispered back, 'All right, all right, Master Potts. I was only kidding on a bit. Her's in the first cubicle up in the attic. But for God's sake don't go telling her I told you.'

'Of course I won't.' Tom's smile broadened. 'Unless of course, you and I ever have any cause in the future to doubt each other's word, if you get my meaning.'

As Tom climbed the uppermost rickety set of unlit stairs, he was forced to feel his way slowly through the darkness. His nervous tension increasing with each step upwards, his vivid imagination picturing what the reaction of Maggie Murphy and her companion might be when he disturbed their tryst.

'She's as savage as any pointer lad, and God only knows what the man with her might be like. I could end up getting my head smashed in by them both!' He was brought to a standstill by an overwhelming impulse to turn around and go back down the stairs.

'I can't do this,' he told himself. 'I just can't risk it!'

'But you must!' another entity whispered in his mind. 'You must!'

Against his conscious will, he found himself again moving upwards as if impelled by an unseen force. He reached the landing and stood stock still, holding his breath and listening hard. Directly opposite him a glimmer of candlelight showed around the edges of the first cubicle curtain, but no sounds came from within. Once again the urge to turn and flee threatened to overwhelm him and he was sickeningly conscious of the fear-invoked trembling of his body. Then a surge of furious self-disgust for his own cowardice blotted out all other emotions and he took two rapid strides, gripped the curtain, tore it aside and gasped in shock.

'Oh my God!'

The naked Maggie Murphy lay dead on the narrow cot, her eyes bulging, foam flecking her livid lips, her hands in tight clenched fists, the soiled bedclothes beneath her soaking from her voided bladder and bowels.

Tom remained motionless as the primary shock of his discovery quickly receded. He had witnessed a similar scene years before when he was a medical student, and now carefully studied what was before him, noting particularly the two dark green gin bottles lying on their sides on top of the heap of clothing on the floor. Noting also the glint of some silver and copper coins scattered out from the clothing. He stepped to the cot and bent low over Maggie Murphy's bloated face, his nose almost touching her livid lips. With one hand he slowly compressed her flabby, not-yet-cold abdomen and sniffed the air expelled from her mouth. Mingled with the fumes of gin and bad breath was another faint odour, which had a resemblance to the scent of bitter almonds.

243

'Could it be prussic acid?' Tom wondered. 'Has she died from poison? I don't think she's been dead for above an hour or so. There's still warmth in her flesh.' He carefully turned her over on to her face and examined her buttocks and back, then turned her face upwards once more.

There were no bloodstains or marks of fresh wounds on the body to indicate that violence had been used against her. If what he could smell from her mouth was indeed prussic acid then it presented the hallmarks of an act of suicide. But deep within Tom's mind there was burgeoning a nagging doubt that this was an act of self-destruction. Women like Maggie Murphy, inured since birth to bitter injustice and hardship, made tough and hard-minded by adversity, did not customarily destroy themselves over the loss of a brutally abusive paramour, particularly while they still had money to buy drink and food with.

Tom inserted his forefingers into the necks of the empty gin bottles and held them up into the candlelight. 'I wonder if I might be able to raise any finger prints on these?' He gently placed them upright on the floor and sniffed them in turn, but could detect only the smell of gin.

The clumping of clogs sounded on the staircase, and Tom moved out of the doorway of the cubicle and drew the curtain closed behind him, blocking any view into the space. Bocker Duggins came up on to the landing, preceded by the light from the lantern he carried.

'I couldn't hear any screaming and bawling, Master Potts. Arn't Maggie up here then?'

'Oh yes, she's here,' Tom told him grimly. 'And you've got more than a few questions to answer to.'

'What's that cow been saying about me?' Duggins demanded and shouted threateningly, 'If you been telling fuckin' lies about me, Maggie Murphy, I'll be giving you a smack in the chops, make no mistake!'

'Come here,' Tom beckoned, and as Duggins approached he jerked the curtain wide, closely observing Duggins's reactions.

'Fuckin' 'ell! What the fuck's happened here? Is her all right? Her aren't dead, is her?' The exclamations tumbled from Duggins's lips, as he stood staring at the dead woman in utter stupefaction.

Tom judged the other man's shock to be genuine, and was satisfied that he had not known of her death.

'I think she may have taken poison, Master Duggins. Who was the man she was expecting? For your own sake you'd better tell me the truth, because if you lie then things will go very hard with you.'

With watery eyes still fixed unbelievingly upon the dead woman, Duggins shook his head. 'I don't know who the bloke was, Master Potts, I swear on me babbies' lives, I don't. Because I never saw him, did I?'

'Then tell me the names of the other men that she's had up here,' Tom pressed harshly. 'And don't hold any back, Master Duggins, because if you don't give me your full co-operation you'll find yourself in very serious trouble with the law.'

'Fuckin' 'ell, Master Potts, be fair!' Duggins complained. 'Her had some regular friends that only her and me knew about because this being a small town we had to keep it secret. But there was others who was casuals that was just passing through the town, and I never seed them afore or since.'

'Who were her regulars? Tell me, or you'll be spending your time in my lock-up.'

'All right, all right, Master Potts. There's no need to take that tone wi' me. I'll tell you everything I knows, believe me.' Duggins went on to babble a string of names, some of whom were outwardly respectable family men and pillars of the local community.

Once satisfied that Duggins had told him all he could, Tom nodded, 'Very well, Master Duggins. I take your word for it and I'll do my best to try and prevent any harm coming to you because of what's happened here.'

Duggins gushed profuse protestations of gratitude, but Tom cut the gushing thanks short. 'I shall have to close this floor off from your lodgers for a few hours. Now I want you to go immediately and respectfully request Master Blackwell to please to come here to me. If anybody else asks you what's happened, tell them only that Maggie Murphy has died suddenly and we are merely making sure that her death is not some virulent contagion.'

'I'll do that, Master Potts. I'll do just whatever you tells me to do. I'll not forget you being so good to me today.'

'Leave me the lantern, if you please,' Tom requested, and while Duggins was feeling the way down the dark staircase, he returned to his close scrutiny of the cubicle and its occupant.

He prized her clenched fists open and spread the fingers, hoping that he might find a truncated top joint of her right-hand ring finger, but to his disappointment found all her digits complete.

Then he carefully examined the discarded clothing and her other pitifully few possessions, but frustratingly found nothing to enlighten him any further. When Blackwell arrived he said, 'I'll need to have the whole contents of this stinking den transferred to the lock-up, and examine them in full daylight.'

'If it is a cyanide poison that you can detect from smelling her mouth, then it certainly appears to be a case of suicide, Master Potts. It could be that the grief of losing her lover was too much for her to bear. Or alternately was it she who killed Harris and she could not bear the guilt? Either way, she is no loss to the world and neither was he.' Joseph Blackwell stared bleakly at the naked corpse. 'I shall utilize the same jury I've empanelled for him and hold both inquests on the same day.'

'With all respect, Sir, I'm not sure it is suicide,' Tom said hesitantly. 'According to Duggins she wasn't grieving in the slightest for Harris, and on the night he was killed she was in the kitchen here drinking with some of the lodgers until dawn of the following morning. I suspect she may have been murdered.'

247

'Why? What gives you cause for thinking this? You already said that you've discovered no marks of violence on her body?' Blackwell frowned. 'And until a post-mortem can be carried out to establish the fact, we cannot yet be certain that she did ingest prussic acid.'

'To save time we can do our own post-mortem, Sir. I assisted my father with several and have had practice in the procedure. With your permission, I can make a small opening in her stomach and drain off the fluids into a jar, and a simple test can then be done on them to demonstrate if the poison is present. May I do that, Sir?'

Blackwell pursed his lips and pondered frowningly, then asked, 'Where do you propose to carry out this procedure, and who is to witness it?'

'There's plenty of space in the lock-up for me to do it, and since I need to have her body removed there anyway, together with the contents of this den, it seems the most convenient site. You yourself can be the witness, Sir, and anyone else you might care to have present.'

Still frowning, Blackwell changed the subject, 'Tell me now, Master Potts, why do you suspect she has been murdered?'

Tom spoke slowly, searching for his words. 'It's as if I were just starting to assemble a jigsaw puzzle, Sir. I can dimly discern indications of meaningful patterns among the various pieces, but as yet have no clear ideas as to what the final completed puzzle will show us.' He emitted a sigh of frustration, and said. 'I've no concrete evidence to offer that she was murdered, Sir. I'm being impelled solely by instinct, but I sense that all these recent crimes, the body snatchings, the robberies and the killings, are somehow interconnected.'

Blackwell stared hard at Tom's face without making any reply. The silence lengthened, and Tom's tension increased to become a tangible discomfort. He was struggling to remain silent himself and not to ask the other man what he was thinking.

Finally Blackwell slowly nodded. 'I am prepared to place my trust in your instincts. Tell me your theories.'

Tom's tension instantly dissolved and he stated confidently, 'I'm sure that Harris was involved actively in the Gould body-snatching and the Chillingworth robbery. His palm prints were at both scenes of crime.'

'Palm prints?' Blackwell raised his eyebrows.

'Yes Sir, for some time now I've been practising the discovery and recording of finger and palm prints. I believe they will prove to be a virtually positive method of identification.'

'I see.' Blackwell mulled over what he had been told before chuckling drily. 'An ingenious theory, Constable Potts, but unfortunately a proof of identity not acceptable to a court of law.'

'I know that, Sir, but such virtually identical prints are very acceptable proofs to me personally.'

'And to me privately also.' Blackwell chuckled again. 'Pray continue with your account.'

'I suspect that two men and a woman stole Mrs Gould: Harris and his woman here, in company with another man. I believe Harris was one of the Chillingworth robbers, and that again he had two accomplices, one of them perhaps being Maggie Murphy. As for the Bates robbery, I suspect the same people were involved, because of the similarities in the method of entry into the premises.'

'What about the Craig body snatching from the old graveyard?' Blackwell queried.

'I've no lead on that.'

'This second man, do you think it's he who has killed Harris and this woman? Perhaps because of a quarrel over the division of the spoils? Have you any idea as to his identity?'

'I can answer yes to the first two of those questions, Sir. But I need to make many further enquiries before I can answer the third with any truthfulness. However I think Bonny Southall is strongly suspect.

'Meanwhile, with your permission, I'd like to have Maggie Murphy and her effects moved into the lock-up immediately. Then as soon as I've got her safely secured there, I shall go to keep watch over Watts' grave. It's best that I wait until I have full daylight to do what I must with Murphy's body.'

'I'll order Charles Bromley to take over the grave-watching until its completion,' Blackwell declared. 'That will ease the present demands on your time.'

'I'm afraid that won't be possible, Sir.' Tom smiled ruefully. 'My lady mother and Master

Bromley are presently visiting his sister in Birmingham, and won't be returning until next week. But it doesn't matter, because truth to tell while I'm grave-watching I've quiet and peace to think about how to best pursue my enquiries.'

'Well I shall ensure that you and Master Hollis both receive suitable remuneration for the cold nights in the graveyard.' Blackwell returned the smile. 'As for my own stiff old bones, I'm returning them immediately to the warmth and comfort of their home. So proceed as you think best, Constable Potts. I shall attend upon you as a witness at the lock-up at nine o'clock tomorrow morning. For now I bid you good night.'

Moments after Blackwell left, Bocker Duggins came clumping back up the stairs to demand anxiously, 'What's he say, Master Potts. Am I in any trouble?'

Tom decided it would be advantageous to keep the other man on tenterhooks. 'Master Blackwell is not best pleased about this occurrence.' He shook his head regretfully. 'He's threatening to withdraw your licence to lodge and board.'

'Oh fuckin' 'ell!' Duggins ejaculated in dismay. 'What am I going to do now? Me and me babbies 'ull fuckin' starve!'

Tom lifted his hand to forestall any further reaction. 'Hold hard now! I've managed to persuade him to allow you to stay in business, for the time being at any rate, and I shall keep on fighting on your behalf, Master Duggins. So don't give up hope yet.'

'You'm a true Christian, Master Potts, and I'm real grateful to you.' Duggins snatched at Tom's

251

hand and pumped it vigorously up and down. 'And anything I can do for you, you needs only to ask me to do it!'

'I need everything in this cubicle, including Maggie here, to be taken across to the lock-up straightaway. You can bring me a sack bag to put her personal possessions in. Maggie can be carried on the cot. But don't worry, everything that's your property will be returned as soon as this matter is dealt with.'

'I'll get some lads and have it all shifted in two ticks, Master Potts.' Duggins rushed down to the kitchen to return in scant seconds with a ragged crew of helpers.

'Just you tell us what you wants us to do, Master Potts. We'm here to serve you.'

Hovering discreetly at the rear of the noisome gang, William Kinchin was avidly scrutinizing and listening, storing in his memory every scrap of information that he could report to Jonathan Crowther.

Thirty-Three

Friday, 1 September 1826

In the cold of the early morning, hoar frost glistened whitely on grass and foliage, and Tom fervently blessed his first glimpse of the sun rising above the eastern horizon.

'Thank God you've come at last. I'll likely be crippled with rheumatics before this job is done with.'

He moved stiffly and painfully from his hedgerow hiding place to stand above the grave of John Watts and said aloud, 'Good morning Master Watts, I trust you've had a more comfortable night than I have.'

'Well I most certainly have, Master Potts!'

Tom jumped in shock, fearing for a split second that the dead man had answered from the grave, then turned to see Hannah Anstiss smiling at him from the graveyard gate. She showed him a silver coffee pot. 'The night was a cold one so I've brought you a warming drink, Master Potts. You must be frozen to the bone.'

'How did you know I was here, Ma'am?' He frowned in mingled surprise and chagrin.

'Oh now, please don't be cross with me,' she coaxed. 'You were very well-hidden, so I'm positive that no would-be grave robber could have seen you. But after seeing you yesterday I put two and two together and realized why you had been here so early in the morning. It needs nine days and nights for a buried corpse to become too decomposed to be sold on to the anatomists, does it not? So you've another seven nights of guard duty to perform. But don't worry. I shan't breathe a word to anyone about your hiding here with pistols at the ready.

'Now please don't be so churlish as to refuse my coffee, Master Potts. Regard it as a peace offering, because I would really like us to be friends.'

Tom felt ashamed of his own bad manners and immediately went to her and offered his apologies. She waved them away and poured steaming coffee into a silver tankard, which she handed to him with a smile.

'Take care not to gulp this, it's very hot.'

He cradled the tankard in his cold hands, and couldn't repress his involuntary fits of shivering.

'Why didn't you wrap up in a cloak or even a blanket, against such a cold night? Come back to the house with me, there's a fine fire to warm yourself by while I cook you some breakfast.'

Tom was sorely tempted to accept the invitation, and found himself once again appreciating her physical charms. 'She's a very handsome woman, and charming company. It would do no harm to spend an hour having breakfast and chatting with her.'

Then he remembered Maggie Murphy lying in a lock-up cell, and felt impelled to regretfully

254

decline her offer.

'Sadly, Ma'am, I've some very pressing duties to attend to this morning, otherwise it would give me the greatest pleasure to accept your breakfast invitation. But perhaps we might find another opportunity to share a meal and conversation.'

'There is no perhaps about it, Master Potts. I'm convinced you and I will share many meals and enjoy many conversations in the future. Now drink your coffee before it gets cold. Leave the pot and tankard here by the gate when you're done. I'll send the maid to collect them.'

She smiled flirtatiously at him and walked away.

Tom found himself staring at her gracefully undulating shapely hips with both aesthetic appreciation and a rapidly burgeoning sexual desire.

'Dear God! You're behaving like a prurient schoolboy! And you're still in love with, Amy,' he castigated himself, but then the voice of his other self whispered in his mind. 'But you haven't got Amy any more, have you? So you're a free man, and can quite properly enjoy looking at a beautiful woman. You may be celibate, but you're not yet a monk!'

Reluctantly, he forced himself to turn away from the visual contemplation of Hannah Anstiss' luscious figure, and to concentrate his attention on the primary tasks for the day ahead:

Draw fluid from Maggie Murphy's stomach.

Make the tests on the stomach fluid.

Copy her prints and closely examine her

corpse, clothing and bedding in the full light of day.

Attempt to raise finger and palm prints from the two gin bottles.

The thought of poison brought the death of John Watts once more into the forefront of Tom's mind. In his father's case note ledgers, he had found two separate descriptions of cases of poisoning which bore a strong similarity to what he had learned about Watts's symptoms immediately prior to his death.

'I can go and speak to John Smith again now that I've got funds to pay him with. I just hope Blackwell agrees it'll be money well spent.'

His empty stomach rumbled and his mouth gaped involuntarily in a huge yawn. 'But first, get some breakfast.'

Once more he took a roundabout route back to the town centre, circling westwards and approaching the crossroads at the Green by way of the Unicorn Hill. Early though it was, there were people already leaving their houses and making toward their workplaces.

'Master Potts.' Tom was hailed by Thomas Oakley, who was leading a string of donkeys laden with empty panniers out from his business yard adjoining the Unicorn Inn. 'I wants a word wi' you.'

Tom came to a reluctant halt. Unlike his son, the elder Oakley was a noted curmudgeon, and at this moment he was the last man that Tom, desperately in need of food and sleep, wanted to have any talk with.

'What can I do for you, Master Oakley?'

'Eddie Harris and his woman? Has they left any money, or is the parish paying for me to bury them?'

'I've no idea.' Tom shook his head. 'As far as I know the matter of their burials haven't been discussed yet.'

'Well, I'll be getting the job, won't I?'

'I really don't know, Master Oakley.'

'You'm a real useless know-nothing, aren't you!' Oakley's coal-grimed face bore an accusatory scowl. 'And you aren't doing a very good job of protecting us, am you?

'You'm the bloody daftest, most useless constable this parish has ever known, and that's a fact, that is! Everybody says so. Because lately we've had thieving and body-snatchings and killings, and you aren't managed to stop nor catch any of the buggers who'm a doing it, and don't look likely to neither!'

He led the string of donkeys away, and one of the mangy beasts opened its jaws wide and emitted a series of loud discordant brays as if it were jeering agreement with its master's accusations.

The encounter left Tom feeling despondent. 'It's true what he says, isn't it? I'm neither preventing these crimes, nor anywhere near to discovering who the perpetrators are.'

He walked slowly over the crossroads, and to lower his spirits still further saw the resplendent scarlet-uniformed figure of Sergeant Sullivan standing outside the Fox and Goose. Feeling unable to face an encounter with the man who had won Amy's heart, he abruptly changed

257

direction and went in front of the chapel and along the far side of the Green.

Entering the lock-up consoling himself with the thought that at least he had a tasty mutton pie to breakfast upon, Tom found the cupboard door wide open and the shattered dish and scattered remnants of the pie lying on the floor beneath it.

With a welcoming miaow and tail held high, Bathsheba came to greet him, and purring loudly rubbed against his legs.

'How could you be so greedy, Bathsheba?' he asked her reproachfully. 'How could you steal my breakfast, after I left you such a big bowl of bread and milk? Enough to feed you for a week!'

The only foodstuffs left upon the cupboard shelves were a hunk of stale bread, three pickled onions and a small piece of hard cheese. Tom went and drew water from the pump in the rear yard, slaked his thirst and wetted the iron-hard bread so that he might chew it more easily. Breakfast eaten, he clambered up the stone stairs to his room to fetch his father's medical chest and his own investigation bag.

The cell where Maggie Murphy and her belongings had been locked in was next to the rear door. Rigor mortis had stiffened her, but the chill air in the cell had not accelerated bodily decomposition and she had not yet begun to smell unduly foul. The cell was dark; its only light source the small iron grille set high in the outer wall, but with the rear and cell doors opened wide, the daylight lit up the cell interior and Tom was able to minutely examine Maggie's skin through his magnifying glass. He found only old bruises and scars, and no sign of any fresh wounds apart from the numerous pustules, flea lumps and lice rashes which were the customary concomitants of life as a slum dweller.

He spent several minutes searching through the contents of his father's medical chest and took out small bottles, jars and other articles, which he carefully arranged in order. Then he went back to his room and pored over his medical books until the doorbell jangled to signal the arrival of Joseph Blackwell, in company with an elderly well-dressed, bespectacled man.

'Dr Price is a very old friend of mine, Master Potts, who is living in retirement in Alvechurch village,' Blackwell explained. 'He has had much experience of poisons, so I requested him to come with me and give his expert opinion on whatever we may discover in Murphy's stomach contents.'

Tom bowed to the newcomer. 'I shall be most grateful to you for your aid, Sir.'

He could see that Price's head was rocking and his hands shaking badly, and the other man smiled ruefully, displaying ill-fitting ivory false teeth, and informed in a quavering voice, 'As you see, Master Potts, I am afflicted with a severe palsy which forced me to retire from the profession many years ago. My sight also is much weakened, so all I can offer you is the services of my senses of smell and taste, which God be praised, are relatively undiminished.'

'Lead on, Master Potts.' Blackwell gestured.

259

'Let's make haste and do the business because I've a deal of other work awaiting me today.'

As he led his companions into the cell Tom experienced a spasm of nervous apprehension, 'What if I make an awful mess of this? It's years since I practised any dissection.'

'But you were very skilled at it.' His other self came to his support. 'And what you intend doing now is a very simple procedure. She's dead and can't be harmed further by whatever you do to her.'

A sense of confidence burgeoned, and his voice was firm when he told his companions, 'I shall incise the intervening flesh and then insert a trocar into the lower stomach and drain sufficient of its contents into a bowl, then suture up the aperture and incision.'

It took comparatively little time to cut through the layered skin and flabby fatty flesh and push the trocar through the stomach wall, adjusting the copper tube so that the stomach's liquefied contents could ooze through it and drip into the small crock bowl.

No sooner had the dripping pale blobs pooled and filled the bottom of the bowl than the mingled odours of cyanide acid, alcohol and sour foodstuffs began to reach all their nostrils.

'Do you recognize the smell, Dr Price?' Tom asked.

'I do,' the old man said. 'It is most definitely a cyanide compound. Possibly prussic acid, or Scheele's acid.'

With the bowl half-filled, Tom withdrew the trocar and used his previously prepared needles and threads to suture up the stomach and outer incision.

'I'll next do the iron test to confirm the identity of the acid. I've made ready the solution of green sulphate of iron, and have potash and diluted sulphuric acid to hand.' Tom was feeling elated with his performance so far.

'If you really must do this test, let us bear witness to it in the open air, Master Potts.' Joseph Blackwell was looking distinctly queasy. 'I confess that I'm finding this stench most distasteful. My stomach is not as strong as it used to be, I'm afraid."

He took Price's arm and led the old man into the rear yard. 'There now, Cuthbert, we've only the good old familiar stink of the privy to fill our nostrils with out here.'

Tom poured some of the stomach contents into a bulbous-shaped clear glass container, selected three of the small bottles from the collection and followed the others out. Holding the container close to Price's eyes, he emptied the contents of the bottles into it in sequence, commentating aloud as he did so.

'Firstly I add a few drops of potash and swirl it around. Then secondly I add the solution of green sulphate of iron. You'll note that almost immediately a dirty greenish-brown precipitate is falling. I'm going to shake the mixture well for a couple of more minutes.'

He lapsed into silence while he vigorously shook the container for some time, until Blackwell complained, 'Surely that's long enough, Master Potts. I have many pressing affairs to attend to this morning.'

'Very well, Sir. I shall now add the diluted sulphuric acid to the mixture.' Tom could not resist making a flourish out of pouring the contents of the third bottle into the container and swirling the mixture rapidly. He experienced a sensation of immense satisfaction as the liquid turned a shade of Prussian blue.

'Is that not the absolute proof, gentlemen? Maggie Murphy was poisoned by a cyanide compound which more than likely is prussic acid.'

'It certainly appears to be so, young man. I could be persuaded to testify to that probability,' Cuthbert Price quavered, then added almost as an afterthought, 'But a very similar cyanide compound can be extracted from ordinary laurel leaves, don't you know?'

'Well done, Master Potts, you have proven your point.' Blackwell congratulated him warmly, then his faded eyes twinkled mischievously, and he added. 'Now all you have to do is to prove your theory that she was murdered, and last but not least, find her murderer. Good day to you.'

Left alone, a wave of weariness engulfed Tom and he yearned to lie down and sleep. But buoyed up by his moment of triumph, he spent the next hour examining Maggie Murphy's shabby clothing and pitifully few personal items of toilette. They gave him no clues or leads, and neither did the two gin bottles.

Only then did he surrender to his need for sleep and go upstairs to bed.

Thirty-Four

It was late afternoon when the ringing of the bells roused Tom. He stumbled down to the front entrance and dragged open the heavy door to find no one waiting there. Puzzled, he took a few steps outside and looked about him. There were people passing about their various affairs but none very close, and no one appeared to be hurrying away from the lock-up. No mischievous urchins could be seen either.

He scratched his head, yawned and stretched his arms wide. 'I must have dreamt that the bells rang.'

Turning to go back inside, he noticed a brick leaning against the wall at the side of the doorway, with a piece of paper sticking out from under it.

The small scrap of paper bore a scrawled charcoal message, *bony suthal done em ded*. Again Tom stared around but could see no one paying him any attention. He studied the note. The penmanship and spelling was that of someone who had received little or no schooling.

'Bonny Southall done them dead!' Because of his own suspicion of the man, Tom couldn't control a surge of excitement, but sternly cautioned himself. 'Now don't get carried away with this.

It could just be someone with a grudge against Southall.' But still the thought persisted. 'Or it might be someone who really knows that South-all is the killer.'

His stomach rumbled loudly and hunger pangs struck hard. 'I need to eat and put something out for Bathsheba.' He smiled wryly. 'Even though she ought by right to suffer for robbing me of my breakfast.' Fetching a jug from inside, he walked across the Green to Morgan's dairy shed and found its proprietor standing at the double doors.

'Can you please fill this for me, Master Morgan? I'll collect it in a minute or two after I've done some shopping,' Tom requested.

The swarthy features of the stocky Welshman did not greet him with the usual welcoming smile and he made no effort to take the jug from Tom. Instead Morgan muttered surlily, 'Well it's to be hoped that you can shop better than you can keep law and order in this parish.'

Tom was surprised at this uncharacteristic reception, 'Why do you say that?'

'It's not me only that is saying such.' The Welshman's sing-song voice throbbed with indignant accusation. 'This town is become like Sodom and Gomorrah! Evil-doers are flourishing. There's been highway robberies, warehouses are smashed open and robbed, the dead are snatched from their resting places, and now Eddie Harris being slashed to pieces. It's disgraceful! That's what it is, disgraceful! And you should be ashamed for letting things come to such a terrible pass. I'll not sell you any of my goods until you do your duty and put a stop to

264

these outrages!'

With that final rant Morgan stepped back inside the double doors and slammed them shut in Tom's face. The shock of this verbal assault momentarily stupefied Tom, and he stood staring blankly at the door panels for a few moments until the sheer injustice roused his own sense of angry indignation. He raised his fist to hammer on the door, then let it fall once more to his side.

'What's the use of arguing with the man?' he asked himself wearily, and set off across the Green towards the shops which stood opposite the front of St Stephen's Chapel.

Several groups of hooped-bonneted, white-aproned housewives stood outside the shops with baskets on their arms, small children clustered about their skirts, gossiping and laughing together. But as Tom crossed the roadway towards them, all eyes turned upon him and voices and laughter stilled.

Made embarrassed by their silent frowning stares, Tom nodded and greeted them. 'Good afternoon, ladies.'

Only one muted voice returned the salutation.

In the bread shop the young baker, Charles Scambler, a noted local wag, threw up both arms and shouted loudly in mock surprise. 'Dear God, it can't be! It can't be! But yes, it is! I can't doubt the evidence of my own eyes. It's our constable! Our very own constable! Who hasn't been seen for ages around this town! Where have you been, Sir, while we've all been waiting our turns to be robbed or murdered?'

Tom refused to be drawn into any reaction. He merely asked quietly, 'Will you sell me a quartern loaf, if you please, Master Scambler?

'I shall be more than happy to do so, Constable Potts, at the very same moment that you do your duty, and catch the bastards who are making this parish a hell on earth to live in. Until then, buy your bread elsewhere.'

Tom didn't stay to argue further. He went the few yards to the grocery shop kept by Balthasar Groby, physically the largest and strongest man in the parish, who matched Tom for height and tripled him in weight. To the relief of the local dominant pugilists and brawlers, Groby was a fervent Methodist lay preacher and practising pacifist, who neither drank strong liquors, smoked tobacco, took snuff, or ever frequented taverns, horse races, prize fights, or any other scenes of ribaldries and sinful pleasures.

When Tom entered his shop, Groby shook his head more in sorrow than in anger, and silently pointed one massively muscled arm towards the door.

His face burning with embarrassment, Tom exited the shop and walked quickly back across the road, and unable to bear the risk of meeting other stares of derision or contempt kept his gaze fixed straight ahead.

Back in the lock-up, he went to his room and sat on his cot, looking down at the warped planks of the floor, waves of depression welling over him. Then his innate stubborn streak came to his aid, and he resolved grimly, 'I'll walk all the way to Birmingham to buy food if needs be.

And I'll track down and capture every killer, resurrection man, and thief no matter how long it takes. So instead of sitting here moping, I'd best get on with it.'

He went into the rear yard, and stripping off his upper clothing, doused himself thoroughly under the gouting jets of cold pump water. As he was drying himself on a strip of rough towelling the bells jangled loudly, and still bare to the waist he went to the front entrance and cracked open the door.

'Good God! Is it you, Amy?' he gasped in shock.

'Well it was still me when I last looked in the mirror,' Amy Danks giggled. 'Now are you going to let me in, or not?'

'Oh, I'm sorry.' He stepped back, pulling the door further ajar.

She entered and Tom could only gaze silently at her in surprise.

'Oh don't think of thanking me for bringing you this, will you?' she snapped in admonishment, as she thrust the cloth-covered basket towards him. 'Are you going to take it, or have I got to stand here holding it for the rest of the day?'

'What is it?' Tom was desperately struggling to overcome the shock of her sudden advent: delight that she was here mingling with dread of what this visit might portend.

'It's food, you great booby!' she chided impatiently. 'I was outside the shops when they sent you packing. I can't leave you to starve, can I? Daft great lummox though you are!'

'Oh Amy! This is wonderful of you! What can I say?' he uttered, as a lump rose in his throat and his eyes began to sting with rising tears. 'How much has this cost? If you'll allow me a moment to get dressed I'll pay you straight away.'

'Never mind any of that now, I've got to get back to work before Tommy Fowkes has a fit. You go and get after them bad 'uns, and catch them quick. Because I don't like having you blaggarded by bloody shopkeepers.' She darted forward, pulled his head down and planted a kiss on the tip of his nose. Then she was gone, running across the Green with skirt and petticoat billowing about her knees, delighted laughter pealing from her lips.

Tom remained completely motionless, staring after her in a daze of confusion until she had gone from sight. Shutting the door, he eagerly stripped off the cloth covering the large basket and delightedly unpacked its contents. There was fresh bread, meat pies, salted butter, golden-yellow cheese, a pot of relish, a jar of pickles, hard-boiled eggs, a bag of oatmeal and a big chunk of ham.

'God bless you, Amy. There's a week's worth of food here,' he murmured aloud, and felt hope happily burgeoning. 'Perhaps she still cares for me, and isn't yet fully committed to Sullivan.'

Miaowing plaintively, tail erect, Bathsheba came trotting to him and he smiled down at her.

'We shall have our feast immediately, Bathsheba. And you shall have a meat pie all to yourself.'

After he had satisfied his rampaging hunger, Tom sat and read until dusk came and it was time for him to go to his nightly grave-watch.

Thirty-Five

Saturday, 2 September

As day dawned in the Old Monks Graveyard, Tom came out from his hiding place, stretching and bending to ease his cold-stiffened joints and muscles. He was experiencing mixed emotions. Frustration that nothing had occurred during the long hours of darkness, mingling with relief that he had not had to use the pistols he carried against another human being. He planned his day ahead: first, eat and sleep. On rising, wash the shirt, underclothes and socks he was wearing and hang them out to dry in the backyard. Then make his enquiries at the apothecary's. Lastly, go and talk with John Smith.

'Prussic acid, d'you say?' Theobald Vaughn, apothecary and druggist, muttered, scratching his shiny bald pate and looking vaguely at Tom through the tiny lenses of the spectacles perched on the end of his long, drink-reddened, thickly pustuled nose. 'Prussic acid is one of the cyanide compounds. Did you know that when taken orally, 50 milligrams of a cyanide compound can cause death within five minutes? A very learned physician once told me that the cyanide inhibits the capacity of the blood to absorb oxygen.' He shook his head regretfully. 'Both lethal and brutal, wouldn't you agree, Sir?'

'Indeed I would, Sir,' Tom confirmed.

The bent-bodied old man turned and moved with a peculiar bird-like hopping gait along the tiers of shelves lined with bottles, stone jars and glass phials, crouching at intervals to peer short-sightedly at the gold monogrammed inscriptions on the drawers of the wall-length cabinet beneath the shelves. He muttered to himself continuously before eventually returning to face Tom and ask, 'Good afternoon to you, Sir. How may I help you?'

Still highly elated by yesterday's encounter with Amy Danks, Tom was having difficulty controlling his urge to laugh aloud at Vaughn's eccentric mannerisms.

'As you see, Sir, I am the parish constable.' Tom held his crowned staff before the other man's eyes. 'I would like to see your sale of poisons register, if I may.'

'Poison register? 'Pon my soul, that's a rare request to have made of me, Sir.'

'Perhaps it is, Sir, but I would really appreciate your allowing me to see it,' Tom pressed politely.

'But of course you may see it, Sir,' Vaughn concurred graciously. 'It's on top of that cabinet there. You can see it clearly now, I don't doubt. It has very fine spinal binding, does it not? My father had it bound at great expense, you know,

270

just prior to his death and my inheriting the business.'

He turned away from Tom again and recommenced his bird-like hopping along the shelves, crouching at intervals, continuously muttering incoherently, before returning to face Tom and repeating.

'Good afternoon to you, Sir. How may I help you?'

Tom was momentarily nonplussed.

'It's all right, Father, there's no need to trouble yourself. I'll serve the gentleman.'

A middle-aged man with a distinct physical likeness to the old man came into the room from a side door and said to Tom. 'You'll have to excuse my father, he's very old and gets tired at this time of the day. What can I do for you?'

Tom explained why he had come and the younger Vaughn immediately assented and brought the large ledger to him.

'We don't sell a great deal of the cyanide compounds. Someone might buy a few grams of prussic to bathe their varicose veins with, or ask us for Scheele's acid if they want to try it to get rid of vermin or put down a dog or cat they've no use for. But as I say, there's not a great deal of demand.'

Tom scanned the list of names, complete with addresses and reasons stated for purchase. He noted that all the local doctors were among them, and some women, but no entry aroused his immediate suspicion. He thanked both Vaughns and left the shop.

He returned to the lock-up and spent a couple

271

of hours poring through his collection of books and his father's ledgers seeking information which would support an idea he had occur to him while studying the poison register. Then he went in search of John Smith, the witch man.

Smith was ensconced in the bar of the White Lion when Tom found him. He greeted Tom with a tipsy grin.

'Well now, I'll wager that you've come to pay your debt.'

'You've won your wager, Master Smith.' Tom placed two shillings on the greasy-topped table. He could smell the strong aroma of brandy emitted by the other man, and grinned. 'Have you spent a pleasant day?'

'I have indeed. But if you've come to have your fortune told or stars read, I'm not able to do either at the present moment. All my powers of divination are temporarily exhausted.'

'No, Master Smith, I've not come to have my fortune told, but merely to seek to tap into your worldly knowledge.' Tom laid a sovereign beside the shillings.

Smith's drink-bleared eyes blinked down at the gold coin, then he glowered angrily at Tom.

'What's this piece of gold for, Constable?'

Tom was taken aback by the other man's abrupt change of attitude. 'It's in payment for the answers to some questions I need to ask you, Master Smith.'

'The bargain I offered the last time that me and you met, was to answer all and any questions you cared to ask me for the sum of one extra shilling, was it not?'

'Yes, I do believe that was your offer.'

'Well Constable Potts, my word is my bond, so don't insult me by trying to bribe me with blood money squeezed from the poor by the pigs who rule us.'

'I meant no insult,' Tom hastened to assure him. 'And I sincerely apologize if you've mistakenly perceived this as a bribe, Master Smith. I swear to you that I was merely...'

'Spare me your swearing!' Smith waved his hand in refutation of Tom's protestations. 'Just pick up that gold, and go from my sight.'

As Tom opened his mouth to reply, Smith cut him short with another wave of his hand and growled. 'I'll listen to no more grovelling false apologies from one of the willing tools of our tyrant oppressors!'

'And I'll listen to no more o' your ravings, you drunken bugger!' Widow Poole shouted furiously as she hobbled into the room. 'That gold 'ull go towards paying some of the rent and board you owes me, so it's me who'll be picking it up, and you that'll be answering the questions this gentleman asks you!'

Smith's pendulous lower lip quivered in alarm and he shrank back into the corner as she threatened him with her bony fists, shouting, 'You'm always like this when you'm in drink, you arsey bugger! It's that nasty streak in you that you got from your nasty bugger of a feyther. He was just such another as you, warn't he. A drunken, lazy, ne'er-do-well!'

She pocketed the sovereign, then stood with

arms akimbo and told Tom, 'Ask away, Master Potts! He'll give you full and fair answers or I'll kick his arse for him! And what he can't tell you, I might well be able to.'

Tom couldn't help but be amused by the dramatic alteration in John Smith's attitude, as the witch man now hastened to meekly concur with his landlady.

'Oh yes, Master Potts. I'm happy to be of service to you. What do you need to know?'

'I want you to tell me all about poisonous fungi, Master Smith.' The memory of Cuthbert Price's quavering voice suddenly came into Tom's mind, and on impulse he added, 'And I'd like you also to tell me anything you might know about the toxic properties of laurel leaves.'

When Tom finally left the White Lion he was satisfied with what he had learned, which included Widow Poole's contribution that Bonny Southall's grandfather had been a thatcher named Arnold Southall, whose grandson, Bonny, had cared for the old man in his final days.

Stars were glinting in the sky and Tom was torn between the necessity to get to his hiding place in the old graveyard, and his compelling desire to question Bonny Southall.

He stood outside the White Lion and from near and far could hear the ringing of bells from mills and factories signalling the release of the operatives from their long hours of gruelling toil. Almost immediately noisy whooping youths, girls and children began to pour out into the streets, closely followed by their older, staider brethren.

On impulse, Tom turned and hurried in the direction of Bredon. Bonny Southall was a pointer at Joseph Turner's mill in Bredon and Tom was hoping to intercept Southall as he made his way back home to a tenement on the Back Hill.

Halfway towards Bredon Tom encountered two men dressed in the pointer's rig and stopped them.

'Do either of you work at Joseph Turner's please?'

'We both does,' one informed him and in return challenged with surly aggressiveness, 'What the fuck am you asking us that for? Now what's we supposed to have done wrong?'

'Why nothing at all, I do assure you,' Tom hastened to mollify. 'I'm merely seeking Bonny Southall. I've got some private information for him. Do you know where I might find him?'

'He'll be laying between some wench's legs, the dirty lucky bugger!' the second man leered lasciviously. 'Left work early he did. Said he'd got a very urgent bit o' business and he could only do it when the coast was clear. So you can bet your arse it's a married piece that Bonny 'ull be shagging right now.'

'Would you have any idea who the woman might be? Only what I have to tell him is very important, and I need to see him as soon as possible,' Tom asked more in hope than expectation.

'Could be any one of a hundred.' The informant's tone was envious. 'He's a real ladies' man is our Bonny, and there's a lot o' women takes a fancy for the lucky sod. He aren't fussy about who he beds neither. So long as they got a pulse he don't give a bugger what they looks like or how old they am. Anyway, if you wants to talk to him, you'd best come down to the factory tomorrow.'

Tom accepted defeat. 'I will do. Thank you both for your trouble.'

He briefly considered returning to the lock-up to get the brace of pistols, but decided that he needed to get to the Old Monks Graveyard without any further delay; so continued on towards Bredon, taking the indirect route across the fields and wasteland. His thoughts remained centred on Bonny Southall. Although he had no definite proof, Tom strongly suspected that Southall was the killer of Eddie Harris, and thought that he could discern a definite pattern of events.

He was certain that Harris, helped by two associates, had stolen both Bates's and Chillingworth's needles, and also Mrs Gould's body. He believed that the two men and a woman heard by the old blind man, John Tanner, on the night that Mrs Gould's corpse was stolen were the perpetrators of that outrage, and that they were Eddie Harris and possibly Maggie Murphy and Southall.

Harris and Southall's savage brawl in the chapel yard could have been a clash over the division of the spoils. Or, knowing Southall's reputation as a notoriously indiscriminate womanizer, maybe even a fight about a woman.

Tom remembered Harris snarling that Southall had been trespassing on his property. Was Maggie Murphy that property?

The thatching knife found on Harris's corpse almost certainly had been Southall's grandfather's, who had spent his final days living with Southall. Added to this was the mystery of Southall's whereabouts on the night of the murder. Tom had made discreet enquiries but had not found anyone who could remember seeing Southall in his usual tavern haunts that night.

There was also the fact that on the day of her death, Maggie Murphy had been entertaining a visitor. Could that have been Southall? And did Southall decide that it would be convenient to dispose of Maggie Murphy also? There were two empty gin bottles, which indicated that Maggie was most probably stuporous with drink and sex. It would have been very easy to slip a few milligrams of cyanide compound into her gin.

Nothing in Vaughn's poison register had pointed towards Southall, but Tom had confirmed in his talk with John Smith that with time and patience it was possible to extract and distil a deadly cyanide draught from common laurel leaves.

'And Bonny Southall lives by himself, doesn't he? There's no one else there to query what he was doing if he was boiling up laurel leaves and distilling their juices.'

The night sky was clear and the low risen new moon gave light enough for Tom to make his way across the fields and waste ground without mishap. Within sight of the graveyard he moved cautiously, keeping to the shadows in case there should be anyone in the vicinity.

The night air was unusually still, with not even the gentlest whisper of wind to rustle the dying leaves on the branches of the trees. Forty yards distance across the Abbey Meadows, lights burned in the windows of the Forge Mill and the adjoining house.

Tom moved along the ditch line of the hedge-row towards the gate of the graveyard and when only yards from it, tripped on a tussock of grass and toppled headlong across the ditch into the tangled branches, staff flying from his wildly flailing hands, unable to hold back a cry of pain as long thorns ripped into his flesh.

On the other side of the hedge, a donkey bucked and brayed in shock and a man's voice cried out, 'There's a bastard spying on us!'

The next instant, a gun roared and lead shot cracked through the hedge, blowing Tom's top hat away, missing his head by scant fractions.

Propelled by the adrenalin charge of mindless terror, Tom tore free of the entangling branches and fled. Another shot came and a third, lead balls hissing past him, and he heard a man shout, 'I'm going after the bastard!'

Legs and arms pumping frantically, Tom charged across the fields, vaulting stiles, jumping ditches, plunging through bushes, wading muddy streams, gasps of breath sobbing through his gaping mouth.

Dogs were barking uproariously around the

Forge Mill and lantern lights came bobbing from its doorways, while booted feet and donkey hooves crunched on the gravel of the narrow lane leading westwards from the graveyard to the main turnpike road.

Thirty-Six

Sunday, 3 September 1826

The first greying of the chill dawn found Tom crouching in the muddy bramble-filled ditch where he had finally collapsed from sheer bodily exhaustion. Shivering with cold, painfully bruised and lacerated in a score of places, racked by shame for his self-perceived cowardice, he had hours since exhausted all his vocabulary of self-directed castigation and insult.

'It'll be full daylight soon, so you can't stay here any longer, you pathetic excuse for a man!' He forced himself to crawl out of the ditch, stand upright and take stock of the surrounding area.

'Oh my God!' He stared with horrified disbelief down the slightly sloping field at the bottom of which was the oblong-shaped border of trees and hedgerow surrounding the Old Monks Graveyard.

'I ran in a circle like a bloody headless chicken! I couldn't even manage running away properly, could I? If I'd had the strength to run a few yards more I'd have fallen into the arms of the very ones who were shooting at me! Useless, cowardly fool that I am!'

The image of Amy rose in his mind, and he found himself asking, 'How can I ever look you in the face again, Amy, after the shameful way I've behaved?' The resplendent image of the dashing Sergeant Sullivan rose to replace Amy, and Tom experienced heartsick despair.

'No wonder she prefers you to me, Sergeant. What woman wouldn't choose a brave man above a coward? The best thing I can do is to leave this town. To walk away from here right now and go to live out my days where no one knows my shame.'

Then, as it always did at Tom's darkest moments of self-denigration, another self spoke from deep within his being, 'If you run away now, then you may as well take a pistol in your hand and put a ball through your brain, because you will not be able to live with the knowledge that you'll have brought disgrace upon your father's name.'

'But it's too late now, I've already besmirched his memory, haven't I?' Tom argued. 'I've already stained his name by my cowardice.'

He turned around and began to walk. 'I'm leaving this town for good.'

But after only a few paces he came to a halt, turned around again and with great reluctance headed down the slope towards the old grave-yard, bitterly berating that other self that existed within him, and was now forcing him to stay.

'I really don't want to do this! Why can't you

stop tormenting me so, and allow me to go and seek a quiet peaceful life somewhere?'

When Tom reached the graveyard, he saw his top hat lying in the shallow ditch and went to pick it up. He gulped as he turned it over in his hands and saw the torn holes perforating the fabric.

'My God, that was a close call. This can't be repaired. I'll have to wear my father's old hat until I can afford to buy a new one.'

In the graveyard itself, he checked John Watts's grave mound and breathed a sigh of relief to find the soil apparently undisturbed. He quickly scanned the neighbouring graves but found nothing untoward.

As he walked back to the gate he saw a couple of paces from the side of the pathway one of the squared brown paper hats favoured by the needle pointers. He took it up and examined it. Although dampened by the night-time dew, it was clean and appeared to be freshly made.

'Could this have been dropped by one of those who were shooting at me?' He folded it carefully and put it into his pocket, then decided that despite the early hour he would go straightaway to report the happenings of last night to Joseph Blackwell.

'By God, Master Potts, but you present a sorry sight!' Joseph Blackwell stared quizzically at his bedraggled, muddied early visitor. 'Have you spent the night wallowing in a pig sty?'

Racked by shame, Tom summoned the scant remnants of his self-respect and forced out the honest reply, 'Not in a pig sty, Sir, but skulking in ditches like the coward that I am.'

'Explain yourself,' Blackwell ordered firmly.

Tom described the events of the previous night, leaving nothing out and making no attempt to excuse his own terror-stricken flight.

The older man betrayed no emotion, his lined pale face remaining inscrutable. When Tom's recital came to an end, Blackwell merely sought confirmation.

'And this morning Watts's grave shows no sign of being disturbed.'

'None that I could see, Sir. Nor any of the other graves. It may well be that whoever fired at me were only poachers, or alternatively of course, that I arrived before they had started to dig the grave out, and fearing the gunfire would bring others there, they ran off.'

'Perhaps that is so.' Blackwell nodded, and then smiled bleakly. 'Listen very carefully to what I have to say, Master Potts. The only criticism I have to make of you is the fact that you did not follow my wishes and take my pistols with you. As for your running away and hiding in a ditch? Given the circumstances that is what any sane man should do, as I most certainly would myself. Remember the old adage, Master Potts, "He who fights then runs away, lives to fight another day."'

'I'm always too ready to run away from a fight, Sir. I'm just a coward,' Tom said despondently.

Blackwell shook his head. 'Whatever else you may be, a coward you are most definitely not.

Somehow you always manage to return to the fray, and for me that is the measure of true bravery.

'Now I feel that you should still maintain the night watch on Watts's grave. Those rogues may well make a further attempt on it. Taking into consideration your ordeal last night, I suggest ... No! I order that this being the Sabbath you take a full day of rest before continuing with your watch duty tonight. Make sure that you take my pistols with you this time. I bid you a good day, Master Potts.' He waved his hand in dismissal, took up his pen and bent his head over the ledger on the desk before him.

Tom left the house and walked slowly across the Green, replaying the interview with Blackwell over and over again in his mind. His low spirits began to tentatively lift, and then abruptly plummeted again as he noticed the scarlet-uniformed man standing outside the door of the lock-up.

'Is he going to make trouble because Amy came to see me? Well I'll not run away from him. I've done more than enough running away for one week.'

Tom steeled himself for what could be an unpleasant encounter and quickened his pace to reach the lock-up.

'Good morning, Sergeant Sullivan, is it me you're waiting for?'

'Indeed it is, Constable Potts.' Beneath the shiny black peak of the shako, Sullivan's handsome features frowned dourly, and his hand moved to grip the hilt of the short sword slung

283

from his belt as if he was going to draw it from its scabbard.

A sharp tremor of apprehension coursed through Tom, but he was determined not to flinch from trouble, and his fingers tightened on his staff as he readied himself to meet an attack.

'What is it you want with me, Sergeant?' Tense though he was, Tom found himself marvelling at how firm and steady his voice sounded.

'I wanted to tell you that my engagement to Miss Danks no longer stands. The young lady has decided that she does not wish to wed me after all.' The soldier's eyes were filled with sadness. 'Because you've behaved as a gentleman, Master Potts, I feel it only fair that I should inform you of what has happened, and of course release you from our previous agreement. I'm returning to my regiment today, and I hope that we part without ill feeling.'

'But of course we do, Sergeant Sullivan.'

Sullivan saluted smartly and marched quickly away, before Tom could say anything more.

Still trying to fully absorb the connotations of what he had heard, Tom went into the lock-up and through to the rear yard. He stripped naked and for long minutes washed away the sweat and mud of the terror-filled night with the icy jets of pump water.

The long iron pump handle eventually slowed and creaked to a stop.

His dripping wet, goose-pimpled body shaking with cold, its numerous bruises and abrasions painfully aching and stinging, his brain reeling with fatigue, Tom lifted his arms skywards and laughed with joy.

'Amy is not going to marry the soldier! So perhaps she might still marry me some day.'

Thirty-Seven

Sunday noon, 3 September 1826

Jonathan Crowther hammered his gloved fists on the door of Mary Watts's cottage, and shouted angrily, 'I know you're in there, so open this bloody door or I'll smash it down.' Breathing hard, he pressed his ear to the weathered, warped panels and listened for any sound within.

Above his head, the gable window opened and Mary Watts's smiling face peeped out of it. 'Calm down, Crowther, or you'll give yourself a seizure.'

He stepped backwards and glared up at her. 'Where the hell were you last night?'

'It's none of your business anyway, but I was here if you must know.' She was still smiling, but there was the glint of resentful anger in her dark eyes.

'Oh no! Oh no! I came knocking twice and you weren't here!'

'Then you should have knocked harder and woken me up.'

'I knocked more than hard enough to wake you up.'

'Well you couldn't have done, could you? Else I'd have woken up, wouldn't I? Or is it that you're getting too old and feeble to knock a door properly?'

Crowther brandished his fist threateningly, 'Don't you be taking the piss out of me, girl, or you'll be finding out how old and feeble I am from the weight of this. Now get down here and open this bloody door afore I smash it in.'

'All right, all right, I was only teasing you.' Her tone softened in placation. 'I'm coming down, just give me a minute to put my clothes on.'

'Why aren't you dressed? It's the middle of the day, so why aren't you dressed?' he demanded suspiciously. 'Have you got a fancy man with you?'

'I've no fancy men, as you well know! I'm a respectable woman and bear the good name for being so! Why must you blaggard me like this? I've done nothing to deserve it!'

'All right, all right, I'm sorry!' It was the man's turn to be placatory. 'It's only that I've been worried about you when I didn't get any answer last night.'

'That was because I took a dose of laudanum. You know very well I've had trouble sleeping since I lost Johnny. I'll be down in a minute.' Her head disappeared and the window slammed shut.

Crowther turned his back to the door and peered agitatedly about him, his clasped hands twisting and jerking. Nearly five minutes passed before she opened the door and curtsied elaborately to him.

'Please be so gracious as to step inside, my lord and master, and let me introduce you to my fancy man.'

'What's took you so long to open up? Have you got somebody hiding upstairs?' Crowther glared suspiciously around the shabby room, then stamped up the wooden stairs to check the two small bedrooms.

'I've been sleeping in the front bedroom, my lord,' she shouted mockingly after him. 'Be sure and examine the sheets to see if there's any love spillage on them.'

'Oh don't you fret, I'll be doing just that,' he bellowed back.

'Good! And I'll be expecting your most humble apologies when you find nothing.'

After only brief seconds Crowther came back downstairs, and she challenged, 'Well?'

'Well what?' He growled but his eyes were shifty and couldn't meet hers.

'Do I get an apology for being called a whore?'

'I called you no such thing.'

'You implied it plainly enough, Crowther. And if you and me are going to be friends in the future, you'd best give me the apology you owe me.'

He glared and shook his head, then cleared his throat and reluctantly gritted through his clench-ed teeth, 'Sorry.'

'Oh no!' She shook her head and angrily stamped her foot. 'That's not near good enough! I want a proper apology, one that's really meant. Or you and me are finished. I mean it, Crowther!

I'll not speak to you ever again.'

'All right, there's no need to go mad at me. I'm sorry if I've offended you, truly I am. Now I've got to go to my trap and bring in a little present I've brought for you. I'll only be two ticks.' He turned from her.

Mary Watts's white teeth gleamed in a triumphant smile as she moved to look through the small open window of the back scullery into the thick woodland beyond, where squirrels darted, birds fluttered and a hungry fox hunted stealthily for prey through the dense underbrush.

Unseen by her, another hunter was also stealthily trailing his prey through the underbrush. William Kinchin was following the man who had hurriedly exited through the cottage's rear door as Jonathan Crowther entered at the front.

Thirty-Eight

Monday, 4 September

Tom left the graveyard as the first hints of dawn showed in the eastern sky. During the night's vigil he had been troubled at intervals by a sense of burning shame as the painful memories of his terror-stricken flight flooded his mind.

'Never again!' he vowed passionately. 'I'll die first!'

Now as he made his roundabout way back to the lock-up he forced himself to recall every single detail that he could remember of what had happened. The tumble into the ditch, the braying donkey, the man's shout, the three gunshots.

Being raised from a child in his military surgeon father's various army encampments and barracks, Tom had acquired an intimate knowledge of varying types of armaments, and now he concentrated hard on the three gunshots.

'I'm pretty sure the first was a long-barrel flintlock firing small shot, as witness the punctures it made in my hat. But the second and third were pistols firing a single ball apiece.

'There were at least two people there, because of the warning being given. Perhaps one was standing lookout and was armed with both the sporting gun and the pistols?

'A braying donkey again? That's the second time there's been a donkey in the vicinity of a body-snatching. And then there were the fresh droppings I found at Forge Mill.'

Tom smiled in wry amusement. 'Is there any difference in size between donkey droppings and horse droppings? Perhaps I should have taken measurements?'

Tom was becoming convinced that Southall was a member of a gang that was involved with the body snatching of Mrs Gould, the robbery of the needle warehouses, the murder of Eddie Harris and the death of Maggie Murphy. The murder of Harris could be as a result of an internal feud between the gang members. In view of Southall's reputation as a womanizer, the mysterious note left at the lock-up could have been one of the gang seeking revenge for Southall's seduction of his woman.

Tom came to an abrupt halt as an absolute certainty whelmed in his mind. 'This gang are the Rippling Boys! They're not just a local fable. They exist in reality!'

He made an instant decision.'I'm going to bring Southall in for questioning this very day! I'm going to arrest him on suspicion of murder. Hopefully that might put the cat among the pigeons.'

As he walked on he pondered, 'Might it be wiser if I go and fetch John Hollis to help me? What if Southall or his friends turn on me?' But the shaming memory of his terror-stricken flight drove Tom to shake his head.

'No! I must do this thing myself. I'll behave like a man and not disgrace my father's name further.'

At the lock-up, he kindled a fire in the grate of his room and hung the small iron cooking pot containing the mixture of watery oatmeal and chopped ham above the flames. While he waited for the food to heat up, his thoughts turned to Amy Danks and he smiled fondly.

'I'm going to ask her to marry me. But I must solve this case before I do that. Because I want her to be able to be proud of me, and not be mocked at for marrying a man who's a laughing stock and a pauper both.'

The tolling bells summoning the people to work sounded from various mills and factories.

Tom mentally pictured the scene of hundreds of men, women and children hurrying to their daily toil and told himself wryly, 'Still, I've got to admit that being the parish constable is certainly a more interesting occupation than spending a lifetime penned up in a dirty workshop being ruled over by a needle master.'

An hour later, after he had eaten, washed and shaved, Tom carefully checked the priming and loading of the brace of pistols and placed them in the satchel slung from his shoulder. He put on his father's battered old top hat, took up his staff and went from the lock-up.

During the long walk down the sloping road to Bredon, doubts began to assail him, and he could feel his stomach twisting with apprehension at what might face him when he reached Turner's pointing shop. But he refused to surrender to the tremors of fear and doggedly marched on, telling himself, 'What's to be, will be. I'm not running away again.'

At Turner's mill, the old blind horse was trudging his endless circles, driving the creaking gin mill powering the factory machinery. Tom halted outside the long low building and checked the pistols in his satchel. His heart was thudding, mouth drying, throat tightening. He swallowed hard and pushed the door open to be met with the din of slapping fast-revolving leather belting, clattering gears, whirring pulley wheels and the deeper trundling of grindstones. The air stank of burning grease and white-hot steel and Tom could taste the gritty dust of metal and stone which permeated the atmosphere in a malignant miasma.

He peered through the gloom at the line of pointers straddling the wooden saddles, hunched bodies bent low over the spinning grindstones. Their close-pressed palms trapped and spread rows of long needle lengths, pressing and turning the points upon the stones, showers of sparks shooting up into their rag-wrapped faces and creating flickering auras of dense-thronged, angry red-white pinpoints around their heads and shoulders.

The nearest pointer turned to drop the finished pointed needles into the box by his side and saw Tom. He rose from his saddle and came to Tom and shouted, 'What does you want here, Master Constable?'

'I want Bonny Southall,' Tom told him.

The man only shook his head and bawled, 'I can't hear you.'

He moved to the wall where the huge drive wheel spun, and lifted a long lever to disengage the drive shaft. The cacophony stilled, and all heads turned towards the two men.

'What does you want, Master Constable?' the pointer reiterated.

'I'm looking for Bonny Southall. Is he here?'

'I am.' Midway along the row Bonny Southall pulled down the rags covering his mouth and nose. 'And what does you want with me?'

Now that the dreaded moment of confrontation had come, Tom found himself marvelling at how grimly and calmly determined he was to arrest this man, and he recognized that he must act without any hesitation whatsoever, and take complete control of this situation. He propped his staff against the doorpost, snatched both pistols from the satchel, cocked them and walked swiftly towards Southall. Halting a yard from him, Tom aimed the muzzles at the man's head and ordered, 'I'm arresting you in the King's name Master Southall, on suspicion of murder. Now rise slowly, step away from your saddle and kneel on the floor with your hands behind your back. Do exactly as I say, or I swear I'll blow your head off. And if anyone of you others attempt to stop this arrest, then I'll shoot that man dead also.'

His words brought a concerted outcry of shocked astonishment from his hearers. Bonny Southall's jaw dropped open as if he were stupefied. A sudden clamour of questions erupted.

'Murdered?'

'Who the fuck's he murdered?'

'Shut your mouths!' Tom roared, and as the clamour subsided to an excited susurration, he told them, 'He's under suspicion of murdering Eddie Harris.'

Another clamorous outburst of shocked exclamations and questions mingled with Bonny Southall's bellowed denials as he slumped down on to his knees. 'Bollocks! That's bollocks that is! It's all bollocks!'

Tom nodded towards two of the pointers. 'You and you, I'm summoning you in the King's name to help me escort this prisoner to the lock-up. If you refuse, then you'll face serious charges yourself for refusing to aid a constable in his lawful duty. Do you understand?'

To his surprise, both men appeared willing, indeed eager to assist him.

'What does you want us to do wi' the bugger, gaffer?'

'Get some rope and lash his arms securely behind him, then take him between you and go in front of me.'

They hastened to obey, binding Southall's arms and lifting him to his feet.

Tom stepped face to face with his prisoner and warned quietly, 'Mind what I say, Master Southall. If you make any attempt to escape, or to call upon your friends to rescue you, then I'll put a ball in your head without any hesitation.'

To his surprise, Southall grinned contemptuously and shook his head, 'I've no need to try and get away, Master Potts. You'm only making a fool of yourself again by taking me in like this. It warn't me who gutted Harris, even though he deserved what he got, stinking pig that he was. You might as well turn me loose now, and save yourself being laughed at for a fool.'

'The court will decide on your guilt or innocence, Master Southall,' Tom replied quietly, and told the escorts, 'Lead on.'

As always in Redditch, the news of any dramatic happening had spread like wildfire, and men, women and children laid aside their tasks, left their work and came rushing from all directions. By the time the lock-up was reached, the progress of Tom and his prisoner had metamorphosed into a carnival-like procession of cheering, laughing, jeering and jostling hundreds.

Inside the lock-up, Southall was unbound and Tom searched him but found only some silver and copper coins, a tobacco pouch, a stubby clay pipe and a large key.

'What does this unlock, Master Southall?'

'Me front door.'

Tom gave him back the coins, tobacco and pipe.

'What about me key?' Southall queried.

'You'll get it back later.'

'Oh I see,' Southall grinned. 'You'm going to be poking through me house am you? Well don't make a mess, because I'm a very tidy man. And make sure you locks it up again when you've done, and will you ask me neighbours to keep an eye on the place, because there's a lot of light-fingered gentry in this town. If I goes back and finds any of me stuff's gone missing, I'll be holding you personally responsible for it.'

After Southall was locked securely in a cell, the two pointers began to cut the binding rope into small lengths.

'What are you doing that for?' Tom questioned. 'That's a useful rope.'

'And it'll earn us some useful money, gaffer,' one grinned. 'We can sell these bits o' rope as souvenirs. Lot's o' folk 'ull pay a farthing for a keepsake o' Bonny now he's going to be hung for murder, and this 'ull be the first time we've ever got a drink out of the tight bastard.'

And this is a good example of the vaunted brotherhood of the pointer lads, Tom thought.

He waited until they had left with their booty before opening the small observation shutter of the cell door. Southall was lying on the narrow wooden pallet that served as a bed and to Tom's surprise appeared to be completely at ease. His white teeth gleamed as he smiled and said, 'I'm enjoying this rest, Master Potts. You've done me a favour because I was feeling like having a lie-down this morning. I had a very busy night of it, if you knows what I mean. Some ladies can be very demanding, can't they? Kept bothering me all night, so she did.'

'And who might that lady be, Master Southall?' Tom asked.

'Oh come now, Master Potts, I'm a gentleman, I am. I never kisses and tells.'

'Neither can your ladies kiss and tell, can they, Master Southall? They're silenced for ever when you leave them, aren't they?'

Southall's handsome features creased in a puzzled frown. 'What d'you mean by that?'

'Exactly what I say,' Tom rejoined curtly. 'I've got Maggie Murphy in the cell next door. The woman you poisoned.'

'Poisoned? Me?' Bonny Southall appeared to be genuinely startled. 'You reckon I poisoned Maggie Murphy?'

'I'm convinced of it,' Tom asserted, yet even as he spoke a fleeting suggestion of uncertainty crossed his mind. The other man's expression of utter bewilderment was not the reaction he had expected.

Bonny Southall rose and came to the door to stare angrily into Tom's eyes as he gritted out between clenched teeth, 'Now you listen to me, Potts, it's bad enough you wrongfully accuse me of killing that piece of shit, Eddie Harris, but now to tell me you reckon I poisoned Maggie Murphy just goes to prove that you'm right off your fuckin' rocker! I've never lifted a hand to, or deliberately harmed any woman in my life.

'So bring me to trial whenever you feels like it, and try to prove what you says in front of a judge and jury, and when the case is dismissed then you really ought to leave this town straightaway. Because if you stays your life won't be worth the living. I've always took you to be a man with brains, but now I can see that you'm just another thick-skulled clown.' Sneering contemptuously, he moved back to the pallet and lay down, pillowing his head on his arms.

Tom closed the shutter and walked away, uncomfortably aware that Southall's attitude and demeanour seemed to be based on something more than the blustering bravado of a guilty man.

As he locked the main door behind him and walked along the Red Lion Street, Tom frowned uneasily at the recognition that the previous fleeting pang of uncertainty that had crossed his mind was now beginning to develop into a wriggling worm of doubt concerning Bonny Southall's guilt in Maggie Murphy's death.

'Could it be that she simply killed herself after all, maybe? But I'm still convinced that he killed Harris.'

Southall's home was on the upper reach of the Back Hill at the top end of a row of small, neatly thatched cottages fronted by a cobbled forecourt and a gabled well shaft. As Tom unlocked the

297

front door, a slatternly young woman bearing a small baby in her arms came out of the neighbouring cottage and challenged fiercely, 'You'm the constable, aren't you? Where's Bonny? What's you doing going into his house?'

'He's in custody.' Tom noted her swollen bruised eyes but thought little of it. In the Needle District, black eyes on Monday were a common sight after weekend roistering.

'Custody? What the bloody hell's that when it's at home?' Her pretty face frowned in puzzlement.

'He's locked up on suspicion of the murder of Eddie Harris.'

'Murder? Bonny? Of Eddie Harris? If you'm saying that Bonny killed Eddie Harris then it's all bollocks! He couldn't have done it!'

Tom didn't mind prolonging this exchange, knowing that when emotions were heated, as this young woman's appeared to be, then sometimes vital information was unwittingly disclosed.

'How do you know that, Miss? I'm sorry but I don't know your name.'

'Harper. Me name's Jenny Harper. And I'm Missus, not Miss,' she snapped. 'And I knows it's all bollocks because the night when they says Eddie Harris was being sliced up, Bonny couldn't have been there at the White Hart because he was wi' me.'

'Where was he with you?'

'We was in his bleedin' bed!'

Tom was momentarily taken aback by this frank admission of adultery.

'But you say that you're married? Or are you a widow?'

'Widow!' she exclaimed. 'I wish I was, but I didn't get these buggers off any dead husband, Mister!' She indicated her damaged eyes. 'The crafty bastard come back from the pub afore I expected him to, and he waited outside to cop me coming out o' Bonny's house.'

'Can your husband confirm this?' Tom asked.

She scowled suspiciously. 'What's that mean? I wish you'd give over using all them words I don't understand.'

'Will your husband tell me the same as you've told me?'

'Oh he'll tell you all right. He's told every other bugger in this street. But he won't tell you as how he was too fritted o' Bonny to try giving him a hammering like he give me. Bloody coward, that he is!'

'Where's your husband now, and what's his full name?'

'His name's Samson Harper.' She grinned derisively, displaying uneven, discoloured teeth. 'That's a bloody laugh, aren't it? Giving the name o' Samson to a fritted little prick like him.'

'Where is he now?' Tom pressed.

'Buggered if I know! He said he was sick and tired o' my shenanigans, and he was going off to 'list for a soldier. The bastard's left me and me babbies on the parish, so he has! God rot him! I 'opes he gets sent over the sea to fight them black heathens, and that they catches him and roasts him to death over a bloody fire. And when he's dead and gone me and Bonny can get

299

married all proper like.'

'Well many thanks to you, Mrs Harper.' Tom felt an urgent need to be alone and think carefully about what she was claiming. Without other confirmation, her story was merely a woman giving her lover a fake alibi. But there was a possibility that the illiterate note left at the lock-up accusing Southall of murder could have been Samson Harper seeking revenge, and thus serve as confirmation of a sort of his wife's claims.

'Look, can I come and talk to you a little later? In an hour or so, perhaps?'

'Yes, o' course you can, Master, no bother.' Her attitude became friendly. 'I likes the way you talks, even if I can't make hide nor tail o' them words you uses.'

The baby began to squall and she scowled down at its tiny, screwed-up red face.

''Ull you shut your bloody rattle. You'se sucked me dry already, you greedy little bleeder!'

Tom entered the front room of the cottage and stood evaluating it. The walls were limewashed, the floor flagstoned, and the room looked and smelled clean. In its centre were a plain wooden table, a bench and a couple of high stools. Two wooden-armed chairs flanked the small fire range, which was gleaming with blacklead, as were the iron kettles and pots on the mantelpiece above the range. In a corner, a tall, fine-quality grandfather clock ticked, its presence suggesting that there had been money to spare for luxuries at some time or other in the family history.

'You spoke the truth when you said that you're a tidy man, Bonny. You put me to shame, so you do,' Tom acknowledged, as he ruefully contrasted this neat room with his own distinctly untidy quarters.

In the small rear room there was a standing cupboard which held crockery and cutlery. Next to the cupboard, a small cubbyhole served as a pantry and was well-stocked with foodstuffs, and several bottles of gin and brandy. Ranged along the rear wall were a large wooden washing tub and a smaller tub set on individual stands with a large copper jug at each base, along with a besom broom, mop, scrubbing brushes and two wooden buckets.

Low on the adjoining wall, a collection of thatching tools hung from hooks: a pair of shears, a whimbel, some rakes, a leggat, shearing hook, two hook-curved thatching knives and hand and knee pads. Tom examined the tools and found that each had been inscribed with the initials 'AS' formed in similar fashion to the initials on the handle of the thatching knife that had been used against Eddie Harris.

'Good!' Satisfaction surged through Tom's mind. 'At least this proves that the killing knife was part of this collection.'

He opened the back door on to a fenced shared yard with a privy shed to one side, which would also be shared by all the tenants of the row, as was the ash and general rubbish pit on the opposite side.

Upstairs, the two small rooms were each furnished with double bedsteads, linen presses and

301

chests of drawers with looking glasses placed on their tops. The rear room had the bed made up and Tom assumed that this was where Bonny Southall normally slept.

He opened all the linen presses and drawers and was surprised by the good quality of the sheets and blankets in the presses, and also by the quantity of well-made clothing in the drawers.

Next, he examined the array of toiletries set out before the looking glass. Tooth powder and brush, several pomades, scented soaps and Macassar oils, fine quality cut-throat razor, silver inlaid combs, hair brushes and curling tongs.

Tom chuckled in grim amusement. 'You're certainly well-supplied with the good things in life, my bucko. Now have you hidden any of the proceeds of crime in this house, I wonder?'

Above his head, the steeply pitched roof rafters and tiles were open to view, as were the underneath of the bedroom floorboards and joists in the rooms below. So he began his search with the flagstones of the downstairs rooms but could find no sign that any of them had been recently lifted or disturbed in any way.

Back upstairs, he emptied the contents of the linen presses and chests of drawers, but again found nothing untoward. No false bottoms in the presses or under the bases of the chests of drawers. No packs of needles, or pieces of a domestic distillery kit.

Disappointed by failure, Tom replaced all the contents taking care to put them neatly in the order they had been and was about to go downstairs when sudden intuition stopped him. Once more he pulled the drawers out in turn, but this time completely removed all of them and laid them in a row on the floor.

'That's it!' Excitement flashed as he compared the difference in height of the rear panel of the top drawer to the rest. He felt beneath the underside top of the chest and his fingertips touched the rough canvas packages stowed upon the cunningly concealed suspended shelf at the rear.

There were two flattish rectangular packages wrapped in dirty blackened canvas sheeting. Tom unwrapped one to discover a myriad of polished, finished needles.

Exultant satisfaction brought a broad smile to his lips. 'These have been stolen, else why would he hide them away like this?'

Tom hefted a package in each hand. *It's surprising how much they weigh for their size, isn't it?* he thought, and as he did so an unbidden mental image flashed through his mind.

'Could that be why?' he wondered aloud. 'Could it? Because if it is so, then it boils up another kettle of fish entirely. So what do I do now?'

He sat down on the edge of the bed. Tens of seconds lengthened into tens of minutes which doubled, trebled, quadrupled, and still Tom sat motionless, deep in thought. Downstairs, the grandfather clock sonorously chimed the hour, and Tom rose to return to Jenny Harper's cottage.

'Now Mrs Harper, are you quite certain about the time that you left Master Southall's bed?' Tom questioned as she opened her door to his knocking.

'O' course I am! Does you take me for a fool?' she bridled indignantly. 'It was just arter midnight, because when his big clock struck the twelve I said to Bonny, you'll needs let me get up and dressed because that little prick 'ull be coming home shortly and if I aren't in bed waiting ready to give him what he wants, then there's bleedin' ructions.'

She shook her head in disgust. 'God Christ! He's a randy little bastard, Samson Harper is. Every night and morning he wants it, so he does. It don't matter how worn out I'm feeling. He's got to have his oats or he makes me life a misery.'

'Yes, it must be very hard for you, Mrs Harper,' Tom murmured sympathetically. 'But I still have to ask you if you would be prepared to go before the magistrates and swear on oath to what you've just told me?'

'Tell 'um about Samson Harper wanting to shag me morn, noon and night?' She cackled with laughter. 'O' course I 'ull. It's no more than a lot o' women in this town has to put up with from their men. And them bleedin' magistrates' women has to as well, I shouldn't wonder. But from what I've seen of 'um, the old cows should be grateful that any bloke 'ull give 'um a seeing to.'

'No, Mrs Harper, you don't have to speak

about your husband,' Tom explained. 'But you will have to testify that you were in bed with Bonny Southall at the time in question. I realize that such a public confession of adultery might well damage your reputation and good name, and so make you reluctant to do it.'

She raised her fingers in a lewd gesture. 'That's what I gives for me good name and reputation. I'll tell the magistrates straight and true that me and Bonny was shagging each other round about the time that they reckons Eddie Harris was sliced up, and that's the gospel truth, that is. I swear on me babbies' lives to that.'

'Very well, Mrs Harper.' Tom smiled reassuringly. 'I shall make sure that you'll have the opportunity to testify in front of the magistrates when the time comes. However, there are necessary formalities to be completed before the hearing can take place.'

'You should be ashamed of yourself!' she admonished shrilly. 'You didn't oughter have locked him up in the first place. My Bonny is a good man. He wouldn't harm a fly! And what's them formalighty things?'

'Nothing to worry your head about, Mrs Harper,' Tom assured her. 'In the meantime, it's essential that you keep what we have talked about completely secret. No one must learn anything of what's passed between us.' He solemnly placed his finger across his lips.

'Why?' She was puzzled. 'Where's the harm in me telling all them spiteful cows round here whom jealous o' me shagging Bonny, that they can shove it up their arses?'

'Because my Lord Aston is the magistrate who'll be hearing your evidence, Mrs Harper. If he suspects that you had so much as whispered a single word of your testimony to anyone but myself before you gave it to him, then he might simply refuse to accept it, and poor Bonny could end up on the gallows.'

'What's testisummat?' she asked plaintively. 'I wish you'd stop saying them long words, Master Potts.'

'It's what you have been telling me about yourself and Bonny,' he explained patiently, and uneasy guilt assailed him as she smiled and told him trustingly,

'I'll do just what you says, Master Potts. I won't breathe a word to anybody. Not even to me own dad if he was to rise from his grave and beg me to tell him. I knows that you'm being a real friend to me.'

I truly hope that will prove to be the case, you poor soul, he silently wished for her with utter sincerity, as he said aloud, 'I'll say good day to you now, Mrs Harper. All being well, you'll be appearing before Lord Aston in a couple of weeks or so, and hopefully Bonny will be released. So say nothing!'

'I won't, I swear it on me babbies' lives!' She kissed her hand and made the sign of the cross.

Walking down the row, he could not resist turning his head to take a quick look back, and guilt struck again as she smiled and waved before disappearing indoors.

'Can I have a word wi' you, Master Constable?' a ragged-dressed, middle-aged woman hoarsely called to him from the doorway of the bottom cottage.

'Of course Ma'am.' He went up to her.

'Come on in quick! I don't want anybody to see me talking to you.' She beckoned urgently and stepped back inside the room.

Tom followed her, removing his hat and crouching beneath the low sagging ceiling to find himself in a dark, stench-filled hovel.

'Is it true? Has you took Bonny Southall in for murdering Eddie Harris?' Her foul breath gusted and Tom involuntarily averted his head to escape it.

'Has you? Has you took him in?' She scowled impatiently.

'Yes, Master Southall has been arrested.'

'I 'ope he hangs and goes to hell,' she hissed venomously. 'He should have gone there years since, the amount of harm he's done in this town!'

'Can I ask your name, Ma'am?' Tom requested politely.

Words flowed in a rapid saliva-spluttering torrent. 'I'm Sissy Craner. Jenny Harper's me youngest daughter. Samson Harper's been a good husband to her, so he has. And now he's gone for a bloody soldier and left her on the parish, and it's all bloody Bonny Southall's fault, so it is. Filling Jenny's yed with daftness about him loving her. Her's a good little wench at heart but aren't got no bloody sense in her noddle! I told her, I knows for a fact he's got other women on the go. But Jenny won't have it. She reckons I'm just trying to be spiteful. She

307

won't even speak to me now. Silly little bitch that she is!

'I followed him just a couple o' nights past, but he didn't know I was following him, did he? And he went to see a woman. Up atween the Crosses it were. He went into an house that's in the woods atween the Crosses. He knocked on the door and the woman come and opened it, and he went inside, so he did. And a minute after he went in, I saw the candle light shift from the downstairs to the upstairs, and it stayed up there for a good hour or more afore it shifted downstairs again, and you can't try telling me they warn't up there together. Neither of 'um 'ud stay sitting by themselves in the bloody dark 'ud they? And it hadn't come downstairs again for more nor a minute or two, when he come out the house and buggered off. He'd had what he come for, hadn't he! But that sarft little cow of a daughter o' mine won't believe a word I says! It'll all end in tears, so it 'ull!'

She fell silent, agitatedly champing her toothless gums, her worn, lined features a mask of despairing sadness.

'This house he went to, where exactly is it between the Crosses?' Tom queried.

'Oh about midway, I reckon. It's got a couple o' them big old graveyard trees in front. What's they called now? Yews? Yews? Is that what they calls 'um?'

'Yews they are, Mrs Craner,' Tom confirmed thoughtfully. 'This woman, do you know her name? What does she look like?'

The old woman shook her head. 'I don't know

her name, and I aren't got very good sight these days. But I reckon she might have had dark hair, and her looks to be a lot shorter than Bonny.'

Her account held the ring of truth, and opened new vistas for Tom which he needed to think hard about.

'I must be going, Mrs Craner.' He felt great sympathy with her obvious distress, and tried to soothe her. 'Now I'm sure that Jenny will soon come to her senses and cut off all connection with Bonny Southall. So try not to fret too much. It'll all come right in the end for her, I'm sure.'

He walked slowly down the steep hill, mulling over this new information, which was making it even harder for him to clarify his own rampaging ideas, thoughts and suspicions, plus his future course of action.

'Do the ends really justify the means?' he asked himself continually. 'And am I right to use any means to establish that the Rippling Boys are a reality, and not merely a myth? Will I be able to live with myself should it all go wrong?'

Finally, reluctantly, he made a grim decision. 'I must bite the bullet and march on! If it ends badly then the guilt and shame be on my own head.'

Back at the lock-up, Tom went straight to Bonny Southall's cell and opened the observation shutter. Southall sprang up from the pallet, grinning confidently. 'Come to let me out have you? I'm bloody dying for a drink.'

Tom pulled the packets of needles from his satchel and showed them to the other man. 'I found the hiding place. You can get hung for warehouse breaking, or at the very least fourteen years transportation for receiving stolen goods. So what have you done with the rest of these?'

Southall's grin faltered, and he blustered, 'I don't know what you'm talking about. I've got no hiding places in my house and I bought them needles years since. And anyway, what's a few needles got to do with you accusing me o' killing Eddie Harris?'

'I've got the knife that you killed him with. It's one of your grandfather's thatching tools. And these needles have shown me the reason why you and Harris were fighting in the chapel yard, and why you finally killed him. You quarrelled over the share-out after you and he robbed Bates and Chillingworth, didn't you?

'Also, it was you, Eddie Harris and Maggie Murphy who body-snatched Mrs Gould, wasn't it? And I know for a fact that you're having carnal relations with Mary Watts. Was it you that waylaid her husband that night? Did you want to get Johnny Watts out of your way?'

'Bollocks! That's bollocks that is!' Southall's handsome face was drained of colour. 'I swear to God I've never killed nobody, nor body-snatched neither! And I come by them needles honestly. May God strike me dead this instant if I'm lying to you!'

Tom shook his head and spoke in a regretful tone. 'I truly believe that at heart you're not an evil man, Bonny. Why in hell's name did you ever join up with the Rippling Boys? They're implicated in all this thieving and body snatching as well, aren't they, Bonny? But you're the only one of them who's going to hang.'

He waited for the last sentence to take full effect, before adding casually, 'Of course, if you were to turn King's evidence against them, you could save your neck from the hangman.' Then he snapped the shutter closed, and left the lock-up.

Assailed with grave doubts about what he was doing, Tom crossed the Green battling with his sense of moral guilt. Reiterating over and over again, 'The end will justify the means. It will! It must!'

His next call was at the barber shop of Professor Aloysius Parr, who fluttered around Tom as if he were a visiting royal personage.

'My goodness, Constable Potts, you are undoubtedly the hero of the hour. How may I serve you, Sir?'

'I just need a shave, professor.' Tom was taken aback by the diminutive barber's fulsome reception.

'It'll be a privilege to shave you, Sir. A veritable privilege! I'll attend to you this very moment.' Parr turned to the shabby-clad old man who was occupying the barber chair in front of the wall mirror and ordered sharply. 'Shift yourself, Henry Collier. Constable Potts takes precedence above the likes of you. He has matters of great importance to deal with.'

'No, professor!' Tom protested sharply. 'I've plenty of time to spare, so please attend to Master Collier. I'm sure that he's got pressing matters to deal with also.'

'Oh no, Constable Potts!' Collier bared his

stumps of blackened teeth ingratiatingly. 'I'm more than happy to let you go fust.' Grunting with the effort, he levered himself stiffly from the chair and tottered to slump down on the wall bench and sit grinning, nodding continuously and rubbing his swollen arthritic hands together.

Embarrassed by this display of slavish deference, Tom sat down and remained silent while Parr took up brush and soap and deftly lathered Tom's throat and jaws and chin.

'The whole town is ringing with your praises, Constable Potts,' Parr gushed breathily. 'Everyone is filled with admiration at your capture of that evil murderer. How on earth did you manage to unmask him so quickly?'

'I'm sorry but I can't divulge my methods of investigation, professor.'

'No of course you can't. A man of your genius must always keep his methods secret,' Parr sycophantically hastened to acknowledge, and stayed silent for a few moments before his curiosity drove him to ask, 'Has he confessed?'

'Please God, forgive me for what I'm about to do!' Tom prayed silently, drew a deep breath and answered with a deliberate casualness, 'No. He's denying murdering Harris. But he's betrayed his guilt himself without realizing it.'

'How so?'

'By asking me would he escape the hangman if he were to turn King's evidence, and tell all he knows about killings, needle robberies, body snatching and God knows what else.'

Parr took a hissing intake of breath and with eyes narrowed considered what he had heard.

312

Tom remained silent, relaxing his body, closing his eyes and softly humming a tune.

The barber finished lathering, laid aside the brush and took up a razor. As he stropped the blade he queried eagerly, 'But if Southall's asking how he would fare if he turned King's evidence, then surely that means that there's a gang who're committing all these crimes? Who do you think they might be? Could they be those Rippling Boys, do you think?'

Tom gave a quick nod of affirmation, then winked slyly and raised his forefinger to his lips. 'Now professor, you know very well that I cannot divulge such information until the guilty parties are brought to trial. I've already said too much as it is. But I know I can rely on you not to breath a single word to anybody about what I've told you. It must remain a close secret between you and I.'

Tom turned his head to frown sternly at his other listener. 'And you also, Master Collier. You are not to repeat a single word about Southall offering to turn King's evidence against the Rippling Boys. Not a single word, do you understand?'

The old man nodding, rubbing his hands, saliva spattering from his blackened tooth stumps as he shouted excitedly, 'Not a word, Master Potts! Not a word! Not a word! Not a word! Not a word!'

'For God's sake hold your tongue, Henry Collier! You're making noise enough to wake the dead!' Aloysius Parr admonished severely, and the old man's shouts quietened to a muted

313

muttering beneath his breath,

'Not a word! Not a word! Not a word!'

Tom made no further conversation, and when shaved he paid the two pennies fee and left the shop exchanging mutual expressions of appreciation and thanks with its proprietor.

He was satisfied that the seed was well sown, knowing very well that neither Parr nor Collier would be able to resist passing on to their cronies what he had just told them. Those cronies would tell others, and as the story passed from one to another and another and another it would become wildly distorted and exaggerated.

'The bait's been laid, let's see who rises to take it.' Tom's sense of satisfaction was interlaced with a degree of foreboding. 'I now have to go and tell Joseph Blackwell what I'm doing. How will he react, I wonder?'

Thirty-Nine

Seated behind his study desk, Joseph Blackwell's reception of Tom's news was initially disapproving.

'I fear that you've acted too hastily this time, Master Potts. This is badly done. Southall will have to be released because you have no certain proof to present to the magistrates that he killed Harris, or the Murphy woman.

'It's fortunate for both of us that my Lord

314

Aston is in London, because if he were here now he'd take pleasure in asserting that this arrest vindicates his belief that you are a fool, and that I am greatly misguided in putting my trust in you.'

'With all respect, Sir, I'm not a fool, and you're not misguided in trusting me,' Tom contradicted forcefully, and pulled the canvas packets of needles from his satchel to lay them on the desk.

'I found these in a concealed hiding place in Southall's bedroom. If Southall came by them honestly, there would have been no need to hide them away like he has. They are proof that he is somehow involved in that robbery, and at the very least we can now hold him on a charge of receiving stolen goods. Also, the knife found in Harris is most definitely a possession of Southall's. His motive for killing Harris could have been a dispute between them over the division of their loot.'

The other man opened his mouth to speak, and Tom held up his hand to forestall interruption, 'I beg you to hear me out, Sir, before you say anything more.'

Blackwell frowned, but then grudgingly nodded in silent assent.

Tom doggedly pressed on, 'I strongly suspect that the bulk of the needles stolen from Bates and Chillingworth are hidden in John Watts's coffin. Now I saw Watts's corpse prior to the burial, and it was so sadly wasted that he would not have weighed more than a child and could have been carried with ease by two men only. I watched six men carry the coffin to the grave, and it struck me at the time that it seemed to be unduly heavy from the way they struggled to bear it. The extra weight could be the needles. If that is so, then Jonathan Crowther must have been fully aware, and party to it.

'I also suspect that Watts didn't die as a result of the injuries he received previously, or from apoplexy. I think he was poisoned, as was Maggie Murphy. Again, Crowther and/or his associates would have had opportunity to commit both crimes.

'In truth, Sir, I've come to the conclusion that the Rippling Boys do indeed exist as an organized criminal gang, and that Crowther is the likely leader of it. I also believe that members of this gang, two of them being Harris and Southall, have committed the various recent robberies and body-snatchings in this district. That completes my report, Sir.'

'Dear God above!' Blackwell exclaimed disparagingly. 'I have to say, Master Potts, that your flights of fancy seem to have become excessively vivid of late. Are you indeed letting your imagination run away with you? Pray tell me how you propose to amass the evidence to prove all these pipe dreams in a court of law?'

Tom was simultaneously feeling both hurt and resentment at this unpalatably contemptuous reaction from a man he so highly respected and admired. He resisted the almost overwhelming impulse to protest, and instead forced himself to answer quietly and firmly, 'I've already set in motion a course of action which I hope, speaking figuratively, will set the cat among the pigeons.'

'And what might that be?' Blackwell's face was grim.

'I've set in train a rumour that Bonny Southall is to turn King's evidence against the Rippling Boys.'

Blackwell frowned. 'What exactly do you expect to happen as a result of that? And have you considered that you may well have put Southall at grave risk of harm from his fellow rogues?'

Tom's resolve momentarily wavered, and he hesitated for a few seconds before summoning his nerve to state with simple honesty, 'I really don't know what to expect, Sir. But desperate straits call for desperate measures. I'm hoping that when this rumour reaches the ears of the Rippling Boys, they will feel driven to act in haste and take risks. I'm sure that the needles are in Watts's coffin and that they will try to remove them, possibly this very night. John Hollis and myself can both be there ready to ambush them, because I don't believe that Southall will be initially targeted by the gang. Watts's grave will be their top priority.'

Blackwell closed his eyes, steepled his fingers and rested his chin upon their tips.

Tom could feel his own fingers twitching involuntarily, as he nervously waited for a further outburst of denigration from his employer.

After what seemed endless hours to Tom, but was in fact less than a minute, Blackwell lowered his hands and asked, 'And Southall? How do you propose to keep a guard on the lock-up during the night hours when you and Hollis will be on grave-watch?'

'I intend to pay old Jimmy Grier to act as watchman while I'm away at night, Sir. I shall give him strict orders that he's not to unlock the doors for anyone until I return. If any attempt is made to break into the lock-up and free Southall, then Grier can raise the alarm by merely shouting and ringing his bell from an upstairs window. He doesn't need to put himself at any risk.'

'Well the lock-up was designed to defy any attempts to break in. It's a virtual fortress and cost the parish a damned fortune to build,' Blackwell grumbled sourly.

His earlier condemnatory attitude appeared to be softening somewhat, and sensing this, Tom ventured tentatively, 'With your permission, Sir, if the gang makes no attempt tonight then I'd like to open Watts grave myself. If it contains the needles, I can transfer them to the lock-up for safe keeping. At least then, no matter what the final outcome of my actions, Messrs Bates and Chillingworth will have the satisfaction of recovering their goods.'

'Why not open it immediately?'

'These men are not fools, Sir. They'll have been keeping a close check on the mound. If they come tonight and discover the slightest sign that it's been disturbed it will warn them off; and I can't arrest anyone for merely walking through the graveyard, no matter at what hour that may be. I need to catch them breaking open

318

the coffin.'

'Very well. But if you find that Watts is in sole occupation, what then?' Now Blackwell seemed more curious than condemnatory.

Heartened by this, Tom answered without hesitation, 'If that proves to be the case, Sir, then I shall reconsider my strategy.' He risked a lighter note. 'Like the Duke of Wellington's plans of campaign, my own plans are fashioned like a harness of rope. If the harness breaks, then I shall just tie a knot in it, and immediately plan another course of action.'

'This is not the time for levity, Master Potts,' Blackwell admonished sternly.

'No, of course it isn't, Sir. My apologies!' Tom replied humbly.

The merest hint of a wintry smile twitched Blackwell's thin lips. He made no reply, but instead took up a quill pen, dipped it into the inkwell and bending his head, began to write in the open ledger on the desk before him.

Tom was nonplussed at this behaviour. 'What in hell's name is he about? Why is he deliberately ignoring me?' His patience became increasingly strained as time stretched and he watched the pen dip into the inkwell and scratch across the large page once, twice, three times, four times, five times, until driven beyond endurance he coughed deliberately and enquired, 'Sir? Do you wish to say anything to me?'

'Only this, Constable Potts.' Blackwell did not raise his head and the pen continued to scratch across the page. 'Within the hour I have to set out for London to join my Lord Aston, and shall

319

unfortunately be detained there in his company for some time.

'So whatever you decide to do, on your own head be it! If your current strategy leads to disaster, then I shall disclaim any prior knowledge of your plan of action; and furthermore, humbly acknowledge to my Lord Aston that his scathing opinion of you is fully justified. If your plan results in success, then I shall modestly claim some plaudits.

'I bid you good day, Constable Potts, and kindly take those filthy packages with you, they're making my desk unsightly.'

'Good day, Sir.' Tom, relieved that Blackwell had not vetoed his plans, picked up the packages and departed to go in search of John Hollis.

As he walked along the road fronting St Stephen's Chapel, young Charles Scambler called from the doorway of his shop, 'Hold on a second, Constable Potts. I've just taken a fresh-baked batch from the oven. Would you like to take your loaf now, or shall I have it delivered to the lock-up for you?'

Suspecting sarcasm, Tom halted and the baker hurried across the road smiling sycophantically, 'By Christ, Constable, that was fine work you did to catch that murdering bastard Southall. I said to everybody, so I did, that you're the smartest man in this parish; no, in the whole of the Needle District, without a doubt. We should thank our lucky stars, I told them, that you'm our constable. Please do me the honour of accepting my sincere congratulations. And I'm confident that I'm voicing them on behalf of every respectable man and woman in this whole parish.'

'Thank you, Master Scambler.' Tom nodded coolly. 'And you may deliver my loaf to the lock-up later this afternoon.'

'It'll be a privilege, Constable Potts.' Scambler bowed, and as Tom went to move on added, 'It's all over the town that Southall's turned King's evidence against the Rippling Boys. That'll have the buggers quaking in their boots, won't it? Knowing that you'll be giving 'um lodgings in the lock-up afore they eats many more dinners.'

Tom was both surprised and gratified at the amazing speed with which his planted rumour was already spreading. He nodded and replied simply, 'Good news travels fast, Master Scambler.'

The other man chuckled. 'Ah well, Constable Potts, you know what they says about Redditch, don't you? If a man farts in Bredon, then the stink reaches Crabbs Cross afore the last bit o' the trump has left his arse.'

Tom walked on, murmuring in wry acknowledgement. 'That's very true Master Scambler, very true indeed.'

Forty

Monday, late afternoon, 4 September 1826

A short distance from the hamlet of Webheath, the unpretentious two-storied red-brick house stood at the end of a narrow, twisting lane and was hidden from casual view by a large copse of trees and a surround of high laurel hedge.

Andrew Adamson reined in his mount on the gravelled forecourt and sat frowning in puzzlement at the closed shuttered windows and the padlocked front door. No smoke rose from the chimneys and the only sounds of life were the distant barkings of dogs.

Booted feet crunched on the gravel behind him. 'Hello, doctor.'

Startled, Adamson turned in the saddle and exclaimed. 'Dammee, you gave me a shock! Where did you spring from?'

'I was setting a few snares in the trees. I'm partial to a nice young rabbit. My uncle should be here shortly,' Benjamin Fairfax told him.

'Why is it all closed up?' Adamson indicated the house.

'When we moved the girls on, Annie Kelper wanted to go and visit her old mam and dad, so Uncle Jonno gave her a couple of days' holiday.'

'Your uncle's note said that I was wanted urgently to check over a pair of new girls. Where are they?' Adamson asked.

'They'll be here very shortly. Sally Dykes is bringing them down from Brummagem. My uncle is meeting up with her at the White Hart.' Fairfax scowled. 'I can't stand that old cow! If it was down to me I wouldn't do business with her! She's too fond of trying to pass off damaged goods on to us.'

Adamson tapped the side of his nose with his forefinger and winked knowingly. 'I'm far too fly to fall for any of Sally Dykes's tricks, Ben. I can always discover if a whore's poxed no matter how cunningly she hides it. That's why your uncle employs my services.'

The other man's answering tone contained a measure of hostility. 'My uncle's far too fly to fall for anybody's tricks, be they woman or man, doctor. Or in his employment or not, as the case may be.'

From round the bend in the lane with a thudding of hooves and rattling of iron-rimmed wheels, the smartly painted pony trap of Jonathan Crowther came into view.

Fairfax grinned wolfishly. 'Here's my uncle come, doctor, and that's my brother Thomas with him.'

'But where are Sally Dykes and the girls?' Adamson frowned. His companion's manner was making him feel somewhat uneasy, even a touch apprehensive.

Fairfax made no reply and walked to meet the new arrivals, taking hold of the pony's bridle and leading it to the hitching rail in front of the house.

Jonathan Crowther greeted Adamson with bluff camaraderie. 'Thanks for coming at such short notice, my boy. We'll go inside and make ourselves comfortable, shall we? I've something very important to discuss with you. Benjamin will see to your horse.'

He unlocked the padlock and went into the house, closely followed by Thomas Fairfax. Adamson dismounted and handed the reins to Benjamin, then began to unstrap his medical chest from the rear of the saddle.

'I'll bring your box in for you, doctor. You go straight indoors now because my uncle's very eager to talk to you about a certain matter.'

The wolfish smile curved Benjamin's lips again, and once more Adamson experienced a frisson of unease. When he entered the well-furnished room, Jonathan Crowther was already seated in an armchair and Thomas Fairfax was opening the internal window blinds and pulling the curtains aside to let in the rays of the sinking sun.

'Stand there, my boy, so that the light will allow me to see your face clearly,' Crowther invited smilingly, pointing to a place directly in front of him. 'My poor old eyes are not as sharp as they used to be.'

Adamson obeyed and essayed a quip. 'I wouldn't have thought that seeing my ugly face clearly will bring any great pleasure to you, Master Crowther.'

Ben Fairfax came into the room without the

medical chest, and the two brothers ranged themselves on each side of Adamson.

Still smiling pleasantly, Crowther requested. 'Now tell me, my boy, how long is it that you've been shagging my stepdaughter?'

The young man's jaw dropped with shock, and Crowther's smile metamorphosed into a threatening snarl, 'Don't you try gammoning me with denials, you little cunt! You were being watched when you went into the cottage last Saturday night, and when you came out of it Sunday noontime. So unless you want my nephews to beat it out of you, you'd best tell me how long it's been going on between you and her?'

Ashen-faced with fear, Adamson's voice faltered. 'I've not been having any sexual relationships with her. We're just friends, that's all. That night we were drinking and smoking some opium, and I passed out on the floor and didn't wake up until morning.'

'I'll kill you if you keep on lying to me!' Crowther shouted and in one fluid motion produced, cocked and aimed a small pistol at the other man's head.

'Arrghhh!' Adamson emitted a cry of terror and cowered back, hands held up in front of his face. 'No! Please! Please! I beg you! Nooo!'

The twins grabbed his arms, brutally twisting them up behind his back and forcing him down on to his knees.

'Now, how long have you been shagging her?' Crowther growled.

'I've not been! I've not!' Tears ran down the young man's face as he choked out terrified denials. 'I swear to you, I've never shagged her. She and I are just friends. I went there that night to help her, not to shag her. I would never shag her!'

Crowther nodded to Benjamin, who immediately rammed his thumb against Adamson's eye. 'Arrghhh! No! No! I beg you! Nooooo!' Adamson shrieked piteously.

'The truth!' Crowther demanded. 'The truth, or you lose that eye; and that's just for starters.'

'I've never shagged her! I've been treating her for her complaint, that's all! I've been doctoring her.'

'Doctoring her? Why? What's up with her?' Crowther scowled suspiciously.

Shaking with fear, Adamson panted. 'The pox. She's badly poxed.'

'What?' Crowther roared incredulously. 'What did you say?'

'The truth!' Adamson's head dropped low, and he began to sob, choking out brokenly, 'I'm telling you the truth! Mary has got the syphilis. I've been treating her for it ever since I moved here. That's the truth, the God's honest truth! I've been treating her with mercury. Go and ask her yourself if you don't believe me.'

'And if I ask her, and she says you're lying, how can I discover which of you is telling the truth?' Crowther challenged.

'She has the reddish macular rash on her body and limbs, and inside her mouth there are sores.' Sheer desperation enveloped the young doctor, and lifting his head to meet Crowther's threatening glare, he babbled frantically, 'And sores are developing on her external genitals, and a profusion of weeping papules on the moist surfaces of the genital and anal regions. She's entering the secondary stage of the syphilis, and there's nothing I can do to cure her. The mercury may well retard the progress of the disease, but it won't effect a cure. Also, it has serious side effects. Before very long her teeth will turn shades of green and begin to rot and fall out.

'Then when the tertiary stage of the disease is reached, her features will become necrosed and deformed, and she may well become paralysed, or insane, or both.'

Adamson drew a long shuddering breath. 'All I've done is to try and help your stepdaughter to the best of my abilities, Master Crowther. I've not had any sexual congress with her. I've only ever been a friend who is greatly distressed by knowing the awful sufferings which lie ahead of her.'

A terrible anger was burning within Jonathan Crowther, but he mustered all his self-control, and nodded. 'Very well, I accept that you're telling me the truth.'

Adamson exhaled a loud gasp as his tense body sagged with relief. 'Thank you, Master Crowther. Thank you!'

'Lift him up and get him a chair,' Crowther ordered.

When Adamson, overwhelmed by relief, was sitting slumped in an armchair facing him, Crowther questioned, 'Was it Watts who infected my stepdaughter?'

Adamson shook his head. 'She's never blamed

anyone for it directly to me, but ... but...' Visibly apprehensive, his voice trailed into silence, until Crowther frowning, urged him, 'Come on, man, spit it out!'

Adamson continued haltingly, 'Well, Master Crowther, when I was treating John Watts I saw no indications that he was syphilitic.' He swallowed hard, coughed nervously and added, 'And she did mention once when we were smoking opium, that for some considerable time she has been friendly with a man named Southall. Bonny Southall.'

As Crowther fully realized the implications of what the other man had said, he lost his iron self-control. He got to his feet and walked out to the forecourt, where after a brief while Thomas Fairfax came to join him.

'Are you all right, Uncle?'

Crowther's eyes were murderous, his voice a menacing rasp. 'She's played me for a fool, Nephew. I've been putting up with all her moods and tantrums and spending my money on her fine clothes and whatnots. And all this time she's been laughing at me behind my back and playing the whore with Bonny Southall and that little cunt in there.'

'What will you do to them?' Fairfax asked.

'Bonny Southall is already bound for the gallows or for transport, Nephew, unless we can get to him first.' Crowther grinned evilly. 'But if by some mischance he escapes us and the hangman, then being transported won't save him from me. I've got a lot of old acquaintances out in Van Diemen's Land.'

'And Mary?'

'Mary, my beautiful stepdaughter? What's to be done with Mary?' Crowther seemed to be musing aloud. 'Well, I'll just have to give that some thought.

'If Adamson has told the truth, then the syphilis will take a very sweet revenge for me. I'll keep her locked up in a secluded place. I'll fill her room with mirrors so that wherever she turns her head she'll be seeing her teeth and face and body rotting away. Every day I'll be reminding her that if she hadn't played false with me, she'd be living in luxury. My satisfaction will be watching the pox bring down the torments of hell upon her. But until that day comes, I'll still have my tracker dog keeping a watch on her.'

'And what about him?' Fairfax jerked his head towards the window of the room where Adamson waited. 'Do you think he might lay a complaint to the magistrates against us for ill treating him? Don't forget his uncle's a powerful man.'

'He'll lay no complaint.' Crowther spoke with absolute assurance. 'He knows very well which side his bread is buttered on. I shall now go inside and apologize most sincerely for thinking wrongly of him. I shall most heartily thank him for his care of my beloved daughter, and beg him to continue treating her at my expense.'

He chuckled grimly. 'And when the time suits me, I'll destroy the little cunt.'

'My Christ, Uncle Jonno!' Fairfax exclaimed admiringly. 'Remind me never to get on the wrong side of you!' Arm in arm they went back into the house, a devoted uncle and nephew.

Forty-One

The night was dark and stormy and sheets of rain were being hurled upon the land by the gusting winds.

'Bonny? Can you hear me? Bonny?'

The voice came from outside the lock-up wall, and Southall immediately rose from the pallet and called back through the grille.

'I hear you.'

'Listen carefully, and do what I tell you.' The voice gave brief, rapid instructions.

Southall grinned with relief, waited for a few seconds, then began to hammer on his cell door and bawl at the top of his voice, 'Jimmy, come here. I needs to speak to you. Come here, Jimmy.'

Upstairs in Tom's room, old Jimmy Grier, wearing his full regalia of town crier, was sitting half-dozing by the glowing grate. When he heard the din from below, he lit the lantern and shuffled laboriously downstairs to open the observation shutter, grumbling petulantly. 'Bloody hell's fire, Bonny, what does you want? Me rheumatics am giving me gyp, and you fetching me down here is making 'um worse. Potts said that I aren't got to open this door no matter what happens. He said that he's fed and watered you,

330

and give you a bucket to piss and shit in, so there's nothing you needs.'

'And what's he give you, Jimmy, to make the hours pass?' Bonny grinned. 'I'll bet he aren't give you a bottle of the good stuff to keep you jolly.'

'No he aren't!' Grier confirmed resentfully. 'And I won't be getting paid for this night's work until the end of the bloody month, so I won't be having any bottle 'til then, and I'm bloody gasping for a sup o' the pongalo.'

Southall held out his hand and jingled coins. 'There's enough here to get us a bottle apiece, Jimmy. I'll have gin, and you can have whatever you fancies.'

'I can't let you out, Bonny.' Grier shook his head. 'Potts told me I warn't to let you out o' this cell, not even if you was a dying.'

'I'm not asking you to let me out of here, am I, you silly old bugger. All I'm asking is for you to go to the Red Lion and buy a bottle of gin for me, and a bottle of whatever you fancies for yourself. That can't do any harm, can it?'

'I been ordered to keep all the doors locked and not to open 'um for anybody or anything! Not if it was the Angel Gabriel come a knocking. Not even if the bloody last trump was astounding!'

'It'll only take you a second to slip out o' the door and you can leave everything locked up behind you, and you won't be gone for more than a minute at most. There's no harm can come o' that, is there?' Southall jingled the coins again, and coaxed. 'Herbie Willis took delivery o' some brandy the other day, Jimmy, and you knows how fond you am of a drop of brandy. Well, for the sake of walking a few yards, you can have a whole bottle to yourself.'

When Grier still hesitated, Southall scowled irritably and made as if to turn away, 'Oh bugger you then! Stay thirsty!'

'No!' The old man quavered in alarm. 'No, I'll go.'

Chuckling with satisfaction, Southall passed the coins over. 'Be as quick as you can, Jimmy, because me throat's as dry as an old maid's cunt.'

Grier shuffled to the front door, the feeble flame of his lantern casting a dim glow of light before him. He turned the key in the lock and pulled the door ajar, cursing as the strongly gusting wind lifted the tricorn hat from his head and sent it flying back along the corridor. Grier turned to see where it had fallen, and in that instant a shadowy black figure loomed from the night and a cudgel smashed against the old man's head.

'Where are you, Bonny?'

'I'm in this 'un.' Bonny Southall peered through the observation shutter, grinning with relieved delight. 'I knew you wouldn't let me down.'

The pistol barked and a blood-gouting hole appeared in Southall's forehead. The shutter closed up and seconds later the front door of the lock-up slammed shut.

Forty-Two

In the early hours of the morning, the storm passed over, the wind dropped to a soughing moaning and the rain abruptly ceased.

Crouched under the dripping branches of the thick hedgerow, saturated to their skins, bodies stiff with cold, Tom and John Hollis were maintaining their night-long vigil.

'It must be getting near dawn, Tom. I don't think we'll be receiving any visitors now, do you?' Hollis whispered.

Tom was reluctant to give up. 'We'll give it a while longer.'

Many more minutes passed and dawn had come before Tom disappointedly accepted that the likelihood of any interlopers appearing was virtually non-existent.

'I think you're right, John. We're just wasting time now.' He pushed free of the branches and stood upright, groaning audibly as his stiffened joints and muscles painfully stretched, and joked ruefully, 'Another night like this and I'm going to be asking old Jimmy what's best for soothing the rheumatics.'

'Ohhh Jesus! I'm as stiff as a board!' Hollis

333

complained, also stretching and grimacing with pain. 'What do we do next, Tom?'

'We'll take a quick look and see what Johnny Watts is sharing his coffin with. He's only about a foot deep, so we can get the job done and the mound repaired before anybody is likely to be about.' Tom smiled wryly. 'The exercise will warm us up, my friend.'

They had brought two spades with them and it took only a couple of minutes to dig down to the head of the coffin lid, then Tom used the sharp-edged shovel blade to splinter and lever off several shards of the thin wood. As he knelt on his knees and reached down to pull the shards out of the coffin lid, he exclaimed in surprise, 'There's no stink coming off him, John.'

'Well it's been coldish weather since he was buried, so perhaps it's slowed the rotting,' Hollis suggested.

Tom lifted the shards aside and peered down into the narrow gap but could distinguish nothing in the darkness of the coffin's interior. He cautiously inserted his hand and his fingers and encountered only a mixture of loose soil and stones.

'What in hell's name is going on here?' he hissed in shock, and rose to grab the spade and frantically shovel dirt until all the coffin length was cleared. Again the sharp-edge blade hacked and splintered until the entire lid could be torn off and the contents of the coffin laid fully open.

Two or three inches of soil and stones covered the floor of the coffin.

Crouching low, Tom plunged both hands into

its innards, carefully sifting and lifting handfuls of the spoil to examine it closely. At last he found what he was searching for: several loose needles which had escaped from their packaging.

He clambered to his feet and with angry self-disgust spat out, 'If I hadn't been such a bloody coward I could have caught the bastards! They must have come back here later that same night and dug the needles out, then rebuilt the mound so that no one would see it had been tampered with. They must have been laughing their heads off, while I was lying in a bloody ditch shaking like a leaf! Bloody worthless cowardly fool that I am!'

'What's happened to Watts's body, do you think?' Hollis wondered aloud.

'Whatever has happened to it, then those who were family to him must know,' Tom said, and his self-directed anger abruptly stilled as the memories came back of his dealings with the dead man's closest relative, and coupled with those memories the earlier uneasy suspicions rose unbidden to nag at him.

After a long pause he told his friend, 'John, will you please fill the grave in and reshape the mound again. I'll see you back at the lock-up later.'

Head bent deep in thought, he walked slowly away and out from the graveyard. He turned westwards along the winding lane leading past the Forge Mill to the turnpike road and his pace quickened, 'I need to put a few more questions to Bonny Southall straightaway.'

* * *

When Tom reached the lock-up, he realized to his chagrin that he had left his own personal door key in his bedroom, but consoled himself, 'Never mind, Jimmy surely has sense enough to find the key board if I tell him where it is.'

He tugged the bell rod to set the bells jangling, and waited.

No one came in answer.

He tugged the bell rod two more times, and waited.

No one came in answer.

'God above! Where is he?' Tom hissed impatiently and walked round to the side of the building to shout up at the windows. 'Jimmy, will you wake up and open the door? Jimmy, are you there?"

The casement opened and Jimmy Grier's head appeared swathed in towelling.

'What's the matter with you? Are you suffering from a migraine?' Tom questioned.

'What's that?' Grier quavered. 'What's a moigrine?'

'A headache!' Tom gritted between clenched teeth. 'Now will you please come and unlock the door.'

'What's you done wi' your key?' Grier wanted to know.

'Never mind that now, just come down and unlock the bloody door, will you.' Tom was struggling against losing his temper with the old man.

'It warn't my fault,' Jimmy Grier moaned plaintively. 'I opened the door and me hat blew off, and when I turned round to look for it some bugger hit me over me yed and knocked me cold! I could have been killed! I was bleedin' like a stuck pig, so I was. I could ha' been killed, so I could. I managed to crawl up here and aren't been able to step foot outside this room since, I'm so shook up!'

A rush of foreboding swept over Tom. 'Is Bonny secure?'

'I'm fucked if I know,' Grier mumbled.

Tom's foreboding became conviction, and he fought to keep calm. 'Just come down and let me in, Jimmy.'

In the gloom of the cell, the blood was a black halo spreading out from Southall's head. Guilt for Southall's death was the overriding emotion throbbing through Tom as he led the old man back upstairs, seated him and carefully unwrapped the swathe of towelling. There was a bruised lump left by the impact of the blow on Grier's bald pate, but to Tom's relief it did not look to be a serious injury, and when he checked Grier's eyes there was no sign of an enlarged pupil to suggest any injury to the brain.

He questioned Grier at length but the old man was adamant that he had seen nothing of his assailant. Knowing that it was pointless to upbraid the old man, Tom finally sighed in acceptance. 'Very well, Jimmy. What's done is done, and we'll say no more about it at present. You stay here and I'll go and fetch you a measure of brandy from the pub. That should help your head to heal.'

'Can you make it more than a measure?' Grier

quavered plaintively. 'I'm feeling very shaky.'

'Then a full tumbler it shall be,' Tom agreed.

As he reached the bottom of the stairs and began to walk along the corridor he noticed the trail of muddy footprints that his own boots had carried in from the mud of the roadway, and realized, 'It was raining since early afternoon yesterday and the roads were muddy well before darkness fell! Whoever it was who shot Bonny must have left boot prints!'

He immediately began to scan the flagstones leading from the entrance door and found he could distinguish a separate patterning of dried mud smudges intermingled with those made by his own boots ... He dashed back upstairs and Grier exclaimed in shock, 'Bloody 'ell, you've been quick!'

'I'm not gone yet,' Tom gasped, snatching up his investigation bag and rushing downstairs again. He opened both front and rear doors wide to cast the daylight across the floor, then sinking down on his hands and knees began to carefully examine the trail of smudges. He minutely studied each one through the magnifying glass, making careful measurements, painstakingly copying some of the clearest with a charcoal pencil and paper.

More than an hour had passed before he sat back on his heels, mulling over what he had found. Prints of footwear smaller than his own which appeared to have squared toes.

'I'm vaguely reminded of something. But what is it?' he asked himself.

'Has you fetched me brandy yet?' Tom started

in shock when Grier's voice sounded from behind him. He clambered to his feet and apologized.

'I'm sorry, Jimmy, it went clean out of my mind.' He reached into his pocket and pulled out some coins. 'Look, I have to wait here for John Hollis to come. So you take this money and buy your brandy. Then you'd best go straight home and rest. You've had a bad shock and need to take it easy.'

The old man greedily eyed the coins. 'But what shall I say if anybody asks me about Bonny?'

Tom hesitated before replying in resignation. 'Tell them the truth, Jimmy, and you can also tell them that I'm admitting it to be all my fault for not warning you sufficiently about what might happen.'

He counted out sixpence and handed it to the old man. 'There, that should be enough for a tumbler full.'

After Jimmy Grier had shuffled away, Tom unlocked the cell door and stood staring down at the dead man, guilt and remorse tearing at him. 'Your death is my fault, Bonny, and I shall blame myself for it for the rest of my life. All I can do is swear to you on my father's grave that I'll not rest until I've brought your murderer to justice.'

An hour later John Hollis came to the lock-up, soaked through and liberally plastered in mud. While he sat before the fire drying his wet clothing, Tom quietly told him what had happened, and how guilty he felt because of it.

'I feel that I murdered Bonny Southall myself, John.'

'That's nonsense!' Hollis stated forcefully. 'Southall paid the price for his own sins. He was a vicious predator who only got what he and his ilk deserve. Now he's dead there'll be many decent people who'll be able to live out their lives in peace.'

He paused for a moment, then added. 'The Rippling Boys have finally been forced to come out from the shadows, Tom.'

Tom shook his head. 'They're still completely out-foxing me.'

Hollis's eyes widened with surprise and he instantly protested, 'I can't believe that. I'm sure you've got something up your sleeve.'

Tom grimaced ruefully. 'All I've got up my sleeve at this moment is desperation. It's as if I'm blundering through a pitch-black tunnel, and periodically deluding myself that I can see glimmers of light at the end of it.'

Hollis stayed silent for some time digesting what he had been told, then requested, 'Tell me about those glimmers of light. It could be that you haven't been deluding yourself concerning them. Perhaps they're true insights. Let me hear your thoughts, my friend.'

Tom grimaced and told him reluctantly, 'Well, for what it's worth, I think Jonathan Crowther is the guiding hand of the Rippling Boys, and that Southall and Harris were one-time members of the gang. Perhaps Crowther had Southall kill Harris for some reason. On the other hand Southall could have killed Harris because of a quarrel over Maggie Murphy. Southall's notorious for chasing anything that wears a skirt and has a pulse.'

'I'm beginning to feel that way myself, it's been so long since I've tasted a woman's sweetness,' John Hollis chuckled.

'You and I both, John,' Tom grimaced ruefully. 'But I'm feared that any search for romance must wait. The first thing we have to do is to make enquiries, to find if anyone was seen coming in here or leaving.'

'Before we go out again, can we have some breakfast?' Hollis beseeched plaintively. 'My stomach thinks my throat's been cut. And an hour's nap wouldn't go amiss either.'

Tom nodded. 'Breakfast and an hour's nap it shall be, and then we start work.'

Forty-Three

Tuesday evening, 5 September

'Eeeny meeny miney mo,
Potts caught Bonny by his toe.
But the Rippling Boys came out to play,
And sent poor Bonny on his way!'

The jeering chant and raucous laughter had dogged Tom and Hollis all that day as they trudged the town and the neighbouring Crosses fruitlessly making enquiries and seeking witnesses who might have seen something.

Now shielded by the dusk of evening, a rowdy gang had gathered at the lock-up and were amusing themselves by gleefully roaring the chant, then ringing the doorbells and running away.

Tom was sitting in his room in company with John Hollis. After one such visitation by the rowdies, as the bells' jangling died away, Tom shrugged resignedly. 'Ah well, they'll soon get tired of baiting me.'

Even as he spoke, the bells jangled again, but this time did not cease after brief seconds but continued dinning. 'Bugger this for a game of soldiers!' John Hollis growled angrily, and before Tom could move to stop him, he jumped up and ran downstairs.

Tom chased after him. Hollis slammed the door open and darted outside. Close at his heels, Tom cannoned into his suddenly motionless friend.

Standing by the bell rod, Amy Danks furiously berated them.

'Have you both gone loony? Coming charging out here like a pair of mad bulls! For two pins I'd box your ears, you great lummoxes!'

'I'm sorry!' Hollis stammered. 'I'm sorry, I thought it was somebody else!'

Her mood altered mercurially and she giggled, 'I bet you thought it was Lady Godiva, didn't you, and you came charging out to take a close look, like the dirty old man you are.'

Tom, uncomfortably aware that curious eyes

were watching from the surrounding shadows, tentatively intervened, 'Would you like to come inside, Amy?'

'Would you like to come inside, Amy?' she mimicked sarcastically, poking her tongue out at him. 'Oh no, Master Potts! I much prefer standing here with the whole town watching and listening to my private business!'

'Please Amy, we're both of us truly sorry if we startled you. Please come inside.' Tom said.

She tossed her head, a smile playing around her moist pink lips, as she released the bell rod and stepped up to them to demand, 'Do I have to climb over or crawl under you to come inside?'

'Sorry! Sorry! Sorry!' the two men chorused in embarrassed unison as they hastily moved back to allow her free passage.

'Close the door and go away, Master Hollis. I wish to speak to Master Potts in private,' she commanded regally, and John Hollis hastened to obey.

The dim light of the solitary lantern hanging from the ceiling midway along the corridor was not strong enough for Tom to distinguish any nuances of expression in her face, but when she moved close to him the fresh young scents of her body and breath filled his nostrils, and the warmth of her proximity filled him with poignant yearning. Driven by intense emotion, he opened his mouth to tell her how much he loved her. But before he could utter more than her name she laid her hand across his mouth. 'No, Tom Potts. Just listen!'

He nodded acquiescence, and she told softly,

343

'The whole parish is mocking at you yet again, Tom Potts. But I'm not. I'm come here to tell you that you must make them eat their words. When you've done that, then I might consider going courting with you once more.'

She moved her hand to the back of his neck and pulled his head down to lightly kiss his lips, then turned, pulled open the door and went running across the Green, skirt and petticoats swirling high around her slender legs.

For the first time that day Tom's heart lightened, as with poignant yearning he watched her disappear into the night.

Forty-Four

Tuesday night, 5 September

John Hollis lay on the bed reading by candlelight while Tom sat on the stool by the window immersed in thought. Since Amy's visit, his mood had fluctuated wildly between surges of elation that she had come, and depression engendered by the death of Bonny Southall.

At this moment, his thoughts were centred on Amy when without any conscious volition remembrance lanced into Tom's mind.

'The latest fashion! All the rage!' he shouted aloud, and jumping to his feet, began to pace backwards and forwards, frowning in concentration, his fists so hard-clenched that his fingernails threatened to draw blood from the palms of his hands.

Hollis stared concernedly at him, but remained silent.

Tom abruptly halted by the bed and bent to lift the two greasy, blackened, canvas-wrapped packages of needles he had stowed beneath it. Next, he took his magnifying glass from his investigation bag, and holding one of the packages close to the candle, studied its surface, then laid the package aside, took up the other and subjected it to the same intense scrutiny, continuously repeating this procedure as one minute succeeded another, and another, and another.

A battle was raging within Tom's mind as his contrary opposing traits of timid caution and wild impulse fought for domination. Finally the battle ended, and staring intently into his friend's eyes he declared, 'I've been looking in the wrong direction, John, but now I'm going to act upon my instincts. If I'm mistaken in doing so, then I'll remain a parish laughing-stock for the rest of my days. So I must do it alone.'

'No you will not!' Hollis shook his head in emphatic negation. 'Where you go, I shall go with you. We stick together and win or lose together.'

He jumped to his feet and proffered his hand, 'Seal the bargain with me, Tom.'

When Tom made no move, Hollis grabbed his hand and pumped it vigorously up and down, laughing triumphantly. 'There now, our bargain is sealed!'

At this moment, Tom loved Hollis as he would the brother he had always longed for but never possessed, and with tears of emotion blurring his sight he muttered hoarsely, 'You have my word on it, my friend. Our bargain is sealed.'

'So, what are your instincts driving us to do?' Hollis demanded.

'Firstly to go counting, John.' Tom replied solemnly. 'To go counting by moonlight. But if I talk about it any more, then it will begin to seem even more of an insane notion.' He looked at his pocket watch. 'It's just turned half past eleven o'clock, There won't be many people abroad, so let's go.'

They pocketed a loaded pistol each, and Tom took up his crowned staff, while Hollis favoured a heavy cudgel. Two sets of shackles, padlocks and keys apiece carried in shoulder-slung satchels completed their equipment.

Downstairs, Tom extinguished the corridor lantern and opened the door just wide enough to see through. There was a full moon but scudding clouds blotted out its light at intervals, and the two men waited until a cloud shadowed the land before slipping out and away from the building. Moving stealthily from cover to cover, Tom led his friend to the Oakleys's walled yard by the side of the Unicorn Inn. The gate was padlocked and Tom led the way around the high walls to the rear of the yard.

'Why are we here?' Hollis whispered.

'To count the livestock,' Tom whispered back. 'Make a back so I can get over this damned wall.'

Hollis braced himself against the bricks, acting as a human ladder so that Tom was able to climb up high enough to grip the parapet. Tom dragged himself clumsily up on to the top, badly grazing his knees and hands in the process. Coal was heaped against the other side of the wall and Tom lowered himself on to the heap, but when he began to scramble down its steep sides he lost his footing and fell sprawling to the bottom, smothering himself with coal dust and knocking the breath from his body.

'If I survive this night I'll practise the Swedish Drill to make myself more agile,' he vowed as he clambered painfully to his feet.

The donkeys were tethered in a line under a lean-to roof on the opposite side of the yard, and it took Tom only seconds to count them. There were seven beasts, but he knew the Oakleys owned eight, and had met with young Billy Oakley driving them back to the yard from his coal deliveries late that very afternoon.

Next he went to the stacks of empty wicker-work panniers and quickly ran his hands around several of their interiors.

He struggled back over the wall, losing more skin from his hands, elbows and knees in the process.

'What did you find?' Hollis whispered.

'What I was suspecting,' Tom whispered back. 'One of the donkeys is missing, and I met with Billy Oakley driving the full team back into the yard this afternoon. He told me he'd finished work for the day and was locking the beasts up for the night.'

347

'Well, perhaps Billy had a later job come up which he needed a donkey for,' Hollis began, then drew a sharp breath of comprehension. 'The donkey that Old Tanner heard braying! You think that it was one of the Oakleys's beasts, don't you!'

'I do.' Tom confirmed. 'There was a donkey at the graveyard when I was shot at, and the droppings of a horse or donkey in the Chillingworth's yard.'

He held his open palm in front of Hollis' eyes as moonlight shone clear, 'Look at this coal dust, John. if I hadn't been so stupid I'd have made the connection days ago. The canvas wrapping of the needles I found in Southall's cottage is filthy with grease and coal dust.'

Hollis's quick wits sparked. 'And the only coal dealers in this parish are the Oakleys. So you think the needles were carried in the panniers of one of their beasts.'

'Exactly so!' Tom confirmed. 'And another thing: it was the Oakleys who coffined and buried Johnny Watts, wasn't it?'

'But you suspect that it's Jonathan Crowther and the Rippling Boys who're responsible for the thieving and body snatching,' Hollis objected. 'And it's common knowledge in the parish that Thomas Oakley and Crowther are bitter enemies. They fell out years ago when Crowther accused Oakley of delivering short-weight of coals to him. They came to blows, didn't they?'

'So I've heard,' Tom acknowledged. 'Come now, we've no time to waste.'

Forty-Five

The Oakleys's single-storey cottage stood by itself at the end of a narrow alleyway leading off the road running south from the Green crossroads towards the Front Hill. There were no gleams of light showing through its latticed windows as Tom and Hollis cautiously approached its front door. Hollis crept around to its rear. Tom waited to give his friend time to get into position, then knocked on the door with his staff.

Nothing stirred within and Tom knocked louder, keeping the hammering going until finally an angry shout sounded. A few moments later, the door creaked open and Thomas Oakley, dressed in a long nightshirt and with a tasselled nightcap on his head, bellowed furiously, 'What's the meaning o' this? Who the bloody hell does you think you am, you lanky pisspot? How dare you come here at this hour o' the night creating a racket that 'ud wake the dead, and dragging me from my lawful slumbers? What the bloody hell is the matter wi' you?'

'I'm very sorry to disturb you, Master Oakley, but I need to speak to your son. Will you get him for me, please?'

'No, I bloody well won't!' Oakley shouted. 'If you wants to speak to him, then go and get him yourself!'

'If you'll let me pass, then I will,' Tom offered.

'Let you pass?' the other man snorted incredulously. 'Does you think he's here?'

'Of course I do. Where else could he be at this hour?'

'He's bound to be where he always is lately, in the White Hart up at Headless Cross, drinking and whoring and gambling. Nowadays I count meself lucky to see the bugger by day, never mind by night, he's so busy wasting his own bloody money, and mine as well! He's become a bloody millstone around me neck that God's afflicted me with.'

'Are you sure he's at the White Hart?' Tom asked.

'Sure?' Oakley bellowed. 'Sure? O' course I'm bloody sure! I knows he's there because one of me neighbours called in to tell me so afore I went to me bed. Harry Abbie it was. Go and ask him if you don't believe me!'

Tom was satisfied that Oakley was being truthful, and apologized politely. 'I'm truly sorry to have disturbed you, Master Oakley. I'll be on my way.'

'What's he been up to this time anyway?' Oakley queried. 'Has he been fighting again?'

'He was involved in a bit of a row, Master Oakley. There was no harm done so there's nothing for you to worry yourself about. I've persuaded the other party to take no other action in the matter. Now I just want to have a word with Billy, and tell him not to be so loud and rowdy in future.'

'Well I got to say that you'm acting very fair, Master Potts,' Oakley grudgingly conceded.

'Then will you shake my hand to show you bear no ill feelings towards me for disturbing you tonight, Master Oakley?'

Tom proffered his hand, and grudgingly the other man took it.

'I'll say goodnight, and sorry again for disturbing you.' Tom took his leave.

'So you should be, you bloody lanky pisspot,' Oakley growled under his breath and slammed the door shut.

Tom was feeling disappointed. The fingers of Thomas Oakley's right hand were all complete and whole.

'Oh well,' he consoled himself. 'Perhaps I'll have better luck with his son.'

He waited in the main roadway, and when Hollis rejoined him they hurried on up the steep Front Hill and the long Mount Pleasant to Headless Cross and the White Hart Inn.

Forty-Six

Nail Styler was outside the inn putting up the shutters when Tom and Hollis arrived, and he greeted them jovially, 'I hope you aren't come to take Eddie Harris away, Master Potts. He's the best lodger I've ever had. Pays well, makes no noise, and costs me nothing for his bed and board. He stinks a bit, o' course, but no worse than the midden heap.'

'No, we'll not be taking him away this time, Master Styler.' Tom smiled pleasantly. 'We're just passing by. Has trade been good tonight?'

'Only middling. Just a few o' me regulars. They've all gone home now, and truth to tell I'm glad of it because I'm feeling a bit knackered.'

'Was Billy Oakley here?' Tom asked casually. 'Only we saw his dad earlier and he said to tell Billy to get the donkey back and stabled.'

'Yes, he was here, and his randy bloody donkey. He aren't been gone more than a couple o' minutes. He's become a regular lately. Spends free and easy he does, as well.' Styler's brown-stained teeth showed in a broad grin. 'I said to him the other night, "Billy," I said, "there must be a hell of a lot o' people dying down Redditch these days, the way you'm chucking your money about. Is Old Nick buying more coals from you to burn the buggers on his hell fires?" The bugger quite got the hump wi' me, so he did. But he knows better than to raise his fists against me. I've ate three like him afore breakfast many and many's the time.'

'That's well known, Master Styler. We'll leave you in peace. Goodnight now.'

'And a very good night to both of you gentlemen too,' Styler wished in return.

The pair walked on into the wood-shrouded darkness of the Rough, and Hollis ventured, 'I'm thinking we'd have met Billy if he was going home, so where's he gone?'

Tom's confidence in his own instincts was

352

strong now. 'He can't be far ahead of us, so let's get a move on.' Both men broke into a fast jog, only slowing the pace when they neared Mary Watts's cottage.

Light glowed from the lower windows.

'Wait here,' Tom whispered and went on alone to reconnoitre, creeping cautiously, listening hard for any sounds from within the building. He was experiencing a conflict of emotions: trepidation churning his stomach, causing his hands to tremble and bringing clammy sweat, but at the same time the excitement of the chase coursing through him.

All was silent within the walls, and Tom crawled to the nearest window and risked a quick look through its distorted dirty panes. The room was empty. He moved to the door and cautiously opened it. Holding his breath, listening hard, he went inside and nerved himself to creep upstairs. Both bedrooms were empty. He expelled his bated breath in a relieved whoop, and went back to where Hollis was waiting.

'What's going on, Tom?' Hollis whispered in puzzlement.

'I'm trusting my instincts.' The excitement of the chase now had Tom completely in its grip. 'There's not time now to fully explain my reasons, but I'm convinced that instead of Crowther, it all centres on Mary Watts. She's the puppeteer pulling the strings! She's somewhere close by with Billy Oakley and maybe others. I'm going to try a sweep around the rear of this place.'

He hesitated. 'Look John, it could well be that

I'm acting insanely, and I'll understand if you don't wish to continue further with me.'

Hollis grinned. 'Are you forgetting that I'm the officially insane one here? I'm not letting you wriggle out of our bargain and make me miss all the fun. Now, lead on MacDuff!'

'Take great care, John. They're all ready and willing to kill,' Tom warned.

Once again they separated, each following wide arcs on either side of the cottage.

In the dense woodland, the moonlight stuck through the overhanging leaves and branches in isolated slivers, constantly appearing and disappearing as clouds passed across the skies. Try though he might to move silently, Tom was sickeningly aware of his feet cracking fallen twigs and loudly rustling through grasses and undergrowth, and he cursed his own physical clumsiness as he stumbled onwards.

Two shots rang out almost simultaneously, followed by a shout of pain and the loud braying of a donkey. Tom started in shock and a terrible dread flooded over him. 'Is John hurt?'

Abandoning all attempt at concealment, he frantically headed towards the direction the shots had come from, ignoring the painful whiplashes of branches and foliage across his face and body, half-maddened by the frustration of being so sorely impeded by the clinging undergrowth.

He broke through into a narrow space of clear greensward and saw the black shapes of people and animals only yards before him.

'Stand fast! In the King's name stand fast! Or

I'll shoot!' he shouted, levelling his wildly wavering pistol, and lifting the crowned staff threateningly. With a thrashing of undergrowth and panted execrations John Hollis forced his way into the clearing just as the shrouding clouds rifted and moonlight brightly bathed the narrow open space.

Tom saw clearly now the man and woman, horse, pannier-laden donkey, and the spasmodically jerking, huddled heap on the ground.

'Drop your weapons, Mrs Watts. They're no use to you now they're discharged, and I've no wish to shoot you for refusing to, unless you force me to do so,' Tom ordered.

She let the pair of pistols fall from her hands.

'Both of you put your hands on top of your heads. You might find it easier to do that doctor, if you take your hat off first.'

The man removed the wide-brimmed hat pulled low over his eyes, to reveal the moon-silvered features of Andrew Adamson.

'Shackle them, if you please, Master Hollis,' Tom instructed. At this moment his overriding emotion was not triumphant satisfaction that he had captured his quarry, but only relief that he and his friend had survived unscathed. 'When you've done so, we'll look to Billy Oakley and see if we can do anything for him.'

John Hollis went to Adamson and momentarily blocked Tom's view of Mary Watts. In that instant, despite her long hampering skirts, she sprang catlike on to the horse and kicked it into headlong motion. The animal smashed the three men aside and went thundering into the twisting path leading from the glade.

Even as the trio regained their balances a volley of shots roared and the beating of hooves transposed into a crashing impact on to the earth.

'Secure him, John,' Tom shouted and ran into the pathway. Before he had covered many yards, the clouds shrouded the moon and he was forced to slow his pace to a hesitant walk in the now almost impenetrable darkness.

He could hear the screaming and thrashing of a beast in mortal agony and as he rounded a bend he saw the flash of a gunshot. Its report echoed through the trees and the screaming and thrashing ceased. Moonlight came again, illuminating the path ahead and he found himself face to face with armed men. He instantly raised his pistol and the nearest man shouted.

'There's no call for you to be alarmed, Master Potts, or to point that gun at me. We intend you no harm. The beast is dead, and the woman who rode it.'

Tom could only stare, completely dumbfounded, as Jonathan Crowther told the two men with him, 'Bring her here, Nephews, and lay her before the constable.'

The Fairfax twins briefly disappeared into the brushwood, and came back bearing a limp, motionless form between them. They laid it gently on the ground in front of Tom, and he stared down at the grotesquely distorted broken neck and contorted, bloodied, yet still beautiful face of Mary Watts.

'This is a most terrible night for me, Master Potts.' Crowther appeared near to tears, his voice broken and hoarse. 'My stepdaughter was a wicked woman, but I'm filled with grief to see her dead. The horse came upon us like a mad beast and we fired at it in self-defence. But if I'd known that my stepdaughter was its rider I would have let the beast trample me to pieces rather than have fired a shot.'

'Tom? Tom?' John Hollis's shouts sounded from further down the path, and Tom called back.

'Keep coming, John. All's well here.'

When Hollis joined them he told Tom, 'Don't worry about Adamson, I've left him shackled to a tree. Billy Oakley looks to be mortally wounded. The donkey's panniers are loaded with needles.'

He glared suspiciously at Crowther and the brothers. 'How do you come to be here at this time?'

Crowther replied in a sad and reproachful tone, 'We are here, Master Hollis, because we are loyal subjects of His Majesty and we uphold his laws. But seeing my beloved daughter lying dead is too much for me to bear at this moment. My nephews will render you any assistance you may ask of them. I'll talk to you again tomorrow morning, when I hope to have summoned sufficient fortitude to bear my grief more steadfastly.'

He turned and went away with the halting gait and bent head and shoulders of a man labouring under intense suffering.

'What now, Tom? What do we do next?' Hollis questioned.

'This is the first thing I have to do, John.' Tom knelt, and lifting the right hand of the dead woman, examined her fingers. The top joint of the ring finger was missing. He looked next at her square-toed shoes, then stood up and exclaimed wryly, 'My God! What a fine actress she was. She took me in completely.'

'Tell me something, Tom, it's been bothering me for hours,' Hollis queried. 'Earlier tonight when we were in the lock-up, what made you jump up and shout out, "The latest fashion! All the rage!"'

Tom pointed at Mary Watts's shoes. 'The footprints in the lock-up left by Southall's killer, John. They were made by smallish, square-toed bootees. I suddenly remembered that Amy's got a pair like that. She bought them a few weeks past and said that squared toes are the new fashion, and all the rage for smart-dressed women. And just lately who's become more fashionably clad and shod than this lady lying here?'

At the end of the path where it debouched on to the turnpike road, William Kinchin was waiting with the pony and trap, and when Crowther reached him asked anxiously, 'Did it go well, Master Crowther?'

Crowther scowled and shook his head. 'No! That lanky bastard, Potts, beat me to it. I've lost the bloody needles!'

'I'm sorry, Master! I'm sorry! I never seen Potts, I only seen them others!' Kinchin cringed fearfully. 'I did me best, honest I did!'

'I'm not blaming you for it, William. I should have acted faster when you brought news of your sightings.' A hint of reluctant admiration quirked Crowther's features. 'Potts is a far flyer cove than I thought him to be. I'll keep that in mind in future.' Abandoning all posture of suffering, he mounted the trap and whipped the pony off at a trot towards Crabbs Cross, with Kinchin running behind like a faithful dog.

Forty-Seven

Saturday night, 9 September

Jonathan Crowther opened the rear door of his house and greeted his late night visitor, 'Good to see you, Charlie. What news do you have for me?'

'Bloody hell, Jonno, give me a chance to take me breath!' Charlie Marsden protested. 'I've been riding like the clappers; and me bloody horse went lame on me when I got to Alvechurch. I had to go back to Hopwood and borrow me dad's old nag to get here.'

'Sorry, Charlie. Come in and sit you down by the fire.'

Crowther waited until they were comfortably ensconced in the fireside armchairs, and had drunk their first glasses of brandy, before asking again, 'What news, Charlie?'

'Semprimus Monkland bought the Gould woman and Johnny Watts, and it was his nephew, Adamson, who sent them to him. Monkland's porter is an old cellmate of mine so I can vouch for him telling me the truth; and from the description he gave me it's pretty certain it was Harris who made the deliveries.'

'I thought as much.' Crowther scowled. 'That bastard Harris! After all the work I'd put his way he betrayed me. It's a sad state of affairs when there's no honour left among thieves, Charlie. Things were different when I was a lad, I can tell you.'

'Ah well, you paid him out for it didn't you?' Marsden consoled. 'Sending Turpin Wright to do for Harris and his woman.'

'Turpin had nothing to do with either killing! And I know that for a fact, because he was here in this house when Harris was sliced,' Crowther asserted forcefully. 'But I sent him down to Bristol to keep him out of the way for a while, because I was feared he'd get the blame for it. He's been very useful to me in the past, has Turpin, and I've use for him in the future now that we can resume business.'

'Then who did do for them?' Marsden showed his surprise. 'Was it Bonny Southall?'

Crowther frowned thoughtfully, 'I don't think so. Southall was a tough nut, but no killer. I swear on my mother's grave, Charlie, that I'm of the firm belief that it was that little bitch herself that did for them. My lovely Mary!

'Dr Laylor examined her body on Thursday and she was no more poxed up than I am,

Charlie. She'd got Adamson, Southall and Oakley by their short and curlies all at the same time.'

He shook his head in wonderment. 'By Christ, Charlie, just look at what she got up to. Needle robbing, body snatching, murdering. And bloody well fooling me all that time! What a phenomenal Rippling Boy she'd have made!'

Forty-Eight

Sunday afternoon, 10 September

Tom had not slept more than a few of hours since Tuesday night and was physically bone-weary, but his elation at that night's outcome was still buoying him mentally when the manservant ushered him into the study. Joseph Blackwell laid down his pen and sat back in the chair with a frown on his face, but his eyes gleaming in satisfaction.

'Well now, Master Potts, this is a pretty kettle of fish you've cooked. I'm told that the parish has been in uproar since Wednesday morning, and that you are being acclaimed as the cleverest constable in England. Tell me what first made you suspicious of Mary Watts and Dr Adamson?'

'It was the death of John Watts, Sir. Adamson said that the cause of death was apoplexy, but

Watts's symptoms immediately prior to death were those that are caused by ingesting Amanita phalloides, the death cap mushroom. It's the most deadly poisonous of all the fungi, and once you have it in your stomach your life is forfeit. In my father's medical records he's described in detail two cases he treated, both fatal of course.

'John Smith told me there are isolated spots in the woodlands around the Crosses and Webheath where he's discovered it growing, and Mary Watts herself once told me she often collected mixed fungi because her husband was very partial to them.'

'I see.' Blackwell nodded smilingly. 'Now let me hear in brief your overall case against her.'

Tom drew a deep breath and confessed, 'In truth, Sir, there is much that I cannot fully prove.'

'No matter,' Blackwell dismissed airily. 'Continue.'

'Very well, Sir. It's my belief that Mary Watts was desperate to change her life, and needed money to do that. Using her beauty as bait she emotionally entrapped Southall, Adamson and Oakley in her net and used all three of them for her own purposes.

'She rid herself of her husband by first assaulting him, then feeding him the death cap fungi to kill him off. I have fingerprint evidence that she directly participated in the Bates robbery and the Gould body-snatching. Eddie Harris was definitely one of her accomplices. He was also present at Chillingworth's.

'She murdered Harris and tried to lay the guilt

362

on Southall by leaving his knife at the scene, then she poisoned Maggie Murphy. When she heard that Southall was turning King's evidence, she broke into the lock-up and shot him.

'On Tuesday night, she disposed of Oakley, and that left all the proceeds of the various crimes to be shared between herself and her latest paramour, Adamson.'

'If you had not caught her, what do you think Mary Watts intended to do next?' Blackwell asked.

An unbidden overwhelming sense of certainty invaded Tom and he replied without pausing for thought, 'She meant to marry Adamson. Then she would have discovered that Adamson is up to his neck in debt, and that would have been his death warrant. Then in all likelihood she would have climbed into Jonathan Crowther's bed. Once she'd persuaded him to make a will in her favour, he would very quickly have gone to the graveyard, leaving her free to enjoy his wealth for the rest of her days.'

Blackwell smiled bleakly, and told Tom. 'I can't help but wish she were still alive and able to fulfil that plan, if only for the future well-being of this parish.

'And what does Adamson have to say?'

'That Mary Watts was blackmailing him. She asked him for some prussic acid to treat a varicose vein in her leg. She then poisoned her husband with the acid, and threatened to blame Adamson for the crime. She forced him to vouch to his uncle the provenance of the bodies of both Mrs Gould and John Watts. He claims that he knows nothing about the other murders, and tried to stop her shooting Billy Oakley.'

Blackwell emitted a short dry chuckle of disbelief, then queried, 'Crowther? Where does Jonathan Crowther fit into all this?'

'I've not the foggiest idea, Sir,' Tom admitted. 'He claims he was in the woods because he suspected Mary Watts and the others of stealing the needles, and that he and his nephews were hoping to catch the gang in possession of the stolen goods. I've no proof that he or his nephews set out to kill Mary Watts. Dr Laylor says it's virtually certain that she died from breaking her neck as a result of being pitched off the horse when it fell. There are no gunshot or other suspicious wounds on her body.'

Blackwell picked up his pen. 'Produce Adamson before the magistrates tomorrow morning to be remanded to Worcester to await trial. He will hang himself with his own lies. No jury in the land will believe him anything but guilty of capital offences. So he'll get his just desserts.'

He nodded with obvious satisfaction. 'As for myself, I shall take great delight in seeing my Lord Aston's expression when I force him in public view to eat his derogatory words concerning yourself. I bid you a very good day indeed, Thomas Potts, constable of this parish.'

Forty-Nine

Tom awoke to the sunlight streaming through his bedroom. He turned over and stretched his body, smiling in absolute contentment.

On Monday he had escorted his prisoner to Worcester Jail. All through Tuesday he had been showered with the plaudits and congratulations of his fellow parishioners.

Best of all by far, this very afternoon he and Amy were going to go courting in the Abbey Meadows.

'I shall tell her how much I love her, and ask her to marry me just as soon as our banns can be called.'

'And if she says, yes, where will you both live?' his other entity whispered.

Nothing at this moment could shake Tom's supremely confident expectations that for he and Amy a new life of happiness and fulfilment was imminent, and he dismissed the doubter with scorn.

'Here, of course! I shall paint and furnish this room and make it fit for a queen. We shall be very happy and contented to live here, until such time as my fortunes improve sufficiently for me

365

to buy her a fine house.'

The bells of the lock-up raucously jangled.

'Oh God, spare me!' Tom muttered in annoyance at being disturbed during this delightful reverie. 'What can be the matter now?'

The bells jangled again, louder and longer.

Tom jumped out of bed and ran downstairs barefoot, wearing only his nightshirt and long-tasselled nightcap.

'You lazy lay-abed hound! You've kept me waiting here in the cold deliberately, haven't you, you unnatural beast of a son!' The Widow Potts's face was puce with rage, her voice a high-pitched screech.

She used the weight of her massive belly to buffet Tom aside. 'Let me get in, will you! Things are going to change here very shortly, you ungrateful wretch! You'll not be able to bully me any more when my Charles moves in. He'll put you in your place, you vile cur!'

'What do you mean, Mother? When Charles moves in?' Tom questioned.

'Charles Bromley Esq. and I are betrothed,' she announced with a simper. 'We are to wed just as soon as our banns are called. And we are agreed that it will be more economical if Charles gives up his present house, and we shall live here. So you'll have to mind your manners from now on, you lanky great spawn of the devil!'

A chill of horror shivered through Tom. His eyes lifted to the skies and appealed with plaintive desperation. 'Oh Lord, Lord, why hast Thou forsaken me?'